# SHADOW FALL

## A MILITARY SPACE OPERA TALE

## P. R. ADAMS

PROMETHEAN TALES

❀ Created with Vellum

# ALSO BY P. R. ADAMS

For updates on new releases and news on other series, visit my website and sign up for my mailing list at:

http://www.p-r-adams.com

## The War in Shadow

*Shadow Moves*

*Shadow Play*

*Shadow Strike*

*Shadow Talk*

*Shadow Pawn*

*Shadow Fall*

---

## Books in the On The Brink Universe

### The Stefan Mendoza Trilogy

*Into Twilight*

*Gone Dark*

*End State*

### Stefan Mendoza: The Human Deception Trilogy

*Split Image*

*Hard Burn*

*Null Point*

### The Rimes Trilogy

*Momentary Stasis*

*Transition of Order*

*Awakening to Judgment*

**The ERF Series**

*Turning Point*

*Valley of Death*

*Jungle Dark*

*Chariot Bright*

*Dawn Fire*

**The Lancers Series**

*Deep Descent*

*Deadly Game*

*Dire Straits*

*Dark Secrets*

## The Burning Sands Trilogy

*Beneath Burning Sands*

*Across Burning Sands*

*Beyond Burning Sands*

## The Second Burning Sands Trilogy

*Inside Burning Sands*

*Over Burning Sands*

*War for Burning Sands*

<u>**Books in The Chain Series**</u>

**The Chain: Shattered**

*The Journey Home*

*Rock of Salvation*

*From the Depths*

*Ever Shining*

# DEDICATION

*For those lost in the shadows.*

**1**

———

Steam rose from Captain Faith Benson's mug, giving off a mix of cocoa and citrus aromas along with the usual deep notes of the coffee she sometimes drank instead of her favored stimulant drink. The taste was rich and layered, providing a warmth of its own combined with the heat from the drink.

The man sitting across from her in her cabin was the real source of heat, though. With the lights dimmed to barely reveal the spread of plates and bowls on the portable dining table, Captain Floyd Thiessen looked like an entertainment star. He was one of the most handsome men she'd ever seen, and at that moment, staring down, face washed in the blue glow of his data pad, he was like a dream. His blue-black uniform jacket was draped over the back of his seat, same as her white jacket was draped over the back of hers. That left only the close-fitting white shirts they both wore. He pulled the look off much better than she could ever hope to, with the sharp V-cut of his frame emphasized every time he stood or paced.

Even sitting, leaning back and studying the reports she'd prepared for him to review, he had a masculine beauty she found herself falling into. There was no mistaking him for Halliwell and his aura of broody danger, but she found she wasn't missing that sense of power and menace.

She sipped the last of her drink and set her cup down with a soft clatter that brought the Gulmar captain's head up. What would she see in his eyes if they were free of this war and their obligations?

She smiled. "Well?"

"Well…" He set the tablet down and rubbed his eyes. "I was never the fastest study, if you want me to be brutally honest."

"Oh. I didn't mean that you should be done reading yet. That's a *lot* of data."

Thiessen chuckled. "How do you do it?"

"Most of it's the software. That and my officers and front-line supervisors. They're the ones who put all the raw data together and filter out the noise."

"I've got similar systems on my ship, and I can't get to this level of detail."

"You don't have a professional military working for you, Floyd."

He frowned. "I don't. And I'm not professional military myself."

She blushed. "I meant—"

"No. I'm not taking offense. It is what it is. We're in a real pickle, and you should have better resources available to you. My people are doing what they can, but we'll never be able to match the Kedraalian Navy."

"We wouldn't be here having this conversation if it not for your task force."

"Maybe."

"No maybe to it. You more than pulled your weight. Unlike Faulk."

Thiessen's frown deepened. "I was happy to see he didn't make the list."

"This is about pleasure, not pain." She blushed. *Pleasure?* How could that slip out?

"You're confident about all of this? Repair rates and this shadow technology network running between our ships being able to replace the lost signals ship?"

"I am." Benson pointed to the table. "Are you done?"

He patted his belly. "Ready for a nap. It was as good a meal as I've ever had on a ship."

"I'll pass the compliment along." She pulled her data pad out and summoned the team from the galley to collect everything. "So, the point I was trying to make was that the executive summary should be our first opportunity to squabble."

"Squabble? Isn't that something married couples do?"

Even though he put on a charming smile to mark the comment as playful, her heart skipped a beat. "Well, a lot of Kedraalian officers consider squabbling duty."

"I noticed. I'm not sure I find that something I'd copy over to Gulmar security, if I had the chance."

"Oh, I wouldn't recommend it."

"But you tolerate it."

"The Kedraalian military has undergone a lot of changes in the last couple decades. Budget cuts, mass reductions in force, training lapses—you could argue that it's a miracle we survived."

"*If* you believe in miracles." The stiff smile he put on said that he didn't.

"Regardless, the fact that we're still operational comes down to veterans who survived all of that. They may be a hot mess, but they're all we have holding things together."

Thiessen turned when her hatch chimed, then pushed up from the table with his data pad and jacket in hand and stood as the stewards from the galley came in and hastily gathered the dinner remnants and the table. They had both been fresh-faced, young men, straight out of training when the *Valor* had launched, and they would both be in line for their second promotions soon. Benson imagined she could see the differences in how thick the shadow of their whiskers were compared to the day she'd welcomed them aboard, both of their fresh faces flushed at meeting their captain.

And then the two of them were gone, leaving behind the smoky remnants of dinner scents and the last clank of dinnerware as the hatch closed.

The Gulmar captain stretched, then pointed to her desk. She nodded, and he folded his jacket over the top. It felt comfortable and casual in a way that made her tingle. Having the jacket there or hanging in her closet —she liked that thought.

She put her own jacket on top of his, imagining what it might be like if it were their bodies pressed against each other instead of what they wore over their flesh.

Before she could turn, he moved in a little closer and pointed to the edge of her desk shelf. "What's this?" His finger tapped the square-shaped discoloration where her dream globe had rested since the day she'd settled into the cabin.

"Nothing."

"It sure left a mark for being nothing."

"It's a reminder to do a better job cleaning up after myself, really."

"Oh." His lips twisted in a frown. "One of the upsides of you never seeing my cabin in person is that you don't get a good idea of how cluttered my life is."

"Cluttered? Are you sloppy?"

"Not...sloppy. That's harsh."

"Sorry."

He waved it off. "I have trouble letting go of memories is all."

She swallowed. Did he know about the globe? He couldn't. "Everyone hangs onto memories."

"It's not healthy. Everything I had from childhood was in my apartment back on Radetta. It's all ash now. But before we left, I pulled electronic copies from the surviving network and had things printed up."

"What sort of things?"

"Stupid things. Certificates and awards and pictures."

"Pictures of you and Leona?"

"What?" Thiessen's brow wrinkled. "Oh. From when I worked for her?"

"Is that what she called it?"

"Well..." He shrugged. "She liked her power. I think that was a big reminder of it for her."

"Sleeping with one of the common people?"

He scratched the back of his head. His hair had grown over the scar from the injury he'd suffered shortly after helping her escape the destruction of Radetta.

That was a memory, too: She owed him her life.

Thiessen looked around the cabin. "I'd imagine it's a pretty big advantage being able to step away from memories, good and bad."

"Is that even possible?"

"You said I was sloppy for hanging onto mine. I thought—"

She pressed fingers to her forehead. "I didn't mean it like that. Sorry."

Thiessen shoved his hands into his pockets. "All right. I think I've made things awkward enough. Sorry about that."

"No, I—"

"This idea—" He held his data pad up. "—of tracking the Khanate fleet. No one's ever questioned you about it that I can see. I feel kind of stupid even bringing this up, but I sort of need to know: Is it real?"

"Tracking the fleet?"

"You've figured out how to find them somehow? It's in the report."

She held her hand out for his data pad, and he passed it to her. It still had his warmth to it. "The part you want is…" She flipped to the table of contents, tapped the link, then turned the display so that he could look at the device over her shoulder. "You see this?"

He tapped the display to drill down onto the image she was talking about. "What're FSDNs?"

"Fold Space Detection Networks. The demilitarized zones."

"No one wasted the money on a real DMZ but the Azoren, Faith."

"I know. But I'm not talking about weapons systems. The detection network is everywhere. You might not have something as robust as they have, but you have a network."

"We do?" He folded his arms across his chest. "I was part of the security apparatus, and I—"

She held up a hand. "Hold on. This isn't an early warning system."

"Okay. Mind telling me what it is, then?"

"Do you know why it's so hard for a fleet to move through Fold Space?"

"Sure. Every ship has to enter the same pocket dimension at the same time, or you'll probably never find each other. It means your computers have to be in perfect synchronization at the time of transition to Fold Space, and then you need to maintain the same velocity. Either you slave everyone to the same system or you run the risk of getting separated."

"And all of that—entering Fold Space and staying in it—requires more energy than just flying through normal space. You may not be traversing normal space physically, but you're passing through it. The energy you're using is detectable. It's a measurable wave."

His face was tense. "I've been trained. I get it."

He was feeling defensive, probably because of the differences in their backgrounds. She needed to find a way to not sound patronizing. "I'm sorry. I had to set a baseline to make this not sound crazy."

"I'm sure it's sane."

"Well, the thing is, just because we can detect the energy of something moving through Fold Space, we can't attack it."

"It's moving too fast—"

"Right! Relatively speaking. But the DMZs—we all have sensor networks. Maybe it's listening stations or some sort of picket ships or whatever. At the bare minimum, we have the message buoys with Fold Space transmitters."

"They track Fold Space movement?"

"Well, no. Not explicitly. But they capture the data I'm talking about, whether they're designed specifically for the tracking or not. It's all the same concept, whether it's a super-sensitive buoy in the Azoren DMZ or a basic Fold Space transmitter orbiting a planet. They all pick up some level of information from Fold Space."

The tension slipped from Thiessen's face. "You're not talking about actually going into Fold Space and tracking them, then."

"No. We just need to know where they've been."

"But how does that help?"

"Well, where would this fleet go? It's a question we didn't have to ask before, because we thought we knew where it was headed: home."

"They must have prearranged resupply points."

"Right. But there are only so many places they can go to replenish fuel and supplies, even if they can rely on the Khanate system to provide them."

"And...you don't think they can?"

"Rely on the Khanate? I guess they can to an extent. They had new ships and weapons systems."

"But—?"

"But I don't think it's a sustainable approach. Fusion reactors don't burn *that* much fuel, even when you fire up Fold Space drives. But everyone has to choose in ship design between carrying large quantities of refined fuel, having a fuel refining system, or picking fuel up somewhere."

He squinted at his data pad. "And since you're talking about this detection network, you think they're going to pick fuel up somewhere."

"I've been studying that fleet. We've destroyed a cruiser, a carrier, and several frigates. Looking through the husks of the frigates, they're mostly built as oversized gunboats."

"They pack a punch."

"They do. And everything points to a focus on weapons—an oversized reactor and limited room for much else. Even their defenses aren't comparable to frigates from our fleet."

"But if they don't have fuel onboard, how have they been resupplying?"

"Those carriers. The way they're built: They're huge, but they don't carry that many fighters. We've never seen more than fifty at one time. When we took that one out the other day, it released a lot of materials: deuterium and tritium. More than would make sense for their reactor to need."

"They were the storage ships?"

"I think so. And if they were, I think that fleet will need to refuel sooner than they were planning. Either those cruisers have a lot of materials aboard or they'll have to go to a fuel-producing site."

Thiessen's eyes widened. "And there aren't that many of those."

"There aren't. So, it's just a matter of getting this FSDN data collected, looking for the signature of a big fleet, and—"

"And seeing what potential refuel sites are in the area." He whistled. "Impressive."

Benson blushed. "Well, it's just a theory so far."

"A good one. I think it's solid."

"Thank you."

He powered his data pad off. "I've been thinking about what you said—about not returning to Radetta or wherever the Gulmar capital ends up being when this is all over."

"Oh?"

"At first, it felt like running from trouble instead of fighting."

"What changed?"

"That's hard to say. I just think going back to Kedraal makes sense." But the set of his jaw made it look like there was more to it.

She bit her lip. "It does make sense, doesn't it?"

"Do you think it would be inappropriate to use you as my sponsor, if I do that?"

"Sponsor?"

"You know. You could vouch for me, get me some sort of refugee status."

"Oh. Right. I would. Absolutely."

"I don't want to put you in a bad place. I'm not using you, y'know."

"Right now, I think I could really enjoy a bit of being used." Heat shot through her cheeks, and her mouth dropped. "Oh. That— I mean—"

Thiessen smiled. "That's okay. I bet it's lonely running the fleet."

"I—" The cabin felt warm with him so close.

He leaned in and kissed her softly. Just a peck on the cheek. "Maybe we should have more talks about our future. Whenever you're ready, I mean."

Her breathing seemed too fast, too deep. Heat bloomed in her belly.

Thiessen backed away. "I should get—"

She grabbed his arm and pulled him in, tasting the coffee on his lips and the chocolate sauce from their dessert. After an eternity, she pushed free. "We're not done with the strategic..." What had she called the meeting?

"Assessment." He kissed her again, this time wrapping his hands around her and rubbing them down her back, pulling her hips against his.

Without meaning to, she found herself grinding against him, tugging on his shirt. She backed away, lightheaded. This was happening too fast. She was rebounding after the breakup with Halliwell.

Except...she wasn't. The feelings she had for Thiessen were...different.

She pulled her data pad out with shaking hands, took a deep breath, then connected to the bridge. Commander Dinesh Chopra—her XO—was there, apparently caught up in turnover with the second shift.

His eyebrows went up. "Captain? Is the meeting with Captain Thiessen concluded?"

"No. In fact, we've...run into a complication. I won't be there for turnover, I'm afraid."

"Turnover will proceed without you."

"Thank you. Would you have the bridge hold all non-critical calls while we work through these sensitive matters, please?"

The light from the big control console reflected off the XO's bald head. "Of course, Captain."

"I'll see you first thing in the morning."

Chopra nodded, and she thought there might be a smirk on his face before he disconnected. Thiessen pulled her close again, his hands hot against her tender flesh. She had a vague awareness of powering the data pad off and setting it down, then she wasn't really thinking but falling into what she'd wanted for weeks now. It was a release that tore her away from the stress of command, something to free her mind of all the death and destruction and fear that had been with her since taking command.

She grabbed onto that release with an intensity she hadn't known before, and she rode it until the world shuddered, then faded to black.

---

Nausea curled in Parkinson's gut. It would've been worse, he was sure, but the needles digging into the creases of his elbows were a burning reminder that there was always something worse in life. He'd been warned about the pain of the transfusion process, but it hadn't really prepared him. Nothing could have.

The cute medical technician Kohl had apparently latched onto smiled and patted Parkinson's forearm. She could have passed for Stiles's younger sister, almost—caramel skin just a tad lighter, dark eyes just a hint bigger, more lean than fit. "Just a few more minutes."

"Thanks."

He shifted on the bed, trying to find a position where it didn't feel like the stiff pillow would break his neck. At one time, he would've looked the technician over with envy and tried to pressure her into a drink in the galley. It would have been the first stage of his charm offensive—or what he'd always considered charm. Regale her with his accomplishments and decorations, puff out his scrawny chest and maybe drop some influential names he had connections with, pull at his ridiculous straw-colored soul patch, then maybe dig around to see if she had any insecurities he could exploit...

A process. Predatory, almost.

For an instant, the nausea grew more insistent, and a chill ran through him. He thought it might be the medical center, which was always a degree or two cooler than the rest of the *Valor*. The coolness ran hand in hand with the medicinal smells and the tomblike quiet of the place.

His discomfort must have been in his eyes, because the young woman's brow furrowed. "You okay, Chief?"

"All good. Tired, mostly." Parkinson put on a brave smile.

Would it look sickly and unconvincing? He'd lost weight and color in the last week, so that his normally snug jumpsuit was baggy, and his cheeks were a little sunken. Compared to her youthful vigor, he was probably giving off a ghoulish pallor, his pale hair barely distinguishable from his failing flesh.

She unrolled a deep blue blanket from the end of the bunk and stretched it over him. "This can leave a lot of people lightheaded or even nauseated. You're almost done."

Of course, he knew better. This was his second transfusion, and he'd timed out the first. He had nearly a half hour remaining.

*Greta would've handled it without complaining.*

Dietrich came out of the doctors' office, head down, eyes focused somewhere far, far away. His shoulders were hunched, his curly hair disheveled. He stopped abruptly, looked back at the office, then froze. It was as if he were caught between two half-formed thoughts.

His head twisted around until he was looking at Parkinson. "Will?"

Parkinson pulled the brave smile back into place. "Hey, Doc!"

The older man straightened, then shuffled over, dismissing the medtech with a glance. When she disappeared inside the nurses' station, Dietrich looked the gear over with dancing eyes. "The transfusion. Change your mind?"

"About cold sleep?"

"It's still early enough on. Finish this up, we put a resuscitation ring on you, then freeze you. Once we have you back on Kedraal, I can guarantee you we'd have you at the best institution for treating radiation sickness and on the road to recovery within a month."

"That's really tempting."

"The odds of a complete recovery are exceptional—close to ninety percent. Someone your age and in good health, I can't see it failing."

"And taking just the transfusions and waiting until we get back for treatment drops the odds closer to seventy percent. I remember."

"Sixty if this idiocy drags on too long." The doctor's pale eyes had a stern, warning glitter to them. "The best we can do at this point is treat your symptoms. Are you experiencing nausea? Fatigue? Any problems with your gums or bowels?"

"Just nausea."

Dietrich took in a deep breath. "I can get you something for that."

"But you'd rather I let you make me a humansicle."

"Science is about data, and the data says it would be the right course."

"I—I know." Parkinson swallowed. "Things are at a really sensitive point right now. I can't let Captain Benson down. She's got me working—"

"Don't be an idiot. She's using you."

"Nah. She didn't pressure me."

"Then what? Is this some sort of unhealthy death wish?"

A shudder ran through Parkinson's body. It sucked being on his back while Dietrich ran through one of his dressing-down routines. Being short, being sick—it left Parkinson feeling more vulnerable than normal. "I don't want to die."

"Good. The Will Parkinson I served with all these years was never a stupid man in need of toting a gun around to show that he was some sort of hero."

"Hey—!"

"Leave that nonsense to the grunts. They chose to have their lives destroyed by violence."

"That's not... Sergeant Grier is as brave as—"

"She's a Marine. All she knows is killing and dying."

"We're all in the same boat. It's…the job we signed on for."

Dietrich's lips pressed tight, then he relaxed. "I suppose it is, isn't it? And you've resigned yourself to this fate?"

"No. I mean, dying scares the shit out of me."

The doctor nodded, the ice in his eyes growing colder. "Good. I'll see to your medication. Excuse me."

Parkinson squeezed his eyes shut. Admitting to his fear felt like an act of bravery in itself. Taylor had told him everyone was afraid in battle, but she'd teased and goofed around up until the second the explosion had torn her shuttle apart. Maybe she'd been trying to make him feel less embarrassed about being a coward.

Whatever. What mattered was that she'd helped him see how wrong it was to let that fear rule him. Now he simply had to conquer it, something he would do one day at a time.

S weat trickled down Grier's arms and ribs. She shouldered more from her face with the sleeve of her damp T-shirt, gasping and panting. She'd pushed her Marines hard today, wrapping the workout session with block sprints and a timed run that was too long to maintain a sprint but too short to approach like a distance run.

Her lungs burned from the effort, but it was a good burn.

Halliwell stood at the hangar bay hatch, calling out encouragement in an echoing voice to the last Marine trailing the formation—a young, baby-faced kid who'd fallen out during the run. He appeared to be on the edge of vomiting.

Rather than yell at the kid, Halliwell had fallen out and checked on him, then jogged with him the last leg.

It was the sort of thing that built strength in the relationship between the CO and his troops. So long as Grier could manage playing the hardass, having a sympathetic ear elsewhere in the leadership ranks worked.

She shook out her arms, blew salty sweat from her lips, then shuffled over to where the lieutenant was stretching beside the hangar bay exit.

He nodded at her over an arm knotted with muscles. "Good workout today."

"Thanks." She began stretching at his side, pushing against the bulkhead with her hands and stretching her right calf out until it ached. "Private Ruck needs a little extra motivation. Maybe we should restrict him from the dessert section for the next month?"

"He's not overweight."

"And he's not doing well during PT."

"That's why it's physical *training*, Toni. We train him how to get better."

"Sure." She switched to stretching out her other calf muscle. "Hey, this an okay time to talk—?"

The lieutenant pushed off the wall and stretched his back. "Actually, I've got to get back to the office. Evaluation reviews are just as important as fitness tests."

She grabbed his arm before he could go. "Hey! Wait a second."

He looked down at her hand, eyes narrowed. "What're you doing?"

"Stopping you because you keep trying to avoid me. We need to talk, okay?"

"We're still on duty, Toni. This may be our PT uniform, but it's still a uniform."

"Clive, stop it. There's no one else around. You've been evading me since I got back from the *Mao*, and you know it."

He pulled his arm free. "I haven't been avoiding you."

"You have, but if you want to kid yourself that you haven't, fine."

"We work in the same office. How can I avoid you?"

Grier brushed wet hair from her forehead. "Seriously? This is how you deal with it?"

"Deal with what?" There was an exasperated look on his face.

She shoved him, and when he tried to push her back, she grabbed his arm, tugged him to her, levered him off her hip, and threw him to the deck.

He hit hard, grunting, face turning red.

Rather than let him get up, she threw weight onto his chest, pinning him down. She drove a forearm against his neck, and he did the right thing: pushing against her arm before she could choke him out.

But she wasn't budging.

Halliwell was bigger and stronger, but she kept pushing, and her forearm kept pressing against his throat.

His gasps became quieter, more desperate, and the fury in his eyes shifted to desperation.

That was what she needed to see.

She rolled clear and got to her feet, shaking, but she didn't offer him a hand up. "*That's* what…I'm talking about, Clive." Her breathing came in rapid grunts, crazy like her heartbeat.

He sat on the deck, glaring and rubbing his neck.

"Don't you glare at me." She walked in a tight circle, shaking her head to clear spots from her eyes. "You're too weak. You're not ready. It's why you fell out with Ruck today."

"I fell out…" Halliwell bowed his head. "You damn near choked me out."

"Because you wouldn't listen. You keep acting like I'm not around. Ever since I did the right thing—"

He pushed up from the floor, nearly lost his balance, then stabilized. "You're way out of line." He headed to the hatch, wobbling.

She stepped in front of him. "Am I?"

His face went a darker shade of red. "Move."

"We need to talk about what you said, telling me not to argue like the captain. You were telling me I'm not smart—"

"You've got it all wrong, Toni."

"I don't think so. You want me—"

He pushed past her, nearly knocking her off her feet.

She rounded on him, grabbed his T-shirt, pulling it away from him with a wet, sucking sound. "You don't get to fuck me, then treat me—"

Halliwell spun around, grabbing her wrist and twisting it hard enough to drive her to her knees. "For the last time, you're getting it wrong. *Sergeant.*"

He let go of her and stormed out, the hatch hissing open, then slamming shut behind him.

For the first time ever, she wanted to punch him, to really let go and hurt him. What the hell was going on in his head? Was he mad that he'd dumped his pretty captain for some homely, low-life Marine?

*Dammit, Clive! Don't you dare break my heart!*

Grier pushed up to her feet, then worked her wrist until it didn't sting anymore. The whole time, she fought back tears. It wasn't from the wrist. She'd hurt him more with the throw and chokehold than he had with the wrist lock. The pain was in her chest, the sort of hurt she'd sworn she'd never let herself feel.

But she'd shown him her heart, and now he seemed determined to stomp on it.

If she let him.

She hooked thumbs on her hips and walked around the course she'd just run a few minutes before. Her thoughts were muddy, clogged up by emotion—pain and fear. Halliwell had always been her world, and he'd finally taken her into his. Now he was…

What? What was going on with him?

She kicked at the air, imagining it was something physical and in need of a good ass-stomping.

It didn't help.

If she wanted to clear her head, she needed exertion. Clive wasn't going to be giving her the good kind anytime soon, so the next best alternative was the gym and the weights. She stomped off in that direction, already flexing her arms. It was a temporary solution. Maybe she could come up with something more meaningful before she saw him next.

Otherwise, she wasn't sure she could keep from punching his lights out.

**2**

———

The Jakkara marched the last meters of the passageway, boots stomping and burnt orange armor jangling. Even with only a third escorting Satrap, they were still the greatest security group in all the Khanate fleet. He did his best to relax on his wheeled platform, taking solace in the smell of oil and polish coming from their weapons and armor. It helped him ignore the attached contraption with its life-sustaining cables and lines, its ampules of medicine and rows of filtration systems, and the bite of the many needles in his arms. Primary among all of that were the displays that announced to the world that he was a diminished and broken man who lived only at the behest of his Khan.

*All hail the Glorious and Holy Khan!*

His bodyguards stopped outside the officers' banquet room, where two of their brethren already stood. There was no sign of Zohar's men, or what remained of the captain's security detachment. That was a welcome sign that things hadn't grown worse with the commander of the *Might of the Khan*. After all, this was Satrap's only ally aside from Ikhama.

He glanced back to be sure the old woman still trailed the procession.

She bowed at him, dressed again in the colorful robe she'd worn the last time they'd held such an important meeting inside the banquet room. That had been months ago, when the fleet had been at close to full strength and some of the most problematic captains had still been alive, Rouhani among them. Now he was gone, along with the *Divine Wind*, his cruiser.

So many of the captains were gone now, for good and bad.

Inside, Zohar sat at the large table that occupied the center of the cabin, handsome in soft blue—his family color. When he stood, the loose material of his dark brown pants seemed to puff out. The man's family symbol—a lightning strike enclosed in a circle—stood out in black on the left breast of his jacket.

Across from him, Captain Ho, commander of the *Blessed Saber of Xenu*, stood. The ship was the only remaining carrier in the fleet, meaning the short man had taken on even greater power and influence. There was an ashen nature about the deep gold of his round face, a loss of color that couldn't be explained away completely by the months free of the burning sun of Azh Choak, his home world. His deep red jacket was wrinkled, the saber emblem on his breast dulled.

The two captains bowed as the Jakkara rolled Satrap up to the table. He muttered thanks to his bodyguards, and they retreated to positions inside the hatch, standing beneath strings of thawed flowers that had been woven into green and orange bunting—the colors of the Holy Khan.

Once again, there were silver trays of meats, fruits, and breads, although they seemed less grand, the gold tablecloth beneath them stained.

Or perhaps that was all in Satrap's imagination.

When Ikhama finally reached the table, he signaled for everyone to sit.

She launched into one of her ridiculous, unending prayers, and his mind wandered. The rich aromas coming from the food made his stomach growl. It wasn't a pleasant experience, not with the inevitable announcement that his life support system was about to launch into preventative measures. It had to compensate for the inevitable wild swings in chemicals his ruined organs were about to experience.

He kept quiet while the old woman droned on, her long, wrinkled face stretched in fervent praise of the man who had shattered Satrap's life.

What mattered such abuse from years ago, especially now that he faced yet another imminent threat?

Finally, the rambling came to an end, and everyone dug into the food, piling meat onto their plates, then drizzling rich sauces over the smoky chunks before surrounding them with slices of bread and assorted pastes.

All the while, Satrap contented himself with appetite and pain suppression injections.

Oddly enough, Zohar seemed equally uninterested in the food, even though he'd spooned things onto his plate. His brown hair was greasy, as if it hadn't been washed in some time, and his green eyes were bloodshot. The vitality that had been so much a part of his youthful image was diminished. This lent an almost beak-like nature to his hooked nose and protruding chin.

Something was troubling the captain.

While the other two ate, Satrap studied his ally. There were no angry flashes or stares, and the younger man didn't once utter some cutting comment about the condition of the fleet. He simply nibbled meat and tore chunks of bread from the end of the loaf he'd taken at the start.

When the feasting was complete, it was Captain Ho who broke the relative silence. "Thank you, Satrap, for inviting me once again to partake of the hospitality of the *Might of the Khan*." The old man bowed.

"You are most welcome, Captain. I think I'm the one who should be thanking you."

"Why is that, Satrap?"

Without looking up from sliding sauce-soaked bread around his plate, Zohar chuckled—a bitter sound. "For having the sense to flee when the enemy fell upon us." His eyes came up at that point, the green in them almost washed out against the fine blood vessels. "Isn't that right, Satrap?"

Satrap bowed. "The fleet is vastly diminished with the loss of the *Desert Sands*."

Ho nodded. "A terrible loss."

"Our Khan's favorite ship."

"Yes. Tragic."

If Zohar intended to interrupt again, he gave no indication. His attention was absorbed in the mess he'd made of his plate. Even when the table was cleared by the mess crew, he remained distant.

It wasn't like the captain, which worried Satrap. Zohar could be a vital ally or a terrible foe.

*A problem for later.*

"Captain Ho—" Satrap did what he could to smile. "As Captain Zohar has said, your canny ability to pull out of the battle before the Kedraalian force could damage your ship has given us a potential advantage we might otherwise not have in this war."

"The continued ability to launch our fighter craft?" The way the old man's eyes sparkled, it was impossible to tell whether or not he was joking.

"That is one of the greatest advantages we have now, yes. But also, we have now seen which officers are disciplined and smart enough to best serve the Khan."

Ikhama's head bobbed up and down. *"Might is measured not in the force of the blow delivered, but in the—"*

"—*but in the accuracy.*" Satrap smiled. "Thank you, Ikhama."

Ho grunted, then bowed toward the old woman. "You say then that it was no lack of bravery that led to the retreat you sounded, Satrap?"

"By bravery, do you mean a hunger for self-destruction?"

"That meaning had eluded me, I'm afraid."

"Staying to fight our enemies' combined fleet would have been suicide."

"We were moments away from launching more fighters, Satrap."

Zohar chose that moment to rise out of his melancholy again. "Only when the sky is full of such a threat do they matter, Captain. Listen to Satrap. He saw this before the rest of us did. It isn't the first time, either."

The ancient priestess bowed her head. *"In my voice is the thunder of the tempest and the howl of the void. In my captains is the fire of the Guiding Star. In my satraps is the wisdom of the eons."*

Ho returned Ikhama's bow. "This is so. My apologies, Satrap."

Satrap waved the old man's concerns away. "A captain who won't speak up should have no voice."

"Your wisdom is of the eons, clearly."

"What if I told you that my wisdom leaves me feeling that we can no longer call this assembly of ships a fleet?"

Color flashed through the old captain's face. "This is the Khan's glorious—"

"We have one carrier, Captain. We are down to two cruisers. With the disappearance last night of the *Tip of the Spear*, we are less than half strength with our frigates. Even with the special missile ships the Khan graciously gifted us, our firepower is optimistically half of what it was."

Zohar's eyes came up from studying the stained tablecloth for a moment, then dropped down again.

Was he disinterested in discussing the next step with the fleet?

Ho cleared his throat. "Then we return to Azh Shivan to await the strike of the sword for our failure?"

"Hardly." Satrap leaned on the table. "We go to one of our prearranged destinations to await resupply and reinforcement. And we put together a change to the strategy that will give us the best chance to survive these misfortunes."

Ho grunted, and his eyes narrowed. "The strategy came from the lips of our Khan. That means the strategy is not the problem but those executing it."

"The strategy never accounted for the level of attrition suffered."

"A lack of execution. We failed—"

"Captain—" Satrap rapped his knuckles against the tabletop. "The failures began with the incessant calls for mutiny."

The old man stiffened and blinked. "Mutiny was born of a desire for success."

It had been a bad idea to coax opinions from the old fool. "Can we agree that the fleet, as a concept, is imperiled? You've seen the enemy force."

"We should avoid them. We should strike easier targets until—"

"What easier targets? The other Gulmar planets? The remaining Moskav—?"

"Yes! Either! Or the Kedraalian home. It is the heart of sin."

Satrap clenched his jaw against a groan. "There will be defenses any place we go now, and not the paltry forces the Moskav sent against us."

The old man glared at Zohar, who didn't look up, then turned to Ikhama. "Our directive—"

"No." Satrap rubbed his aching legs. "Captain Ho, please listen."

After a second, Ho folded his arms over his chest. "I listen."

"We must demand reinforcements. We must insist upon the ships we were promised at the start: the *Stroke of Vengeance* to replace our lost carrier; the *Purity of Fire* to replace the *Divine Wind*. And we must have frigates to replace the ones lost in battle."

Ikhama raised her hands high. "*From Khan comes the power of the Guiding Star. His sword strikes true and lays low the asp and the crocodile.*"

Satrap smiled patiently. "That may be true, but it's from the Khan's shipyards that our salvation must be sought."

"Our Khan is greater than any shipyard."

"Yet he must remain on Azh Shivan, and that means the robots he took in exchange for keeping the Kedraalian hostages alive must continue building more ships. Without those ships, the war cannot continue."

Ho's chin jutted out. "Our failings come from the lies these Kedraalians tell."

"Do they?" Satrap fought back annoyance. "There is no mistaking the spacecraft these shipyards produce. We are in one now."

"But the systems fail—"

"The systems perform better than we could have expected. The robots have worked without stopping for years now, first building the two ship-yards, then the fleet. While the promised shadow technology might have disappointed, it is the work of you and your fellow captains that matters most. When you follow orders, we succeed. The first Gulmar fleet, Radetta, Moskav—my leadership has gifted you with successes."

"And failures, Satrap."

"When you conspire against me, yes. If everyone had followed my orders, the *Desert Sands* would not have been extended so far out beyond our systems' ability to protect it."

Ho's chin jutted out even more: defiance without speaking it.

Satrap leaned back. "Think of these Kedraalians, Captain. How short-sighted are they, to not see that they were dooming if not themselves then the generations to follow? Can you imagine destroying your own chil-dren's lives?" When Ho didn't answer, Satrap turned to Zohar. "Captain Zohar?"

The captain's mouth opened, then closed.

*Where was his mind?*

Then, Zohar cleared his throat. "Satrap is correct. Our situation troubles me. No one could have seen the fleet collapsing as it has."

Satrap relaxed. "And so we must head to our next destination."

Ho's cheeks puffed out. "And where is this?"

"I've sent an emergency message to our Khan. I've requested reinforcements—what I just mentioned to the both of you. The loss of the *Desert Sands* has been described as the failure of its captain."

Zohar squinted, as if he might finally be fully engaged. "A dangerous choice. Our Khan was close with Captain—"

"Dangerous, yes." Satrap frowned. "Necessary, though."

He wanted to question whether the closeness of the two men—the Khan and his favorite captain—might be proof that incompetence was a contagion, but Ho would seize on such a joke as unacceptable blasphemy, and Zohar might not even rise in defense or condemnation.

Was Ho's behavior a sign of trouble brewing with the captains, another mutiny?

The captain of the *Blessed Saber of Xenu* wasn't about to divulge anything along those lines, which meant extending the banquet any further was pointless. If there were answers to be had, they would come from Zohar.

Satrap wiped his hands with a linen napkin, and Ikhama stood. She led them through another prayer that stretched for an eternity.

When she was done, Ho stood. "Thank you once more, Satrap."

"This was a pleasure, Captain Ho. Your words leave me much to ponder."

The old man bowed, then exited.

Before the hatch had even closed, Satrap turned to Zohar. "Is this another insane conspiracy to execute me?"

Zohar didn't even acknowledge the question, instead staring into space.

Satrap slammed a hand down on the tabletop. "Captain Zohar!"

The younger man overcame whatever had dazed him. "Yes?"

"Do you and the other captains conspire against me again?"

"What?" Zohar's brow creased. "No. You think because Ho refused to heed you that the rest of us have lost our minds?"

"Well…" Satrap hadn't expected such a reply. "The way he behaved—"

"Ho fears for his life, same as the others."

"But not you?"

The captain shrugged. "Life has taken on a bitter taste, I think."

Not bravery but apathy? Resignation? "What has changed?"

Zohar drew in a deep breath, then squeezed his eyes shut. "My wife. She sent a message with the last reinforcements. I had put off watching the video out of a sense of…foreboding."

"About?"

"About everything. What has gone on at home has eaten at me. And now…" The captain's face pinched in pain or sorrow. He dabbed his eyes with a napkin.

Sorrow, then. "I apologize. Can I help in some way?"

"Not unless you should rise to Khan yourself and change the collective madness of our people."

Ikhama gasped, but Satrap waved her to silence. "What happened, Zohar?"

"My son. He has been accepted into training for the piloting program."

"Training? What training does he need to have explosives strapped to him?"

"Yes. I laughed at the wording myself. It means that the boy is already being fitted for the flight suit that will keep him alive while his fighter hurtles through space. And since it is nothing more than that, it would seem most likely he will be on the next shipment out."

*The carrier I have demanded.* Satrap's stomach threatened to flip. "If the *Stroke of Vengeance* is sent to us, as requested, I can have him brought to our ship, but the carrier was still weeks from completion when I sent that message."

Zohar shook his head. "Everything speeds forward with the weight of war."

"You cannot push the robots faster than—"

"My wife says this has already been done. Those who fancy themselves engineers among Khan's staff have pushed *everything* beyond the edge of safety."

"That's reckless."

"It is war. It spreads like fire. Like fire, it must consume everything around it or die."

Ikhama leaned over to pat the young captain on the shoulder. "Your daughters remain safe. That is something."

The captain's eyes squeezed shut again. "No. Not even they have been fully spared this madness. The younger one has been sent to the Khan's palace. Her rebelliousness was apparently identified as a thing of curiosity. They consider her now as an Ikhama requiring only stern indoctrination."

Those words set Ikhama's lips to trembling. "It is not so."

Zohar laughed—angry and pain-filled. "It is very much so."

"But..."

The captain took her hand. "What does this mean, Ikhama? You told me before that the life of your kind is a blessed one."

"It is. I have been blessed many times in my life. Nothing might hope to replace the glory of service to our Holy Khan."

After a moment, Zohar released her hand. "Thank you."

He stood, bowed to Satrap, then strode from the banquet room, his boots as quiet as the passing of a ghost.

Satrap waved his Jakkara over. The night had drained him, even if there hadn't been a conspiracy to uncover. Demanding reinforcements from the Khan had been frightening enough without now discovering that such an act might have accelerated the death of Zohar's son.

As the Jakkara wheeled Satrap back to his quarters, he noted their alert posture and the way they moved through the ship. He was as safe as he had ever been, protected by those drawn from the ranks of his enemies. This was as it should have been from the start. Still, he worried now that he might have tempted the Khan's attention with what had been done to reinforce the ranks depleted by the acts of traitors. The captains—surely at least Ho—must have complained.

And yet, it was necessary. Satrap's life had never truly been secure before now.

It wasn't as if he'd acted out of a desire for power. He posed no threat to the Khan. The single desire—voiced from the start—was to be free when the bloody mission was complete.

Maybe the trust that this might happen once the final enemy fell wasn't misplaced. Maybe there was a chance to escape the madness of the Khan.

Except, success would mean that all the other people who had once stood against the Khan would be broken, probably annihilated. Where would there be to hide then?

It was actually a clever lie. The Khan had known such a promise was pointless. Freedom? There is no freedom when you're born into the twisted, incestuous disaster of the Khanate, even if you knew it was madness. If anything, awareness was a curse.

*You lie to yourself, letting the pain twist your mind. Freedom awaits when you deliver the promised victories.*

"Satrap?" The captain of the Jakkara stood at Satrap's side, nodding to the pile of pillows that made his room a little more tolerable.

"Thank you."

The bodyguards lifted their master's broken form from his chair and gently settled him in a corner. In the few moments where they adjusted his life-sustaining gear, he fought back panic that they might have been compromised and would leave him disconnected until the poisons built up in his blood and he slipped into an agonized state of collapse.

He thanked them again as they left, and he thought one of them turned back and bowed slightly.

Or maybe it had been meant to hide a look of loathing.

Seconds dragged by as the system labored to return him to a modicum of tolerable pain. His bones ached; the atrophied muscles twitched. It seemed like he was slowly cooking, the sweat beading on his upper lip.

"I need to sleep. I need to have the pain taken away. Please."

The system sensed the rising indicators more than his voice—chemicals building up; elevated heart rate and temperature; brain waves that were dangerously outside acceptable ranges.

Drugs burned in his veins, then turned into a cool tingle.

A hint of relief shrouded his mind. Troubling thoughts of being responsible for killing Zohar's boy, of pushing the captains too hard and angering the Khan, of abusing Ikhama more than she could stomach...

...faded.

The drugs were glorious. There should be an endless supply, a chance to slip away from the pain every day.

But even with the drugs in his system, there were lingering pains and problems.

Still, it wasn't new data but data he kept pushing back in the queue. Everything was a crisis right then, every piece of information received more important than the piece received before it, until eventually he had a mountain of data to work through.

This, though? It was important. He needed to dig into it. Soon. When he woke from his mostly pleasant but dreamless sleep.

After all, they moved through the protective realm of Fold Space. They were safe.

He could push it off. For now. For a little while longer.

## 3

———————

The sensation of falling played through Darien Caville's mind over and over again, until he wasn't sure if he was still falling or dreaming. In the moment of absolute silence, he fell through an inky darkness that wrapped around him, while a circle of light overhead shrank to a pinprick before disappearing completely. He sucked in a frozen breath of what seemed like ancient death, then called out to the young woman who had fallen with him.

Except he couldn't recall her name.

Then he smashed against something soft and giving and blacked out.

When he woke, it was an eternity later, and the slightest shift of his limbs told him the cycle was ready to begin anew—falling through the black, watching the light shrink to a pinprick, desperately sucking in the air.

But he didn't fall again.

All around him, there was nothing but the black of a deep cave. Cool, fine sand brushed against his flesh—dry now and he thought possibly rough with goosebumps.

The one thing that told him he wasn't at the beginning of the cycle again was the absence of the circle of light.

Wait.

There had been heat, too. He'd been wet with sweat. Even in the death-tinged air, he could still smell the salty musk on him.

So…

He had fallen. Fallen from the light. Fallen into darkness.

From the burning heat into the cold of a tomb, he had fallen.

But he hadn't been alone. There had been a woman—tall, with full lips, and pale brown eyes. He had inevitably compared her to someone…

Stiles!

His sister in training. She'd been taller, pretty where the woman who'd fallen with him had softer features. She was softer in every way. Could she have survived such a fall, then?

What was her name?

Denise Gallo. A Khanate spy, a traitor embedded in the Kedraalian prime minister's staff.

But she had also been confused. A naive and foolish child poisoned by her mother.

She had to be nearby, same as she'd been above. There had been a twist as he fell, the result of the ground giving away beneath him. Had he seen her falling the opposite direction?

Caville sat up, and despite his conditioning, let out a moan. The muscles of his back protested, lancing his spine with pain. His foot—his pinky toe—burned like fire. Lightheadedness nearly stole his awareness, and a wet fullness in his sinuses quickly turned into the taste of blood at the back of his throat.

He hacked, twisted his neck gingerly, brushed his hand over the cool sand, then spat.

And that was it. The lightheadedness went no further than a momentary dabbling with nausea. Aches in his joints and back didn't turn into the brilliant pain of grinding bone.

His breathing had been shallow up to that point. He tested his body, drawing in more of the foul air, pushing through the bruised feeling in his ribs.

Then again. And again.

Free climbing was out of the question for now. Full-contact sparring, too.

Living was good enough.

He got his knees beneath him, fought for balance, pushed back against vertigo, then stood.

Besides the Gallo woman, what had fallen with him?

An assault rifle. Water. Food. A light. His duffel bag.

Even more than the woman, those were necessary for survival. Training told him to drop back to his knees and reach out in a slow searching pattern.

Instead, he cocked his head, listening for any hint of breathing. "Denise?"

Not a shout…not even conversational volume. That would have been the same as a shout in the silence.

A thready breath seemed to come from somewhere to his right. He had no way of knowing if it came from above or below, inside something or muffled by material. In the dark, the mind tried to fill in details and failed miserably. It created impossible scenarios.

Caville went to his knees and then to his hands, and with teeth gritted against the pain, he began the agonizing process of stretching his left arm out to first determine if the ground was level, then to see if it was nothing but sand, then to search for his belongings.

A slight slope. All sand. No gear.

He shuffled sideways like a crab, rotated, and repeated the process, slowly mapping out his surroundings in his head.

The top—or near the top—of a mound. All sand for as deep as his hand could plunge without trying to dig. There were spots of warmer sand, but it was mostly cool to the touch and in some spots colder than it would be before dawn.

When the thready breathing came again, he froze.

There were possibilities. One of them was that Gallo had survived, same as he had, but she was hurt—maybe unconscious. Another was that Gallo had died, and there was something in the darkness waiting to strike. Still another was that Gallo hadn't fallen with him after all, and he was the one who was unconscious, and his wounded brain was imagining everything.

Gallo surviving the fall and being nearby was actually a slim possibility. It seemed more likely that a nocturnal hunter was in close proximity, clawed hands curling and opening, watching hungrily—

*The mind plays tricks. It fills in the gaps.*

"Denise?" It came out hissed, directed to where he imagined the breathing had come from.

The breathing transitioned to a moan. "Darien?"

It was her voice, and it came from where the breathing had been.

He relaxed. "Are you all right?"

"No. My ankle hurts. I hit really hard. I…I think I cracked a tooth. There was something in my mouth—blood, too. Now there's a sharp edge when I lick my back teeth."

"Okay."

"A-and my jaw hurts."

"An ankle and a cracked tooth aren't bad. Are you on sand?"

"Yes. It's all over me."

"Do you have anything around you? The water bottle? A backpack?"

Sand rasped not too far away, as if sheeting down over a cliff face.

That was the mind filling in blanks again.

Gallo gasped. "There's a bag. I think it's yours."

Something clicked softly, then a light as bright as the sun hit him in the eyes. He'd been stupid, looking right at the sound of her voice instead of keeping it in his peripheral vision. Now, spots danced in front of him, even when he squeezed his lids shut.

He shielded his eyes and turned away. "All right. I'm blind."

"Sorry!"

"No. It's good. I'll be fine in a minute. Look around you. Tell me what you see."

"Um. Sand. Some of it's red, but most is black."

"Black? Like volcanic rock black?"

"I— Maybe?"

"Don't worry about it. Did you find my duffel bag?"

"It looks like it. Oh. And my ankle is swollen. It's dark."

"Can you move it?"

She whimpered. "It's really tender."

"But it moves?"

"Yes."

"A bad sprain. You'll survive. What's inside my bag?"

The throaty scrape of the zipper tore through the darkness. "Ammunition. Protein bars. Water bottles. Clothes. A pist—two pistols. Is this Captain Goldman's?"

"The same type." It was the duffel bag. "Keep the flashlight pointed at the bag, okay?"

"I'm sorry."

"It's fine." Through the exploding lights and strange dots that danced all around him, he could make out her shape hunched forward, one knee raised, the other leg stretched straight out. The flashlight beam leaked through the thick material of the bag.

He crab-walked toward her, processing what the light hinted at between them. She was about midway down a mound of sand—sparkly black most of it. He was closer to the top of an adjoining larger mound. At the edge of the glow, the slope downward became more pronounced. As he moved toward her, the whisper of sand scraping over the face of rock rose from below.

Her head turned toward him, and the flashlight beam came out of the duffel bag enough to foul his vision a little. "Darien? Where is this?"

Caville stopped, eyes squeezed tight and covered again. "The Place of the Fallen."

*Fallen.* He almost laughed. It hadn't been meant literally, yet...

"These were ruins. I heard about the videos. One of the women I talked to worked on—"

"That was decades ago, right?"

"Yes."

He looked away from her, slowly turned his head until he could just barely see the light again, then he moved closer. "Keep the light pointed into the bag."

"Oh. I didn't think—"

"That's fine. You can point it away from me, but if you point it toward me—"

"I know. I wasn't thinking."

The light pointed away, revealing what might have been a stone wall at the edge of the beam maybe twenty meters out.

When he reached her side, he grabbed the wrist holding the light and took it from her. It was gentle but fast, removing any chance of another inadvertent blinding flash. Then he set the light down so that it pointed at her extended leg.

"This is the swollen ankle?"

She nodded. "It's a dull throb. When I move it at all, it turns sharp."

"Yeah." He'd wrenched an ankle during training once.

He ran fingers down to the bottom of the robe and pulled it above her knee. Her legs had the shape of a youth of leisure—neither well-muscled nor totally soft. They weren't thin, so the bone and joints weren't prominent, but there was no discoloration and nothing seemed out of alignment. When he massaged her thigh and worked down to the knee, she didn't yelp, but the closer he came to her ankle, the more her breathing sped up.

A good five centimeters above the swelling, she swatted him. "Stop!"

"We can't stay here. When we get to a place where we can rest, you'll need to stay off of it and keep it elevated."

"I can't wait." She squeezed his shoulder. "Do you know where we are?"

"No. There's something over there, at the edge of the light." He pointed to where she'd shone the light earlier. "I want to give it a look."

She nodded, but there was fear in her eyes and the implicit plea not to be abandoned.

As he creept toward what had seemed to be a wall, he searched around with the light. Beyond where they'd landed, the sand was almost completely black. It sparkled in the light, and it had the same consistency as the red sand, so it was the same thing other than the coloring.

About fifteen meters out from where Gallo sat watching, the details of what the light had revealed became clearer. It was a black wall of glass or crystal. It wasn't flat but chiseled yet still smooth, as if molten glass had been poured over the surface of rock and allowed to take on its form. The sand sloped down maybe five meters short of that wall, dropping until it reached a level spot of the same sort of black material, and from there, the surface dropped away.

Caville played the light overhead, now making out the edges of a perfect tube of the same black crystal that ended just at the edge of the light.

So, they'd been standing above the tube, which must have opened, then closed. How far from the desert floor above to the sand below? More than twenty meters. They could easily have died, sand or not.

He circled the sandpile, getting a feel for its dimensions and shape, listening to the echoes when the sand rained down.

When he returned, Gallo had her arms hooked around her raised knee and was rocking. "I could see you. The light, the way you moved up and down the dunes. Even when you went on the other side, there was still the glow."

"They aren't dunes."

She shrugged. "Whatever you call sand piles."

"Lifesavers, I think." He stretched, extending the light as far above his head as he could. "We probably fell twenty meters. If we'd been farther out —" He pointed the light to where the sand sloped steeply down. "—it could've been another ten meters."

"That's…a long way."

"I don't think it was a fall the entire way. It felt like it, but I'm betting that roof overhead dipped down rather than just collapsing. No, not collapsing. Opening. I saw a circle of light shrink, then disappear."

She blinked at him. "It's not supposed to be like this."

"You said that."

"The Khan sent scientists out a long time ago. They poked around here, then everyone died. It was a place you could walk around in. It rose up out of the ground."

Caville nodded. "Before this was all sand, right?"

"That's what she said—the person I talked to. We had scientists—real ones—back then. She said they theorized this was what caused everything to die off."

"No wonder the Khan didn't want more scientists."

"Because that goes against the belief that he controls everything?"

"Exactly." He pressed the base of the flashlight against his chin. "This thing we're on top of, it used to rise above the ground. We're not getting out the way we came in, so I need to see if we can go down deeper."

"Down?" There was a desperate, whiny tone to her voice. "I can't—"

"I'm not leaving you. This is about us finding out where we are. Without knowing that, we can't get out. Okay?"

She wrapped an arm around his thigh. "You *do* want out."

"When I'm done here. If we can escape, we will."

"O-okay." She sounded skeptical, anxious.

"Look, the first thing you do at a time like this is assess your situation. What's your condition? What are your resources? What are your options? Right now, we've got a good idea of our condition, right?"

"Not good."

"Not bad, you mean. We're sore, but we don't have broken bones. We can move."

She massaged the flesh above her ankle. "*You* can."

"We'll get you moving. The next problem is resources. We need water. A day or two without it, and we're in real trouble."

"I'm already thirsty."

"That's your brain messing with you." He rotated slowly, shining the light at every promising shadow. "Let's conserve that water for now, okay? I didn't see our other bottles anywhere."

"Right. And our rifles?"

"Same thing. They probably—" He nodded down the slope. "Down there. Which is our next thing to explore."

"What if there's nothing down there? If it all just falls away, what do we do?"

"We figure out other options. Or we stretch out that water and those protein bars as long as we can." He didn't need to tell her what would come when things ran out.

Her shoulders slumped. "Don't leave me here."

"I won't."

"Promise?"

"Promise. You're sore and scared. It makes perfect sense to feel that way. I'm no different. We're in this together, all the way to the end. But for now…" He pointed the light down the sandy slope.

Gallo released him.

It was treacherous after a few meters. When the sand started to give beneath him, it quickly picked up speed, whispering down like an avalanche, hitting the flat top of whatever was below him, then spraying out and disappearing in a sparkling shower. He took to plunging a hand into the sand to slow his descent, but that quit working about halfway down.

That's when he just sort of ended up being launched down to the black surface below.

He felt it coming, but there was nothing he could do about it. During his youth, some of the trainers used sandglasses to track time. Seeing the sand whisper through the narrow channel to collect on the bottom—that's what he was on top of now: the piled sand. And it was hurtling him toward the bottom.

Clutching the flashlight meant he only had one hand to grasp the sand and slow his fall. Releasing the light wasn't an option—they were blind without it.

So he threw himself onto his back and spread his legs.

And slid.

It slowed him some, and when he hit the bottom, he bent his legs and threw himself onto his belly.

That wasn't enough to kill all of his momentum, though. All of the sand that had collected on top of the bottom acted like ice, which he skidded along, teeth gritting, free hand searching for purchase on the glassy surface.

Sand sprayed out into the black, then his free hand shot out. A leg. The other leg.

Then he was over the lip of the bottom, the light showing nothing beyond.

He had a vague sense of a glass-smooth, curved wall that might fit within the empty tube above.

But there were recesses in the tube. Grips.

His free hand had already shot past.

With a curse, he let go of the flashlight and stretched for one of the grips. A finger touched one, smooth and sturdy—a rung.

It slipped from his grasp.

He clutched at the next and missed.

Another—desperate, terrified.

Then his fingertips finally slid over the top of one, and he squeezed. His grip held, and he was slammed into the recess, his knees smacking against the glass with a clap. Pain jolted from his hand to his shoulder, down his tortured back, and through his legs.

Caville glanced down, saw the tumbling light...

It struck, finally, hitting another flat, black surface and winking out.

An instant later, the light flickered back on, strobing softly, to reveal a spill of things that weren't as perfectly black as the surface. It was too far away to be sure, but...

One of the rifles? A ruptured water bottle?

The rungs ran down as far as he could see, maybe all the way down to the much wider flat surface below. If he hurried, he might be able to reach the light, possibly recover it, maybe spot something down there: a way in, perhaps.

But if the light went out...if the rungs ended...

Would it matter without the light? They could lie on top of the sand until they died of dehydration. That would be their only choice without light. Descending the sand to the rooftop he'd slid off of?

Suicide.

The light died again, then it came back. Weaker.

Had Gallo called his name?

His body ached.

He began the descent.

I t was storming out, a blizzard like Stiles couldn't recall ever seeing before. The snow was fat and heavy, the wind fierce, creating a blinding whiteout. All the heat had been sucked out of her body, leaving her shivering worse than...

Someone had left her naked in a freezing room, feet soaking in a bucket of liquid. They'd hooked electrodes to her and clamped leads to areas thick with nerve clusters. How many days had they hit her with jolts that nearly made her crack her teeth?

This was like that. Maybe worse.

Like falling into a pool of ice water and having the top closed over you.

Her body seemed to have lost all of its strength. She couldn't lift her arms or legs. No amount of effort could move her head.

Yet she was moving. There was a sense of gliding.

"Do you understand the mission?"

The voice came from the snowy void. Maybe it was her brother, Caville. He'd been nearby before the blizzard. He'd taken the gun from someone, the gun...the same gun he'd carried with him on their trip to Dramora.

What was so special about that gun? What was it he'd done?

They jogged through the snow, each now in their teens, filled out with the bodies of an adult. At some level, she knew that they were beautiful, that people would be drawn to them without even wanting to be. Unsophisticated thinking called it the male gaze, but it was the human gaze. Caville could make any of her sisters react to him, the same way she could make any of the boys react to her.

But she'd learned to control herself during training. Now she could admire the physique beneath Caville's charcoal skintight suit the same way he could admire hers, but neither of them would succumb to animal needs.

He trudged over the deep snow until he reached a gray-white tree trunk that appeared out of nowhere. He waved her over to his right, and she found a tree there as well.

"Do you understand the mission?" His voice was in her ear.

Electronics built into the suit: radio, optics, armor. The suits were supposed to insulate them, too. They were supposed to provide grip and a level of tactile sensitivity that made opening a door or plucking up a millimeter-thin straw as easy as using naked flesh. Easier.

She tried to remember how the communicators worked. "Darien?"

"The mission."

"I heard you. I can't remember it."

He groaned. "You need to. Try harder."

Typical. Rather than provide a hint or a tip, he pushed away from the tree and went back to the silly-looking snow hop they'd used to get to the tree, pulling a foot out of the deep-piled stuff, poking it out, then plunging it back in a little farther ahead.

She fell in close behind, struggling a bit to keep up. He was taller, produced more testosterone that created muscle mass easier. Genetic design couldn't undo the evolutionary differences between the male and female body, not without blurring the lines.

But her body had advantages over his. For one, she handled pain better than he could.

Caville stood at a door and whipped his masked head around. "Are you ready?"

"Darien, something's wrong. I'm freezing to death."

"You're alive."

"No. The suit's not working. When I run, I don't feel like—"

She fell against the wall—not hard, but it was as if she had no control over herself.

Her brother stared down at her. "You're running out of time. Do you remember?"

"The mission?" She rubbed her face.

The mask came away. Snow clung to her skin, wet and cold. When she brushed the flakes away, there was sensation in her fingertips.

No gloves, she realized. "Darien?"

He knelt beside her as something boomed somewhere beyond the door. "We trained from childhood. There's nothing we can't do."

"My head's a gummy mess. It's hard to think."

"You took a good hit. You'll be fine. The mission, though. You need to—"

"—remember the mission. I get that."

A smell like alcohol and heavy-duty soap hit her then. Her gut clenched, and she thought she might throw up until cinnamon flashed through her awareness.

Cinnamon.

They hadn't reached puberty yet. It was a day where training hadn't left them all sagging with fatigue and soreness. One of their trainers—a big, muscular woman with her hair shaved down to stubble on either side of her head and a small crest of black rising like a fin from the top—had escorted them to the dining hall and told them to take a seat at one of the benches.

Stiles and Caville had settled across from each other, the intense rivalry that normally laced every moment between them with an electric sense of imminent violence gone for an instant.

He glanced at the others, then leaned in toward her slightly. "What do you think it is?"

"They didn't break us today. When they don't break us, there's usually a mental lesson."

"Yeah." Maybe he'd thought of that, but the way he looked around—the corner of his mouth twisted up resentfully—made it seem like he'd just now realized it.

Before he could ask another question, Black Fin rolled a cart out of the kitchen area. Steam condensed on a clear top covering a tray centered on the cart top. She stopped in the center of the group table and pulled the top off, releasing steam heavy with an aroma that made Stiles think of bliss.

On the tray, white glaze slithered down the side of golden bread. Dark brown particles poked out from the end of the nearest of the bread mounds.

A ribbon. The bread was a thin ribbon that had been rolled up.

Black Fin knelt and took a platter of cups filled with milk from the row beneath the tray. "Cinnamon rolls. Grab a plate and a fork. You'll want this milk, too."

The bread was warm—almost hot—and the glaze was even hotter.

And it was ecstasy.

"Life is simple." Black Fin licked icing from her fingertip. "You work hard, and you succeed. You get lazy, and you fail. Success brings rewards —like these cinnamon rolls. Failure brings punishment. For you, that's death. Do you understand?"

The Genesis 3 brood nodded enthusiastically. Black Fin could have ordered them to butcher the kitchen staff at that point, and they would have.

"You have one mission. Remember that." The big woman stared right at Stiles. "The Kedraalian Republic must survive. Your enemies might be foreign or domestic. It doesn't matter. When you know your target, you will eliminate them. That's how the republic survives."

Stiles dragged a finger through the sweet icing, eyes wide in awe. It was sugar. There must be a fluid mixed in, too. Something must thicken it all. She felt Black Fin's glare. The woman wanted an answer of some sort.

The mission. Stiles smiled. "Eliminate our enemies. The republic survives."

That put a smile on the trainer's blocky face. "Exactly."

Stiles drew her finger closer, studying the icing...

Which turned into snow.

That melted.

A deep, throaty whine rumbled beneath her, and she sat up.

She was in a car.

Rain pelted against a window to her right. Someone had buckled her into a front seat—passenger side. Hot air blasted her chest, rustling the light fabric of the loose shirt she wore. It was a hideous plaid pattern and was too big. It smelled musty, as if it'd been stored for a long time.

To her left, a tall man with silver hair was looking out the driver's side window.

Looking out and down, she realized.

The whine: an air car. They were airborne.

And then she realized who he was. "Colonel McLeod?"

He spun around, eyes wide. "Brianna?" He relaxed. "They said you could be days coming around."

"What—?" She shivered. The snow was gone, but she was still freezing.

"I'll explain it all. Why don't you get some sleep."

Sleep. It sounded like a great idea. She leaned against the door and closed her eyes.

She had a mission. He would tell her what it was. Later.

**4**

———

When Benson was able to, she showed up shortly after 4 a.m. at the officers' fitness room, which was about twice the size of her cabin. The equipment was rarely in use so early. Most days, it was just like now: polished and bright in the LED light meant to emulate a clear Kedraalian noon sky. At least a few times a week, she tried to hit the weights for thirty minutes, and every time she came into the small room, she committed to an hour of cardio. After a night with Thiessen, she wasn't sure that she could last *half* an hour at a walk.

*What were you thinking?*

As she slowly accelerated to a jog on the treadmill, that thought seemed to play in a loop. It was bad enough that she'd let herself get involved with the Gulmar captain, but some of the things they'd done...

She blushed and smiled at the memory.

Who said you were ever too old? Besides, she wasn't even forty!

Her heart pounded, and her sneakers thudded on the rubber tread, but the noises from the night before almost certainly had to be spilling out of her head. They would be too loud for the hatch to hold them in. The towel wrapped around her neck was damp with sweat, and she thought she could smell Thiessen's cologne coming from the material.

He was a part of her. It was a comforting thought and wholly inappropriate after a single night together. Yet there was so much more about him that she connected with than she ever had with Halliwell. With him, it had been two pained souls finding comfort in each other.

Thiessen was *different*.

Yes, he had a painful history with a hard childhood.

And he'd survived tragedy.

He resented the situation that had him in his current military—security—service. But where Halliwell seemed always ready to lash out at the rest of the world without explaining exactly why he was so mad, the Gulmar captain had a cool calm and an understanding about his situation.

There was certainly anger and resentment. How could there not be?

Yet he held them in check and viewed the universe through an eye that wasn't jaded but wary.

What mattered more, though, was that the connection they shared allowed him to communicate.

It built trust.

The hatch opened, and Benson twisted around just enough to see who'd come in.

Commander Dietrich looked around the room like someone who'd entered a dance studio while searching for a nightclub. Toothpick-thin legs poked out of what looked like fresh-printed gym shorts. A loose blue T-shirt that had probably been used more often as a nightshirt than its intended gym top jutted out where his small belly protruded. The arms that hung at his side were only slightly sturdier than his legs because he used his hands all the time.

His brown eyes jumped from the weights system to the pull-down treadmills and exercise bikes. He wandered over to the station beside hers, pulled a slender bike down and let it unfold and snap into place, then climbed onto the seat. It looked like he might fall off at any moment, and he fumbled around clumsily before figuring out how to slide the tips of his sneakers into the pedal straps.

When he started pedaling, his eyes widened, and his head dropped to the small control panel.

Benson pointed to the top left corner. "It defaults to an uphill gear. You can knock the resistance down to low until you get a feel for it."

His cheeks puffed out as he huffed. Once he had the setting where he wanted it, he nodded. "Thank you."

"I can't recall the last time I saw you on a piece of fitness equipment."

"I only come…when I feel sufficient…self-loathing."

She wiped her face. It was nearly time to head back and shower, but if she left now, the doctor would have to come up with some other way of confronting her in private. Better to let him get it out of his system.

He started sweating quickly, his brow glistening and his cheeks flush. His hands locked onto the handlebar grips, which he squeezed like a swimmer clutching a lifeline in a gale.

When he seemed to be struggling to form words, Benson tried again. "I thought exercise was recommended as a good means of maintaining mental health."

"So is doing what entertains you. I happen to have a job I love."

"That sounds like a dangerous excuse to avoid dealing with work-life balance issues."

The doctor turned on her, scowling, cheeks turning even redder. "I can't believe you'd even pretend to care about something like that."

Benson stopped her treadmill. "What's that supposed to mean?"

"It means your job is to kill, and many times a little bit of scrutiny and objectivity might reveal there's little differentiation between the enemy and those operating under your command."

"Are you accusing me of being reckless?"

"Callous seems more appropriate."

"Callous." She wiped the treadmill down, careful not to look at the doctor. "You think I don't care when my people die?"

"That's a question you should answer for yourself."

"I value all human life."

Dietrich snorted. "You've pushed your chief engineer to the point that he's facing long odds of survival. If I were to create an entry for a medical journal describing callous disregard for personnel, I would embed a video of that situation as a prime example."

She folded the treadmill up into place and listened for the whirr of drying fans before turning back to the doctor. "What's wrong with Chief Parkinson?"

"I sent you the report last week."

"The radiation poisoning? That report indicated he had a full transfusion."

"And another yesterday, yes. And those are appropriate initial steps to halt the immediate threat. But to ensure the greatest likelihood of survival, the next step would be to use a resuscitation ring and put him in cold sleep. Facilities on Kedraal are far better suited to deal with the dosages he was exposed to than what we have aboard the *Valor*."

Benson wiped her arms down. She remembered the arms she'd had in her youth—leaner and firmer. Age killed just as effectively as anything else. It took everyone eventually. "What are the odds of his survival with your treatment?"

"That's your question?" Dietrich's sneakers came free of the pedals and smacked against the deck. He pushed up from the bike with some effort, nearly falling over. When he stood before her, his cheeks shook. "The correct question is, How do we make him see the error of his decision to avoid cold sleep?"

She shook her head. "I asked the question I wanted answered: What are the odds?"

"Sixty percent."

"A Marine in a combat posting would take those odds in a heartbeat."

"That's hardly relevant."

"Is it? Are you saying they're less valuable than Will because he's an engineer?"

"Of course not. The difference is that they've chosen to embrace the idiocy and waste of war. They charge full—"

"No." She balled her hands into fists and rested them on her hips. "You're not going to do this."

"Do what?"

"Turn this into another of your rants against the military."

"You can't tell me—"

"Ernie, no. This is the career you chose to go into. You've sworn to uphold the safety of our nation. Instead of a gun, you wield a scalpel and dispense medicine. You're still serving our cause."

The doctor's cheeks puffed out, but this time it wasn't from exertion. "I won't have you twist my oath. I won't accept that!"

"You're going to have to. It's long past time for you to ask yourself where you really stand. I've put up with you for the same reason the Navy did for all these years: You're the best surgeon we have. But—" She held up a hand to stop him when his mouth opened to interrupt her. "—you're going to have to make a choice, Commander. Are you a naval officer out to save the lives of sailors and Marines, or are you just drawing pay and acting as a stick in the mud, trying to undo the war effort in any way you can?"

"My concern is always with saving lives."

"Good. Then do that. Stick to that one thing, and stop with the sniping about the unfortunate need to kill the enemy."

"You can't tell me—"

"Ernie, I *can* tell you. I *am* telling you. You've been dangerously insubordinate and unprofessional. You've abused peers and subordinates, and you've crossed the line with senior officers. The protection you always had in the past won't be there much longer."

"Protection?"

"People like Martinez failing to document your alcohol problems and your lack of discipline. People like me covering for you when you decide you can tell an admiral that he doesn't know the first thing about valuing human life."

"I have a right to my views!"

"You do. But you don't have a right to express them. It's just one of the freedoms we give up when we sign on for service."

His eyes narrowed. "You get your promotion, and you become the enemy."

"There. That's a perfect example. You can't say that. You can't tell me that I'm the enemy. You can't tell me that I'm a callous butcher. Not only is it unprofessional, it's wrong. And when you say it, you undermine me."

"Sending people to their death. Killing civilians. That's a butcher, Captain."

"*Think* about what you're saying. You're equating what I do to what the Azoren or the Moskav or the Khanate do. Do you really believe that?"

Dietrich's back stiffened. "Killing is killing."

She sighed. "That's false equivalence. I hate war just as much as you do. I feel pain every time I send anyone—*anyone*, not just an engineer—into harm's way. It weighs on me."

"You hide it well."

"That's my job. But no commander worth a damn simply *accepts* that death is part of the deal. It is part of the deal, but it doesn't mean you don't wrestle with the pain of decisions gone wrong. If you can't control that, it could cripple you."

"What you do is *murder*." The doctor's nostrils flared.

"All right. What happens if we pack up everything and fly back to Kedraal? What happens if we shut down the Navy? Will the Khanate forget us? The Azoren?"

"We tell them we're neutral and uninterested in their squabbles."

Benson groaned. It was like talking to a child. "That's not how these extremists operate. They eradicate their enemies. Completely. You know that."

He clenched his jaw in reply.

She wasn't about to let him walk away with the idea that he'd *won* the disagreement, simply because he refused to accept her point. "We fight back for survival. If we don't, people die. *Our* people. Civilians. Children. If I don't make decisions in that struggle, someone else does. I happen to feel like I have an understanding of how to win this war. It doesn't involve *wishing* these demented people away."

"You have no idea what would happen if we disassembled our military."

"Actually, we do. We saw what the Azoren tried to do once we stripped our military down to the point where—" She stopped herself short of saying that people like him and Martinez should never have been allowed to remain in the service. It was the truth, but Dietrich wouldn't hear it, and saying it would have closed him off completely.

She took his hand and squeezed it lightly. "Think about it, okay? You're a good man. You have the skills to help the military. But things are changing. This task force? Us coming out here? The changes going on back home? What comes after?"

"After?"

"When the war ends. If there's no Khanate threat, no Azoren or Moskav threat: Will Parliament continue to fund the military at this new level, or will they gut it again? At some point, we'll be redundant. *All of us.*"

The hatch hissed closed behind Dietrich. His sneakers swished across the passageway deck outside the fitness room, and fresh air replaced the stuffy smell of the nasty place. His face burned, and his jaw ached. Thankfully, no one else was awake to annoy him. He could deal with the absurdity of the moment on his own.

Redundant. *Redundant!*

Benson was losing her mind.

There would always be a need for a surgeon of his skill and experience. Even if the military were to shrink down and release him, he could turn to a civilian job in a heartbeat. How many offers had he turned aside over the years?

And the ridiculous premise she built everything upon? That someone had been protecting him all these years? How preposterous!

He let himself into his cabin and settled into the chair before his desk, wondering at the way his heart was still hammering away, so loud in his ears in the silence, even though he'd finished his workout long ago.

Lights settled at just a bit brighter than a pre-twilight gray, and he turned to look his quarters over. As a commander, he rated a comfortable cabin. On another ship, he would've shared a larger space with another officer of equal rank. On the *Valor*, that wasn't necessary. Space wasn't that hard to come by.

They were the *flagship.* How else could someone better emphasize their importance?

How many years ago had he told Melissa that he would take care of her forever? She had yet to enter officer training, and he was already commissioned and moving up the ranks. Benson hadn't even started to take university prep classes yet at that point. She would've been a child trying to understand the onset of puberty, nothing more.

And *she* was telling *him* that he had a choice to make. A choice?

He snorted.

Sweat trickled down his cheeks, salty on his lips. He must have exerted himself more on the bike than he'd expected.

Except, it wasn't sweat. Tears blurred his vision.

How could Benson say the things she'd said?

She was smart. She cared about people. He saw it in her eyes: humanity and decency that so many others clearly lacked. Obviously, she understood the pointlessness of war, of killing. Destroy one enemy, another rises up in replacement. The problem was a lack of humaneness. What was needed was an outreach and education process. Help the enemy see that they were their own problem, that humanity was a single, bright light in the firmament, a light that would wink out if not properly cultivated.

He pulled his data pad from the desk corner and signed in.

The image of Melissa smiled back at him, frozen for eternity in her youth. They both wore navy whites—him a lieutenant, her a fresh-pressed ensign.

His fingers traced the gentle curve of her jaw, then tracked over the lips curved in a smile of bliss that couldn't possibly last.

*"They won't give me a posting to a research station, Ernie. They lied!"*

Melissa had been furious. She became bitter, fighting the broken institution. He tried to explain to her that his own postings would obviously need to be aboard ships until he finished his training and showed everyone that he offered skills and intellect far beyond what they were expecting. A few years, some experience as a surgeon—he would be able to pull an assignment back on Kedraal and demand she receive a posting nearby. Her skills were equal to his, her intellect something magnificent to behold. How could they waste her on a battered, old piece of trash?

She hadn't had the patience he'd asked of her. There was no satisfying her with a few weeks of passionate vacation when their ships happened to have schedules that overlapped.

*"This isn't a marriage. We barely know each other."*

It wasn't children. She had no interest in that, at least not until she had established herself. The world was too dangerous, anyway.

*"If you love me, you'll leave the Navy. Show me I'm what matters."*

But he couldn't. Not at that point. He needed more experience.

Her frustrations became his. Her impatience and inflexibility mapped over his own flaws. Understanding her positions had always been something that came naturally for him. Before long, he found himself echoing her words verbatim.

And she wasn't wrong. When she divorced him, she had every right. He'd failed to deliver his promises. How surprising it had been to discover a promising surgeon actually held far greater value aboard ships where people might be injured. And a lieutenant? A lieutenant commander? Those ranks weren't enough to make demands as he'd imagined.

So how could he hold it against her—any of it—when she'd turned acid-tongued toward him and broken off communication except for the rare update on how exciting her civilian life was?

Her words had brought such pain, although none of that was her fault. He was the one who'd made and failed to keep promises, after all.

Dietrich swiped the back of a hand over his eyes, clearing the tears.

It was one failure out of a lifetime of them. And those failures were compounding, growing greater and greater. Benson was right about the way he'd mistreated people, especially Kohn. It was uncalled for. The boy had so much potential, and he was a good soul who cared about his patients. Throwing bitter words his way was pouring poison into his life, ruining him.

*I had no right to parade him around as a trophy, dammit.*

Benson had seen how patently obvious a bad idea that had been, but she'd supported her senior doctor.

*Covering for me.*

"I should have joined you." Dietrich ran his fingers over Melissa's image again. The ship she'd eventually signed on for had an opening for a doctor. He would have been making less than his pathetic Navy pay, but he would've been with her. They could have disappeared together.

So many mistakes. So many regrets.

There was only one way to wash it all away, something he'd turned away from for too long.

Dietrich squatted before the small closet where his uniforms hung. There was a box there, hidden beneath his boots. Inside the box was a bottle, and inside that, the caramel-colored liquid that could warm him and clear his head so that he could better deal with the demands of his job of sewing back together the people torn apart by war.

He unscrewed the lid and took a drink of the smoky fluid, let the warmth settle into his gut, then relaxed.

The Engineering Bay fabrication system made a racket when assembling complex systems, and the drone Parkinson had programmed in would definitely qualify as a complex system. He leaned against the heavy plexiglass cover that shielded the fabricator mechanisms from humans who might be too curious for their own good. Beyond that cover, robotic arms whirled and whipped, placing printed panels and assembling components with frightening speed. In the span of an hour, the drone pieces had been printed out and nearly fully assembled. It was a process that would've taken him days to do by hand.

A wave of nausea ran through him, like having his innards freeze in an eye blink then melt just as quickly. He shuddered and sucked in the air, which was warm from the fabricator. Or maybe it was just the nausea.

Parkinson popped one of the pills Dietrich had provided. The chief engineer remembered that he'd left his cold drink in his office and turned.

Captain Benson—dressed in the same jumpsuit as his team—was talking to Petty Officer Hu, one of the junior engineers. Hu was a short, skinny kid with short black hair and small eyes with a severe enough epicanthic fold that it looked like she was always on the edge of falling asleep. She was saving up for a cosmetic process to have that fixed, although Parkinson couldn't figure out why. It didn't affect her performance. She was one of the high-potential members of his team, and he was leaning on her now more than ever.

Benson looked up, brow furrowing for some reason, as Parkinson approached. "Chief. Everything okay?"

A sort of perplexed look wrinkled Hu's broad face. She stuck a finger between her lips.

*Oh. Shit.* Parkinson yanked the pill from between his lips. "Sorry. I was going to grab my drink, Captain."

Understanding and what must be pity settled on Benson's face. "I'll join you."

She muttered something to Hu, then fell in behind the chief as he navigated the cluttered bay. After glancing back, she closed the hatch to his office and leaned against the bulkhead.

He washed the pill down with a drink of chilled water. "Everything okay?"

"I think I should be asking you that."

"The pill?" He shrugged and dropped into his seat. "Nausea meds."

"Are they working?"

"I'll let you know."

Benson jerked her head toward the bulkhead between them and the section of the bay that held the fabricator. "Petty Officer Hu said you're printing up a pretty advanced drone model."

"Telly."

"I'm sorry?"

Parkinson activated the desktop terminal, which flashed to life with a bright blue, rotating wireframe of the drone's guts. "That drone. It's probably the most capable model in our inventory. I can do all sorts of telepresence work through it. We had an older version on the *Pandora*. Roddy, remember?"

Her eyes widened the way they did when she figured something out. "Yes."

"If Telly works out, I figure I'll print up a few per ship."

The captain crossed her arms. "You were...close with your drones on the *Pandora*."

"They were reliable. You don't need to send people out when you've got a good drone."

"You don't." She pushed off from the hatch and crossed to his desk, squinting at the drone components on the display. "How are you doing?"

"Great. I mean, I could do without the pain of the transfusion, but it beats the alternative."

"Commander Dietrich told me he advised you to go into cold sleep."

"I—" Parkinson spun around to study the display, tapping a button that dressed Telly in his thick ceramic skin. "I've already had one resuscitation."

"Someone like you, I don't think there's a limit to that number."

His ears burned. It didn't sound—it didn't *feel*—right, not with Taylor a charred ruin left to float forever in the black of space. She'd deserved another chance at life, but no one had given it to her.

He tugged at the small patch of whiskers beneath his bottom lip. "There's a lot to do. I would've printed up more drones by now otherwise."

Benson settled on the end of the desk. "Chief, I need to know this is you."

"Me?"

"Your thinking and choosing. I need to know you're not acting out of pain."

"The meds control the pain—"

"Not from the radiation. I'm talking about the pain of what happened to Greta."

Why hadn't she called her Chief Taylor?

The answer was in the captain's posture—leaned in—and the way she squinted her eyes. She might as well have said that she knew he was confused and hurt and angry, that she could appreciate what it felt like to have someone so easily touch the confused core that he had lugged around his entire life. It was something no one else could understand, but Benson was special like that.

His throat constricted. "I—" He had to take a deep breath. It should have been cherry syrup soap and summer blossoms, but that wasn't the captain's scent. A tear threatened, but he blinked it away. "I liked her."

"Commander Karras said she was special—like you."

"Greta made me see how some of the things I did and said were easy to misunderstand."

"That's a real gift."

He brushed a finger across his eyes, which were damp despite him not wanting them to be. "She told me she wouldn't put up with my bullshit." A chuckle slipped out unexpectedly.

"I just finished writing up a posthumous commendation and a recommendation for consideration for the Navy Bronze Cross."

"She would've liked that."

"We've reviewed the audio and video. She went into a combat situation knowing the risks, did everything anyone could reasonably hope to do, then assisted getting the wounded out. It should go through."

"Thanks." His cheeks were damp now. That was odd. He'd decided against mourning her loss until later.

For some reason, Benson didn't seem satisfied. She kept leaning in, and her lips seemed squeezed tight when she wasn't talking. "You miss her."

He nodded. That was easier than talking. "Sure." That sounded like a squeak.

"Have you used an online counselor?"

"No. I'm fine. This is my decision. I…miss her, but it's not why I turned down resuscitation. I mean cold sleep. We have work to do. I want to see that it gets done. I have obligations, just like she said. This mission."

"She told you that?"

"When I was going out to the *Mao*. She said everyone's afraid. Because I was. I didn't know she was, but it's what she said. And she was right."

He had to use the cuff of his coveralls to dry his cheeks. Fortunately, his computing pad chimed: Telly was done.

Parkinson smiled and tapped the display. "He's ready to go."

Benson squinted at the terminal. "The drone?"

"Just needs some battery packs. I'll take him to one of the maintenance airlocks and give him a test run."

The captain stood, adjusting the jumpsuit's legs where they'd bunched. "Don't let your hatred of these people kill you, Chief."

It was a funny thought. Kill *him?* His job was to kill *them.* All of them. "I won't. No worries."

He followed her out, and when she left the bay, strode over to Telly. The drone looked wonderful, the smooth slopes of the exterior managing a grace and aesthetic appeal that seemed almost unnecessary. His fingers slid over the skin, and he was momentarily surprised it wasn't soft and warm.

*A drone, not a human. I need to remember that. Drones don't die.*

## 5

Through the limited view of the video showing Captain Faith Benson aboard the *Valor*, Field Marshal Dietmar Faulk had sufficient appreciation of the other ship to catch the unspoken message.

Her voice alone managed a significant message beyond the spoken words: calm, authoritative, certain, even alluring.

The powerful notes filled the air.

To his left, his brother—as the Children considered themselves—Leopold Hart seemed oblivious to the signaling from the Kedraalian captain.

Or maybe the captain was already a believer.

It was hard to read the other man's features—softer and less defined as they were. They might be nearly the same when standing, the two of them, other than the captain's softness extending to a slight paunch.

The eyes, though... That was where Faulk lost the ability to truly know his brother.

Rather than Faulk's gray, Hart's eyes tended more toward a sea blue with hints of green that—along with the streaks of red in his thinning hair—spoke of some miscalculation in the work of Minister of Purity Jack King.

Perhaps their creator had hoped some variation might create a new line of development. If so, that development was in the way of functionality and followership rather than brilliance and leadership.

Faulk imagined he might even be able to smell a difference in his brother sitting so close by in the *Warsaw*'s meager conference room, the sort of thing a child might have sensed during a scuffle to tip him off to the false identity of a stepbrother or even a changeling insinuating himself into the family. That difference amounted to a muted, spice-like twist to the all-too-familiar odor they all carried while repairs restricted access to anything so trivial as showering. Those repairs left the air barely recycled, as thick and hot as any jungle.

But one needed look no further than their uniforms, which spoke volumes about this difference between them: Faulk's was the well-tailored black tie and suit, with a Silver Wolf emblem on the breast. Hart's was the sky blue jacket and pants of the Azoren Navy.

Only a black tie and white shirt acted as a commonality between them.

Hart eschewed a distinctive emblem, wearing instead that of the *Warsaw*.

When Benson glanced away for a moment, Faulk muted the conference room microphone and rested his chin on a thumb, covering his mouth with his fingers. "Quite the intriguing babble, wouldn't you agree?"

Hart seemed drawn from a hypnotic state, his eyes only slowly coming around to the field marshal's. "You don't find the idea intriguing?"

"Should I? She proposes we begin a hunt and that we embark on wresting initiative from our radical enemies. If such a thing were possible, we would have shut down Kedraalian intrusions long ago."

"Would we? What evidence do you have there were so many to be detected?"

"We know they penetrated the DMZ many times." Faulk's eyebrows rose. "Ah. Yes. I see the problem. We within *the High Command*. I should take some level of pleasure in knowing that at the very least, General Weber didn't breach his trust by making this common knowledge among his senior officers."

"I've only heard of the occasional spy ship testing our sensor network."

"It was no spy ship that obliterated the *Hammer of Heaven*. We know for certain sabotage eliminated that destroyer with all hands."

The Azoren captain stretched his neck. "As you say."

"This isn't women gossiping about the supreme leader's indiscretions over a slice of apple strudel. These were reports straight from our people implanted within the halls of their defense ministry."

"I'm sure they were. I'm also sure these spies of ours are vulnerable to planted intelligence ripe for the harvesting."

Faulk tensed, then relaxed. Although ill-presented, Hart had a point.

On the viewscreen, Benson was still looking down at something on the table in front of her. Although her conference room wasn't ostentatious, it was nearly double the size of the *Warsaw*'s, and every centimeter was polished and bright, while even the seats of the Azoren warship creaked with age. Her white jacket was similarly a message of superiority and vibrancy, better fitting and made from a superior material to his own.

She was still going on about the condition of the Kedraalian and Gulmar ships, which had escaped the Khanate ambush with far less damage than his own task force. Apparently, they also were more efficient at repairs, because they were days ahead on that front.

The field marshal's seat groaned as he shifted. "She means to intimidate."

"Intimidate?" Hart's brows arched. "She's sharing progress on fleet preparation. Transparency like that is only intimidating in what it says: She doesn't fear us using this knowledge against them."

"What fear should she feel? They have us vastly outnumbered now."

"They had us outnumbered at launch, Field Marshal."

Faulk waved the other man's words away. "Those ships are crewed by inferior people. Only now do the numbers make them a concern."

"The real concern is our own crew." Hart glared for a moment. "A crew reduced in manpower by tragic and unexpected deaths and horrific executions, don't you think?"

It was hard holding back a smirk. "A culling of the weak. That is always the unfortunate reality of battle."

"The unfortunate reality we face is a crew asked to do too much."

If Faulk hoped to head off an argument, distraction was called for. He waved a hand at the screen. "What about her claim? Do you sincerely believe she can come up with a solution such as she proposes?"

After a moment, the heat drained from the captain's face. "The Kedraalians have always shown a propensity for resourcefulness."

"That's neither a yes or no. Do you believe her?"

A slight but noticeable tilt of the head gave the captain a look less of curiosity and more of...aloofness. "It's strange the way the dynamic has changed between you and her, isn't it?"

"Dynamic?" Heat pricked at the back of Faulk's neck.

"She realizes just how thoroughly she holds the upper hand now. What leverage there is in our tenuous relationship is exclusively hers."

The heat spread to Faulk's face. "I have no idea what you mean, Captain."

"This Benson has put forward the idea of tracking the Khanate fleet through the existing detection networks, including our own. In fact, she put forward the idea that using our own network would be ideal and challenged you when you said no such thing would be possible."

"It wouldn't be. And exactly how does this say anything about our *dynamic?*"

"Well, Field Marshal, obviously I had no part in the deliberations of the High Command, but you were there. Did she put forward such an idea while under your tender care?"

"She did not. There was little time for anything beyond the most basic discussion of strategies thanks to the assassination attempts and the other rebel activities."

"I see." The captain shrugged. "It seems no less a change of dynamic."

Faulk's chin jutted. "You think there's something to this idea of hers."

"I do."

"And it does not trouble you that she knows about our detection system?"

"Troubled?" Once again, the captain tilted his head. "Did you think this technological extravagance was secret? We expended years and a significant portion of our budgets to build this border protection. Obviously, we wanted our enemies to know about our efforts."

"Obviously." The field marshal turned his attention back to Benson, who was now looking directly at him. Had she addressed him? "Captain Benson..."

She still stared, but there was confusion in her eyes, as if she hadn't heard—

Faulk muttered under his breath and unmuted.

Hart had distracted the field marshal. Such an annoyance would have to be dealt with later.

Faulk cleared his throat. "Captain Benson, my congratulations on the accelerated repairs you've managed to your ships."

"Thank you, Field Marshal. Did you want to update the status on your task force?"

"We are—ah—waiting for the latest set of diagnostics to complete before creating a rollup of the most recent work. A few...setbacks have crept into our otherwise remarkable achievements."

"I'm sorry to hear that."

"Not at all. We truly have managed the best outcome—the best. All things considered. Our task force is wonderful." Faulk thought Hart might have rolled his eyes but if so had done it without giving himself away.

Benson leaned forward, resting her head atop a graceful hand. "Now that you've had a moment more to think about it, what are your feelings about the idea of tracking the Khanate fleet through the existing Fold Space Detection Network?"

Faulk straightened in his seat, wincing at the squeak it made. "Captain Hart and I were discussing that just now."

"A group of ships the size of the Khanate force, assuming they're moving together, should be pretty easy to detect."

"Yes. The point you make is obvious. What is less obvious is the value of such detection."

His challenge apparently surprised her. Was it something she simply had failed to think of on her own? Were such obvious questions beyond her own ability to see once she fell in love with her precious notion of tracking the enemy?

The pretty Kedraalian captain cleared her throat. She needed time to deal with the setback, no doubt. "Once we know the direction they're taking—"

"Captain, direction in space is meaningless. The vastness lends itself to an infinite opportunity to hide. Once they exit Fold Space, they could proceed anywhere undetected."

"They could. My thinking was built around the idea that they *wouldn't*."

"Obviously."

Was there a smirk on her face? "I'm sure Captain Hart has already shared with you the way a fleet operates, but to explain my assumption, I'll need to state the…obvious."

"Yes." Faulk waved impatiently at her to get to the point.

"A fleet relies on resupply. Food, water, atmosphere—we recycle and reduce waste as efficiently as we can, but at some point food runs out and water is lost to the reclamation process. More importantly, the reactors will use up fuel."

"Fusion reactors are extremely efficient. We carry sufficient deuterium and tritium to last a year."

"Under normal circumstances, yes. Our ships follow similar designs. I'm not so sure that holds true with these Khanate ships."

Faulk glanced at Hart, but the man's attention was laser-focused on his counterpart. The field marshal couldn't afford to look like an idiot, so he smiled at Benson. "Their frigates look like oversized gunship corvettes to me. Has my lack of naval experience misinformed me?"

"No. That's a fair observation. The thing is, I was using our gunships as an example for my thinking here. Unlike ships the size of the *Warsaw*, our corvettes can't carry a full year of reactor fuel or even enough water to operate for several months without resupply."

"You have tender ships, though, same as this Khanate fleet."

"Yes, but that fleet is made up mostly of those frigates, and those ships look even more unlikely to have space set aside for things like fuel and water. What I was going over earlier—the estimates my weapons officers have put together on the frigate configurations? Maybe I didn't do a good job emphasizing the importance of that?"

"It is possible." Faulk saw Hart's mouth open and tensed, but the captain swallowed whatever it was he'd been about to say. It was unlikely, but there was always the chance he'd been ready to complain about Faulk talking over the Kedraalian captain's briefing.

Regardless, she looked away from her camera again. "Here."

An image appeared on the display, replacing her. It was a mockup of one of the Khanate frigates, with weapons and other features highlighted. If anything, the image made the similarity to the Kedraalian gunships more pronounced, as if the frigates were older brothers. Long, rectangular, with gently sloping drops from the edge of one deck to the next, and weapons systems allocated to most of the same basic locations —the only visible difference was in the number of guns and the larger size.

Faulk frowned. "I'm not sure I follow, Captain Benson."

Her face appeared in the upper right corner of the display, still looking off-camera. "Well, let me start with the biggest difference. Do you see how the number of guns has increased over the number on a gunship?"

"Yes. That would be hard to miss."

"That's because the ships have been designed to have a greater focus on offensive capability. It's a risky focus. Based on our estimates, it comes at the cost of shields, armor, and point defense systems. Also, they've shown a lot of maneuvering and thrust. That means they haven't sacrificed space for their drive systems."

"Oversized gunships. They've been brutally effective hammering home the point of their design."

She nodded in her small corner. "They have. But as I said, that design comes at a cost. It means larger reactors and more fuel consumption. And since they've jumped into Fold Space quite often, the strain on the reactors is only increased."

"I still fail to see—"

Hart pointed at the display. "They haven't the capacity to last even as long as one of the Kedraalian gunships operating at such a load. Would that be your point, Captain Benson? You estimate, what—half as long?"

Benson nodded. "Conservatively."

Faulk had to fight to maintain his calm. There would be a discussion with Hart at a later point, a reminder that one does not undermine a superior in the presence of an enemy. "Which takes us back to the point that this Khanate fleet has tenders. Or did your bold hunt of the retreating forces net the entirety of that group of support ships, Captain Benson?"

"It didn't. But by our estimates, those tenders carry food, water, and maybe raw materials used in the manufacture of some of the weapons systems."

"No reactor fuel? That would be a strange design shortfall."

Hart's eyes narrowed. "Not necessarily, Field Marshal. Reactor fuel is best kept in shielded areas. That consumes space, which would be vital to those tenders, if the captain is correct."

That interruption brought a smile to Benson. "We believe that's the case."

"It's the most efficient design. Better to use a ship with ample space that could be given over to heavily shielded areas than to compromise a design like you assume with the tenders in question."

"Exactly."

Faulk's tongue ached, and he realized with surprise that he was biting into it. "Humor my ignorance for a moment, please, *Captains*. That fleet has exactly what you describe: large ships with no doubt ample area that could be dedicated to shielded storage."

Now Benson spared one of her obnoxious smiles for him. She could be so patronizing. Perhaps that was what Hart meant about the dynamic changing. "That's our thinking as well, Field Marshal. And after what we saw when we destroyed that wounded carrier, we believe that's where the spare reactor fuel for the frigates is stored."

There! His point had been made for him! "Thank you, Captain."

Unfortunately, Hart missed the message to let the matter go. "Captain Benson—this thing you saw when you destroyed the carrier? Could you explain?"

She licked her lips. This wasn't something she'd planned to delve into, apparently. "Well, we observed what appeared to be secondary explosions. At first, we attributed those to runaway magazine detonations, which assumes explosives of some sort. The more likely cause was suicide mechanisms to protect the ship from being taken."

"But you've reassessed."

"The video and the sensor readings point to something more than conventional explosives."

"Ah." Hart's head bobbed up and down foolishly.

"My weapons officers think it's possible the Khanate storage design was flawed. Maybe the shielding was inadequate, or maybe there were compromises that led to fissionable materials being stored with the tritium. It's also possible the conventional explosives stored aboard the carrier for those suicide fighter craft include fissionable material. Whatever the reason, that carrier ended up being torn apart from the inside by a nonconventional explosive that gave off a sizable radiation signature."

Hart pinched his chin. "And there were only two carriers."

"Meaning that if the fuel was spread evenly across them, their fuel supplies have been cut in half."

The Azoren captain turned to Faulk with a meaningful look. "There is the answer."

Faulk bristled. "What answer?"

"Why their destination matters."

"Because their reactor fuel supply *might* have been cut in half. That is the extent of the discussion?"

It was Benson's turn to take offense. She crossed her arms. "We're looking at a way to seize the initiative, Field Marshal."

"Building a strategy around shoddy guesswork is hardly the way forward."

"We don't feel it's all that shoddy, thank you. It's sound. We've seen the inside of these Khanate ships."

"You can't derive meaningful data from examining the blackened husks of these fanatics' vessels."

"I think you can, but I mean operational ships. I've had two Marine squads aboard one of those cruisers."

That revelation brought Faulk out of his argumentative mood.

Was she bragging? Could this be a moment where she lied to get what she wanted?

Or had she just revealed something critical. Getting Marines aboard an enemy ship—that took daring and skill. Azoren Marines only performed boarding once a ship was subdued or surrendered.

Even Hart seemed intrigued by this.

The Azoren captain shot a glance at Faulk that clearly was a request to follow up on the claim; Faulk nodded.

Hart clasped his hands in front of him. "Captain Benson, would you be able to reveal how your Marines gained access to one of these Khanate ships?"

Her mouth pulled in, the full lips becoming thin strips of red. "I'm not sure that's relevant to this discussion."

*So!* She wasn't ready to open herself fully to her allies! That was answer enough.

Faulk stretched an arm across the table so that it was beyond the camera angle recording him and his captain, then held a finger up to signal to Hart to hold off on further probing.

When Hart gave his subtle nod of ascent, Faulk tried a disarming smile: blinking happily, the corners of his lips raised painfully high, his teeth almost exposed but not quite. "Captain Benson—this cruiser your Marines boarded?"

"Yes?"

"What makes you think that reflects on the carrier?"

"They found explosives stored in adjacent or near-adjacent areas. There wasn't anything shielding the explosives from each other. A simple satchel charge managed to cause a chain reaction." She relaxed a little. "The more we see of this fleet, the more we question the quality of construction. We also believe that it's not optimally designed. Instead, it seems created with an eye toward fast-hitting and focused offense followed by speedy relocation."

"Retreat."

"If they face a powerful enough force or something goes awry, yes."

Faulk could see that. The delay in retreating once the battle tipped to the Kedraalians could easily have been necessitated by a desire to finish off the helpless troop transports. "This attack we suffered upon arrival in Moskav space—?"

Benson's head bowed slightly. "We believe that was nothing but bad luck."

"A sensible assumption. The destruction of the Moskav was clearly their focus. But the fact that you were able to destroy a carrier leaves me uncertain about the idea that this is purely a strike force not intended for standup engagements."

She sighed. "Without having all of the data, I'm reluctant to judge the performance of another captain. If you're pressing me to do that—?"

Faulk nodded. "Please."

"I think the commander of this fleet is either incompetent or not in complete control of the ships under his command."

"Not in complete control? That seems unlikely."

"Which leaves incompetence. The problem with that idea is that we've seen indications that the fleet is run effectively, at least in the early stages of battle. When they have missiles and fighter craft in play, they seem capable of completely devastating an enemy. The Gulmar fleet was nothing but debris when we found them. They crippled one of my destroyers. It's only after those initial resources have been removed from the battle that things fall apart."

"You describe an undisciplined rabble."

"Which is, I think, the problem." She showed the palms of her hands, possibly signaling surrender. "It's possible that this fleet commander doesn't have the self-discipline to keep his fleet focused on task. But given what we know about the Khanate, I think it's more likely that the various ship captains simply get caught up in their own blood lust."

Hart's back stiffened. "Meaning that the longer a battle goes, the greater the odds of defeating this enemy?"

"That's what my captains and I feel, yes. Captain Thiessen feels the same."

The Azoren captain turned to Faulk. "Field Marshal, I believe we should confer with our officers as well."

Faulk almost snorted at the idea, then realized the intent was to talk without the Kedraalian captain listening in. He grunted. "Captain Benson, we'll get back to you shortly with our repair situation and with our assessment of the Khanate fleet."

"What about the idea of using the detection network to track—?"

He waved her question away. "Any use of the Azoren Fold Space Detection Network must necessarily go through the *Warsaw*."

"But we have—"

"The point is not negotiable, Captain. We will be in contact." He killed the connection.

Hart turned, his face more animated than ever. "Her idea is sound. You could say that it's revolutionary. This technology which hides their ships can't hide them from the detection systems."

"Or so she assumes."

"But it's an easy enough thing to test. The ambush of the Gulmar fleet —that was accomplished by the original Khanate fleet. She put the numbers at greater than thirty. Those carriers and cruisers alone would be sufficient proof."

"Assuming she is right—" Faulk was becoming more convinced she was. "—what does this prove? That we know where they go. The delay between receiving this knowledge and acting upon it renders the information useless. We will arrive to empty space at best, and it's quite possible we could find more of their specialized missile systems waiting."

"True. Except she's proposing that they have something dictating where they *must* go eventually."

"The reactor fuel issue? That seems built upon a structure of unreliable scaffolding."

"I don't agree. Every force faces limitations of some sort."

"And logistics is one of the most common." Faulk took a deep breath. At one level, he knew he was being emotional and petty. Benson's strategy was as sound as anything he had come up with to deal with the Khanate monsters. Ultimately, his plan had been to leave everything exposed and to charge straight for Azh Shivan. After all, with the way fleets could maneuver through Fold Space, only fixed targets mattered.

But if there truly were some way to find this Khanate fleet in a moment of vulnerability...

"How would she do something like this?"

Hart pulled a data pad from his pocket and set the device on the scuffed tabletop. He took control of the display, filling it with a star map centered on the Azoren holdings, then shifted focus to a section of space closer to Khanate space.

"Here." The captain highlighted the Khanate worlds. "Their ship production facilities must be in one of their systems. Most likely, it is near Azh Shivan."

"Do you propose—?"

"No proposal. This is establishing where their resupply must ultimately be assumed to come from." Hart moved the map around, highlighting where the Gulmar fleet had been destroyed, where Radetta was, and where the Moskav home world was. "These are where we know the fleet has been. The most likely paths through Fold Space are fairly obvious."

Faulk tracked along the proposed paths, eyes narrowed. "And where they would go?"

A dozen or more places on the map lit up, many of them close to well-defended space or far out from Khanate holdings.

Hart pointed to the map. "Thirteen viable targets exist if you want to refill water and reactor fuel. Fourteen if you assume Azh Shivan has such a refining capability. Deuterium and tritium aren't complicated materials to manufacture or store. You could even do it with your reactor, if you're willing to use some of your precious water reserves. That's not efficient for a fleet on extended missions. Better to keep your own supply of the fuels."

"Unless you face the design constraints you believe this fleet does."

"I see no reason to doubt this Benson. She seems as competent as we are likely to find in any fleet."

"Careful you don't fall for her, Captain."

"This is merely observation. Her reasoning is sound. Of these fourteen possible resupply sites—places with fuel and water available for a ship to onboard—we need only..." Hart tapped his screen, and the most distant of the sites disappeared. He repeated that until only three remained. "And there you have the most likely targets."

The captain pushed the view in closer until the three sites were at the edge of the display.

There was no obvious reason for the shift to Faulk's eyes. "What is this?"

"This—" Hart tapped the data device, and another dot appeared in the center of the three points. "—is where I would propose moving our forces to."

"The middle of nowhere?"

"The middle of the three most likely places for the Khanate force to move to."

It was a risky idea that would take them farther from Azoren territory and also from the remaining Moskav holdings. If something went wrong, Supreme Leader Graf would have every reason to demand the head of the officer behind such a gamble.

Faulk leaned in. "If this is her plan, you would support it?"

"Although there is risk—"

"Would you support her in this?"

Hart thrust his chin out. "I would."

"Then I hope you are correct." Faulk pushed up from the table.

"You are done?"

"One of the Khanate spies killed himself last night. I must talk to the other one. I have to understand how they became what they are. As improbable as it is for other spies to exist, I find myself wondering how even one came about."

The captain nodded slowly. "And this matter of Benson's idea?"

"Reach out to her. The two of you can work out the details. Let me know what you agree to."

Surprise crept across the captain's face. "As you command."

Faulk smiled before exiting the room. "Should you turn out to be correct, Captain Hart, the Supreme Leader will know about it."

Hart's cheek twitched. "As he will if I turn out to be wrong."

"You understand how command works."

There was a spring to Faulk's step as he left the conference room. Creating a scenario where he was protected from fallout was probably the most valuable lesson he'd learned in his youth. It had led to a career that propelled him past rivals at an early age.

He wasn't about to let that career founder against the rocks of the crazy Khanate fleet.

## 6

————

Time took on weight, a mass that pressed against Benson's chest more intensely with each passing minute. Her heart pounded louder than the soft, steady rhythm of the air recycler. She found herself fighting the urge to chew on a fingernail, and when she pushed that aside, the damned headache that always haunted her settled just above her eyes. This time, the pain was so intense, she smelled color and numbers gave off a spicy scent.

What was it? A treat from childhood. Some sort of bread or roll her mother had made when scores from school were as high as they should be —top of the class. Had that alleviated pain in those days?

Now, nothing worked but time away from stress.

The stress at that moment rivaled the start of battle.

Her XO glanced down from his command station, lips sucked in and one eye squinted.

Finally, Chopra cleared his throat. "We could lower the lights, Captain."

"Thank you. It only delays the headache."

"The data coming in through engineering might be better. Unfiltered and immediate, I mean."

Mahama twisted around, unconcerned with the weapons station at the moment. There wasn't a threat, and he seemed connected at the hip with Chopra. "Chief Parkinson's going to know just as quickly as we do, ma'am."

At the opposite end of the broad console that served as communications, helm, and weapons control, Lieutenant Nuñez nodded agreement.

Beyond the chunky weapons control officer and the supple communications officer, the giant display was pitch black other than the green boxes marking the source of her anxiety: Gunship-81 and Gunship-99 were ready for the jump into Fold Space.

All systems were green. Two smaller green boxes—Parkinson's drones—hugged the hulls, running scans and recording video.

What could they possibly hope to find?

Data. It was exactly as Chopra said: The data was what mattered.

Benson adjusted her flight suit, which seemed determined to cling to the soft flesh handles that were forming above her hip, no matter how much torture she put herself through in the gym. "I'll be in engineering."

The passageways were an anonymous gray that shuddered and shifted as she hurried to the lift. She barely caught the greetings of a few of her crew hurrying about their business: "Good morning, Captain!"

It seemed like she managed to recover and smile effectively, but she could never be sure, not when the pain was like it was this morning.

Engineering had a welcome dark about it, the on-duty team hunched over in their areas, faces lit by terminals. They would be focused on the gunships, looking for any piece of evidence that strengthened or undermined the theory being tested.

Her theory.

To an extent, Parkinson's theory. And to a lesser extent, Thiessen's.

Ships moved through Fold Space by tearing open a hole into the collapsed pocket dimension, and to continue moving through that space, they had to feed a lot of power into the Fold Space drive. The bigger the ship, the greater the power consumption. Ships as big as the Khanate cruisers and carriers...

The network of Fold Space detection systems *had* to be able to detect the Khanate fleet. The shadow tech didn't account for that level of power use.

It *had* to be a vulnerability, something they could exploit.

She slipped into the chief's office, hovering at the entry until her eyes had fully adjusted to the near-complete darkness. His scent was everywhere, amplified either because of her headache or because there was little else to distract her. The engineer's computing pad was in low-power mode, the display it was attached to barely lit. He was seeing the universe through VR goggles that blocked out everything else. Matching gloves covered his hands, which moved with delicate precision over virtual flight controls.

"Go on, Telly. What's in that crease? Hm? Radiation leak?" The scrawny engineer tut-tutted. "Somebody's getting sloppy. Let's make a note of that."

Parkinson seized what was probably a yoke in the VR but was thin air in the real world. "Petty Officer Hu, I'm sending you a message for Gunship-99. They've got a small radiation leak—"

From out in the main bay, Hu's voice was a whisper, too soft to understand.

The chief nodded. "Yeah. Thanks."

Benson leaned against the bulkhead and massaged her brow with the palm of her hand. The dark helped. "Chief?"

"Huh?" Parkinson whipped around, then he raised the goggles. "Captain?"

"Mind if I sit down here with you? To see the data when it comes in?"

"Oh." He pointed to a chair pushed in against a small section of desk that ran perpendicular to his main station. "You can use that terminal. Greta—"

He pulled his goggles back down and returned to piloting.

As Benson sat down, the terminal came to life. The colors were brilliant, the skins of the two gunships so sharp that they could be real, a meter away from her. It was stupid, the urge to touch the hulls, but it was also instinctive. Effective virtual reality work required a mastery of immersion that was beyond her. Parkinson's expertise with it made him doubly valuable.

"Thank you, Chief." Despite herself, she leaned in a little closer to the display. "They ready to launch?"

"That was the last set of scans. Telly found a minor radiation leak—"

"I heard."

The engineer's head came around, even though he couldn't see her with the VR goggles on.

After a second, he returned to what he'd been doing before, looking straight ahead, gripping a non-existent yoke. On the display, the gunships fell away until she was looking straight down on them, getting a clear view, stem to stern. For as small as they were, they seemed dangerous, bristling with weapons mounts.

Blue fire ringed the engine nacelles, and the drones climbed higher. The gunships nudged forward, accelerating slowly. Data tracked inside windows on the left and right of the display. On the left, the window was labeled 88. On the right, 91. Everything stayed in the green, although an amber notation in the right-side window seemed to be modifying some of the values.

*Radiation signature. The leak. He's removing that interference from whatever they're tracking.*

As the ships accelerated, the images on the display spun. It was slow at first, then sped up. Vertigo combined with the biting pain of Benson's headache. She squeezed her eyes shut and slammed against the chair back, fighting back a wave of nausea.

Parkinson wasn't squealing about losing control of his drones, so she had to assume he'd been playing with them. When the urge to vomit had passed, she looked at him.

He was smiling like an idiot, spinning an imaginary controller, letting out a soft, dry chuckle.

She shook her head. It wasn't his fault. He was fully immersed. "Chief?"

"Oh! Shit. Sorry." His hands returned to the imaginary yoke.

On the display, the gunships were flying straight away now, continuing to accelerate.

The world returned to normal. Benson concentrated on the data. At this point, everything was about building a baseline, seeing what sort of energy signatures the gunships gave off before they transitioned into the other dimension. In a few minutes, it would all be about checking normal space after the ships were gone.

Everything rode on this. Controlling the Azoren, ending the mission as aggressor instead of having to always react, tracking the Khanate fleet down before they could rebuild...

Her combined fleet *needed* this.

A new sub-window popped up over the 88 and 91 windows—a countdown. On the display, the ships became almost hazy. They were smaller now, too far out for the retreating drones to maintain the same level of video detail as before. Green energy flickered around the ships, then the distorting blur became more pronounced.

And suddenly, they were gone.

Parkinson pumped a fist. "That's some sly video."

"It is." Benson blushed when the engineer twisted around; he hadn't been talking to her. She bit her lip. It was just the distraction of the headache. "A clean jump like that—what sort of readouts would you expect, Chief?"

His head twisted around, as if he were searching the stars above them. "What you're seeing there. There's a big heat spike when they engage the Fold drive. That's on our end. This is the first time I've ever done a broad array of scans from the outside looking in."

"I'm not seeing much of a readout."

Blue lines flashed on his goggles. "Yeah. Huh. Is that a surprise?"

"Is it the detection network? Is it just a big delay?"

"Could be. I don't think the Moskav were very big on maintaining or upgrading their systems. Maybe they don't have a lot out there."

"Can you show me where?"

His fingers swept through the air, then tapped against something that wasn't there, and the display took on a three-dimensional grid. The view shifted, pulling out until the grid shrank noticeably.

Parkinson tapped and swiped, and a string of icons attached to grid corners heading away from Benson. "As far as we can tell, this is the extent of the Moskav early warning system. I've pinged the systems, and I had a shuttle carry Telly out to get a look at the closest. Everything seems to work, but as bad as they had their asses kicked by the Azoren, you never know."

"These numbers—" She tapped the closest and most distant of the icons. "Is that the delay?"

"Yeah. Roundtrip in seconds. That's an ideal number, not really a practical one."

After a second, two green lines extended through the grid, running beneath the line of Moskav early warning sensor buoys: the gunships' path.

The grid was a flimsy aping of the Azoren DMZ, fractional in size to the point of being useless, at least if the intent was to redeploy starships for defense. Apparently, the Moskav had simply used the warning to get their leadership into defensive structures spread across the planet.

Yet even accounting for the delay, the sensors weren't picking up the gunships.

She pinched her bottom lip. "Could the Khanate have knocked them offline?"

"It's possible."

"But you don't think that's the case."

"No. The one we inspected didn't have any meaningful damage to it. It responded to the ping. I think they're functional."

"That wasn't what I needed to hear."

"Sorry." Parkinson took the goggles off. "Y'know, it could be a sensitivity issue. These older systems, small ships like those corvettes, the advanced stealth designs even without the shadow tech. It's not really comparable to what you're trying to do."

She massaged her forehead. "That won't matter. With Faulk, I don't know if anything matters, but at least a successful test would have shown the concept has merit."

"He seems like a dick."

"I've dealt with more difficult, but when you combine his racist dogma, it really is hard to maintain my composure."

"Is he stupid? Does he understand the difference between the footprint of one of those cruisers compared to two corvettes?"

"He understands control, and he refuses to surrender any at all."

"As in, he won't let you use the Azoren DMZ network?"

"He insists it would have to run through his ship."

"That old clunker? Great."

"I'm less concerned that his ship couldn't handle it than I am about him being honest sharing the data."

"I get that."

"We can't let this data get out. If Faulk finds out this didn't work, he'll push his idiotic agenda and become an even bigger pain in the ass."

"You think someone might leak it?"

"I know you won't let that happen." She smiled.

Parkinson ran a thumb over the top of the goggle frames. "I still owe you that shadow tech information. I didn't forget."

Benson stood and absently adjusted her jumpsuit. "You've been busy."

"I like doing that kind of work. It keeps me...distracted."

The way he looked down, the pain in his voice—it was a sting. "Chief —" She straightened her back. "Will, are you taking care of yourself? You look thin."

"I'm good. Dietrich's whipping up something that should be easier on my stomach. Big calories in small packages, right?" The engineer snorted, but his lips trembled. "I don't want to let everyone down."

"You won't. You've been doing—" Her data pad buzzed. "Excuse me."

"Sure." The little engineer's eyes tracked her movement, then when she was passing through the office entry, he set the goggles back on his head and slumped in his chair.

She wondered whether she might do better giving him a direct order to take the cold sleep route. Her task force was running out of senior engineers, but Parkinson already seemed ready to collapse. What good would it do to push him to the point that he couldn't contribute?

Maybe the high-calorie food would help turn him around.

Her tablet buzzed again: Nuñez. That was odd.

Benson took her headset from a pocket and put it over an ear. "Lieutenant Nuñez?"

"Message for you, ma'am."

"Commander Chopra couldn't take care of it?"

"It's Eyes Only."

Eyes Only. Wonderful. It would be keyed to the task force commander's encryption, and the communications officer would be the only one notified when it came in. That wasn't a good sign.

The earlier headache came back at full intensity when she reached the passageway outside Engineering, throbbing with her heartbeat. It was like a vise squeezing tight, then loosening a little, then squeezing even tighter. Once she was in the lift, she closed her eyes and leaned against the wall for support.

Maybe it was time to talk to Dietrich about a deeper look. He'd never found anything in previous tests, but she was certain this wasn't psychosomatic. The pain was too visceral.

Rather than head to the bridge when she exited the lift, Benson turned toward her quarters. "Lieutenant Nuñez?"

"Yes, ma'am."

"Could you forward that message to me now? I'll take it in my cabin."

"You should have it now."

The data pad vibrated. "Received. Thank you, Lieutenant."

"My pleasure, Captain." Nuñez killed the connection.

Once inside her cabin, Benson dropped into the chair in front of her desk with a groan. She powered the lights off, then stumbled over to the sink and splashed cold water onto her face. That helped a little, as would the aspirin she took once she found the bottle in her belongings. It was high-dosage, something she'd been given just before entering the academy.

She dampened a washcloth, pressed that to her head, and returned to her desk. After a few minutes, with the pain receded enough that she could handle the light, she opened the message.

A glow resolved into a room that seemed almost familiar, an office with an impressive desk and other appointments. Behind that desk, an admiral she *wasn't* familiar with stared at the camera. He was old, with heavy jowls and bags under dark eyes. Deep wrinkles made his chestnut skin look almost like scales.

Ames, she remembered. Head of fleet security. He'd been angling for a spot in the senior advisory group when she'd been selected to command the *Valor*. Tight with some of Zenawi's people, if she was remembering right. With the headache, though, she couldn't be sure.

"Captain Benson." The man had a raspy voice that bent gravity. "I don't believe we've formally met, but I'm Admiral Wesley Ames, current head of Naval Operations."

So, he'd gotten the position he'd been shooting for after all.

"I realize this message would be seen as an inconvenience under the best of circumstances. After all, you were granted autonomy and discretion at an unprecedented level, which no doubt leaves you wondering what I could possibly have to say to you."

The man's dark eyes seemed to grow even darker, dipping into pitch black.

"Political matters have become more complicated than anyone could have anticipated at the time of your task force launch."

Benson snorted. Did the man know anything at all about complications?

"At the time of this recording, certain Parliamentary members have taken the first steps of a procedure that was until now considered a mere theoretical measure. Rather than wait until such time as allows to render a challenge through the standard voting process, this group has chosen to pursue an unproven and frankly questionable course to force Prime Minister Zenawi out of office before the normal duration."

The headache seemed to intensify again. Benson wasn't a politician, but she'd grown up around someone who lived and breathed the intricate network of laws and procedures that made up the Kedraalian legislative system. If something was in that network of laws and procedures, then there wasn't anything *theoretical* about it.

But Ames was obviously one of Zenawi's people. If ordered to, he could imagine this was a coup. That was what had happened previously, when the SAID operatives had nearly brought everything crashing down.

And there was no doubt that Zenawi had been behind that.

Ames clasped his beefy hands in front of him, then lowered them so that they were out of sight. It transmitted the earnestness of the moment. "If the members of that political body decide that the procedure in question is legal and valid, and if they proceed with this incautious and dangerous political maneuvering, the ultimate goal will obviously be the removal of the prime minister through means he can't challenge. Granted, a challenge is being prepared at this moment, with the intent to ask the high court to intervene and undo this fraudulent effort."

Fraudulent. Coup.

Why was it the use of tools in the framework of laws and remedies was a danger when the target was someone who had provided political favors? What should matter was the good of the nation. If Zenawi had done something egregious enough to push his rivals to enact a procedure for removal, then that was his problem.

She glared at the data pad. "Don't you dare say it."

The admiral sighed deeply. "Sadly, if the prime minister is removed from power, the validity of your mission will be undermined. The task force represents a substantial element of our military strength. Only the prime minister would have the right to send such a force into action, and his removal... Well..." Ames shrugged, hands rising up into view and spreading wide, saying without saying: *What can you do? They've taken this out of our hands.*

Except that was absurd.

This was retaliation. It was bald-faced repudiation of the captain who just so happened to be the daughter of one of Zenawi's biggest rivals. Even if Sargota wasn't involved in the esoteric procedure in question—and Benson couldn't imagine her mother missing out on such a maneuver—it was still a slap in the face to those issuing the challenge.

Of course, a lap dog like Ames wasn't about to present things that way.

He pressed a sad smile at her. "A new prime minister will need to be named. And, of course, as part of the new leadership, there is the right to decide military objectives and implementation of those objectives. The *Valor*'s mission must be considered paramount in any such discussions of executive control."

Benson paused the recording. She had to splash cold water on her face again. Nausea was creeping up through her gut, leaving her shivering and sweating.

This message wasn't just a poke in the eye for Zenawi's rivals. It was a dangerous—a reckless—maneuver to undermine Kedraalian security.

She paced the cabin, sucking in deep breaths.

The task force had been created to act as an iron glove wrapped in velvet. If she hadn't lost the Gulmar main fleet before even meeting it, she would have been able to hammer the Azoren defense fleet and send a clear message to that antagonistic group that their days of aggression were over.

Now?

She wasn't sure the Azoren would survive another decade even absent a crushing blow from her task force. And the threat that was still out there —a threat that was even more dire?

*That* couldn't be walked away from.

What other groups were operating to remove the prime minister?

According to the latest reports, her mother's coalition had grown in power. They were either the majority coalition or close to it. They might not have the numbers to force another election to push the prime minister out, but they had the power to bring this mysterious provision into play.

Benson made a mental note to research what the hell procedure could even apply.

Later. When the headache was gone.

For now, she returned to the desk and resumed playing the message, while still pacing.

Ames now shook his head and took on a somber look. "Even as distant as you must be at this point, you've probably heard the rumblings of the stated objectives of the growing minority. This is the same faction that made deep and irresponsible cuts to the military the last time they had the budget in their control. Their rumored remedy to what they call over-reach is to look to the Gulmar model of a security force that's paid only when needed." The old man shook his head morosely.

It might have been high drama, but the idea was actually easy to believe. Sargota and her allies were delusional when it came to the role of the military. None had ever served. They thought everything could be turned on with the flip of a switch, but they believed even more strongly that there wasn't an actual threat that required a professional fighting force.

Would they change their minds if they saw the ruins of the old Gulmar seat of power?

To Benson, Zenawi and his rivals were playing a childish, short-sighted game that would put the Kedraalian Republic at risk of collapse. And for what? For a few more years in power? For a chance to test the theories of a group of peaceniks who apparently were incapable of seeing the enemy at the gate?

She growled. The *imbeciles!*

On the screen, Ames drew himself up. "So, we'll need you to turn the task force around immediately and return to Kedraalian space. Your charter to resolve this…threat—" He shook his head disapprovingly, more she was sure to signal that she wasn't the right instrument for the task than to question the task itself. "—has been revoked. Perhaps you might return to our space to find everything resolved in a way that allows for a continued effort against our enemies. If so, that will be something you and I discuss. I admit that I'm curious about what you've accomplished by the time you see this and what lessons we can take from your experiences. The academy might do well to interview you. Or there's always the chance you could provide instruction directly."

In other words, she wouldn't be returning to complete the mission.

Ames fell back on his sad smile. "Those are your orders, Captain Benson. Or, if Captain Benson has been lost, then whoever commands the expeditionary task force, I look forward to seeing you upon your return."

The message ended.

Benson wanted to throw the device, as if the message had been created within the tablet.

That was the most ridiculous response possible.

Instead, she stripped out of her flight suit and put on her Navy whites, raising the lights enough to check herself in the mirror. She looked ghostly, her forehead damp, her eyes puffy. A quick wash under the cold faucet and a few strokes of the brush helped with that.

Professional, she thought. It was the image to project.

She sat in front of the data pad and smiled pleasantly as the record light activated. "Admiral Ames. Thank you for your message. It *does* sound like things have become stressful on Kedraal. I can only imagine what it must be like, moving from meeting to meeting with a cloud over your head, never knowing if your position is secure or not. That's not the way to run a military."

Her throat constricted. She swallowed. "For that reason, I'm going to have to decline to follow your order, Admiral. The charter I was given wasn't tied to a specific political party, ideology, or politician. Your predecessor and I made absolutely certain that I had the leeway—the *freedom*—to see this mission through with an objective to ensure the survival of our people. When that mission is complete, I'll return with the task force and will accept the repercussions of my decision. I hope you'll understand. Thank you, Admiral."

It took a bit, but she held the smile until she closed the recording. She paced, then replayed the message.

She couldn't do anything to make it plainer.

*No. Thank you.*

She encoded it, then sent it to Nuñez to transmit back.

After that, Benson took her uniform off and crawled under the shower to vomit and wash away the feeling of betrayal. All the dreams of her youth were bitter ash now. Everything she'd done to get to this point in her life was a lie, a dark deception.

And the worst was yet to come.

## 7

Muscles twitched in protest, and Caville thought he might finally have pushed his highly trained body too far. Fire burned beneath the flesh of his shoulders. Spasms clenched and released in the small of his back, and at the end of each cycle of pain, it seemed his legs developed more of a mind of their own, twitching and jerking.

It had been the fall, the damage from the impact. He'd been impatient climbing down, and it might be about to kill him.

He held position on the rungs for a moment, letting his legs take his weight and breathing in the cool air. The smell of death and rot was even stronger here, maybe twenty meters above the spot where the dropped flashlight's dying light flickered. Descending to the black rooftop below might not kill him, but it could leave him weak and vulnerable enough that whatever had slain the decomposing corpses hidden somewhere out of sight could make short work of him.

There wasn't really any other choice. Either he made it to the light before it died or he and Gallo both would perish. On the rungs, on the roof above, or on the broader roof below—they would perish. They would run out of food or water, or the unknown cause of the rotting corpses would get them, too.

It sounded like Gallo might be calling to him again, her voice bouncing around, distorted in the dark heights above. Calling back would only alert whatever didn't already know he was down here; she wouldn't understand his words anyway.

They should have taken radios from the Khanate soldiers. Maybe they would have worked underground. Even if not, they would have provided a semblance of security.

He'd rested long enough. Time to continue down.

After two rungs, his body protested even more than before. Dropping the rest of the way was out of the question, but so was descending at the rate he'd been going.

He managed two more rungs, then stopped again.

His heart pounded. Despite the cool air, sweat trickled down his back.

Water. Food. Security.

The two of them needed those things in that order. That meant getting into whatever was under the broad roof below. This place had been explored at least a little by whatever passed for scientists in the Khanate culture and its interior recorded. Using logic alone, he knew there was more than the tubelike part he and Gallo had fallen onto, which wasn't big enough to require an entire team of scientists to search.

This place was big—that much he was sure of.

He started back down, then stopped.

In the flicker of light from the dying flashlight, his eye had caught a shadow just below and to his right. He descended a couple more rungs and stopped again.

The flashlight died.

Caville bowed his head against the rungs. A part of him screamed that this was the worst possible time—a nonproductive and stupid waste of his mental resources.

Things could *always* be worse.

Should he continue down? Go back up?

Or there was the shadow. He'd seen it clearly, a darker crease in the black skin of the thing they were on. It was the sort of crease that could indicate a door.

He reached out, running his fingers along the surface, probing...

There! An indentation!

Caville tried to squeeze a fingertip into the crack but couldn't. A fingernail wasn't going to move anything. He pushed against the section of wall that would likely be a door. It didn't budge. That left trying to slide it open or to lift it.

He pressed the palm of his hand against what he hoped was the door, and—

A hiss of cold air, the smell of death amplified, and the door pulled away from him, almost tugging him from the ladder. Silvery light rippled away.

*Physically rippled.*

It took a moment to get over the strange sensation of seeing light move like the surface of a pool disturbed by a rock. When Caville felt steady enough, he poked his head around the near end of the revealed doorway.

Inside, everything was black, crystalline, with the edges and defects in the surface lit silvery white. The light revealed what must have been a set of stairs or a ramp leading down several steps in.

He could get from the rungs to the opening by extending his right leg and planting a foot at the base of the opening, or at least he could if his body didn't give out. And if he did that, he would be committed. Coming back out would be almost impossible.

Below, the flashlight came to life again.

His guns were down there. The broken flashlight was, too.

Would the door stay open if he continued down? Would he be able to climb back up?

Uninjured, fully rested, and alone, he would've risked the door. As banged up as he was, he needed all the resources he could gather. Plus, there was the smell of the dead. Going in without the assault rifles just seemed like a bad idea.

So he continued down, listening for the inevitable whisper of the door closing. It did that when he was still maybe five meters above the lower roof.

And the flashlight died again.

Caville groaned. He should have been ready for something like this, as if there were some way to be ready for…what had happened? The site he'd been sent to find had simply disappeared, withdrawn under the ground. How was that possible?

It was possible because the designers weren't human. That was the point of coming here, the thing that had lured the Khanate scientists in as well. Half of the hostages taken when the revolution had splintered the religious radicals off had been Kedraalian scientists and technicians trying to solve the last puzzle of the place. The promise and threat of the alien technology—the shadow technology—had been too great to leave behind when things started to look dangerous.

One of the points of emphasis during training for the mission had been not to expect anything conventional. The first team to enter the place had disappeared completely, and only a few of the bodies had ever been recovered by subsequent teams. *Lots* of people had died inside the alien structure, apparently including all of the Khanate teams.

Caution was the watchword.

He continued down, fighting through the fatigue and pain, until his booted foot tapped against something broad and firm.

The roof he'd seen below.

To reduce the risk of it giving away like the surface above, he lowered himself until both feet and all his weight were firmly on the surface but never let go of the rungs. He jumped up and down. He stomped.

The roof held. More importantly, it didn't sound like anything slid away.

Sturdy and flat, then.

He released the rungs and dropped to his belly. Better to fall with some control if things gave away again. Sand scraped and scratched beneath his fingers as he stretched out in search of the rifles and anything else that might have fallen. Where there wasn't sand, the roof felt like polished rock or crystal: hard and glassy.

His fingers bumped against a metallic surface that turned out to be the barrel of one of the rifles. He drew that to him and searched it in the dark, pulling the magazine out and sliding it back in, working the action—everything seemed to be operational.

There had been other things on the roof. Maybe the flashlight could be salvaged.

It took a few minutes, but he found the slick spot where the water bottle had ruptured, then the flashlight. There were a few pieces of sharp-edged plastic near the device, which he assumed caused the intermittent behavior. But when he gently tapped the side of the case, the best he could get was a dull glow from the light panel.

That was like a fiery star in the pitch black.

He clipped the lamp to the assault rifle strap and searched around, eventually finding another assault rifle and a water bottle with a crack down its side. There was still plenty of water within. He tasted it to be sure it hadn't been compromised: sweet and cool. Finally, he stuffed the bottle inside his shirt.

Now he had no choice but to climb back up and try the door. Getting all the way back up the rungs to Gallo was…

Impossible.

He sighed.

The light failed a couple more times but always came back before Caville reached the crease again. To his surprise, the door opened again—no drama or exertion or shock this time around.

Before trying to make the jump to the opening, he tossed the rifles inside. Their clatter against the floor was so loud, he cringed. But now he knew that the floor was solid and wouldn't give way when he put his boot on the opening.

Stretching to get a toe on the opening produced a pop somewhere in his back. A tingling ran down to his thighs, which felt weak for a moment.

But he was committed.

He put weight on the front of the boot.

His ruined pinky toe burned, and his arms shook from the strain, but he couldn't pull the foot back. His balance was forward, on the extended foot. And the boot of his second foot was slipping on the rung, as was the grip of his left hand.

Caville threw out his right hand, sought a grip in the doorway, a small lip where the door would embed itself. There was barely anything to hold onto…

His left foot came off the rung, then his left hand came away.

The fall would be nearly twenty meters, this time without sand…

He threw his weight to the right side, to the doorway. His boot slipped sideways, and his fingers slid in the doorframe crease.

The fall began.

Then his boot hit the corner of the frame, and his fingers caught in some imperfection in the groove. That was enough for him to exert himself fully and to drag his weight forward, into the opening and onto the floor.

He bounced against the right wall, then collapsed against the floor, scraping on top of the assault rifles.

Once again, the surface was flat and didn't give way.

Caville laughed.

It was a desperate and relieved sound, but the way it echoed in the hallway stripped away the authenticity. He'd spent years storming buildings, running through the tight confines of spaceships, parachuting and diving. Never before had he felt so close to death.

He pushed up to his knees, then to his feet.

After a moment, he stretched his back and arms, then his neck, listening for pops and other warnings. The muscles were tender and tired, and something was definitely wrong, but he was functional.

With one rifle over his shoulder and the other held high ready, he headed to the ramp or stairs. It turned out to be a ramp, which set him at ease.

Until he saw the skeletal form at the base.

Just beyond the form, tattered and bloody robes covered the floor.

Khanate.

A closer examination showed gouges and breaks in the bones. The death hadn't been accidental, and it hadn't been a gunshot.

No one had ever figured out exactly what had killed those who'd been recovered, but there were indications it might be an animal. The killer was simply called "the sentinel."

How many of those sentinels there were, Caville would find out.

The way the Kedraalian bodies had been mangled seemed similar to what he could make out of the Khanate bones.

Beyond the mangled bones was another assault rifle. The magazine was still half full. The casings were several meters ahead, pressed against the walls.

No blood. No indication that the shots had landed.

The hallways here were narrow. It would be hard to miss something coming right at you.

Caville retraced his steps and checked the bloody rags. There was a sash, and attached to it were some other pieces of gear: a shattered radio that looked like the guts had fallen out; a knife; a pouch with chemical lights; and a couple batteries.

Batteries.

There was one good thing about the Khanate and the other forces that had split off from the Kedraalian Republic: They all had stolen technology and stayed with what they'd stolen.

He set the rifle against the wall and took the flashlight apart, stopping occasionally to listen carefully for any sound of approaching threat. When he had one of the replacement batteries in place, he tested the flashlight. It wasn't a complete fix, but it was better. The light panel would need to be replaced to get it back to where it'd been.

Caville used the sash as a strap for the flashlight, securing it to his chest. Then he followed the corridor in, sniffing and listening to see if he might pick out other corpses or any sounds other than his own.

He stopped when he spotted a shadow in the wall to his left, another crease that might indicate a door. A repeat of the tests—push, press— revealed the same functionality as the exterior door.

Inside, the stench was stronger, taking on more of a tomb-like quality. The corpses—there were three—hadn't been torn to pieces. Instead, they seemed to be mummified, skin dry and muscles like paper. There were no visible signs of injury, either. Each corpse had an assault rifle or pistol and a lamp.

Security. Or maybe Khanate researchers carried guns around with them. The society seemed psychotically obsessed with its weapons.

Foil energy bar wrappers littered the floor, and there were empty canteens, the lids removed. These people had probably died of dehydration. There was no way in other than the door he'd found. No way...

He spun around as the door closed.

But it opened with the same press it had taken from the outside.

Then what?

Caville searched the corpses more closely but gave up after a few minutes. Dehydration had to be the cause. It *had* to be.

The magazines of their weapons were empty, but there were full magazines in pouches tied to their sashes. Other pouches held more batteries and…radios. And these radios were intact. And they had data pads. The batteries were long ago drained, but it wouldn't take much to transfer power from external battery packs to one of the data pads.

One of the lamps looked like a better option than his, so he switched to that. The light was bright and reliable. He took a second flashlight and put a battery in it, just in case.

For redundancy. For Gallo.

He took all the gear and piled it in a corner, keeping only a couple batteries and a magazine for himself, then he dragged the corpses out and set them at the base of the ramp.

Whatever had killed the one in the corridor, the three in the room had survived it. That meant the room possibly offered the most important thing he was looking for at that moment: security. He and Gallo had a place to sleep, assuming he could get back to her.

It was easy tracking the way back to the ramp and the outer door, but the Kedraalian researchers had reported the place was huge and the passageways labyrinthine. That meant it would be easy to get lost.

For other people.

Like Stiles, Caville had an excellent memory and his spacial problem-solving capabilities were far above average. He was already mapping out the interior, even if his data pad failed to do so for some reason.

He'd have to check on that, eventually.

Before proceeding farther, he stopped by the room and began transferring battery power to one of the Khanate data pads. Maybe it would hold helpful information.

That was optimistic. Maybe stupid. Maybe.

He returned to searching the corridors, stopping and listening, sniffing. There were more corpses, and there were a few rooms off the winding hallways. The rooms were uniformly empty, at least from what a quick glance could see. This wasn't the time for thorough searching. He needed to find a way up, to get to Gallo.

Finally, he found another door, and beyond that a ramp that led up. There hadn't been any bodies for a while. In fact, the place seemed colder, and it felt like a separate section from the rest.

Although he hurried up the ramp, he forced himself to stop and listen on occasion. The dead smell was completely absent in the ramp passage.

Then the passage ended at a door overhead. Caville couldn't be sure if he'd gone as high up as he'd climbed down the side of the structure. It didn't seem likely, not with the way moving on the ramp was so much easier than going down the ladder rungs. Even if he hadn't reached the upper area, he'd made progress. At the worst, the overhead door would probably open into another ramp passage.

He listened at the door as well as he could, then repeated the process to open it.

It slid aside, and sand rattled down, raining on the ramp and sliding away.

Caville climbed out, assault rifle at the ready. To his left, the base of the sand sloped up. To his right, maybe three meters away, there was another abrupt drop-off, exactly the same as what he'd shot over and lost the flashlight.

Someone was sobbing close enough that he could hear it clearly. He stretched up toward the rising sand and listened. "Denise?"

"Darien? Where are you?"

"Can you see the glow of the flashlight?" He waved it.

"Yes."

"Can you—"

"I'm crawling to you."

"Go slow." He set the rifle down beside him. "Don't come down the sand, okay?"

"Why not?"

"Because you'll pick up speed to the point you can't control yourself, okay? I overshot and nearly fell. It's a long way down."

"So…what do I do?"

He waved the flashlight again. "Come to me and let me see you."

The door closed behind him, but he was comfortable opening them now. He listened for the shush of sand, then when he heard it he watched for her crown of black hair and the eyes he'd found himself missing in their short time apart.

She poked her head over the top of the piled sand and smiled. "I see you!"

"Push the duffel bag down."

Gallo disappeared for a second, then returned with the bag. "What'd you find?"

The bag slid down, and he braced for it, catching it without getting knocked back or off balance. "I found a place for us to sleep tonight. Is that okay?"

She almost sobbed again, but there was a smile on her face. "I could kiss you."

"Sure." He waved her down. "When we get to the room. For now, I need you to come down."

"I will."

"Wait. I want you coming down face first. Keep your hands out wide, like this." He made a wide *V* with his arms. "Fingers splayed. And you need to do the same with your legs. Dig your hands into the sand until you're just about down to me. Got it?"

"Into the sand?"

"To slow you down. If you come shooting down at full speed, you could take both of us over the edge. Understand?"

Her head bobbed in acknowledgment, then he waved again, and she came over the side, arms wide, hands plunged into the sand. She yelped when her foot caught and tugged on her ankle but otherwise did as he'd told her to do.

But when she reached him, she was going too fast. He missed her hand, but she flailed and caught his leg, knocking it out from under him.

Then they were sliding toward the edge, him on top of her, flailing wildly for purchase on the smooth surface.

Sand now covered the hard, black top, and he couldn't get a grip.

Gallo screamed, but she managed to slow herself somehow. When

Caville seemed ready to go over the edge again, she wrapped her hands around him until her nails dug into his flesh.

Together, they spider-scrambled across the black surface and pushed away from the shadowy depths.

After a moment of silence, she groaned and rolled onto her back. "Never again."

He got to his knees, found the door, and pressed it open. "We need to be quick and quiet, okay? You carry the bag, and I'll carry you."

She nodded, eyes wide, then hooked the bag handles over her neck.

His muscles protested at her weight, but it was a pleasant sensation holding her so close, hearing her breathing and seeing her eyes dart around. It had been an eternity since he'd been with her, a distracting and misinformed idea that he couldn't push aside. Danger was all around them, and they were both hurt, yet the entire way down the ramp and through the halls, he had to concentrate or he'd forget to listen.

When he finally set her down in the room that had held the old corpses, the aches and quivering nearly put him down, but she clutched his face between her hands and kissed him, momentarily driving the fatigue and aches away.

A sigh escaped her. "This is it? Our room for the night?"

"Longer."

"I guess it'll have to do."

He turned out the light and rested his head against the wall, his thoughts turning to the corpses he'd found. At that moment, the room might be the only thing keeping Gallo and him alive.

## 8

The *Valor's* main conference room was standing room only, and by the look of things in the large video display, the rest of the task force wasn't much better. For something so momentous, Benson felt it was important to have everyone present. Passing the situation down through the chain of command, telling someone that they were going to have to choose between heading back to Kedraal or staying and facing a court-martial or some other discipline…

That required the personal touch. She needed to see the pain, to feel it.

It was still necessary to start with the senior staff, which was what she was doing right now. Chopra, Halliwell, Dietrich, Parkinson—those were the most familiar faces, and they were closest to her. They weren't a support network, but they were her way of reading the room easily.

She'd worn her dress whites, even though they did a terrible job hiding her stress. At that moment, no one was going to see the flush in her cheeks or the dampness around her shirt collar or note how strong her perfume was.

Not yet.

If they did, they could attribute it to the warmth in the room, the heat coming off all the bodies.

Benson smiled, swallowed coffee-tinged saliva, and cleared her throat. That killed the soft chatter. "Thank you for being prompt. I don't want to hold you up from your off time, so I'll get right into this. Once I get through this, I'll be happy to answer questions."

Heads nodded in understanding. That was the easy part.

"A few hours ago, I received a message from Admiral Wesley Ames, the current head of Naval Operations."

On the display, Tuleyev made a sour face. Apparently, Ames belonged on the commander's long list of disappointing officers who hadn't done enough to help his career along.

"Admiral Ames conveyed to me the changing nature of the political landscape back on Kedraal. The biggest changes apparently involve members of Parliament exploring a never-before-used procedure to challenge Prime Minister Zenawi's legitimacy."

There. The shocked look on their faces. It wasn't loyalty to the prime minister but a sense of dread. These people all knew about the attempted coup that had led to Zenawi's rise. They were right to question what this meant.

She fought the quiver in her lip and voice. "There's a very real possibility this challenge will be allowed by the high court. If so, the admiral feels that Prime Minister Zenawi will be removed from office."

A few of the officers looked at each other, flabbergasted. Tuleyev scowled.

Benson breathed in slowly through her nose. "Admiral Ames has informed me that my charter to see an end to this threat to Kedraalian existence has been voided and has directed me to set aside this mission and return the expeditionary task force to Kedraalian space as soon as possible."

Gasps. Wide eyes. On the big display, Tuleyev gaped.

No one could have seen it coming. She hadn't, and she was supposedly the one with her finger on the Kedraalian government's pulse.

She exhaled. This was the hard part. "I've informed Admiral Ames that I don't consider this a legitimate command decision, that it runs counter to the exact nature of the charter as drafted, and that I will *not* honor this request."

There. That was the other bombshell, and it had the exact effect she'd expected. Some of her people were aghast. The most shocked seemed to be Chopra.

No. Commander Karrass was almost red in the face. Maybe that shouldn't have been a shock. She was often a stickler for the regulations, even if she wasn't the best at following them herself.

Something to think about later.

Benson clasped her hands in front of her. "So, that leaves us the disposition of the task force. I'll be briefing everyone personally. I'll be sending schedules to each ship captain for me to meet with your enlisted. I think I can wrap this tomorrow."

Karrass stiffened visibly. "Enlisted?"

"Just a moment. I'll take questions next." This was going to be a problem. Benson could see it in Tuleyev and Chopra's eyes. "For now, please keep the details of this to yourselves. I want everyone to feel that they've been treated the same."

Tuleyev frowned. "Disclosing this to us over video while meeting with the enlisted in person, this is not the same, is it?"

"All right. That's the briefing. I'll take questions now. Alexander, to your question, I wanted my senior staff to hear this first. Your decisions are going to have the greatest impact. You're my ship captains and my Marine commanders and my chief engineers. My line officers and non-commissioned officers look up to you. If you choose to return to Kedraal, that's going to mean a lot."

Karrass held a hand up. "Return?"

Benson nodded. "First, I hope I answered your question about briefing the enlisted personally. I—"

"No. But I guess I'm confused." The older woman's face became pinched. "Are you saying *everyone* is going to make a decision about whether to stay or not? Even the enlisted?"

Halliwell twisted around to look at the display, red-faced. "Why the hell wouldn't enlisted have a say, Commander?"

"Because they're *enlisted*, Lieutenant. We're their commanders."

"Yeah? And this is a career-altering decision." The big Marine leaned toward the display. "People need to know what they're getting into. You can't just order someone to—"

Karrass shook her head. "That's your *job*, Lieutenant. You make decisions about your people every day."

"Not something like this."

Benson held her hands up. "Okay. I can see there might be disagreement on a few points. Let's get that cleared up. Commander Karrass, this isn't something we can order someone to do, whether it's me telling you or Lieutenant Halliwell telling one of his Marines. I've been given a direct order by my superior. I don't view that as a legal order. This scenario of being recalled because of political pressure was one of the ones we went over when we crafted the charter. I refused to take this command without guarantees that every chief of staff was behind the accomplishment of our objectives and that they supported me as the person to see this through. Prime Minister Zenawi approved the charter and we have Parliament's vote making it law. A prime minister feeling that he might want to punish his successor—that's not acceptable."

Tuleyev folded his arms over his chest. "Captain, such a statement draws close to the line of political commentary."

"It does." Benson bowed her head. "I don't know how else to phrase it. This decision to recall the task force is a political one. We all agreed from the start that if I saw the need to pursue the enemy—Azoren or other—into someone else's territory, that was my prerogative. The Kedraalian Republic needed a hammer to crack the enemy's skull, and that was the *Valor*. Nothing has changed. Our people still face an existential threat. It just so happens to be from the Khanate now."

Dietrich thrust his chin out. "Wouldn't we be able to shield junior officers from repercussions by using our authority to force them to hold their positions?"

"I don't believe so. Every member of the military is obligated to answer this question as an individual. If you feel Admiral Ames gave me a legitimate order, me telling you to ignore that order is an illegal order. You would be obligated to reject my order as a result."

"But you're creating an opportunity for complete chaos. No offense to Lieutenant Halliwell, who seems intent upon championing the enlisted cause, but you can't expect some eighteen-year-old Marine to have the sophistication—"

Halliwell took a step toward Dietrich, but Chopra stepped between them. The Marine jabbed a finger at Dietrich. "That's a pile of shit, Commander."

Chopra patted the lieutenant on his shoulder. "Commander Dietrich's words could have been better chosen, I agree."

The Marine glared down at the smaller man. "The captain's right on this."

"She might be." Chopra's lips turned down at the corner. "We're all aware of the regulations, Captain. The problem is—as Commander Dietrich and Karrass have pointed out—we are dealing with a dangerous precedent."

Benson had expected some pushback. It looked like Chopra was supporting the challenge, which hurt. "First, let me be clear. Lieutenant Halliwell is absolutely correct. You're doing a disservice to your enlisted personnel by assuming they can't process something like this. Second—" She nodded at Chopra. "—the precedent was established centuries ago. Right or wrong, we've always held everyone in uniform to what you could argue is an impossible standard. They have to risk their careers when it comes to something like this. Even if they're shown to be right, they could still face a court-martial."

Chopra glanced down. "But we now put forward the idea that every order must be analyzed. The potential for challenge of every command given…it's too much."

"That's why it's on us to give the right sort of commands, isn't it?"

The tension went out of Halliwell's shoulders. He returned to where he'd been earlier and turned slitted eyes on Benson. "Enlisted people can think for themselves. And if you don't think they can figure out something this complicated, make sure they understand what's being asked. It's that simple."

She smiled. "That's our role."

There was color in Dietrich's cheeks. "You're asking too much of them."

Benson locked eyes with the doctor. "What you mean is that I'm asking too much of *you*. I expect all of us to do our best to communicate all the intricacies behind this situation with our personnel. I expect you to have a healthy debate amongst yourselves about what this means."

"This is about education." The doctor glanced at Halliwell. "You might think anyone can untangle a complex series of interwoven puzzles, but it's not true."

The big Marine twisted around to glare at Dietrich. "You want to make this about education? It's not. It's about dignity and honor."

Dietrich rolled his eyes. "You can't fall back on calls to emotion."

"I sure as hell can. And I can see the problem with all of you. You're afraid of losing control. Giving everyone the chance to choose their own fate weakens your stature."

Benson started to raise her hands again, but she spotted Parkinson looking around uncomfortably. "You have something to say, Chief?"

For a second, the little engineer seemed angry, jaw clenched tight, then he relaxed. "I understand the concerns about challenging this order." His eyes darted around. "It's a bullshit order."

Tuleyev leaned forward on the display. "Is this to be an argument about the political aspect of the order we have been given, Captain?"

"No." Benson smiled at Parkinson. "I don't think that was intended."

Parkinson shook his head. "Sorry. I'm trying to say I get the idea that we're dealing with something dangerous. Better?" He glanced back at the display, where Tuleyev drew back in on himself. "If I can put this in terms I'm comfortable with?"

Benson beamed. "Please."

"We've got a decision tree. It's a complex one, just like you've said. It's not A or B. It's A or B with different choices underneath. Those are just the gates to subsequent gates. You need several conditions to be true for the ultimate choice to be true. Do you believe the captain's statement about our charter? Do you believe this is a political act? Do you believe it's legal? And, I guess, do you think your career matters more than what's right or wrong?"

Karrass jabbed a finger at the camera on her end. "Trying to make this about careers is insulting."

The chief engineer's eyes went up. "It doesn't play a part in your decision?"

Rather than answer, the captain of the *Seattle* looked away.

That was as good a signal as any that the meeting had reached its conclusion.

Benson straightened. "Please consider the challenge before us. If you find yourself in need of more details or clarification, reach out to me. Finally, please be sure to have your crews ready to report to the briefings I've scheduled. Some smaller ships, I've asked to have your people come to the *Valor* for the briefing."

Tuleyev blew his nose, then folded his soiled handkerchief. "Will the original message be released? Doing such might perhaps assist in the decision-making process."

"It was Eyes Only, Alexander. If I could quote it verbatim without risk of compromising that security qualifier, I would."

The commander bowed; he understood.

No one else challenged or questioned anything.

Benson swallowed. "Dismissed."

She waited until everyone had filtered out of all the conference rooms, taking the opportunity to meet the look of any who wanted her gaze. When she was alone, she powered off all the connections, then settled into a chair.

Her knees were shaking, and her shirt clung to her wetly under her jacket. For her, the moment might have been seen as the start of insurrection. The repercussions might extend beyond forced resignation.

She accepted that as the price of leadership.

No one else could be allowed to face such charges, though. If that meant she commanded an empty *Valor* in the fight against the Khanate, she would have to do just that.

***

Grier was pulling her pants on but stopped halfway. Her head hurt from trying to make sense of what Halliwell had just said.

She turned, calling over the noise of his shower. "Are you serious?"

"What?" He turned the water off, and the noise shifted from the thunderous blast the showerhead normally gave off to the drip of water from his body.

"I said: Are you serious?"

"About being recalled to Kedraal?"

"Yeah." She pulled the shower door open, letting out the sweet musk of his soap, along with the steam that settled soft on the goosebumps of her skin. Normally, when she saw him like he was now, her attention was drawn to the muscles or scars of his body or to the handsome face that rested on the foundation of his angular jaw. Not this time.

To see if he was joking, she had to see his dark eyes.

He wiped soap foam from his forehead and squinted. "I'm serious. Do you mind?"

She shut the door. It wasn't some weird prank. "I—I don't get it."

The power blast of the water rose up again. "Don't tell anyone."

"I'm not going to." She leaned against the shower door. Their shift began in a couple hours, and that meant his roommate would be returning soon, but she had to know.

She *had* to.

Halliwell turned the water off and pulled his towel into the small shower. When the slap of the heavy material stopped, she pushed off from the door and waited for him. He glared at her as he draped the towel over the rack. "What's the big deal?"

"What's the—?" She rolled her eyes. "Swear to me that this isn't a big joke."

He tugged a fresh pair of underwear on. "It's not."

"She can't do that. You should've told her that."

"Can't do what?" His words were almost lost in the rustle of his T-shirt going over his head. "She's the captain."

"Yeah, and that means she needs to make the big decisions."

"She did." Halliwell pulled the bottom of his T-shirt down to his tighty-whities. "I don't understand what you're so pissed about."

Grier yanked her shirt up from the floor, where one of them had tossed it. The material prevented it from picking up wrinkles from being left in a crumpled heap for an hour or two, but she felt like ironing it anyway. There needed to be *some* kind of order in her life at that moment.

She pulled the shirt on. "I'm pissed because this is a classic screwup."

"Then you should've expected it. The fact that we made it this far without being recalled is the crazy part."

"Not the recall. That's…" What was it? Stupid. "I'm talking about her."

"Faith?"

That hurt. Grier still ached at the reminder that Halliwell had been that intimate with their captain. "Just make the decision. Either we're going back or we aren't."

"She made the decision: *She's* not going back. Now everyone else has to do the same."

"But…"

"But what? Our survival's on the line. How hard is the choice?"

"That's not the point. I mean, that's exactly the point. She should just tell everyone we can't do this. Some pinhead wants to worry about how he looks to his constituents or doesn't like how the popularity polls look or some stupid thing, and she can't let that interfere. That's not what matters."

"Right. So why would you even get worked up?"

"Because that's *her* job. Tell us that."

The lieutenant plopped onto his bunk, head tilted curiously. "She's going to tell you what your options are. You should already have the appointment."

"I do. That's why I asked you what this was about."

"Then—?" He shrugged.

Grier growled. "Stop doing that! She's trying to push a huge decision on me—on people like me."

"Wait. What's that mean?"

"It means I shouldn't have to make this sort of decision. It's above my pay grade."

Halliwell cupped his face in his hands. "You didn't just say that, Toni."

"Did too."

"You're being given the chance to make a choice. You can't be mad about that. It's what you should *want*."

"Nope. I signed on to take orders. I don't want to deal with complicated choices."

Halliwell grunted. "Listen to yourself."

"What? I'm afraid, Clive. This is huge. She wants me to choose between something illegal and something unethical? Really?"

His dark eyes narrowed. "Why is this such a problem?"

"Making a complicated choice?" She rested her hands on her hips. "I'm not ready for it." The words came out soft and weak, like she felt.

"Make yourself ready for it. You're a Marine. You train for the toughest situations. Treat this the same way."

Grier settled on the bed at his side. "Did you?"

"Did I make my decision?"

"Yeah."

"It's *my* decision. Make your own."

She took his hand. "Tell me. You're staying, right?"

At first, he wouldn't meet her gaze or respond, then he nodded. "That's just me. You need to figure things out for you."

"What about your career? You could make a lifetime job out of this. You're going to throw that away? Another couple years, you're a captain. You could make major. If you stay in long enough, you could go higher. It's a good life."

He turned to her. "Why do you think I'm staying?"

*You want to get her back.* Grier pushed that idea away. It was immature, her insecurity talking. "Because you think the Khanate's a real threat. If we don't stop them now, they could wipe us out."

"And if she's right, this isn't a legal order."

"But her boss gave it. He's speaking for the prime minister. She *has* to follow it."

"That's a lazy viewpoint." Halliwell twisted her hand around and stared at her knuckles. "That woman who stabbed you back on Kedraal after the bomb attack on the parliament building—was she following a lawful order?"

"She wasn't military."

"Doesn't matter. People like to act as if we're special, hiding behind our mission and our structure and oaths. It's all the same. If a cop is told to shoot a pedestrian who isn't doing anything wrong, does the cop shoot? If a scientist is told to dump toxic chemicals in a river a million people get drinking water out of, do those chemicals get dumped?"

"I don't—"

"Everyone has to make choices, Toni. The only difference is that we get scapegoated. We didn't take prisoners from that carrier. Someone's going to learn about that one day. They're going to try to say we're cold-blooded murderers and monsters."

"But the ships never offered to surrender."

"It doesn't matter. People like to hold us to a different standard. They've never seen a friend turned into red paste right in front of them. They don't know what it's like to have someone try to kill you one second, then surrender when things turn hopeless. They don't understand."

A strange pressure squeezed Grier's chest. She could barely breathe. "This is too big. I don't... I can't..."

"Grow up. You wanted to be like Faith? Put in the work."

The pressure grew greater and became a heat. Grier pushed up from the bed. "Gotta go."

Halliwell didn't try to stop her. When she stumbled down the passageway to her quarters, he didn't come running after her to apologize for telling her to grow up. He was the first person she'd ever wanted to get serious with, and now he was telling her she wasn't good enough, that she had to be something she wasn't.

How was she supposed to understand this and make a decision for herself? She'd never paid any attention to political courses or ethics classes. Her job was to destroy the enemy. Someone else was supposed to figure out who that was, then point the way and move.

Why did everyone want to make this so difficult?

Grier stumbled back to her darkened quarters, kicked off her slippers, and crawled under the covers of her bunk. She wished someone else were there, that she could listen to the steady breathing of a deep sleeper and use that to drift off herself.

Maybe she would skip the appointment. Or she could just do what

Halliwell was doing and choose to stay. Who cared why? Go with your gut.

But Halliwell would know. He'd call her lazy again.

She threw off her covers, searched for her data pad, and powered it on. It was less than two hours to the appointment. She'd have to figure out the complexities of legal orders before then.

The doctors' office was quiet, the only occupant a sullen and fidgety head surgeon. Dietrich preferred that title to Commander, Task Force Medical Operations.

He preferred a lot of things that weren't normal: the smell of alcohol and detergents that clung to everything in his medical center; the coolness that made his work easier; the hum of life-saving machines.

And right then, the darkness that was broken only by the lamp on his desk.

Solitude. He liked that, too.

Except now solitude made it possible to hear the arguments raging in his head.

The brave idealist Melissa had drawn out of him demanded to know why he hadn't stormed away in protest before the *Valor* even launched. Wasn't he bigger than this war?

The surgeon raged at the idea of abandoning those in need. Didn't it all come down to saving lives?

And the pragmatic whisper of his former self—the man he'd been before meeting Melissa—asking what was so hard about this decision. This was a comfortable life. Working in the military was a safe environment in its own way, wasn't it?

He snorted at that. Those were Melissa's words.

His mind drifted to the whisky waiting for him in his cabin. That could silence pain and doubt.

Or maybe it was the easy ticket out, a way to screw up and draw sympathy while still getting what he wanted. Wouldn't that just be like him—forcing someone else to act as a spine?

Maybe it was time for him to be the man he couldn't be for Melissa.

The door opened, and Kohn poked his head in. "You getting some sleep?"

Dietrich glanced at the cot deeper inside. "All yours."

Kohn pulled the door shut behind him but stopped before going to the cot. "You okay?"

"No. No, I'm not."

"Still messed up over the recall?"

"Ultimately, yes. The particulars are hard to define. Becoming furious over some admiral playing god while hiding behind political expediency seems justifiable to me."

"Yeah." The young man ran fingers through his dark hair. "Is that it, though?"

"You mean do I still resent the captain's approach to resolution?"

"It sure sounded like that was your main complaint."

"I'm reassessing."

"Okay."

"You sound skeptical."

Kohn frowned. "It's nothing. I've been trying to process it all myself."

"You have a brilliant career ahead of you."

"Sure, except that I can't afford the cost of medical school if I get kicked out. I need this."

"Yet you find it unpalatable to abandon the task force."

"Our patients need us. More patients will come in. And, yeah, I think what we're doing here is the right thing. What more do you need to see than what we went through on Himmel to understand we have an obligation here?"

"Stand behind the shield and oath, and you'll be fine, whichever decision you make."

"No offense, but that's more than a little cynical."

Heat rushed into Dietrich's cheeks, but rather than offering up a stern scolding, he stared into the desk lamp light.

Only Kohn could call such a truth out and make it stick.

Dietrich lowered the brightness of the light and stood. "I believe it's time I checked on our patients."

He closed the door to the office and slipped out to the infirmary.

The job was about caring for patients, after all, not about his righteous indignation.

Maybe that was something Melissa had never understood.

9

It would have been easy for Benson to let the dull rumble of the shuttle lull her to sleep. Traveling from ship to ship for the personal briefings had been strain enough, but on top of that, she'd gone nearly a full day without sleep. Stress from the meetings had wrecked her appetite and left her too nauseated to sleep.

To make things worse, she'd torn her dress white uniform pants while leaving the *Seattle*'s hangar, requiring the printout of a new pair that were stiff and pinched at her waist.

Now, as her shuttle neared the *Warsaw*, it felt as if she were being slowly baked. The numbers and names that had been rolled up from her task force captains were worse than could have rightly been expected. A full quarter of her people were opting to return to Kedraal, including Commander Karrass.

Benson powered her data pad on again to make sure she wasn't misremembering. Maybe she'd read something wrong, or maybe the device had been off by a decimal place.

But that wasn't the case. In the blue glow of the display, it was painfully clear: The numbers were terrible.

To her left, Thiessen leaned back in his seat, impossibly comfortable in his harness. Hers felt like a torture device, crushing the air from her chest.

His uniform was sharp, his hair immaculate. There was a pleasant, fresh-from-the-shower smell about him, even though the duty day had just ended.

He stroked his close-trimmed beard and cocked an eyebrow. "You sure you're up for this?"

She swallowed, her saliva as bitter as her breath was stale. When she tried to answer, her throat tightened, so she settled for a nod.

The Gulmar captain glanced around the empty passenger cabin, then curled his hand around hers. "This Ames did a job on you."

That seemed to unlock her throat. "On us."

Thiessen's hand opened. "On…us?"

"The combined fleet."

"Oh." He squeezed her hand again, eyes squinted at the cockpit area, where the pilot and co-pilot were hunched forward, faces covered by VR visors. "You figure out which ships to send back?"

She sank in her seat a little. "I can't afford to send back one of the cruisers. That's too much firepower."

"It also requires a lot of crew to run."

"I know. We can pull off a lot with automation and doubling up assignments."

"In battle?" He patted her hand when she shot a withering look at him. "You need to have a contrarian at this point, not a cheerleader. These are huge decisions."

"What I *need* is for my own government not to decide that it's time to put politics ahead of national security."

"Maybe that's something you can address later—after you return home."

"*If* I return home."

"We can still win this." He sighed. "Maybe you *could* give them a cruiser."

"No. The firepower—"

"Hear me out. My task force is technically understaffed. I've had people working extra shifts to keep up with your pace on damage control. We lost too many good people when the Khanate hit Radetta."

Benson squeezed her eyes shut. "Just because you and I get along doesn't mean I can put some of my people in your crew."

"No. I wouldn't recommend that."

"Then…?"

"Give your people returning to Kedraal their cruiser. Give them a destroyer if that's not enough. Don't try to squeeze too many into too small a space. They'll see that as punishment, and you said you wanted them to feel that what they did was the right thing."

"The right thing can't leave me with a task force unable to complete the mission."

"We hurt the Khanate fleet last engagement. I think we hurt them bad enough that they can't really recover. We just need to get your capital ships in close enough to cripple theirs. Now that we've seen what they're capable of, I think we win that battle straight up."

"Without my cruisers offering support, your destroyers can't stand against their fighter craft. You'll lose ships. *I'll* lose ships."

The calm slipped from Thiessen's face for a moment, then he relaxed again. "Maybe."

"You might be willing to take that gamble. I'm not."

"That doesn't change your situation. You need to send a lot of people home. You're going to lose ships doing it. Making things hard for the people leaving runs the risk of not only upsetting those people but those who stay behind."

Benson's stomach gurgled in protest. "I know."

"So, give them enough ships and reassign some of your crew to one of my destroyers. I'll pull the crew off and distribute them to the rest of my force. The design and systems aren't really different enough to pose a challenge, not for your people."

The co-pilot turned around, lifting her visor. "We've got clearance to dock in the *Warsaw*, Captain. Five minutes."

"Thank you."

Looking the two pilots over provided a little relief for Benson. They were both combat-experienced Marine pilots, the shuttle one of the stealth units with a deadly rail gun turret. There were also assault carbines mounted in a weapons rack in the passenger bay. If Faulk thought he might make trouble, she at least had a little surprise up her sleeve.

Benson squared her shoulders and smiled at the Gulmar captain. "It's a good idea. Let me think about it."

"When you get hit with something unexpected, things always look hopeless."

"It's not hopeless. I just..." She powered down the display that showed the *Warsaw*'s nearing underside. The port-side hangar bay door opened. Inside, amber warning lights flashed. "I always hoped to keep casualties to a minimum."

"And you probably feel like these people leaving aren't just following orders—they're rejecting you."

Her head came up involuntarily, and heat flushed her cheeks. "They are."

"They're doing what they think is the best out of a bunch of bad choices."

"*And* they're abandoning me."

The shuttle maneuvered, shifting them around in their harnesses. Tones sounded inside the shuttle, and lights cycled off, then on, then shifted to new colors.

After so many years, the familiar cycle was reassuring, or it would have been if they weren't about to meet with Faulk to discuss the change in the Kedraalian task force. Even if she did as Thiessen suggested and sent a cruiser and a destroyer home, her force still dwarfed the other two.

But the psychotic Azoren field marshal wouldn't see it that way.

Exactly as feared, Faulk was waiting for them when they exited the shuttle. Braced by six of his commandos, all of whom looked like his stone-faced younger brothers, he offered a smug smile as Benson and Thiessen approached. Behind the black-uniformed soldiers, Captain Hart stood alone, head bowed, strangely serene in his pale blue uniform.

Faulk squinted past Benson at the shuttle. "Do you take an armed vessel to every meeting, Captain?"

"Only those I'm dreading." She nodded at Hart. "Captain Hart."

The corner of the Azoren naval officer's mouth crept up. He covered his mouth with a hand and coughed, then turned away and waved broadly toward the exit. "Captain Benson, Captain Thiessen, if you would follow me, please."

They followed after the red-headed officer, who managed a comfortable pace. His gait was stiff, but he nodded at any crew who passed.

At one point a young man who didn't look so much like a twin as a distant cousin fell in to share a whispered conversation without breaking stride. A few words were loud enough for Benson to catch: complications; point defense array; new systems failures.

And she didn't even need to hear that.

Despite the path being chosen by Hart, they were still passing clear indications of frenetic maintenance activities. In her reviews of the engagement with the Khanate fleet, Benson hadn't seen any significant hits on the *Warsaw*, but it was clearly in need of significant maintenance.

She would have to talk with Thiessen later to get his take.

As they walked, Faulk watched his captain through slitted lids but moved alongside Benson. "This meeting you've requested—why is it matters couldn't be discussed over communications?"

She glanced around. "After the assassination attempt on you, I'm not sure I trust your security."

The field marshal's face reddened. "Those involved in the attack are quite dead."

"But you've refused to cooperate on a broader security sweep."

"My people are not so vulnerable as yours or..." He sneered at Thiessen. "I'm sure Captain Thiessen understands."

In reply, the Gulmar captain chuckled. "Oh, I think I understand you pretty well, Field Marshal."

It wasn't until Hart led them into a modest conference room and Faulk stationed his men outside that the field marshal seemed to understand that he might have been slighted by his Gulmar counterpart.

As they settled into well-worn chairs that groaned and squeaked, the field marshal turned his full attention on Thiessen.

Faulk leaned forward, his face still red. "Is it really necessary for *both* of you to have come?"

Benson clasped her hands in front of her. "We're a combined force."

"The Gulmar—"

"Are an integral part of the force, Field Marshal. That's even more true now, as you'll understand once I've briefed you." She squeezed her fingers tight and curled her toes. A part of her was screaming that she needed to get out of there, to cancel the whole operation and return to Kedraal and let the politicians play their stupid games. She was tired of the talking, of being a pawn, of having to breathe the same air as someone like Faulk.

Apparently, Faulk took the hint. He leaned back in his seat. "Please proceed."

*Count to three. One. Two. Three.* "I recently received a communique from the head of Kedraalian Naval Operations—"

"A Fold Space message?" The field marshal made a ridiculous show of surprise.

"My assumption is that you failed to decrypt it. Otherwise, you wouldn't be so annoying right now, probing me about why I asked for this meeting."

"I've heard nothing about it." Faulk tilted his head toward Hart. "Captain?"

"Not two days ago. As Captain Benson said, the encryption couldn't be broken."

"I see. Good to know that we tried." The field marshal turned back to Benson. "So this head of Naval Operations sent you a message."

"Recalling my task force to Kedraal. Immediately."

The field marshal's eyes bugged out, but he otherwise hid his reaction. "I see."

"Political jockeying inside the Republic has escalated."

"The inferiority of a parliamentary structure could be no more apparent."

"Of course. I'll propose to that body a more enlightened approach. Maybe we could model some sort of gladiatorial resolution method to better emulate your people, Field Marshal."

Faulk's face darkened. "I suppose your cowardly retreat will begin immediately."

"We have personnel readying for departure tomorrow morning."

"Personnel...?"

"I informed my people of the edict and gave them until the end of early shift today to choose whether to stay or return. About a quarter have chosen to return."

Hart's eyes darted from Faulk to Benson. "You are not returning yourself?"

"No. I'll be keeping the bulk of my task force and completing my original mission."

"But that would be considered a breach of your—"

"I'll be facing discipline when I return. I expect it will be a court-martial." Benson was sure the Azoren officers could see how white her knuckles were.

Faulk's eyes were barely visible through his narrowed lids. "The High Command would have you before a firing squad."

"It's a good thing I don't work for them, isn't it?"

"It is." The field marshal rubbed the tabletop with his forefinger, as if trying to erase a stain. "One quarter."

"Nearly."

"And how will they return?"

"I'm finalizing which ships they'll take."

"Your corvettes, surely."

"Our gunships wouldn't be able to hold that many people, but I expect one of the gunships will be sent back, yes."

"Along with a destroyer?"

"That wouldn't be enough, either."

"Two, then."

"I'm considering two, yes. And—" She nodded at Thiessen. "—one of my cruisers. Captain Thiessen and I are in discussions about having some of my crew take over one of his destroyers."

Thiessen beamed. "That would allow me to reallocate my crew to other ships."

Faulk grunted. The finger rubbed more vigorously, then stopped. He sucked in a breath. "Unfortunately, I can't approve this. These people are deserters. The ships they wish to take—"

Benson's breath caught. This was what she'd thought might happen. "Approve?"

"Your cruisers are too important to my plan."

Her fingers ached, she was squeezing them so hard. "Field Marshal Faulk, do I need to remind you that your own Supreme Leader put me in charge of this task force?"

The field marshal waved her words away. "For appearances."

"*Not* for appearances, no. It was explicitly stated, and the reasoning was clear: You're in over your head. Your role in this operation is just a figurehead. Captain Hart—"

"Captain Hart knows his place, Captain Benson. It would be wise for you to follow in his tracks." Faulk pushed up from the table. "Your weakness is the cause of this recall from your military leader. They sensed that you weren't capable of completing your mission. Now it's time for someone with a greater aptitude for strategy—"

Benson fixed her eyes on her hands. "This is *not* going to become another one of your bungled—"

"Do not talk to me as if you—"

"—operations that leads to unnecessary—"

Faulk slapped a hand against the tabletop. "You will be silent when your superior speaks!"

Thiessen started to push his chair back and stand, but Benson grabbed his wrist and shook her head.

She took a deep breath, then she stood. Slow. Controlled. She tugged her jacket by its hem. Once again, she refused to actually look Faulk in the eye, instead staring at his silver wolf's head emblem. "I'm going to make this as clear as I can, Field Marshal. And I think you should do yourself a big favor and listen."

The Azoren officer's face shook. "I could have you shot and dragged to the nearest airlock to be thrown into space."

"You could. It would be your last act." Now she met his gaze, and there was a coolness coming over her that was even more troubling than the nausea and fear she'd felt during the flight over. "Do you think your pathetic little task force stands a chance against mine? The *Valor* alone could vaporize the *Warsaw* before you have a chance to fire a single weapon. Your ships are old." She leaned in. "And I already went up against your best captain. He's just another part of the universe now, along with his fleet."

"You will find that I am much more capable than Bryce Morganson."

"I doubt it. You commanded an army that couldn't even finish off the Moskav."

Faulk drew a hand back as if to slap her. "You will not—"

Benson brought her arm up in defense. She was no expert in hand-to-hand combat, but she knew enough about self-defense to deal with a slap.

The field marshal caught himself before delivering the blow, but his nostrils were flared and his eyes were wide. He turned a twitching eye on Hart. "Captain Hart, you will escort our guests to their shuttle and see them off the *Warsaw*. Immediately."

Hart had seemed pinned to his seat up until that moment. He stood and bowed his head.

Then Faulk stormed out without another word.

Seconds passed, then Benson lowered her arm. She was shaking, the adrenaline draining away and leaving her weak after so long without food. At one point, she had thought of wearing a sidearm to the *Warsaw*, a brutish message directed at a brutish man. Now she was glad she hadn't. It was entirely possible she would have shot Faulk at that moment. Things would only have escalated from there.

Hart cleared his throat. "Would you like a drink, Captain?"

She thought about that. "Do you...?" Her throat tightened again. "Wine?"

He bowed and smiled. "Of course. This must be on the way to your shuttle. You understand."

"Thank you."

The charm and calm Thiessen had exuded earlier were gone now. He led her by the elbow and kept himself positioned so that he protected her back and Hart protected her front.

They passed down passageways that were busier than before, with crew working or hurrying along. None of them paid much attention to their guests, but there wasn't the sense of overt hostility Benson had felt while on Himmel. These were people doing their jobs, nothing more.

Hart took them through a hatch into what must be the officers' mess. He pointed them to a table in a raised area. "I won't be a minute."

Benson stood beside the table, watching the Azoren captain's back until he disappeared through a set of swinging doors. "Is it me, or is he—?"

"—nothing like Faulk?" Thiessen snorted. "Maybe he's a good actor."

"I don't think so. The way he behaves…" She shuddered. "He seems *human.*"

"Maybe."

She leaned against Thiessen. "I screwed that up."

"Don't you even try. You gave that bastard every opportunity to behave like a professional, and he proved he's just an unhinged, entitled moron."

"I should have seen it coming."

"You did. You told me he was going to try to turn this to his advantage."

"I mean the violence."

"Isn't that why you brought that shuttle? That was a pretty clear message, even if you didn't mean to send it."

Hart came back through the swinging doors before they'd completely gone still. He had a bottle of wine in one hand, three glasses in the other. There was a grim smile on his face as he ascended the steps. It remained as he poured the red fluid. "I applaud the way you stood up to the field marshal, Captain."

She took the glass he offered. "I should know better than to provoke."

"For some, everything is a provocation. 'Good morning' is an insult that cuts to the quick. 'How are you doing?' is an intolerable slight that must be punished. The act of someone else breathing demands retaliation."

The wine was tart and warm and carried a surprising heat into her gut. With an empty stomach, she had to be careful. "Would I be out of order saying that you're a problem for me, Captain Hart?"

"A problem?"

"You don't seem like your brother."

Hart stared at his wine. "Yes. Thank you. I take no offense from that."

"Are they all so unreasonable as the field marshal?"

"The Children?" The Azoren captain took a long drink, nearly emptying his glass. "Who can know. So many of us die before we have the opportunity to understand ourselves or to question the universe."

Thiessen sipped his wine, then set his glass down. "I can understand the frustration of having to fight your entire life."

"I can't be sure which of us have the harder life, Captain. You have risen above challenges I have never known, while I have never known the opportunity to choose my fate." Hart finished his drink off, then put his glass beside Thiessen's.

Benson took another drink. "Thank you. I'm sorry, but I can't recall your name."

"I'm not sure it was given. Leopold." His smile was pleasant.

The entry opened, and a tall, slender woman with yellow hair so pale that it almost seemed white entered. She wore a uniform similar to Hart's, but there was an emblem on her modest breast. The woman glared at Hart. "Captain."

Hart sighed, then dipped slightly toward Benson. "Are you ready?"

She was.

Once out of the mess, Hart continued confidently down the passageway. He seemed to have a different understanding of "immediately" than Benson did. She appreciated that, although being trailed by the other woman was uncomfortable.

The Azoren captain waved toward one of the repair crews. "As you can see, Captain, we're understaffed, same as your forces will be."

Thiessen grunted. "I think the reasons might be different."

"The execution of Weber's loyalists? Sloppy and shortsighted. That unfortunately defines the field marshal perfectly."

Benson smirked. "It's good to see I'm not alone in that assessment."

"Hardly, Captain. His only concern is coming out of every situation advantaged. Someone like me on the other hand only cares about the mission. I am somewhat less enthralled with the religion of my creators."

"That seems…sacrilegious."

"It is. Yet a little research is all it takes to realize that the genetic variances between everyone are negligible. Even our minister of purity has said true superiority is a fragile treasure that can never truly be attained."

The minister. "What was his name again?"

"Minister King?"

"Yes. Thank you. He doesn't believe in racial superiority?"

"His goal, at least according to the early notes I've read, was always to craft a human free of flaws, not a superhuman race to master others. He wanted to end suffering, not create it. But his work was subjected to service Supreme Leader Graf's ideology."

"I see."

The slender, blond-haired woman physically inserted herself between Hart and his guests. "Captain, the impression I was given was that the field marshal directed you to have these officers removed from the ship with haste."

"That would be the same impression I had, Famke."

It didn't seem possible, but the woman's gaze grew even colder. "You must remember the policy—"

Hart's lips compressed into a hard, narrow line. "Yes, I must recommit myself to the policy and to the will of Supreme Leader Graf. There's no need to remind me of my failings." He turned to Benson. "Famke is my minder. A direct line to our dear leader, you might say. Literally. It's in the circuitry, isn't it, Famke?"

The woman's cold eyes flashed angrily. "You are out of line."

"I am. And you are a necessity to keep me sane." He poked his head around her. "One of the gifts of our creation—our fragile mental state. Famke cares for me as only a mother can. Can't have any unhealthy thoughts, you see. Like the idea of independence and freedom. Nasty."

"Your attempts at goading are childish and banal. The disappointment I experience is only that you have after all these years failed to find a new level of aggravation."

"That doesn't prevent you from using your chemical wiles, does it?" The Azoren captain winked at Benson and Thiessen. "When I said she cares for me as only a mother can, that assumes I haven't researched what a normal relationship looks like. Famke and her sisters do their best to rein us in. But Faulk has managed to eliminate his dependency, hasn't he, Famke? No more drugs and sex for him, hm?"

Benson recoiled. "What did you mean by circuitry?"

Famke's cold gaze turned to Benson. "He misrepresents—"

Hart shook his head. "She's like me—designed. Minister King perfected androids before my brothers and I."

*Androids!* There had been a time when people had proposed replacing the bulk of the military with synthetic humans. Had her father been involved in that push? At least it sounded like he'd at one point advocated for something other than Supreme Commander Graf's racial superiority. Perhaps her disappointment in her father had been premature.

Hart turned down a passageway, then pointed ahead, where a familiar passageway intersected the one they were in. "The hangar bay is just ahead, sadly."

His tone was refreshing.

Benson stopped at the hatch, then peeked inside to be sure her shuttle was still intact. She must have visibly relaxed, because Thiessen patted her back.

She extended a hand to Hart. "Thank you, Captain."

"For?"

"Showing decency and professionalism, mostly."

Hart chuckled and shook her hand. "I cannot wait to hear Famke's assessment of my performance. I do not think it will match yours, but at least I know that she has my best interests at…heart."

The android's earlier hostility was gone, now replaced by boredom.

Benson turned for the control panel to open the hatch, but she didn't go through when it opened. "Captain, do you think you might be able to get the field marshal to at least test the Azoren detection network?"

"Test?" Hart frowned. "Ah! Your experiment."

"Yes. If I can at least test that—maybe follow my ships when they depart…?"

"Your experiment has merit. Once the field marshal has calmed down, I will approach him about the idea."

"I'd appreciate it."

Hart smiled at the android. "I think Famke might enjoy provoking him with her support."

The android looked away.

Thiessen stepped through the open hatchway. "We should go."

Noting the urgency in his voice, Benson followed.

She wasn't so sure Faulk would ever calm down, but that was a problem for the Azoren captain. Thiessen's urgency was infectious; she didn't relax until the shuttle was well away from the *Warsaw*.

Things were unraveling in ways she hadn't foreseen, but if she could just hold everything else together, they still had a chance.

The question was, how good of a chance?

**10**

When Stiles woke again, she was leaning against McLeod. He was holding her against him with a hand wrapped around her waist and grumbling under his breath. They were in a small room—dim and empty except for a small terminal that was providing most of the light. Alcohol vapor and body odor seemed to be part of the decor, maybe soaked into the paint-chipped walls by years of use by roughnecks and hoodlums. A watery trail led from where they stood to a small breezeway with semi-opaque glass doors. She thought there might be lights coming through the outer one: a parking lot.

Her outfit hadn't changed, other than being soaked through, but she wasn't as cold as she'd been. Still, she couldn't fight the shivering, and her fingers ached.

A soft whirring came from inside the terminal: a cooling fan.

On the display, a middle-aged man scowled. He was a cheap simulation that skirted dangerously close to uncanny valley in appearance. Mostly it was the way the skin had pores and whiskers that ended up looking rubbery. There was also a problem with the eyes, which were black and lifeless.

The simulation looked down as McLeod tapped through the interface, as if watching him through a window. "We fumigate the rooms."

McLeod sighed. "Thank you. Why can't I select two single beds?"

After a moment, the simulation nodded. "We're out. You can get a double or a queen."

That drew another sigh out of the colonel, who tapped queen-sized bed. After that, a floor plan filled the display except for the top left corner, where the simulation still seemed to be studying McLeod's selections. The colonel scrolled through the three floors and took a corner room on the top floor. He flashed his data pad at the terminal, and the transaction was completed.

Stiles did her best to keep herself upright when they went back outside, pushing stiff legs until she was almost propelling herself. The rain and wind had slackened to a modest drizzle that came down vertically.

McLeod opened the back of a car and pulled out two travel bags. One of them looked like it had just come off the shelf. He slammed the trunk with a grunt. "I didn't feel it was right waking you to ask your size, so I picked up clothes that should be baggy but won't look out of fashion."

"Thanks."

Navigating the stairs to the third floor was a challenge she wasn't ready for. The steps were slick, as were the handrails. Without a word, the colonel took on most of her weight and guided her up. He had to pause before starting up to the third floor.

He was breathing hard. "Not quite the young man I was."

His data pad opened the door, and lights kicked on. Barely. The room had a cloying, chemical smell—stronger than the biting detergent smell.

Fumigation. Rough customers.

A simple bed abutted the outer wall, covered by a tattered, dull gold blanket thrown on with an imprecision that said the cleaning crews didn't waste any time. Opposite the bed was a cheap, printed dresser with four drawers. Above that was a scratched and askew display that looked older than the blanket. The failing light was just enough to reveal a sink and countertop at the far end of the room.

She pushed free of McLeod. "I want to try this on my own."

He let go but hovered until she dropped onto the bed. The look on his face was either worry or fear. "How do you feel?"

"Cold, still. It could be the wet clothes."

"There should be hot water."

Stiles glanced toward the sink. There would be a bathroom to the right. "I know. I wanted to ask some questions first."

"Where are we?"

"For starters."

He dropped the luggage and went to the window, pulling back the drapes. "Dramora. Specifically, Norristown. It's a mining area on the outskirts of the major city."

"Near the—" Something stung the side of Stiles's head. She brushed fingers over the hurt area. "—starport."

"Yes. Not too far. Those stitches—we could get something better. The mortician didn't have any skin sealant. I mean, not the sort that would stand up to wear and tear. His subjects don't usually move around much."

"I was dead. How?"

"That was going to be my question. When you were ready."

"I'm...hungry. Thirsty, too."

"Why don't you warm up and try some of the outfits on, see if anything works for you. I'll get us some food."

Stiles nodded, then stretched out to grab the bag that looked like it had never actually been used before. Inside was an eclectic mix of jeans, shirts, sneakers, socks, undergarments, and a dress. Maybe they were fashionable. It seemed more likely they wouldn't draw attention. The sizes were actually correct.

She took out underwear, a flannel shirt, and a pair of dark jeans. "Coffee, please."

"I can do with some myself. What can your stomach handle? I saw a Mediterranean place that was still open on the way here."

"That sounds good."

"Won't be long."

When he exited, the door locks slammed shut behind him.

*How did I die?*

There were so many questions, so many uncertainties. First and foremost, she had to ask if she was actually alive. Would a dream tell her that it was just that? She had a pulse—in her wrist, on her neck. Her heart was beating. She was breathing. She ached, felt cold, and was dealing with confusion.

*Alive. Don't waste time on the question.*

She tossed the wet plaid shirt and jeans onto the grungy carpet and didn't give a thought to the lack of underwear. McLeod had mentioned a mortician. She'd been dead.

A gunshot rang out as she staggered toward the sink; she fell.

Just a memory.

Caville. There'd been a look in his eyes: sorrow, resolve...something else. Hope?

Stiles pushed up, gathered her fresh clothes again, and shambled to the sink. When she stopped there, the bathroom light slowly woke. It was brighter than the one in the room, revealing a stained toilet and a shower with lime-coated door. Everything smelled like bleach and disinfectant, and while they were clean in the most technical sense, the place hadn't seen a good scrubbing in a while. That wasn't her responsibility.

She put her clothes on the towel shelf, pulled a towel off and folded it over the bar on the shower door, then let the water run until steam billowed out like a fog. Only after her skin tingled and took on a red undertone did she shut the water off and dress.

Steam fogged the mirror, which she wiped down with another towel. The stitch on the side of her head, the puckered skin, the hair that had been shaved away—

A gunshot rang out again, but she kept herself upright this time.

Caville had taken her up to a ship—the *Ollie*. Goldman the pirate was the captain. That was who Caville was working for. She knew about Goldman because of his association with Devanshi Patel.

Who had he been? A smuggler. Stealing mining materials. Moving more.

Stiles had come to Dramora to kill the Patel matron and had made a mistake.

Then Caville had put a gun to his own sister's head and shot her.

He had a mission. It was even more important than hers. And...the look of hope in his eyes...

The hotel room door opened, and McLeod bustled through with a box. "Dinner's served."

So many aromas filled the room as he set his data pad and the box on the countertop next to the sink and opened the food containers. They were labeled with the restaurant's name: Olive Grove.

Olive oil, garlic, dill…

Saliva flooded her mouth.

And there was a plastic carafe.

She poured herself some black coffee first, letting the strong, bitter fluid scald her tongue. It was a small price to pay for the jolt of caffeine.

McLeod piled salad, spiced meat, and the dark green leaves of dolma onto a plate. "You look better."

"I feel better. I thought I remembered us flying."

"When I decided to come out to Norristown, I switched to something less ostentatious. We want to fit in, just a father and his irresponsible daughter who likes to party a little too hard."

"You're my father?"

He chuckled. "It's a little more believable than husband and wife. You're far too beautiful and young for anyone to believe that."

"Are we…on the run?"

He crunched on the stuffed olive leaves for a bit, then poured himself some of the coffee. After blowing off steam, he took a sip. "Here's what I know. You came to Dramora to finish the Patel job."

"To kill Devanshi. I remember that."

"Something went wrong. About a month ago, I received word that you were dead." He pointed at her neck with his coffee cup. "The chip embedded in your neck sent me two transmissions: NLA and RSC."

"NLA. No Longer Available. When I died. RSC…?" She squeezed her eyes shut.

"Resuscitate. Your system had been frozen with a resuscitation ring."

"Resuscitate." Who could have done that? "Darien?"

"Who?"

"Darien. My brother Darien Caville. He's the one who shot me."

McLeod's eyes lit up. "That makes sense."

"What?"

"That wound. It's from a blank. More accurately, it's a specialized round that amounts to a blank. The tip looks real, but it's lightweight enough to fragment without transferring too much energy. It hurts getting hit by one, but ten or twenty meters out, they're harmless. When you go deep undercover around trigger-happy people, it's advised that you figure out what weapons they use most often. Be ready to sabotage those weapons, or maybe steal bullets with fingerprints on them. And create some blanks."

"Why?"

"In case you find yourself on the wrong end of their guns. Swap out a few rounds in their magazines, and it just might buy you the time you need to escape or kill them."

Stiles touched the wound. "I was right next to him."

"And if it had been me, I'd almost certainly be dead. With Genesis 3 designs, your bones are denser, and your skulls have been reinforced. Of course, a real bullet at that range would've killed you."

She fixed herself a plate, starting with a fragrant stuffed chicken breast and artichokes. "But everyone thought I was dead. Why are we on the run?"

"Because Devanshi Patel is still alive."

"You want me to finish the job?"

The colonel poked at his salad before biting into an olive. "That may be our only choice. She thinks I came here to kill her myself—that or I sent assassins. I was supposed to leave."

"You could leave me here. I'll be back on my feet in a few days."

McLeod's eyes widened. "I think that's optimistic, even for someone like you."

"I need my stealth suit and—"

"No. For now, we're going to lay low. If you're feeling better in the next couple days, we'll get off Dramora and hopefully avoid her notice."

"But I was close. I could get close again."

"We—" His data pad vibrated and the display glowed.

As she finished her chicken, he wiped his hands and tapped his way through something that reflected a silvery blue in the mirror over the sink. She helped herself to some of the dolma, as his reaction shifted from curiosity to surprise to alarm.

He set the device back down. "As if we didn't have enough complications."

"She found us?"

"Devanshi? No. Not yet. That was some backed up Fold Space transmissions. It's all updates from the office."

Rather than ask what the updates were, Stiles sipped her coffee.

The colonel sighed. "You know better than to ask, so you won't. That means I have to tell you, because I want your opinion."

"Yes, sir."

"There's a fight going on in Parliament. Captain Benson's mother has the numbers for a coalition to take down the prime minister's party. He's refusing to accede to a vote he knows he'll lose, so she's pushing an obscure legislative procedure that's going to force the matter."

"Does that concern us?"

"Not directly. But it would seem that the prime minister has decided to perform some sabotage on his own. He's having the expeditionary task force recalled. Captain Benson's going to apparently be turned into his pawn to get her mother to set this procedure aside."

"Representative Sargota didn't strike me as the type to back down."

"She isn't. She's as stubborn a person as you'll ever meet."

Stiles smiled. "That's one of the few traits the two of them seem to share."

McLeod grinned. "They're a big mismatch in most ways, aren't they?"

"They are." Stiles filled her coffee cup again. "What was Darien—Agent Caville—doing working with the SAID?"

"Hm?" The colonel appeared surprised for a moment, but it was unconvincing.

"He's deep undercover. That much I remember him telling me."

"I wouldn't be surprised. He was supposed to be good at gaining confidence."

"But the people he was working with—Lev Goldman—he's a pirate. He's an SAID agent. He worked for the Patel organization."

"I see."

"They were..." What had she seen? Crates. In the secure room aboard the *Ollie*, there had been crates of precious gear. "There were crates of shadow tech on the pirate ship. The same sort of things I helped get aboard the *Pandora*."

The colonel nodded. "Do you have any idea where they were going?"

"No. But you do."

"I—"

"I know how to read people, Colonel. You weren't shocked that Darien was the one who shot me."

"That's not quite true. There weren't many people who it would've made sense for them to kill you, then resuscitate is all. I had my hopes it was one of ours."

"But that means you knew we had people in this area, people involved in the Patel operation."

"Hm." McLeod set his plate down. "It does, I guess."

"And you know that Devanshi Patel is involved in this weapons smuggling."

"I don't 'know,' but—"

"Colonel, you sent me in the field to complete a mission that I think you might never have expected me to finish."

He held up a finger. "That's not true, Lieutenant."

She set her cup down. He wasn't tensing for an attack, but his heart was racing. Her body had too recently come out of shock for her to try to influence him with her pheromones, and she wasn't sure that was something that would work against him anyway.

If he wasn't contemplating violence, he was at least hiding something from her. She levered herself up onto the counter. "I think you owe me the truth."

"I've given you the truth—"

"The entire truth, Colonel. I've worked for you for a while now. I've provided results. But it was becoming harder and harder to make headway, as if someone might be selling me out."

McLeod straightened and bowed his back. "That's enough, Lieutenant."

"I don't mean you, sir."

"I'm sure you don't. The implication is that you think *someone* in our group is behind your failures, but I think you might do well to look in the mirror for the cause."

Heat shot through Stiles. "I am *not* a traitor."

"Of course you're not, but you had started to develop a dangerous tendency toward risk-taking in the last several months."

"Because of the feeling that things were slipping away."

His hand shook slightly when he picked up his coffee cup. "I asked a lot of you. I think it's fair to say that some of the risk-taking you exhibited was the result of me pushing too hard."

"Or of our systems being compromised."

"Perhaps." He sank in on himself a little. "I think you're right, though: I owe you some answers."

She crossed her arms. "I'm listening."

"I'm aware of Caville's mission. I didn't directly assign him to it, but when I took over, I was given access to his files. The thing is, he's extremely deep undercover. He's been isolated from the agency for a long time. When an operative goes through such an experience, they're officially considered dead."

"Dead? He's one of *us*."

"Maybe. To protect you, and to protect us, when you operate this deep undercover, your records are completely changed. You saw how we fabricated a background for you. Had the *Pandora* been destroyed in Azoren space, you would have officially been listed as a petty officer with medical technician training. If your brother reports back in, everything changes."

That was the game. It was what she and her fellow Genesis 3 siblings had been created for. And yet... "But he's still alive. He's still focused on his mission."

"I understand. It's actually reassuring that you ran across him."

"Maybe we should pull him out. If you know his objective—"

"No. He accepted the mission. It's not uncommon, Brianna. We've had operatives in the field for decades who never directly update us on their status."

"But how do you know?"

"Sometimes, we infer everything from the environments they're in. For instance, this Gulmar situation."

"Which one?"

"Their capital is gone. You were probably out of communications when it happened."

"Gone."

"Destroyed by the Khanate."

"That…" Her head felt light. "They had a defense fleet."

"And they had a greedy, short-sighted leadership group that ran things very poorly. We learned long ago that you can't operate a government like a business. They found out the hard way."

She bit her lip. "Wasn't Captain Benson trying to form an alliance?"

"She was. The point is that we knew problems and vulnerabilities plagued their security force because we had spies with access to the leadership. Those executives were becoming dangerously greedy and reckless. If we'd managed to recruit them in time, maybe Radetta would still be viable. Now…?"

"Is this tied to Darien's mission?"

"Indirectly. Everything is. We have so many operations running at any one time—us, SAID, even CED—that it's inevitable we'll have people operating with counter-objectives."

"That's wasteful."

"It's necessary. We try to keep that to a minimum, but when you have someone like Devanshi Patel out there, willing to risk her children on her own objectives, people are going to die."

Stiles had been so close. If she'd felt killing Devanshi Patel had been the only thing remaining in the hunt to shut down the Ravens and root out the corruption troubling the Kedraalian government, death would have been acceptable in accomplishing that mission. "I think I should stay here and finish the job."

"I'm thinking about it."

"Would it help Darien? His mission?"

The colonel clasped his hands. "I can't give you all the details, obviously."

"I understand."

"What I *can* tell you is that what he's up against is considered an existential threat easily comparable to any of the major threats we face—the Azoren, the Khanate, or the Moskav."

"The smuggling is tied to this threat? He was helping this pirate smuggle weapons. I got the sense they were..." The memory of the Khanate spy—Denise Gallo—bubbled up in Brianna's mind. "The Khanate. There was a spy on the ship. Gallo."

"Denise Gallo. I know. She's not a threat. We tracked her operations for years. She was a naive kid. We had two people acting as converts, using her to find the real threats."

"But the pirates—Goldman, the SAID...they were smuggling weapons to the Khanate."

McLeod sucked in a breath, and his fingers clenched. It wasn't the reaction of someone surprised by the revelation but by someone who was surprised they'd been caught. "That's...a long-term problem."

"But you knew about it?"

"Prime Minister Zenawi spent years working on a scheme to gain power by securing the rescue of the hostages held by the Khanate after the War of Separation. His entire career could be drawn back to this SAID endeavor."

"And the Patels?"

"They have a good deal of money at stake."

"Through the smuggling and piracy?"

"It's all interconnected, yes. They avoid paying taxes that they consider onerous and unfair. They exploit insurance and push up rates for everyone else in the process. At the same time, they work with Gulmar privateers to feed technology to the Azoren and send some of that technology to the Khanate themselves. The Gulmar government turns a blind eye in exchange for the Patels fighting to protect the prices charged by pharmaceutical companies."

"That..." It sounded like an odd price to pay. "What do the Gulmar get out of it?"

"Hm? Oh. The government—the old government—made huge profits off our government. We spend billions each year buying medicines from the Gulmar at a premium. Every time someone tries to bring up a policy to address this, the Patels use their Dramoran representatives to stop it. Or they create a drama to distract from it. That massacre your Marine sergeant aboard the *Pandora* survived was one of those distractions."

It was impossible to forget the story, but it had been the corporal—Grier—who'd told Stiles: a battalion wiped out by artillery fire. It couldn't have been an accident, but the Dramoran officer responsible for the screwup had never really been punished.

There was so much corruption. And the Patels were tied to all of it.

Stiles clenched her hands into fists. Her arms felt weak; the muscles quickly shook from fatigue. "I need to kill Devanshi Patel."

"She needs to die, I agree. Taking her to court won't solve anything. Her connections and influence will protect her. And she doesn't have a competent replacement, although she started grooming a granddaughter recently."

"If we remove the Patels, we break this chain holding everything together."

"That was our hope, yes. One of the problems with something as intricate as they've put together is that it comes undone easier than a simple plan."

"I just need some time."

"And equipment." McLeod unclasped his hands and grabbed his coffee cup. "I didn't bring you a new stealth suit, and the old one didn't make it into your possessions at the mortuary. The mortician said the only thing you had on you when you were brought down was a bloody outfit. And that resuscitation ring."

"I left a lot of my things stored down here before we went up to the *Ollie*. I'll have to get to them."

"I can get us weapons."

"Us?"

"You're in no condition to do this alone."

His offer wasn't all that surprising. She *was* compromised, and it would be months before she could hope to do what she'd once been capable of doing before, assuming she hadn't suffered lasting brain damage. Part of her design had been focused on quick recuperation, including a brain that was faster at building new neural pathways when old ones failed, but everything took time.

Stiles looked the colonel up and down. "You're too old, sir."

"I'm not saying I'll be much help, but I've been at this for longer than you've been alive." He patted his belly. "It'll do me good."

It might. But there was the fact that he'd known about Caville's mission and never shared it. And he knew about the Patels and all their traitorous works, and he'd never shared those particulars, either. Siloing mission information was to be expected, but it felt like McLeod had put her at unnecessary risk multiple times in the name of protecting GSA security.

Did she really want someone like that at her back?

She realized after a moment that she didn't have a choice. He was her boss. If he'd wanted her dead, he wouldn't have bothered to revive her.

Except that she was the key to accomplishing his mission: Destroying the Patels. For him, Stiles was just a tool, a means to fix the problem.

The Genesis 3 agent pushed off the countertop. "Colonel?"

"Yes?"

"When this is done, I want to know everything."

The tall man frowned. "Everything? Even someone in the position I hold doesn't know everything."

"You know a lot more than you've ever let on. I want to know all of it."

"I—"

"All of it, sir." Her glare finished the thought: *Or you won't make it back to Kedraal.*

**11**

---

Surreptitious glances; shared whispers; perspiration trickling down stupid, doughy faces—Faulk didn't miss a single oddity of the *Warsaw* bridge crew. They'd stared at him wide-eyed when he'd come to the bridge early with his bodyguards, and in the minutes since had become almost agitated. Their fear was the musk of sweat. Their anxiety was the hiss of terse communications.

He clomped across the deck in his boots, squinting at the large display while they hunched over their smaller versions, which were highlighted with the overlays pertinent to their stations—communications, helm, weapons. None of them asked why he was so early or commented on the activity their sensors were picking up.

Kedraalian activity. People being maneuvered from one ship to the next.

*His* fleet being torn apart. *His* orders being disregarded.

The anger burned within him, a fire to rival a furnace. His undershirt was damp. Sweat collected on his upper lip. His prowl was a black knife darting among the pale blue of his hapless Navy brethren.

Finally, Hart appeared, another soft and vacant-eyed fool in sky blue uniform. Like the crew who were templated off of him, the captain's thinning red hair glistened damply.

He slowed when he passed the bodyguards with their hard, gray eyes, and stopped at the base of the raised command station, then turned to squint at the giant display. "They've begun moving those who return home."

The dullard at the communications officer station twisted around enough to make eye contact with his captain. "They radioed a warning, Captain."

"Of course. The Kedraalians are professionals."

It was a dig aimed at Faulk, although he wasn't sure exactly what was meant. Was Hart implying his commander wasn't a professional? Was the captain trying to say that a professional would obviously do what Benson had done? Maybe it was purely a comment about Faulk's competence.

He sidled over to the command station, placing an arm across the opening, effectively blocking the steps up to the raised platform. "A professional, Captain?"

Hart's head tilted. "I'm sorry, Field Marshal?"

"You said these Kedraalians are professionals."

"I did. Naval vessels in relatively close proximity communicate openly unless they actively seek accidents. When ships as massive as ours move about with the thrust we're capable of exerting, there is no such thing as a minor impact. That is my meaning. The Kedraalians did what they could to reduce the odds of an accident." The shorter man looked at the arm barring his way but didn't complain.

A wise decision. Faulk leaned closer to his subordinate. "Captain, professionalism begins with promptness. This morning, you were late arriving at your station."

"Technically, no, Field Marshal. I was here for the shift turnover."

"But you weren't here for the actual time of shift start."

"Ensign Behn had the conn." Hart nodded toward the simpleton at the communication station.

"Who had the conn doesn't matter. *You* weren't here."

"Commander Aidt requested I report for attention at the infirmary."

"Commander Aidt. Your policy officer?"

"Famke. Yes." The captain smiled, an act that presented the gap between his teeth for all to see and gave him even more the look of a buffoon.

"She worries about your health?"

As one, the crew straightened and craned their necks to watch the exchange. Hart smiled at them. "My mental well-being, mostly. There is the stress of the job, obviously."

"Is there something I should be concerned about, Captain? The influence of your Kedraalian counterpart, perhaps?"

"She is spirited and attractive, I must admit. And smart."

"And she offers a dark influence. Your Commander Aidt must see that."

"She does. Exposure to foreign ideas is such a terrible risk, isn't it?"

Faulk squinted. There was a dangerous rebelliousness about the captain. "Remember, Captain: The glory of the Azoren is at stake in this operation."

"Is that the concern I should have: glory? I would have thought survival—?"

"Survival without honor and dignity is a diminished form of life."

Hart nodded. "That is a philosophy that might be at odds with your history, Field Marshal."

"Careful, Captain." Faulk stepped closer so that rather than stretched out to block the other man, they all but shared the same space. It allowed the field marshal to whisper but still be threatening. "There is a hint of insubordination in your tone."

"My apologies. I merely meant that your ascent into the ranks of the High Command came with its fair share of violence."

"There can be honor and dignity in violence."

"You are correct. I had been under the impression that wasn't your goal. Didn't you embrace the title of the Butcher of Groznov once?"

"It was intended as an honorific."

"Not among the soldiers who died in your service, I would imagine."

"Those were merely humans, not so different from the Moskav animals we slaughtered in our victories."

Hart's smile became strained, as if his face might have grown tired. "A clear distinction I was obviously missing, Field Marshal." He glanced down at the arm blocking him from his post at the top of the command station.

Faulk curled the offending arm across the other man's shoulders and guided him aside. "Captain, I will need you to see to it that this nonsense ends before matters spiral out of control."

"Nonsense?"

"The Kedraalian idea of diminishing my fleet."

The smaller man drew up. "I thought Captain Benson had made it clear during the visit last night that this is an internal matter."

"Her delusion must be addressed through concrete measures."

"You have in mind what such measures might be?"

"I do. Now that we know which ships are intended to transport the Kedraalians home, we will position the *Derfflinger* and the *Lutzow* in front of them."

"I see." Hart nodded toward the giant display. "Perhaps you missed that one of those ships is a cruiser? It outguns and has a greater mass than the *Warsaw*. That's our largest ship."

"Blocking departure is meant to send a signal, not to destroy the enemy ships."

"That's good."

"Yes."

"Since we almost certainly lack the firepower to effectively attack the Kedraalians."

The heat Faulk had been feeling earlier while waiting for the captain's arrival returned. Now it was being fed by the man's impertinence, which was becoming a real problem. "Captain Hart, I worry that you have lost perspective."

"And I worry that you have lost your mind."

Faulk snapped his fingers, and his bodyguards rushed to his side. "Escort the captain to his quarters. He is under extreme duress and requires the attention of his precious Commander Aidt. Send two of your brothers to the bridge immediately."

One of the commandos nodded and whispered something into a cuff-mounted communicator.

Hart didn't struggle but glared at his superior. "You should know, Field

Marshal, that Famke's greater concern was about your influence, not Captain Benson's. Benson never killed her policy officer."

The commandos escorted the captain out then. To his credit, Hart maintained a modicum of dignity, keeping his head held high.

With the rebellious captain out of the way, Faulk took the command station himself. He wasn't familiar with the operation of the equipment, but it seemed simple enough: a smaller version of the giant display that offered multiple views, including a mirrored version of what the big screen projected, a version he could operate on his own, the ability to control what was shown on the giant display, and various levels of detailed control to rival what the bridge crew systems were capable of.

Even though it was simple, it would take time to work his way through, and the Kedraalians weren't going to wait. He looked up, clasped his hands behind his back, and exhaled. "Put me in contact with the commanders of the *Derfflinger* and the *Lutzow*."

The dull-faced man on the left—the communications station officer—spun around, blinking his stupid, empty eyes. "You would like to speak to Commander Adel and Commander Pelham, Field Marshal?"

"Do they command those ships?" Faulk tried to remember the ridiculous naval ranks. The man had an epaulet with a single bar of silver. That was the same as a lieutenant. Ensign. Such a silly rank. "Ensign."

"They do, sir. Commander Adel is captain of the *Derfflinger*, and—"

"Then those are the men I wish to speak to."

After a moment of hesitation, the young moron spun back around. Minutes passed, then he called something over his shoulder. A second passed, then he twisted around more fully. "Commanders Adel and Pelham, Field Marshal."

"Yes?"

"They're waiting for you." The ensign pointed toward the small display on the command station. "You can take the call on there, or you can—" He tapped the headset on his head.

The device was an extension to the personal data tablets everyone on the bridge carried in their pockets, a collapsible, palm-sized thing that could stretch a thin, plastic arm over the top of the head and extend a microphone to the corner of the mouth.

But Faulk didn't have one of the headsets.

He waved the ensign over. "I'll need one of those."

It took the dullard a second to realize what the field marshal was requesting, but then the idiot hurried back to his station and pulled one of the devices from a clasp beneath it. "Sorry, sir."

Black plastic sealed the little headset, which had almost no mass. Faulk fumbled with the adhesive, trying to tear it open gently, then abandoning that and simply ripping the container open and tossing the packaging aside.

Once the device paired with his data pad, he settled the plastic arm on his head and tried to find the communications interface on the command station panel. It wasn't readily apparent, so he waved the ensign back over and had him establish the connection between data pad, command station panel, and headset.

Finally, Faulk had a video feed of the two commanders on the panel and audio in his headset. "Commander Adel and Pelham—good morning."

The two looked like even weaker creations than Hart. Both had empty, blue eyes and the beginnings of jowls on chubby faces. Faulk had to squint and summon his imagination to see any hint of familial resemblance in the men. Rather than calling them brothers, he felt they might best be distant cousins from a remote section of the world where inbreeding was common.

A look of recognition flared in the thinner of the two men's eyes, and his broad forehead wrinkled. "Field Marshal Faulk? Where is the captain?"

"Captain Hart has been—"

Realization finally settled on the other commander's bland face. The nostrils of his broad nose flared. "Captain Hart should be communicating with us, Field Marshal. This is a breach of protocol."

"Captain Hart is unavailable at the moment. I am in—"

"If the captain is unavailable, he should have passed task force command on to Commander Brummell."

The other commander nodded vigorously. "That's the proper protocol."

Now Hart's frustration dealing with these commanders became more understandable to Faulk. "*I* am in charge of the task force."

"Of naval operations, Field Marshal?" The thinner one—Pelham—scowled, revealing a furrow that ran not just across his forehead but down the side of his face, disappearing above his left ear. It must have been some sort of birth defect, because there was no scar tissue.

"This is *my* task force."

"You don't have naval operations experience, sir."

"I don't *need* experience. I have a mandate from Supreme Commander Graf. You remember him, Commander?"

"We were briefed from the start that naval operations would always stay within our—"

"You were not briefed by *me* on the matter, Commander. I have orders for the two of you. You will take those orders and…" What was the naval terminology for implementation? Surely, they had some obscure and nonsensical language of their own. "Follow my orders. Both of you. Do you understand?"

The heavier of the two men—Adel—raised his chin. "Where is Captain Hart?"

"*I am in charge!*" Spittle flew from Faulk's lips onto the display.

"I would need to hear this from the captain, sir." The man's jowls shook.

Behind and to Faulk's left, the hatch opened, and two more of his commandos entered the bridge. The thought occurred to him that he could contact the small contingent he had aboard the two destroyers and have the commanders tossed out an airlock, but there were easier solutions.

Faulk disconnected and snapped a finger until the three bridge crew officers turned. "We have the ability to remotely control ships? Our own?"

That question set off a round of the three simpletons looking back and forth, but the communications officer eventually nodded. "If we have not been blocked out, Field Marshal."

"Good. That is what I want done. Now. Immediately."

"Remote control of one of our ships?"

"Yes. Command override."

The young man nodded slowly. "Which ships, sir?"

"The ones I was just communicating with—the *Derfflinger* and the *Lutzow*."

Once again, the three junior officers exchanged worried looks. Now the one in the middle—the helm officer—took on what he must have assumed was a stance of attention. "What would we do with them, Field Marshal?"

"Move them in front of those Kedraalian ships."

"The Kedraalian..." The young man sagged slightly. "How far—?"

"I want those Kedraalian ships to be blocked from leaving. You understand that? I want the *Derfflinger* directly in front of this cruiser—the *Seattle*. And I want the *Lutzow* blocking this destroyer the other shuttles are darting back and forth from."

"The *Ganges*, sir?"

"Fine. Yes. That one. Block those—"

"They're also loading one of the corvettes. Gunship-126, Field Marshal."

Faulk waved that away. "It's inconsequential. The message I wish to send requires only blocking the cruiser and destroyer."

"But..." The ensign made a sound close to a groan. "The crew can wrest control of their ships back."

"Can it be prevented?"

"They would need access to Engineering."

The field marshal turned to his bodyguards. "Call your counterparts aboard the *Derfflinger* and *Lutzow*. Tell them to secure the engineering section against intruders." One of the bodyguards nodded and turned away, and Faulk arched an eyebrow at the ensign. "Do you see how easy this is? When a problem arises, you seek a solution. Captain Hart has failed to adequately train his crew."

"Yes, Field Marshal. But the Kedraalians—"

"What about them?"

"They could simply maneuver away from our ships."

Faulk sneered. "This is why you are just an ensign. The message we send is that they cannot leave. Maneuvering away invites an escalation and assaults the pride of the captain. She will insist upon us moving our ships. She *has* to."

"Y-yes, Field Marshal."

"Once you've positioned the ships appropriately, get me Captain Benson."

The communications officer gulped. "She will almost certainly call us, Field Marshal."

"Let's test your theory." Faulk slapped a hand against the wide ring of plastic that ran around the command station. "Now!"

That set the bridge crew to their tasks. They once again hunched over their stations, only looking up to stare at the black-uniformed commandos or sometimes to study the hatch that separated the bridge from the rest of the ship. It was easy to imagine that they wished for their precious captain to return and resume control.

Sentimental nonsense.

If there was any better sign of weakness, Faulk couldn't think of one. Loyalty existed through a mixture of fear and discipline. He would rather have those elements driving his crew than any other.

Minutes passed, then the communications officer held a finger to his headset. "Cap—" The young man frowned at the command station, not meeting Faulk's eyes. "Field Marshal Faulk, Captain Benson requests to speak to Captain Hart."

At last! Faulk smirked. "Put her through to me." He leaned closer to the command station control panel, now feeling a little confidence about the workings of the communication interface.

But the connection from Benson wasn't there.

He glared at the young man. "Ensign, is there a problem?"

Seconds ticked by, then the ensign nodded. "Captain Benson said... She refuses to speak to you."

"Refuses? You told her it was Field Marshal Faulk?"

"Yes, Field Marshal. She will speak to Captain Hart only."

Faulk nearly stumbled going down the step. The insolence of this Kedraalian woman! He held his hand out to the ensign, pointing to his headset. "Now, Ensign."

The young man pulled the device off and handed it over.

Before realizing what he'd done, Faulk tangled the ensign's headset with the one already in place. The field marshal yanked his own headset off and tossed it aside.

When he had the ensign's headset in place, Benson was already talking. There was considerable heat in her voice. "—*Warsaw*, warn your destroyers off. Do it immediately. Do you copy?"

A deep laugh rumbled out of Faulk's throat. "Captain Benson! Refusing to talk to your superior officer? Really?"

Silence. Then Benson sighed. "What are you doing, Faulk?"

"Field Marshal, please."

"I'm getting communication from a Commander Adel aboard the *Derfflinger*. It would seem he's not in control of his destroyer. Is that correct?"

"It is."

"That destroyer is maneuvering through my battle space. It's passing dangerously close in front of one of my cruisers."

"Not dangerously close, Captain. It will arrive directly in front of the *Seattle*."

"What the hell do you think you're doing?" Benson wasn't so much yelling as putting a surprising coldness into her voice.

"As I told you last night, your deserters cannot abandon my fleet."

"You're having a hard time processing something that's actually very simple: These aren't deserters. These people have chosen to follow an order that they feel is legal. That's not just their right, it's their obligation. And it's my obligation to see that they return home safely and in a reasonable level of comfort."

Faulk's jaw had clenched while being spoken down to. He swallowed. "I am hardly the one having a hard time processing something that is very simple. My government agreed to cooperate with yours in destroying this Khanate threat. That agreement assumed a certain level of military presence. Your actions put that presence at risk."

"We have a more than adequate fleet composition to deal with this Khanate force."

"That is not for you to say."

"It is, and I'm saying it. Now, I would advise you to tell your commandos to allow Commander Adel's people access to their systems so that proper control can be restored."

"I will not, Captain Benson. Your ships—*all* of your ships—are a part of *my* combined fleet. Surrendering to your absurd request risks my command."

Remarkably, the captain didn't snap. She was in an impossible position and must have been losing face with her crew, yet she didn't shout or scream. He had expected histrionics and cursing, perhaps even crying. She was just a woman—weak and ready to fold under the slightest pressure.

Faulk wished he could have managed video with the call somehow, but the reality was that he would rather have the captain in front of him. Would she be so attractive with her spirit broken?

She went silent, not even breathing. Had she muted her connection to him?

He paced.

Silence was a new tactic, a clever game of wills. If he fell for her trick, he would be the one to look weak. She was using the crawling seconds to formulate a plan, no doubt. It would be diplomatic, perhaps an appeal to his good sense, the need to concentrate on their common enemy.

But she would break. He had found the perfect approach to corner her, to strip away her insolence. Maybe she had the superior force, maybe it would be superior even after the ships left, but she couldn't possibly—

"Field Marshal!"

Faulk stopped and turned to the bridge station. One of the ensigns had spoken, but they all looked so much alike.

It was the one on the right, the weapons station. Faulk fixed his eyes on the young man. "What is it?"

Rather than answer, the young man pointed at the giant display, where a battlefield overlay had been placed over everything. On that display, the Azoren ships were green, while the Kedraalian and Gulmar ships were amber. The Kedraalian ships were flipping to red, as were the Gulmar ships.

Now the weapons officer spoke. "Their ships have powered on shields and weapons systems. Electronic countermeasures have also been activated."

*Impossible!*

Yet the ensign continued, feeding even more inaccurate information. "They've locked on, Field Marshal. Multiple weapons systems."

Was that how her histrionics were exhibiting themselves, then? A sad display of depraved and misguided anger? It was reckless and irresponsible. An Azoren officer who had performed such a foolish act would be facing court-martial followed quickly by firing squad.

This Benson was desperate to make her enemy break the silence. She realized she'd put herself into a position from which she couldn't escape, and now—

The communications officer had replaced his headset with another one from below the console. Now he pointed to that headset, nodded, then the main display showed Benson's face.

To her credit, she had wiped away the tears and managed to hide that she'd even cried. Neither eyes nor face were discolored. Instead, she presented a completely calm and confident visage. Her head was tilted back; her eyes reflected the same coldness her voice had held.

What was it she was exhibiting? Arrogance? Haughtiness?

Yes. Haughtiness.

For some reason, the communications officer had given her not just a video connection but audio. Her nostrils flared ever so slightly. "Field Marshal Faulk, this is Captain Benson of the combined Kedraalian and Gulmar task forces. You have threatened safe operations of our ships and continue to do so. You have five minutes to return control of your destroyers to their rightful captains and to restore Captain Hart to command of your contingent."

Faulk snorted. "She has gone mad!"

The bridge officers stared. Faulk realized that the helm officer actually looked at the commandos, as if gauging whether or not they could be overpowered. It was a laughable idea, but it was no crazier than what Benson was doing.

She drew in a deep breath, but she somehow managed to hide her obvious fear and to instead make it seem like an imperious act. "Failure to take these actions will leave me no choice but to destroy the *Warsaw*."

Benson's image disappeared from the display.

Immediately, the weapons control officer put a hand to his headset, then hunched over his control panel. "Field Marshal! More Kedraalian and Gulmar weapons systems have locked onto the *Warsaw*! Missile ports have opened!"

It was a brave bluff, a clever ruse.

The captain saw the need to undermine her superior's authority. She needed to make him look weak and to generate mistrust and desperation in the ranks of Hart's people. Such an act reflected a flawed understanding of the dynamic, the animus that remained between the naval personnel and his own commandos following the necessary punishments.

But it was a mistake. Faulk had instilled fear and discipline. His force wouldn't crumble in the face of such an obvious attempt at intimidation.

What was called for was a message to that extent, something to clear this misunderstanding from the captain's head.

Faulk returned to the command station, back straight, shoulders squared.

The bridge officers looked at the commandos, then at him.

He smiled, projecting the confidence they needed to see. "Have the task force power up shields and weapons. Target the *Valor*. And inform Captain Benson that she has *four* minutes to stand down, or we will blow her ship out of the sky."

His officers gaped. They visibly shook. They blinked.

Obviously, he had impressed them with his command decision.

Good! That meant that Benson would be cowed, as intended.

Faulk smiled at the prospect.

**12**

---

General Quarters alarms blared, the hammering sound a distraction that was the last thing Benson needed. She leaned against the command station support rail, eyes fixed to the display that showed the Azoren ships that had maneuvered into position directly in front of the *Seattle* and *Ganges*. Below her, Chopra calmly moved among the bridge crew officers.

This was the worst time for Faulk to put his idiocy on full display, with so many of her ships now running with crews unfamiliar with each other. Her XO was doing well with Ensign Grehan, who had replaced Nuñez at the communications station.

Grehan was younger, shorter, and had the sort of round, soft face that spoke to a dramatically different upbringing than her predecessor. There was anxiousness in the new communications officer's pale face, which looked worse with her frizzy, red hair pulled back into a tight bun.

Benson knew that feeling. Anxiety gnawed at her gut, leaving her cold inside.

One mistake, and things could go terribly wrong.

Tuleyev and Chopra both had approved of her idea of punching the bully in the nose, but consensus didn't mean much with Faulk's bizarre behavior.

Was he a bully or a clueless psychopath? Hart had hinted at the latter.

She took a sip from her drink container, barely noting the cool, bittersweet fluid and the faintly citrusy scent that clung to her lips. Normally, she would derive some pleasure from the drink. Now it was all she had to energize her.

Chopra glanced up at the timer counting down on the big display: four minutes.

He backed away from the helm control panel until he almost bumped against the command station. Without fully turning, he caught her eye. "We could still simply have them fire reverse thrusters."

"That might be all this moron needs to claim he was provoked."

"If we power our weapons down…"

"Too late." Benson's stomach seemed ready to flip. She sucked in a breath. "He's set down an ultimatum."

"Who blinks first. That's what it comes down to?"

"It does. And it can't be us."

Her XO bowed his bald head. "I begin to wonder if this alliance was the proper course to take."

"You're wondering that just now?" She smiled when he looked up, hurt.

"Do you believe they're truly being controlled remotely?"

"Yes. Commander Adel looked as frightened as I feel. He knows what's at stake if he can't regain control."

"Could we possibly do better engaging this field marshal with an alternative?"

"No. As soon as he turned this into a test of wills with guns, he committed us both to this course." Benson squeezed the support rail. "Ensign Grehan, get me Commander Karras."

Chopra's eyebrows went up, but instead of asking what Benson had in mind, he hurried to the young communications officer's station. He whispered to her, and a moment later, Karras's drained face appeared on the command station display.

Benson accepted the connection. "Commander."

"I sure as hell hope you've got a solution to this, Captain." The older woman brushed back gray hair. "I've got no doubt I can blow this destroyer to pieces, but it's right up on my ship."

"I understand. I'd rather avoid firing if at all possible."

"Might not have a choice." Karras looked around. She was on her command station, so she would be taking in her crew and the bridge of her ship. "This is tricky. Shields do better handling energy weapons than a multi-ton ship, if things come down to getting physical."

"We'll do our best to avoid that. I want to take advantage of the field marshal being inexperienced in naval operations."

"Oh?"

"What would you think of you taking the *Seattle* straight up a kilometer, then moving a kilometer forward at the same time the *Ganges* moves straight down and forward?"

"The *Seattle*'s a big ship to try rapid maneuvers."

"You've got a good helmsman."

Karras nodded. "When would we do this?"

The timer showed two minutes. Faulk's ultimatum had forced the issue. "In twenty seconds."

"Hm." That was all the older woman said, then she disconnected.

Benson flinched. It wasn't a perfect solution, what with the risks involved, but every option facing them was flawed. Ultimately, it came down to the least bad of terrible alternatives.

She drilled down on the display showing her imperiled ships, wishing she could be in Karras's place. "Commander Chopra, please alert the rest of the combined fleet of the impending maneuvers."

Not half an hour ago, the combined fleet had meant all three task forces. It had been her group to command, something granted to her through a broad-ranging charter that had been worded loosely enough to protect her from exactly this sort of madness. The Azoren supreme leader had accepted this when he'd subordinated his maniacal field marshal to her.

But that field marshal had apparently decided that no leash could hold him, and now the fleet stood ready to blow itself to pieces.

The easiest solution would be to accede to Faulk's demands and let him run the fleet. Except that would be disastrous.

He had no experience with fleet operations and apparently had no interest in changing that shortcoming. Even if he did, she wasn't about to let her people be his training wheels, not with their enemy being as capable as the Khanate fleet had shown itself to be.

Maybe she should have taken Thiessen's advice and simply opened fire on the *Warsaw*. They could have given the remaining Azoren ships a chance to surrender after that, although she wasn't sure what that would have led to.

Disaster.

Every path led to disaster.

That was what Prime Minister Zenawi and the senior military commanders had known the moment they'd given Benson's task force the green light. How could there be anything but catastrophe when every element she was sent to deal with was an inflexible, crazed group? All of them were broken: corporatists who refused the idea of responsible behavior; communists who demanded everyone bend to their ideals of a society stripped of individual rights and means; fascists who worshipped a flawed concept of racial supremacy; and religious militants who couldn't conceive of a universe where anyone other than their own fanatical group might exist.

On the display, the *Seattle* suddenly blasted upward, rising above the Azoren ship blocking its way. At the same time, exactly as ordered, the *Ganges* dropped below the ship in front of it. Both of her task force ships moved with a crispness that came from experience and a focus on detail. Once they reached their assigned vertical positions, they began to move forward.

Neither of the Azoren destroyers budged.

Benson smiled. "Get me Field Marshal Faulk, please."

Chopra had been watching the large display. He immediately snapped to and returned his attention to the communications officer, who seemed ready to collapse.

Had she ever expected to be in such a situation when she'd signed on?

After a moment, Chopra turned, brow furrowed. "The *Warsaw* isn't acknowledging, Captain."

She squeezed her eyes shut. Faulk would be in a panic. His ultimatum was coming due, and he'd been caught unaware by the maneuver of someone he considered inferior. He couldn't possibly commit his meager task force to a suicidal strike—

On the small display, the two Azoren destroyers began their own maneuvers. They weren't crisp or even efficient. Each launched at an ugly angle to get back into proximity with the Kedraalian ships.

Benson's back stiffened. Whoever was maneuvering the ships was taking wild risks. "I want to speak to someone on the *Warsaw*. Now!"

Grehan yelped. "I'm trying, ma'am!"

"Don't try, do!"

The ensign's pale face turned crimson. Chopra was talking over his headset now, his voice slowly rising.

Finally, Faulk's face appeared on Benson's screen. She accepted the call, but the sight of his smug smile nearly broke the last of her control.

Before she could say anything, he laughed and clapped his hands. "Captain Benson! Well played!"

"Your ships are taking great risks with those maneuvers. They're moving too fast and their angles are poor!"

He made a surprised face. "Really?"

"If you have to put them in front of my ships again, wait until—"

"Captain, I believe this is a problem caused by your decision, isn't it?"

On the display, smaller ships carrying personnel and cargo to the two Kedraalian vessels were moving out of the way of the speeding Azoren destroyers.

She should have realized the field marshal would be reckless in his response. At worst, she'd expected one of his shouting bouts. Moving destroyers at such speeds through what amounted to tight-packed space?

Irresponsible couldn't go far enough to describe that.

She muted Faulk. "Commander Chopra, have the *Seattle* and *Ganges* come to a stop. Allow these Azoren ships to do the same."

Chopra paced slightly, but he was already connecting to the other ships.

Benson wiped her damp palms against her pants legs. Dealing with someone unhinged...

How could the man have made it to such a senior position?

When she unmuted, Faulk seemed to still be caught up in his celebration. There was an unexpected, almost unnatural color in his face. His eyes bugged out. He jabbed a finger at her. "You still have lock-on, Captain!"

She checked the countdown. He was seconds away from his ultimatum. Could he possibly go through with it—a suicidal attack?

Benson muted the connection again. "Tell the fleet to break lock-on with the *Warsaw*."

Then she came off mute again. "Field Marshal, you need to back down."

"Back down? Captain Benson, you're in no position to ask—"

"I'm not asking. I'm telling you. You're putting lives at risk. This behavior is unhealthy." Her stomach twisted. She shouldn't have tried to stare the man down. He was broken and beyond repair.

"Ah! I see your ships have begun to break lock-on. Good! Now as you can see, I am a reasonable man."

He turned suddenly, and the maniacal fervor that had been slacking from his face returned. "Ah! Commander Aidt! Come to see the performance of a true Child?"

Aidt? Benson couldn't recall the name, but whoever it was seemed to have pushed Faulk over the edge.

Someone else caught the field marshal's attention.

On the command station display, the destroyers continued speeding toward the *Seattle* and *Ganges*. The Kedraalian ships were coming to a stop, and now the destroyers were adjusting course, continuing with their dangerous maneuvering.

What could she do? Attacking the destroyers would be punishing the victims, but if she didn't do something, her people could be hurt.

She leaned in close to the display. "Field Marshal?"

He snapped out of the conversation with whoever had distracted him. "What?"

"Have your destroyers stop. They're moving perilously—"

"Didn't I tell you not to order me around?"

"We don't have time for your ego, Field Marshal. If you continue to put my people and ships at risk, I'll have no choice but to—"

*"Do. Not. Threaten. Me!"*

There was a commotion, and the camera caught movement—a physical engagement. Benson spotted the sharp profile and silvery blond hair of the android Hart had referred to as Famke. It must have been the Commander Aidt Faulk had been talking about, because as she wrestled with him, the field marshal shouted her name: "Aidt! Aidt!"

The chaos intensified, with some of the field marshal's bodyguards trying to drag the woman away.

She struck one down with a crack loud enough to come over the field marshal's headset. In the wild swinging of the camera, that commando slumped against a bulkhead, nose bloody and smashed. He was dazed and limp.

On the larger part of the command station display, the Azoren destroyers continued forward.

Faulk hadn't ordered them away.

Benson muted the connection. She had to do *something*. "Commander Chopra, tell the *Seattle* and *Ganges* to do whatever they have to do to preserve their safety."

Chopra nodded. Mahama turned from his weapons station, dusky cheeks damp with sweat. The look in his dark eyes was clear: He was ready to fire.

On the *Warsaw*, the struggle continued. As far as Benson could tell, Commander Aidt was declaring Faulk unfit for duty. Her jacket and shirt were torn, and the second of the field marshal's bodyguards looked like he might have an effective chokehold on the woman, then he was doubled over, and she was on Faulk again.

The android had something in her hand: a mask.

Faulk looked terrified. He disappeared, then the camera shifted to somewhere else on the *Warsaw*'s bridge.

He'd jumped off the command station and was struggling with something on the ground as Aidt closed.

A carbine—the weapon of one of his bodyguards.

He raised it, pointed it at the woman.

*Android. She's an android.*

"Captain!" It was Chopra.

But Benson saw what had set her XO off. On the part of the display allocated to the *Seattle* and *Ganges* situation, one of the Azoren destroyers —the *Derfflinger*—had adjusted course to match the *Seattle*'s maneuvers. The adjustment was even sloppier and more erratic than the earlier moves.

Too late, the *Seattle* tried to change its course again.

The Azoren destroyer slammed into the larger ship, coming up from below, hitting the cruiser on the starboard side, slightly aft of midship.

On screen, both ships seemed almost to shudder, to blink, then the Azoren ship erupted in flame and flew apart.

It wasn't much better for the cruiser. Fire belched from the impact point.

How? The whole thing was incomprehensible.

Chopra gasped. The command station display lit up with private connection requests from Thiessen, Tuleyev, and the remaining Kedraalian captains.

It was the moment, the time to strike. Everyone could smell the blood.

But killing the Azoren wasn't the solution. There were already too many dead.

Benson muted the connection to the *Warsaw*. "I want the entire fleet to hold fire. Get the word out now. Now!"

She didn't wait to be sure Chopra and the overwhelmed ensign did as ordered but unmuted.

On the display, a bloody Commander Aidt had a mask over Faulk's face. His eyes rolled up, and the hands he'd clutched around her arm fell away.

The android looked at the camera. Half of her face was gone. "Captain Benson." Although garbled, the mechanical woman's voice was under-standable.

"Yes?"

"Field Marshal Faulk has suffered a mental breakdown. This was an outcome Supreme Leader Graf was concerned about after the field marshal abandoned his policy officer. I have removed him from command and will see to his well-being. Captain Hart will be returning to the bridge soon and will set matters aright."

In Benson's head, fire erupted from the *Seattle*'s belly again. Those had been her people. "Understood."

She disconnected and looked down at the bridge crew. "I want all hands committed to rescue operations. If people can be saved, we save them."

The command was easy and obvious, but she wondered if anyone could be saved.

She wondered if the mission could be salvaged.

---

When Dietrich had been a young man, he'd visited a charnel house —not a place where bones were stored, but the bodies of the dead awaiting final preparations. The bodies had been recovered from a crashed passenger shuttle. Terrorists had blown out an engine a minute after launch, and the thing had plunged back to the ground and been torn apart.

The medical center was like that dread place now, rank with the ruin of death. Bodies were piled in a maze of bags at the center of the reception area. Other bags contained parts that might be identified through DNA. Stacked against the wall were sample bags that contained things that were less than parts that might still provide evidence that could close the book on the dead.

He moved from gurney to gurney, sometimes stopping to check vital signs, other times to cover a charred husk that even resuscitation couldn't hope to save.

Groans and gasps filled the air, and everywhere he looked, where there wasn't death, there was pain.

Ice-cold fingers stroked his guts.

Kohn looked up from the twitching form of what must have been a young woman once. He gave a nurse instructions on medication to dispense, then threw a bewildered look Dietrich's way.

The words didn't need to be spoken: *What sort of madness is this?*

Doctors were trained to deal with injury. Dietrich had spent years in search and rescue. He'd seen this before. Where the terrible handiwork of vacuum might cause some moderate visible damage to a body, the frightening masses of ships impacting with unimaginable force might pulp someone into nothing but a smear.

But what he was looking at here—what had Kohn distressed—was at an entirely new scale. Hundreds were lost; some might never be recovered.

"Doctor Dietrich?"

He turned, as numbed by all the death as the whisky he'd been drinking to lament his decision not to return to Kedraal along with the others. Yet another example of his weakness and fear. Melissa had been right about that. He'd never had the courage of his convictions.

After searching around bleary eyed, he realized the call had come from one of the people responsible for hauling the bodies up from the hangar deck.

This was a Marine. He pointed down to the fractured glass of a ruined cold sleep unit. "What do we do with this?"

Dietrich staggered over, blinking to be sure of what he was seeing. The body within—in suspended animation, resuscitation ring like a necklace—might have survived the ordeal if not for the horrific hole in her chest. Some piece of debris had shot clear through the cryogen device and its occupant.

A maniacal snort almost slipped free. A tear did. "Put her in with the dead."

It had been Benson's idea to send as many of the cold sleep units back as the *Seattle* could handle—something he'd warned against. The ship was already going to be overtaxed. If they ran into any problems at all, the captain would have to choose between solutions that risked the living and the frozen. For most captains, the choice would be obvious.

But Benson had insisted that sending the units back to Kedraal at the earliest opportunity meant increasing the odds of survival.

It was her fault. It was all *her* fault.

Kohn was at Dietrich's side, watching the Marine and his comrade pry the ruined sleep pod open for a second, then putting a hand on Dietrich's arm. "You okay?"

"I'm fine."

The young man put his mouth close. "You're slurring your words. I can smell whisky."

"A few drinks. I needed to calm my nerves."

"I'll take care of this."

"You're not ready, Chuck. Our captain created a bloody mess again. You need me."

"You're making a scene." Kohn glanced over Dietrich's shoulder.

He turned. Halliwell scowled from the open doorway, where he and Grier had set down the body of a Marine—not a victim but a wounded rescuer.

The big Marine officer stepped into the medical center. "Wounded."

"I can see that, Lieutenant. Thank you. If you have complaints, take it up with your precious captain."

Halliwell's meaty fists bunched at his side. "You might want to rethink that."

Grier grabbed his arm from behind. "Clive."

But the Marine pulled free. His face grew red.

It should've been a clear enough signal, but Dietrich felt his own rage building. He wasn't the one in the wrong. "She's out of control, Lieutenant. Look around you. She's a bloodthirsty monster!"

The Marine launched himself—so fast for being so big.

His sergeant dove and took his feet out from under him; they both tumbled to the floor.

Dietrich had already lunged forward, uncaring that he was far out of his depth against the Marine. Kohn's wiry arm had somehow gotten around Dietrich's waist, and the young man was directing them toward the surgical bay.

Behind them, Halliwell wrestled with his sergeant. "You're a drunk! You're unfit for duty!"

When Dietrich tried to get his footing and fight against Kohn, the younger man simply ducked lower and powered them into the surgical bay. He swatted Dietrich's hand away when he tried for the door controls. "Ernie, stop!"

"Did you hear him?" Dietrich shook a finger at his own reflection in the glass wall.

"He's right. You said you were going to get this under control. We've got medicine to fight off the addiction."

"I'm not addicted."

"Then why are you drunk? You can knock the alcohol out of your system!"

"I…" The doctor blinked. Beyond his reflection, it wasn't just the Marine lieutenant looking through the surgical bay glass. There were nurses and medical technicians and other doctors. Even some of the wounded peered from where they'd been set on the floor to await treatment.

And the reflection in the wall: red-eyed, haggard, puffy.

*Is that me?*

Dietrich tore free of Kohn and stumbled against the glass, which rang softly from the impact.

His breath… His uniform…

*Dammit.*

Melissa had been right. He'd been too weak to do what needed to be done. Maybe this was what he'd needed all along: something to make his decision for him.

Because now, his career was over.

---

A cloud of red sand scraped along the side of the rental car, obscuring Stiles's view of the squat, fortress-like Patel HQ. She lowered her binoculars and leaned back against her seat, massaging her neck.

McLeod looked up from the driver's seat, where he'd been studying his data pad. "You need a break?"

"After she leaves."

"We've got cameras tracking her coming and going. This is unnecessary."

Stiles pulled a drink container from the bag on the floorboard. Like everything about them—their clothes, the cars they rented, the food they ate—the bag and drink container were innocuous. No one would see them or pay them any mind, her in another of the baggy, soft cotton shirts he'd picked up for her, and him in a conservative pullover and jeans a shade darker than hers. The drink was a spiced, sweet coffee almost thick enough to be a syrup. It helped keep her focused and warm.

After a second pull from the container, she capped it and set it back on the floor. There was a break in the rain of sand, so she put the binoculars back to her eyes. "We need to change this car out tonight."

"You think someone might've spotted it? We've moved through three parking lots."

"It's picking up our smell. I guess that's giving me a headache."

He nodded. "There's a larger vehicle with mirrored windows. We could take turns napping."

"I'd like that."

McLeod held his data pad out to her. On the display, lines crisscrossed the city. "Color coded by day and keyed to time of day. You can search on those criteria and on function to see her patterns."

Stiles checked the function options: business, unofficial, other. "She doesn't have much of a personal life."

"She's made it clear that the company is her life."

"When does she head back to Kedraal?"

He took the data pad back and poked around. "Three weeks."

"We'll need to do this before then."

"You sure you're up for it?"

"We'll have to be."

The colonel puffed his cheeks out. "Did you give the guns a look?"

"They're solid. I'd prefer more ammo if we're planning to deal with her security."

"I'll arrange for it. They never leave her."

"I noticed." Stiles brought the binoculars up again. "Colonel?"

"Hm?"

"What's all of this mean? Who does she ultimately serve?"

"Devanshi? Herself, I guess. Her business. Her family."

"But her kids were in SAID. What does that mean?"

"Not all of them."

"The ones who aren't wasting away on drugs. I don't think she cares about the rest, does she?"

"No." McLeod looked in the mirror, but there wasn't anything behind them. "SAID was compromised a long time ago. Maybe with the purges, it can be saved."

"If Zenawi really is as corrupt as what you've said, maybe nothing can be saved."

"He's not the worst we've had. I do worry he's the start of a new wave of problems, though. If he gets away with what he's done, it could signal that corruption of this scale is acceptable in our government."

It hit Stiles how hard it must be to carry the years of experience McLeod did and not to sink into a dark cynicism. "Is this part of the rivalry between GSA and SAID?"

"The purges?"

"The investigations and undercover operations. How far back does it go?"

McLeod powered his data pad off. "It's part of the design."

"To not trust each other or to have people become compromised?"

"When you have people operating in the shadows, they're going to be tainted. That's inevitable. To get around that becoming a problem, each agency has to keep an eye on the other. You stop the spread of this bad group of actors, and you keep the sanctity of the organization intact."

Stiles could understand the idea, but it seemed inefficient. "So, we have purges every few years?"

"In theory, it's not purges but arrests, resignations, and sometimes retirements. You report the problem up the chain, and the government does house cleaning."

"What happened this time?"

"Zenawi. When you have someone like him—someone who's either part of the corruption or unconcerned with it—the rot spreads like a cancer."

"It's because he cared more about his political career than the nation, right?"

"All politicians care about their careers—"

"I meant that he was willing to put his advancement ahead of security."

"That's a fair assessment. But, like you said, the big problem at the heart of it all—" He tapped the window Stiles was looking out of. "Devanshi."

"And that's where we'll start the cleanup."

**13**

———

The day had begun like most other recent days, with Satrap waking to nausea and chills. Only after shuddering and pushing himself up did the monitoring systems that kept him alive even notice there was a problem. That's when the alarms activated, flashing red lights in his mind and wailing loudly. His Jakkara charged into the cabin at that point, pulling him fully upright and staring at him wide-eyed until he gasped out assurances he was fine.

But he wasn't. The chalky taste of death showed no sign of leaving him, even after he drank water.

For a week now, his failing body had dragged him dangerously close to the abyss he could never return from. There was a darkness in that place and a cold. It would be the end of him, the eternal resting place for his mind once nothing remained of his shell.

Should he fear such an end? It was, after all, an end. But it frightened him.

As the life support system flooded him with cleansing chemicals and nutrients, he tried to stabilize his breathing, to even out his heart rate. The cabin lights were on, but his little home in space seemed dark and small. The pillows needed to be replaced, soiled as they were by his sweat.

Once the monitoring systems assured him that he was fine, that his needs had been tended to, that the toxins had been drained from his remaining organs, he turned his attention to what mattered most: the data.

It occupied his days and kept him awake late into the night. In a sense, it was killing him, keeping him distracted from his misery.

Yet it was also his only hope of survival. Salvation was buried in there.

His first priority was security: the location and condition of his Jakkara. They were all that he could trust now, their transformation as close to complete as it could be until they went through the final process.

That would never happen. It would require a return to Azh Shivan. He would be dead before he ever set foot there again.

There was no reason to lament that. They were his now—loyal.

The next priority was the fleet condition. Repair updates, status reports on weapons and systems fabrications.

And then there were the updates from the Glorious Khan.

Satrap dreaded those.

Progress on ship repairs was slow. That was inevitable. Not many competent technicians remained, not after so many years of attacking education as a fundamental flaw in the human spirit. Knowledge was a lie; objective assessments of the universe were false information; thoughts that weren't given by the Ikhama were blasphemy. Curiosity, imagination, critical thinking—those were the stones on the path to heresy.

So Satrap was left with the handful of literate crewmen available to each ship muddling through the online manuals and videos to figure out what was broken.

If only computer thinking weren't the dark conspiracy of the universe, fighting to undermine the Khan, there might be machines to help.

But for now, there was a message was waiting for Satrap...from the Khan.

He opened it, anxious.

It was a video of the black-eyed old man. White whiskers covered flabby jowls that could only have come from indulgences denied others. Wrinkles webbed the coppery flesh of someone who'd spent years in the harsh sun and still did. That weathered face reflected disappointment and loathing despite the message being intended for the despicable man's creation.

"Satrap." A deep sigh. "What am I to do with you? My words are guidance; my prayers a shield against the enemy of my people. You left the embrace of our mighty empire with the lightning and thunder of the heavens and the fire of the stars. And now?"

Khan shook a data pad at the camera. "Now?"

He hurled the thing away, and the camera caught the sound of the device shattering. *"Lose not my son, lest it be the one come from the woman I no longer love.* You understand this, Satrap? The *Divine Wind* was my favorite. Lose none of my ships in battle, but if you must lose a ship, don't let it be my vaunted carriers, and if you absolutely have to lose a carrier, it must not be the *Divine Wind!*"

Perspiration trickled down the man's cheeks. "How can you lose my divine ship?"

The fury that shook the man and pushed his voice to the heights it had reached also took a toll on his energy. He heaved and gasped for a moment. It was long enough for him to find another data pad and slam it against the floor with the splintering of glass.

Then the Khan jabbed a delicate, fat finger at the camera. "Reinforcements come to you now, like the cavalry charging into the valley to secure the day against calamity when the Sons of Zuro betrayed me and destroyed my army on the Plains of Gibraltar. See to it these reinforcements are not squandered."

With that, the recording ended.

Satrap couldn't shake the image of the old man glaring, seething. It was the look he'd had before engaging in the destruction of a young man's body and committing that young man to a life of slavery.

That had been a body Satrap had felt adequate for a life of happiness.

*Your general. Your satrap. You motherless monster.*

There was a chime at the hatch. Satrap didn't even look to see who it was. "Open."

The device hissed, the hatch opened, and Zohar stepped into the cabin. The captain looked around, eyes narrowed. "I heard a voice."

"Our Glorious Khan."

"You've seen his message, then?"

"Just now." Satrap sagged. "There's a terrible pain in doing all within your ability only to be accused of incompetence."

Zohar's face softened. "Your Jakkara captain warned that your life support system failed to attend to you properly again this morning."

"I have been pushing too hard."

"Then stop. You've forced me to tie my fate to yours. That means that your death will surely lead to mine."

"If I don't push so hard, the fleet won't be prepared for our next engagement."

"We choose the time and place of fighting."

Satrap shook his head. "That cannot last forever. The sorcery of our surprise and inventiveness is being undone with each battle and with each day our enemy has to examine us."

"The Khan must be able to see our need. He will send reinforcements."

"So he claims." Satrap shrugged. "We have no need of more food for our subordinates. What we need is ships. We need to replace the *Divine Wind*. We need to replace the *True Light of the Way*."

"Did he promise such reinforcements?"

"Our Khan chastised me for my failures. There was no acknowledgment of the Gulmar being brought low. There was no praise for eliminating the Moskav from the field."

"But the reinforcements—?"

"The reinforcements were described as simply that. Nothing specific. No promises of giving us the ships left behind for protection against a foe who isn't coming. No guarantee of anything meaningful being deployed to our force, which keeps our foes drawn away and protects our people."

Zohar paced. "There was another carrier being built from the start. I know people who oversee operations at the shipyards. The danger posed by these fighters, and the limitless supply of...volunteers hoping to serve our leader...it's the weapons system he loves most."

"Nothing could better be shown as a testament to his power."

"Then he will send one."

"If he wants another strike of any significance, he'll send a cruiser along with the carrier. We have pilots to spare, and—" Satrap grunted, then looked away. He'd forgotten about Zohar's son being one of the pilot "volunteers." If a new carrier *were* sent, it might include the boy.

Would that be so bad, though? Wouldn't it show Zohar just how mad and inhuman their ruler was?

To what end?

Khan wanted victories. He demanded a constant stream of victories. His anger at the loss of the *Divine Wind* was probably worsened by the lack of a meaningful victory being attached.

Destroy Kedraal or Himmel, and the old man would be contented for a while.

Whip the Azoren and Kedraalian dogs, destroy their willingness to stand against the onslaught, and there might be parades and virgins awaiting Satrap.

As if virgins were something to be desired, even if his ability to indulge in the pleasures of the flesh hadn't been taken from him. A virgin had no understanding of a man's desires. Knowing the Khan, the virgin would be too young to even carry on a conversation.

Zohar stopped his pacing. "Did he direct you in your next target?"

"No. Our successes and failures have combined to define that target for us."

"This fleet that we stumbled upon?"

"The fleet that stumbled upon our special missiles. If they hadn't, it seems likely that all our earthly concerns would have been ended."

"To engage them again without significant reinforcements—"

"—would be suicide." Satrap pressed his hands against the crease of the joint where his thighs and hips met. There were times where even the painkillers couldn't erase the effects of the Khan's crippling blows. "Not suicide but a death verdict."

"That's mad. If we die, the Khanate dies."

"It need not be madness."

"And how is that?"

"The way he sounded and behaved. There was more to it than just anger in the old man's eyes. He seemed…desperate."

"How can he be desperate? He's safe inside the walls of his fortress. We'll be blasted ruins long before anyone comes for him."

"But it says something nonetheless."

Zohar pinched his chin. "Does it?"

"I think we're nothing more than a distraction for him right now."

"A…distraction? We are the great fleet he was convinced would secure the future of our people."

"We *were*. What if things have gone wrong back on Azh Shivan?"

The captain's head came around. "Gone wrong? What do you mean?"

"I'm not sure. Would someone be positioned to make a play for the throne?"

"This fleet is commanded by the most ambitious of his people."

It was a fair point, Satrap realized. His own lack of interest in the intrigues of the Khan's court made him the odd man out among his captains. "But there could always be someone unexpected."

"A possibility, yes." But he clearly didn't believe that was the case.

Satrap rubbed his belly. He'd lost weight in the last few weeks, enough that he could feel the life-giving machinery under his skin, the things that had replaced his ruined organs. "I've complained before about the ships we were given last time."

"The tenders?"

"I think now that we must consider making do with what we have."

"What would you do, then? Manufacture weapons to be attached to their hulls? They aren't meant to handle the demands."

"I mean the weapons they produce—these anti-radiation weapons. They are keyed to this shadow tech the enemy uses. All the electronic countermeasures and counter-countermeasures, all the sensor packages we now use are derived from that same technology. You have seen how much we must rely upon this technology. The same applies to them."

Zohar grunted. "It changes the scope of capabilities—moving unseen, seeing what is hidden."

"Yes. Their ambush of the *Divine Wind* shows the broader applications possible."

The captain's eyes narrowed. He apparently wouldn't soon forget the losses he'd suffered from that attack. "You propose to use these missiles differently? Would you seed the galaxy with them?"

"Not the galaxy. You can see their value, though?"

"This captain stumbled into a trap. He will not do it again."

"He might not. But traps come in many forms."

"Then what? We can only carry so many of the missiles."

Satrap grinned. "We must think different. If the reinforcements fail to give us what we need, only resourcefulness can save us."

"That look in your eye says you feel that you have a clever plan."

"We can only carry so many of the missiles *inside* our ships. If we manufacture more, we can secure them to the hull."

Zohar snorted. "Your life support systems have driven you mad."

"Hear me out."

"Leaving the weapons outside the ship denies them shielding against attacks targeting their computers."

"We disable the computers. The risk of remote hijacking is negligible."

"The missiles would be vulnerable to impacts, even outside of battle. If something struck the warheads just right, the missiles could detonate within our shields. It would be worse than an enemy missile strike."

"We would keep the detonators inactive."

"With no brains and no detonators, what use would the weapons be?"

Annoyance threatened to make Satrap snap. The questions were fair. They were good, even. Zohar's lack of imagination was typical for someone in his position. The Khan had chosen Satrap to lead for this exact reason.

He sighed. "We must find people we can afford to lose, those who are competent and brave but not irreplaceable." He couldn't say the obvious— the volunteer pilots. "We train these people in vacuum suit extra-vehicular operations. These would be the ones to secure the weapons to the hulls and to activate the computers and detonators when the time came."

"And the value of doing this?"

"We could easily double the number of these special missiles available to us when we lay our next trap. Or we could launch them with our conventional missiles. So many missiles at once, even a fleet such as our enemy has could be overwhelmed."

Zohar stared off into space for a moment. "Do not take offense, Satrap, but this will not save us. What you said earlier was true: We need replacements for the ships we've lost. If our promised reinforcements are nothing more than more food and missiles, our next engagement will go poorly for us."

The captain's words felt true, but Satrap wasn't going to give up. His idea was sound. Maybe it wouldn't win the battle, but it might buy them time to flee again.

How many more times could he report failure to the Khan and not face death, with or without meaningful reinforcements? Not many.

And so Satrap dove back into the data.

**14**

———————

Benson could have seen the ruins of the *Seattle* from the *Valor*'s cameras. She could have taken in the slow progress of gunships and shuttles scouring the area where the cruiser had been impacted by the Azoren destroyer for bodies, critical components, and the unlikely survivor. For some reason, that felt inadequate, and she'd asked her shuttle pilot to make a stop on the periphery of the ruins. Now everything felt a little more authentic, the void of space a little less vast.

When she zoomed the belly camera in, she could pick out scratches on the gunships' hull. Brilliant lights crisscrossed the area in a coordinated pattern that enabled the ships' computers to scan the video feeds for promising reflections. Those lights gave off a heat she imagined she could feel through her own shuttle's hull and through her environment suit.

That heat couldn't reach her core, though. She was frozen there. Shivering.

This was her doing—her miscalculation.

In the silent shuttle, it was easy to imagine what those aboard the *Seattle* must have heard and felt: the shriek of metal and composites giving way an instant before the atmosphere evacuated and emergency airlocks slammed down.

And the fire. That strange burst of flame would have come first. It would have swallowed so much of the atmosphere, chased it out into the vacuum.

Her people had been cooked by that fire. Some had been crisped to the point that flesh and sinew came away in blackened, glistening sheets, revealing bone that had been discolored by flash-charring.

The smell of those bodies…

She shuddered and blinked back tears. *Her* people. "Captain Patanga, please proceed to the Gulmar ship."

Her Marine pilot twisted in his seat. "On our way, Captain."

A second later, a gentle tug that pushed her against the seat harness told her they were accelerating. Her mind wandered until Patanga's voice was in her ear. "Captain? We've landed."

Had she felt it and it hadn't registered? She was too damaged to go on. She had caused so much death. Perhaps Thiessen would take over for her…

The co-pilot hurried past and took a carbine from the rack, throwing the strap over her shoulder and switching off the safety as she headed for the airlock.

Benson pushed out of her harness. "Lieutenant Yun, what—?"

"There's an Azoren shuttle. It landed just before us."

"That's Captain Hart. He wasn't responsible for the *Seattle*." Benson waved the younger woman down. "He was trying to fight the field marshal who caused the accident but was put under arrest."

"Oh." The Marine didn't lower the gun but stepped back from the airlock hatch. "You want an escort, ma'am?"

"No." Would that project weakness? Did she even care? "Captain Thiessen has things under control."

The outer airlock hatch showed green, so Benson cycled through and made her way down the ramp. She didn't trust her balance, although everything seemed to be working. When she set both booted feet on the hangar bay deck, she realized that the problem ran deeper: She didn't trust *anything*. Not now. Not ever again.

"Captain Benson?"

Her head came up. Hart was strolling toward her, showing the same sort of caution about gravity and balance that she was feeling.

Several meters away, she could see why: His face was puffy and discolored.

She stepped toward him. "Are you okay?"

His fingers traced the edges of a dark bruise. "Faulk's men wanted to be clear about my status. I suppose I am lucky they didn't help me out an airlock to be sure the lesson settled in fully."

"How is our dear field marshal?"

"Sleeping the sleep of angels." Hart's face was frighteningly still. "Unconscious for now. Famke—Commander Aidt—will hold him as long as her systems keep her operational."

"Your androids…are…counselors?"

"Doctrine officers. They act as Supreme Commander Graf's eyes and ears. When we're honest with ourselves, we acknowledge that they're also subservient to our Minister of Purity. It's easy to ignore the role he plays."

The mention of her father's name—or at least the name he'd taken with the Azoren—stung. "How is it possible for someone like Faulk to reach the position he holds? I would've thought you'd want leaders who were stable and disciplined."

Hart smirked, but it quickly turned into a rueful wince. "Supreme Leader Graf values bloodthirsty fervor and ambition above all else. Those who are competent and disciplined might make it so far as—if this doesn't sound too self-serving—captain or colonel."

"Are all the Children…?" How could she ask about sanity without being insulting?

"Mad? I think the odds are high that most of us are or will be."

"Is that part of the fervor you mentioned?"

"Minister King once told me this is a design feature. By that he meant a flaw that was accepted as necessary. Our DNA is essentially derived in the same way one would inbreed: isolate ideal combinations, repeat them, refine, repeat, and so on. A lot of positive traits are engineered out to achieve the ideal."

The hangar bay door opened, and Thiessen stepped through. A small group of security personnel hovered in the passageway outside. He looked handsome in his uniform, but there was a sadness in his gaze. "Captains, welcome aboard."

Hart bowed. "Thank you for hosting us, Captain Thiessen."

Benson's eyes dropped to the floor. "I can't say thank you enough for taking some of our wounded."

Thiessen waved for them to follow. Once in the passageway, he led them past the security detail, which fell in at a distance. He took his guests to a small conference room, and the security team assumed positions outside.

Once the hatch closed, the Gulmar officer relaxed. "Captain Hart, are you under threat or surveillance? This room has shielding capable of blocking most signals."

"I am not. Thank you."

"The bruises..." Thiessen tapped on his own cheek where the ugliest injury would be.

"Faulk's commandos. As I was telling Captain Benson, there was a message behind it. His commandos may not be willing to go against one of Graf's doctrine officers, but she is damaged beyond repair and will not last much longer."

"Can you...?" Thiessen looked to Benson for approval.

She straightened. It was time to broach the subject. "Captain Hart, when Faulk comes around, what happens?"

"He resumes command, of course. His commandos outnumber my men now and have superior weapons. We have a few sidearms." Hart looked between the two of them. "I assume you are probing about the possibility of permanently removing the field marshal. Even if you weren't, my officers would support the idea. They resent the tyranny and above all the incompetence. Unfortunately, we lack the ability, even with him subdued for the moment."

Benson had expected as much. The dynamic was strange but had its own sort of logic. "We need this fight against the Khanate to succeed."

Hart grunted. "We all do. I would expect that you've already surmised that our High Command shares your desperate fear of this fleet? Once word reaches them of what happened to the Moskav, that fear will become cemented. The Moskav were a particularly vexing enemy for the supreme leader, and he will be heartbroken over the loss of this world."

"My time is limited, as you know." Benson glanced at her hands to see if they were shaking. "At some point, my superiors are going to receive my refusal to follow their orders. They'll be forced to take action that will bring things to a conclusion—probably me being arrested."

"Truly unfortunate. It seems that incompetence is lighter than air universally."

"Lighter than—?" Benson got the joke: that leadership rose everywhere because of incompetence rather than despite it. "We all agree on the threat we're facing. What can we do to ensure we bring it to an end?"

"You mean, how can we deal with the field marshal?"

"Is there a way to get him to allow you to do your job?"

"Short of assassination?" The Azoren captain gently touched the darkest bruise. "The evil you see in the Khanate? It is the same thing that is cultivated in our leadership. Someone like Faulk is forgiven his faults because his strengths are those most valued. He cannot see what transpired as his fault. The death and destruction are a consequence the universe brought about when faced with his rational and logical approach. So, when you ask if there might be a way to deal with the field marshal? I do not believe there is. His entire life has been constructed around the idea that he is perfect. In his eyes, we are the obstacle preventing success."

Benson caught the way Thiessen sagged. He'd been hoping for some sort of miracle solution, same as she had.

She massaged her brow, where pressure was slowly building. "Captain Hart—"

"Leopold."

"Leopold, we're going to do everything we can to see to it that this mission succeeds. We'll also do what we can to support you."

Hart sighed. "Which will not be much, unfortunately."

"No. We don't have the leverage to force Faulk to behave. I don't even have enough Marines to risk removing his commandos, no matter how tempting that idea may be."

"Merely knowing that the two of you understand that—despite our differences—my people and I are not the problem is a relief. While Commander Adel was not someone I considered particularly competent, he was a decent enough man. I am certain his final thoughts included embarrassment over his fate and the damage his ship caused."

"Thank you."

"One small benefit from this debacle: I can now give you access to the detection network. The *Valor* will have the access codes within the hour. Your theory about movement within Fold Space can be tested."

Benson blushed. "We'll begin monitoring immediately."

Hart brought his heels together. "Captain Thiessen, your gracious hosting is appreciated. What I saw in my tour was more impressive than we have been led to believe about your people."

Thiessen smiled at the compliment, apparently not seeing any malice in the words. The relationship between the Azoren and Gulmar was a strange one. He led his guests out of the conference room and back to the hangar deck, standing by Benson's shuttle until the oscillating amber lights came on.

She brushed her fingers against his wrist. "Would it be all right if I visited your infirmary?"

He squeezed her hand. "Let's do that now."

They waited in the passageway, watching through the porthole until the Azoren shuttle departed, at which point Thiessen dismissed the security detail.

Benson marveled at the craft and care of the ship. The way the Gulmar executives talked about their security forces, Benson had expected everything on the ship to be minimalist and poorly maintained. Apparently, the Gulmar designers and security teams took pride in their work, even if their superiors hadn't.

That same sort of care was visible in the infirmary, which was modest but clean. There were the same smells of alcohol and detergents as in the *Valor*'s overwhelmed medical center. Benson's people filled the beds throughout. She spent a minute with each crewman, despite her sense of shame. Most had relatively minor injuries: broken bones, moderate burns, cuts and tears that would heal. Not one of them said a thing about her being at fault.

It was even more painful than accusations would have been.

Thiessen guided her out when she was done, and when she saw that the passageways were empty, she leaned on him for support. He seemed to enjoy her weight against him. "What would you think about dinner? Nothing as nice as what we had aboard the *Valor*, but it could be in my cabin. Maybe you could recover a bit."

She breathed him in and smiled. "I don't think I could eat anything—not after everything that's happened."

"I understand completely. Some wine, maybe?"

"I'd like that. And maybe a chance to…rest. If you're making that offer?"

"That'd be nice."

"Could my pilots grab a bite in your mess hall?"

"They're more than welcome." The Gulmar captain pecked her on the cheek. "We'll get through this, Faith."

"I know."

Although she found strength in his embrace, it wasn't enough to drive off the fear that even if they did succeed, the damage had already been done. There would be no overcoming their history—not for her, not for him, and not for humanity.

---

Grier pushed up from the chair beside the hospital bed that held her youngest Marine. A private who barely looked old enough to shave, the kid stood a good chance of losing his left arm, which had been pulverized during rescue operations aboard the *Seattle*.

She patted his shoulder, smiled when his steady breathing rhythm didn't change, then slipped out of the medical center. It was so much brighter and warmer in the passageway outside, the air strangely sterile and plain after being surrounded by the wounded. And the silence—it was stark after the constant tones and beeps of medical machinery and nurses shuttling things in and out of the patient bay.

Overwhelmed, Grier leaned against a bulkhead and cried.

The tears came from nowhere, rolling down her cheeks in hot runnels before settling on her twisted lips in salty pools.

Days ago, she'd told herself she was learning—growing. She'd made a real effort to study Benson and to try to understand what made her tick. The woman had spent years coming across as the only adult in the room, a rational and disciplined rock that was immune to the wild swings and unpredictable antics of her peers and subordinates. That had seemed to be the thing to emulate, to model for a career.

But the captain was looking at a career cut short now, and hundreds of her people—the people she'd refused to condemn for abandoning the mission—were now being prepped for burial on a burning planet.

Grier wiped the tears away, pushed off from the bulkhead, and headed for her quarters. She couldn't remember how long she'd been in her uniform, but the creases felt like they were digging into her flesh.

Halliwell was seated outside her cabin, elbows resting on knees. He had changed into jeans and a T-shirt but didn't look much better than she felt.

She sniffled. "You okay?"

He held a hand out and let her help him up. "Better than Faith. Most of our losses came during the rescue."

It took a second for Grier to realize it didn't sting to hear him call Benson by her first name. "Want to talk?"

"If you're up for it."

Grier let him in and stripped out of her uniform. She grabbed a change of clothes and towel. "I'll be back."

When she returned from the head, she felt a little better but still tired. She was as emotionally drained as physically. Halliwell had collapsed on her bunk, but he straightened when she came back into the cabin.

He rubbed sleep from his eyes. "Sorry."

"Nah. I feel the same way." She stretched out her towel and tossed her dirty uniform in her locker. "Is this it?"

"This—?"

"The mission. Do you think it's over?"

Halliwell's jaw jutted. "She won't give up. She'll get over it."

Get over it. Like losing the *Seattle* was a scraped knee. "Y'know, I thought being like her—being the only adult in a room full of clowns— would keep her safe. Now I see that no matter how good she is, we're all limited by the clowns."

"I came close to being one of those clowns."

"Hitting Dietrich?"

"Yeah. He's an embarrassment. That whole superiority act has worn out its welcome."

"But you didn't hit him."

The big Marine grunted. "Because you stopped me."

"Sure. You know, you need to be careful. Everyone's on the warpath, and someone who can't control their temper—"

"Yeah, yeah."

"I'm not kidding."

"I know." Halliwell stared down at his hands. "I've got a problem."

"Admitting it's the first step." She squeezed his thigh. "I've been there."

"This is different."

"Is it? Alcohol can ruin a career."

"This…anger…" He sighed. "It comes from always being looked down on. Everyone's better than me. In school, I was the poor kid. Then you run across all these people with better educations. Maybe some are smarter. Maybe they come from influential and connected families."

"You don't have to tell me, Clive. You know how I grew up."

"Sure. But you learned to shrug it off. I never did. I always wanted to be seen for what I did, y'know? It didn't matter if I was some private or sergeant or whatever. If I did better than an officer, I wanted to be *seen* for that."

"Everyone does. It's all bullshit."

"No. It's worse for me. I *need* it. When I don't get it, I get offended."

"You've got to stop that." She gave his leg a more aggressive squeeze.

He winced. "I know. Dietrich, though, he gets under my skin. He hides behind his degrees and accomplishments and acts all smart and sneers at everyone…"

"Just because he's smart doesn't mean he can get away with being an ass. He can't go around diminishing everyone."

"He's done it his whole life."

"Yeah, that'll change. If they get him for being drunk on duty—"

Halliwell brushed that idea away. "Faith protected him before."

"This was different. He made an ass of himself *in front of everyone*."

"Maybe." Halliwell closed his hands into fists. "I want to change all of this, Toni. I can't go on letting things run the way they do."

Grier leaned against the bunk. "Change what? Your temper?"

"Sure. But more. All of it. Like…" He brushed a hand through her hair. "Like when Faith wanted to give enlisted people a chance to make up their minds, people pushed back on the idea. That's backwards. It's a stupid mindset."

"You can't change a thing if you get booted out for losing your cool."

"I know. I'll work on it."

She kissed his hand, then hopped up onto the bunk. "Maybe you could work on it tomorrow?"

Halliwell chuckled and settled back on the pillow. "First thing. Promise."

"Good." She turned the lights out and settled against him. The cabin was all hers now, her roommates both lost in the *Seattle* fiasco, but being alone was the last thing Grier wanted at that point.

She wasn't going to let Halliwell go. Not tonight.

**15**

———

Blackness thick and deep surrounded Caville, suspending him like an ocean of oil. It was shadow within shadow—layers of darkness that grew even deeper than black into something he couldn't conceive. And in that void, pressure encroached on him, choking him, draining his life.

He sat up, suddenly awake, and craned his neck, listening.

There—the slightest scratch of metal on metal—not on the door but more distant.

When the rustle of cloth came from his left, he reached out and covered Gallo's mouth before she could speak. "Sh." He barely whispered it.

Her head moved: a nod. She understood.

Caville pushed up without making a noise, then crawled across the floor on hands and feet, as a cat might, cautious of his mangled toe, probing with fingers to be sure he didn't place any weight against anything loose. The floor—metal or composite—was cool and smooth to the touch. With the movement, he became aware of his stench and of the foul taste in his mouth. If the door was still closed, that wouldn't matter. Whatever was outside it couldn't possibly smell through what had seemed like a fairly strong seal.

Could it?

There was the sound again—something hard and sharp against a resistant surface.

And whatever it was, it wasn't light. There was an unmistakable solidity to the sound. It wasn't just beyond the door, but it was close. What could move in the darkened passageways?

Caville had a decent idea of what he was dealing with: the sentinel.

He crept back to where he'd been sprawled out next to Gallo, feeling the warmth still in the floor. "Something's out there." This was again whispered.

Her reply came just as softly. "Can it get in?"

"No."

Caville felt around for the weapons, finding the distinctive stock of one of the assault rifles. He made sure nothing rested on it, then lifted the gun. Now armed, he searched for one of the lamps. "Eyes closed."

He flicked the light on. The beam was bright enough to permeate his eyelids, but he let his eyes adjust to that before turning his head away and opening them. Even reflected light took getting used to after sleeping in absolute darkness. That was probably a trick of his mind, though— remnants of the dream of floating in a limitless black void.

Finally, his pupils settled, and the spots of light faded from view. Gallo opened her eyes and searched around, settling on one of the weapons, which she picked up with quiet care.

White salt caked her robes where her sweat had dried, same as it did his shirt. Her ankle was swollen and dark.

When she cocked an eyebrow, Caville nodded toward the door. That surprised her, but the alarm drained from her face and was replaced by resolve. She nodded, then he moved to the door so that he wouldn't block her line of fire.

If he was right, the thing outside was nearly twice his size, but it was still fast. Fast enough to get through the door if it was opened then shut?

He'd have to see.

With the assault rifle aimed at the entryway, butt set against his right shoulder, Caville opened the door with his left hand.

The scraping sound was there, impossible to miss, and he thought he saw something dark and shiny at the edge of the opening, then the thing pulled back, and there was the bang and scratch that could only come from the thing bolting away.

Caville poked his head out of the opening, keeping low and searching left, above, then right. The things could cling to almost any surface, at least as far as he knew.

But the passage outside was empty. There was no sign of damage to the walls or floors, and it was quiet other than his breathing.

It hadn't been imagination. He'd *felt* the thing. And—

The bones.

Where he'd set the bones of the dead Kaliphate security, there were signs of disturbance: torn clothing spread out from the bodies, bones even more disordered and stretched away.

That meant the thing's caution didn't extend to dead bodies.

Maybe that could be of use.

Caville drew back into the room and closed the door. "It's gone."

"It?" Gallo's eyes narrowed. "What's that mean?"

"Robot…or at least the equivalent."

"I still don't understand. You know what this place is?"

He set his weapon down and checked her ankle, drawing a hiss when he touched the swollen and discolored area. "How tender?"

"You're lucky I wasn't pointing my gun at you—that's how tender."

"Okay. We need to keep it elevated."

"I did." She pointed to the water bottle her foot had been resting on.

"It takes time. Stay off it as much as you can and keep it—"

"Quit trying to avoid my question. You know this place—this robot?"

"I have an idea about it."

"How?"

"This was a Kedraalian planet originally, remember? We have records about this place."

"Records? How would you have records?"

"My people—the Kedraalian government had research teams in here before the rebellion happened. We tried digging around a few places like this throughout known space."

"There are other places like the Place of the Fallen?"

"Yes. Each one's unique, but they're all from the same…people. Aliens."

Gallo leaned forward. "This is an alien site?"

"Not just an alien site. There are hundreds of those throughout space. Most are blasted ruins. They don't offer much of value. Places like this and the ruins on Jotun—those are mostly intact. And they exhibit the signs of the same species or at least the same technologies."

"Wait. You came to Azh Shivan to find an alien ruin? You weren't really a part of Goldman's team?"

"Goldman's objective was a good one, but it wasn't as important as what I came for."

"Did *he* know about this?"

"The Place of the Fallen? No. Or at least he didn't know that was my objective."

The Khanate spy snorted. "I can't figure you out."

"I'm not like most people."

"You can say that again."

Caville paced around the room. "The shadow technology—were you involved in that? Smuggling it?"

"Shadow technology?"

"Stealth technology. Advanced electronic countermeasures and sensors technology."

She frowned. "No."

"Goldman was involved. His group has been filtering the tech out to the Azoren and to your people for a while now."

"All right."

"It's technology derived from equipment discovered here years ago. It was supposed to be protected technology, the sort of thing that would give our navy the advantage to counteract all the crazy military spending everyone else was doing."

"I guess that didn't work. I've heard the Khan has a big fleet now."

"I—" Caville scraped to a stop. "My focus has been on getting inside Goldman's operation so I could make my way here. The specifics of fleet and army power aren't really my concern. But the fact that the technology we spent years creating slipped out to our enemies—that's a problem."

"Because only you know how to handle this shadow tech?"

"Maybe." He gauged her reaction. She'd said *the Khan* instead of *my people*. That was something. "I think it mostly comes down to us losing the edge we invested so much time into. The technology leaking out means the arms race we hoped to avoid is a reality again."

The young woman bowed her head. "I know I agreed that this was a one-way trip, but did you come here with the intention of dying?"

"No. It's just that the odds of escape aren't good."

"Because of that robot?"

"It's the biggest threat. But your Khan is a problem, too."

"He's not my Khan."

"He's going to find out about the prisoner rescue, and that's going to eventually lead to people finding out that we stole a troop carrier."

"And that's going to lead him here?"

"You have to plan for it, even if it never happens."

"But we know a way out, right?"

"We'll have to find a different one. There was a dropdown from a lower roof. That might be our only option."

"Great."

"Don't get discouraged. It looks like this place was designed to pull down from the surface. Maybe there's another escape route, but it's not something our people ever found."

"Do you have a map?"

Caville tapped the side of his head. "I know what they found years ago. A place like this, that might not be as useful as it seems."

"You mean this place changes? The halls and doors?"

"They thought it had in the past."

Gallo shook her head. "You don't look old enough for something like this."

"What's that mean?"

"You look my age."

"You were old enough to spy."

"Sure, but apparently I was just a way to get an ear inside Zenawi's cabinet. No one bothered to debrief me."

"It's just different priorities. While you were memorizing parables and internalizing hatred, I was learning how to do…" He pointed at the assault rifle, then at the room around them. "This."

"As a kid? You barely look old enough to pilot a vehicle."

Caville shrugged. "My training started when I was a kid."

"What a great childhood."

"No worse than yours."

"My parents didn't teach me guns."

"Your mother taught you not to trust your father or the people around you who were giving you opportunities. I think that's worse than anything I learned."

"Someone made you capable of shooting a friend in the head." Gallo jutted her chin out defiantly. "That's teaching hatred, isn't it?"

Caville strode to his duffel bag and pulled out a box, which he typed a combination into, then applied a thumb to. The lock popped, and he opened the top. He held up a pistol. "Recognize this?"

The young woman's brow wrinkled. "Is that the gun you shot her with?"

"The same make." He popped the magazine out and held that out to her.

She took it. "What—?"

"Count the bullets." When she fumbled with removing the bullets, he took the magazine back and popped each round out. "Eighteen. You see?"

"Okay."

He reloaded the rounds, then handed it back to her. "Now you do it."

Gallo worked each bullet free with some effort. "Sev-seventeen."

"You forgot this one." He held up the bullet he'd palmed during reload, then he waved for her to give him the magazine. He emptied and reloaded it again, then handed it back.

"How can you do that so fast?"

"I can do it in the dark. I can tear the gun down and put it back together blindfolded. It's called training."

She pushed the bullets out of the magazine again. "Eighteen."

Caville plucked one of the bullets from her hand. "You see this?"

"Yes."

He took the magazine back and loaded the bullet, then pointed it at one of the old flashlights resting at the far end away from him. The roar of the gun made the young woman jump, but then she looked at the lamp, which hadn't moved or been visibly damaged.

Her mouth dropped open. "What...?"

"I shot her in the head with a blank. It wasn't ideal, but it was the only way to save her life and preserve my mission."

"But the bullet—?"

"It *looks* like a bullet. And up close like that, it could still kill you. There's too much force coming out of the barrel like that for even the false round to be non-lethal. But we're special."

"We?"

"Brianna and me. The woman I shot."

"Oh."

"What we do—it's not just training, it's how we were *made*."

Gallo covered her mouth with a hand. "You're...an android?"

"No. We're engineered, that's all." He took the other bullets back, reloaded the magazine, slapped it back into place, then stuffed the gun into the small of his back, where his belt would pin the weapon against his skin. "I'm still flesh and blood. I still have human DNA. It's just..." Caville considered for a moment, lips pursed. "It's just that we have a lot of optimizations."

His comrade shook her head. "They made you. I mean, they created you to be this..."

"I'm a soldier."

"Are you? I thought soldiers had a choice? It sounds like you were bred and brainwashed."

Caville didn't consider his training to be brainwashing, but he could understand an outsider seeing it that way. "My training includes learning to think independently. We were never taught to just accept things."

"You don't believe the Kedraalian Republic is perfect?"

"Of course not. It's a good set of ideals derived from the best of what we learned from our history on Earth, but it's only as good as the people who try to implement those beliefs."

"Well..." Gallo frowned. "All right. If you say so."

"I've killed Republic citizens. We have people who embrace terrible beliefs. Does that sound like brainwashing?"

"No. Maybe. It still sounds like you never had a childhood to form your own opinions through experience."

"You did. Look what that led to."

Gallo looked away. "Is she alive?"

"Brianna? I hope so. It depends on whether or not Devanshi Patel destroyed the body."

"Why would she do that?"

"Because she's paranoid. If it wouldn't have put my mission at risk, I would've killed her long ago myself. I needed her to make this technology transfer happen. And if I survive, I'll find her and finish the job."

"That sounds savage."

"The people we're dealing with gave away valuable technology. They put millions of lives at risk. That Azoren attack against Kedraal? Devanshi Patel and her people made that possible."

Gallo looked down at the assault rifle she'd held earlier. "It still sounds like murder to me."

"Justifiable. If she didn't have so much protection, she'd be sentenced to execution after a trial. What's the difference?"

"Nothing, I guess. It just sounds like something that would happen here."

"Something the Khan would do?" Caville grunted. "Maybe your people have a couple good points."

That drew a sour scowl. "So what do we do now? Is that robot coming back?"

"It will. It knows we're here." He crossed to the door and patted it. "It won't go through doors, though. If you keep this closed, you'll be okay."

"If *I* keep it closed? What about you?"

Caville stretched until his back popped, then gathered up his assault rifle, some extra magazines, and a spare lamp. "Remember what I said about finding a way out?"

"You're going out there?"

"I need to check the areas around us. If the passages and rooms are like they should be, we've got at least a little chance of finding a way out."

"What if they aren't?"

"Then we'll have to look for something new."

Gallo started to push up, wincing as her heel banged against the floor. "Let me come with—"

"No. You'd only slow me down. And if that robot's keeping an eye on us, then you'd be the signal for it to attack. You're hurt and slow. That's exactly the sort of thing to provoke it."

"But—"

He glared at her. "This isn't a discussion. You'd be putting us both at risk."

The young woman slapped a hand against the floor. "What if it kills you?"

"Then you stay in here until that ankle's healed up and make a run for it."

"A run…?" She rolled her eyes. "I have no idea where to go."

He held a hand out to her, and when her eyes lit up and she reached for him, apparently thinking he'd changed his mind, he shook his head. "Your data pad."

Her face darkened, and she fumbled around inside her robe. "What do you—?"

"Unlock it." When she pulled the device out and activated it, he took it from her. It was only a few seconds of work to transfer a copy of the crude map he'd sketched. "You know what I know now. Good enough?"

"No, it's not good enough. I can cover your back."

It was an authentic offer. She really did think she could be more helpful than harmful. "Maybe tomorrow." He checked his lamp, stuffed a spare battery into a pocket, then patted the door softly. "Let me show you how to open and close the door, then I'm off."

"But—"

"I have to do this. Even if the Khan doesn't send someone, we don't have enough food or water to last forever."

Tears welled up in Gallo's eyes, creating a surprising sting in Caville's chest. "You have to come back."

"If there's any way possible, I will."

As he walked her through the process of activating the door, though, Caville wondered just how realistic he was being.

He was injured, too, and it was the sort of injury that could slow him down. His arms and legs felt weak and stiff. Although he couldn't tell Gallo, the briefings about the sentinel had been bleak. It had killed soldiers in heavy armor, and as far as the scientists who'd escaped the various surveys could tell, the thing couldn't be damaged by small arms fire.

What were the odds the thing would lay in ambush down one of the darkened passageways and strike before he could detect it? Or maybe it would simply announce its presence and have some fun stalking him.

No matter what, the odds of survival were low.

But that's why he'd been sent. No one else stood a chance, and the fate of humanity depended on what he'd come to do.

**16**

———

As with every previous conference call between Zohar and the other captains, Satrap felt trapped. Even with the arrival of reinforcements, his captains clung to arguments about how terribly the fleet had performed and who should accept the blame for that. He was tempted to point out that every single surviving captain had chosen to abandon the last battlefield when ordered, but someone was sure to twist that into an attack on their bravery.

Ikhama had warned against antagonizing the captains, even though they were now in Fold Space and challenges to authority would be diminished. She sat below the display now, studying the captains who had just echoed her prayers.

With the fleet nearly at full strength again, would they betray her? Would they betray Satrap?

He sighed and massaged his belly. He'd managed to develop a pain greater than in his hip joints. With the pain came a stench like flesh necrotizing and a taste to match.

No mystery—this was the result of his life support machine failing.

The drone of the petty arguments distracted him from part of the pain. Other than Zohar, his captains were fools lacking even a hint of practical command. Their fine uniforms filled the wall display, as did their imperious faces.

Satrap was still trying to evaluate the new captains. They were younger than the men who had accompanied the fleet when it had departed Azh Shivan, perhaps more rigid and lacking in the cynicism that came with age.

Or perhaps they were young enough to still question the basic premise of the Khan and his belief system.

Commanding the replacement carrier—the *Stroke of Vengeance*—was Sudin. He had a long face that was still darkened from what must have been some length of time in the sun. Beneath a narrow nose was a small mouth with dark red lips.

Zohar's son was aboard the vessel, ready to fly into obliteration for the Khan.

Sudin seemed the sort to welcome such zealotry. His blue eyes held no emotion as he listened to his elders squabble.

The cruiser that had finally come as replacement for the *True Light of the Way* was the *Purity of Fire*. Although half the age of his predecessor Rouhani, the ship's captain—Portis—managed the same stubborn, scornful glare. His black hair was clipped close to the scalp, reducing the severity of the high widow's peak. When he got involved in the squabbling, it was only a nod of agreement to something irrefutable.

"Our ships are finite in number." That comment from a fellow captain brought a wise nod from Portis.

"Should we break their shadow technology, our fighters will be even more effective." Eyes narrowed shrewdly, Portis gave another nod at a different captain.

The young captain sought safety by not being offensive. That had to be it.

Finally, Zohar had heard enough. "My fellow captains—silence, please!"

Satrap roused from the torpor that had started to settle over him. Zohar sounded genuinely impatient and ready to put the arguments to rest.

Good! This was what was needed!

If he wanted the role of senior captain leading the blubbering masses, Satrap was fine with that.

The captains grumbled, Portis nodded at their words, then everyone quieted.

Ikhama turned from the display and bowed slightly at Satrap. Things were progressing as she had said they would. All that was required was to continue the effort to bring the more troublesome captains under control.

"Thank you." Zohar closed his eyes dramatically. "There was a specific reason for this call."

The youthful Sudin leaned closer to his camera, which captured the deeper redness in his cheeks. "Forgive me, Zohar, but is it customary to silence the words of your peers when discussing strategy?"

"When they speak about strategy intelligently, obviously not."

"We have questions about our destination. Why were we not allowed to program the Fold Space course ourselves?"

"No question can be answered when people babble on nonsensically."

"I see." Sudin leaned back.

"What we want to speak about today is too important to allow petty arguments to drain away the time. We near our destination."

"A destination we have no idea about."

Zohar pinched his chin. "Then listen more and argue less."

Sudin shrugged. "It is my understanding that healthy debate is the means—"

"No." Zohar waved the younger man to silence. "Satrap has something to share with us. It will explain our course. The longer this bickering goes, the less time there is to discuss this idea."

That was the signal, and it roused Satrap fully. He bowed toward the camera. "My thanks, Zohar."

Scowling captains stared out from the display. Apparently, there was something worse than Zohar calling for an end to squabbling: the satrap offering up his strategies for consideration.

Still, that *had* been the point of the meeting. Weeks in Fold Space with no declared destination had left everyone irritable.

Satrap did his best to sit up straight. "My captains, our mission comes close to the turning point."

Sudin squinted. "My understanding is that you have failed in your attempts to complete your charge but have yet to strike a deadly blow against the enemy. Did the Khan misrepresent your effectiveness, Satrap?"

"It is more likely that you misunderstood, Sudin."

The young captain grunted but let any challenge go unspoken.

Rather than risk another captain seizing on the challenge, Satrap hurried on. "I see a way forward, now. We speed toward our destination. It won't be easy. In fact, this is a bold strategy."

One of the captains—an old fellow with polished head and bushy, white eyebrows that looked like caterpillars curled over bright green eyes —held a hand up. The man commanded one of the newer tender ships. "Satrap?"

"Yes?"

"Was it boldness that foiled us before?"

"What has consistently put us at risk of failure—" Satrap caught Ikhama's warning look. *Don't antagonize. This isn't a time for lessons but a time for solidarity.* Her words, but they were true. "—has been a series of unfortunate incidents that have left us unprepared for the way the enemy has responded to what should have been backbreaking blows."

The old captain screwed his lips up. "You have something to counter this resiliency?"

There. It was exactly what Satrap had needed. "I do. To defeat this sort of enemy, we must draw them out. We must force them to extend their forces and leave them with a choice of flight or accepting the engagement they've been seeking. But that engagement will come at terrible disadvantage. And if they abandon the hunt for us, we strike—another Gulmar planet, then another Moskav planet, and finally Himmel. Eventually, the enemy must face us again, and that is when we will destroy them."

Sudin rolled his eyes. "Where is our answer about our destination, Satrap?"

"Patience. Our Khan knows our destination. That's enough for now. I wish to explain the strategy."

"This fails to clear the bar set for discussion of strategy."

"Does it? Could you tell me what you seek?"

"Details? You talk about drawing them out and forcing them to overextend. This is a fine idea. How do you plan to make it happen? Do we fly to meet them?"

"A fair question. My answer should explain everything." Satrap breathed deeply. "Our enemy knows there are only so many places a fleet such as ours can go for resupply. Without the fuel we need, our reactors run out. If we do not receive resupply from home, the options are dramatically reduced."

"Fuel can be taken from numerous sources. There are dozens known of."

"That is correct in a limited way. Fuel can be gathered from mineral-rich planets like the ones you're counting in your estimate, but only a few currently present themselves as ideal for such refueling, especially for a fleet like ours. If there *is* a refining capability somewhere, that's better. Even that presents a problem, as most such planets are protected."

Once again, the old tender captain raised a hand. "We *are* a wartime fleet. We are self-sufficient."

"We are. That changed with the destruction of some of our ships. We lost a good deal of our fuel supplies, obviously."

Sudin bowed his chest. "My ship carries fuel, same as the *Desert Sands*."

"Yes, but our enemy has no idea of that. Your assignment to the fleet is known by the Khan and a handful of his most loyal people. The enemy must assume that we need fuel at some point."

Zohar tilted his head. "You propose to strike a place for fuel?"

Satrap bowed slightly. This was something the two of them had rehearsed, but it needed to come across as unscripted. "I do."

"One that offers the least resistance."

"Actually, the resistance isn't what matters. We operate on a timetable. Our Khan wishes to see results in our purifying war. For that reason alone, our target must be within a reasonable distance. But there are other reasons as well."

"Such as?"

"We want our enemy to find us."

Portis, the captain who seemed to address every revelation and comment with a nod, froze. "Did I hear you correctly, Satrap? Did you say that you want the enemy to find us?"

"You heard me correctly."

The young man ran a palm over his close-shaved scalp. "That seems...odd."

"Remember that our intent is to engage the enemy."

"Yes, but we would want to do so while on the offensive, not while attacking a fuel resupply."

Satrap had planned on having either Zohar or Ikhama ask the setup questions. This young man provided a much better ally, unwitting as he was. "We'll be resupplied by the time the enemy arrives. This target isn't a *real* target, after all. We might not project such, but we will in fact be lying in wait."

"I..." Portis shook his head. "How will they know to find us but not know we plan an ambush?"

"Remember that the premise of the plan is that they assume that we must take on fuel at some point—whether on Azh Shivan or some other place."

"Yes."

"We destroyed Moskav, but we wouldn't have had time to pillage fuel, assuming any survived on the planet. The enemy is led by a crafty captain. He must know by now that his arrival in Moskav space was unexpected. So, what options remain? Think as this crafty captain would."

Portis looked around on the display. He was deferring to others now.

It was the old tender captain who took the question. "The closest fuel supply point that would draw them in would be in Gulmar space—the planet Petrovan."

Satrap smiled. "It also provides the most promising target for another of our strikes, which is why it is our destination. After Radetta, Petrovan is home to the second largest group of corporations and population centers. And only a small task force protects it: a frigate, a few gunships. The rest of the defenses are atmospheric fighters."

Sudin waved a hand. "That is no challenge."

"Actually, for the plan to work, we need this to appear to be a problem."

"Why?"

"To draw the enemy in." A signal flashed from the Fold Space drive system: They were approaching their destination. "My captains, the time comes. In less than an hour, we exit Fold Space. When we do, you each will have a part to play, and it must be played exactly." It was tempting to point out how failure to follow orders had put them in the situation they were in, but Ikhama's determined stare convinced him otherwise.

Zohar must have sensed that the other captains were too surprised by this to offer challenge. "This plan, Satrap?"

"Yes. As promised, the details. Our fleet exits Fold Space. To be more cautious after what happened in Moskav space, we exit in a very safe part of space. At that point, we split off: a few tenders, a few destroyers, and the *Might of the Khan*. The rest of you remain behind—hidden."

Sudin stiffened. "Hide?"

"Let me finish, please. The *Might of the Khan* will proceed to Petrovan, engage the Gulmar defenses, then back off."

Now it was Portis whose mouth dropped open. "Flee? From that small force?"

"Our objective is subterfuge. We want this enemy captain to arrive thinking we're caught up in a desperate engagement with the Gulmar." Satrap licked his lips. He was thirsty, and the life support system was once again falling behind in meeting his needs. "Every week or so, we mount another attack with the same small force, and we retreat."

Portis shook his head in disapproval.

But Sudin seemed to be putting the plan together. "And this combined fleet—they jump in where we're waiting? We attack them?"

"This captain is cautious and will be wary. I suspect they will use a different exit from Fold Space." Satrap brought up a map of the system. "Above the plane of the ecliptic. Here." He tagged where he suspected the enemy would exit, marking the spot with a bright red dot.

"Is this where we will be positioned?"

"Yes. Our fleet will be waiting nearby. And the area will be littered with the special missiles we have learned to produce. So when the enemy exits Fold Space, they will find themselves facing the same ambush as before, but this time it will be much worse."

Portis and Sudin looked away from their primary cameras, their attention focused on the glow of what could only be other devices.

They were communicating with each other, plotting.

It was Sudin who turned back first, jaw set. "You have taken your captains to a destination you chose without consulting us, and now you ask us to accept your strategy. If there were a record of success for us to embrace, we might do just that."

And this was the problem of not only taking in new officers but not setting straight the fleet's sad history with them. At minimum, Satrap wished he had sent the records of the previous engagements along with his objective and thorough analysis of what had happened.

But Ikhama's warning had included not doing that, so now he could only force a smile. "I understand your concerns, Captain."

"Do you, Satrap? Portis and I have been charged with preserving our ships."

Zohar snorted. "All captains have that same expectation."

"They do. And so it says something when our Great and Glorious Khan makes a point of it?"

Satrap held a hand up for attention. "What would our new captains propose?"

Portis raised his chin. "The greatest threat is the Kedraalian Republic."

"It is. That was why I proposed attacking it last."

"But this fleet is mostly theirs—right?"

"Yes. And the captain is most likely Kedraalian as a result."

Sudin smirked. "That means that Kedraalian space is without its greatest ships and most likely its best captain. We must strike while they are weak and vulnerable."

It took effort for Satrap not to gasp in disbelief. "They are also the farthest away from our own space. Once committed, we will be many weeks out from our own holdings."

"Have we not established that ours is an attack fleet?"

Was this one of Khan's stratagems? It could even be a test. Allowing such a rash and irresponsible idea to proceed unchallenged might be enough for the new captains to call for Satrap's replacement.

He squeezed his hands shut, lamenting the weakness in his limbs. If he were a whole man, he would fly to the youthful idiots' ships and strike them in the face. "Would it be wise to test your skills against the enemy before trying something so…bold?"

Portis's dark eyes narrowed. "We were chosen for that exact reason. We are ready."

"I did not mean to say otherwise."

"Crushing Kedraal would make the rest of the operation easy."

"Of course. Unfortunately, the latest intelligence we have from the Republic is months old. We know they have expanded manufacturing capabilities—capabilities no one even knew of a year ago. They could have several new ships online already."

"A fleet to match ours, Satrap? Unlikely."

It was Sudin who nodded now. "Portis is right. Our time to strike is now."

Sweat trickled down Satrap's face. He hated such negotiations more than anything, even more than Khan's iron authority. In fact, such unquestioned power was exactly what the leader of such a fleet should have been given. Better some broken and callow figureheads running the ships of his fleet than stubborn old fools and hotheaded youths.

But these were the greatest threat to the Khan, and so they were shipped off.

Satrap smiled as well as he could. "Your idea of an attack directly against the heart of our greatest enemy holds appeal. Would you indulge me for a moment?"

Sudin bowed his head, but it couldn't hide his sneer. "We always listen, Satrap."

Of course they did. "We are already in place for the planned ambush."

"Without our consultation."

"Yes. I apologize. My point is that we have an opportunity to practice what we would do if we attacked Kedraalian space. I propose the following: We exit Fold Space, as planned. Immediately, I will send a request to our Great and Glorious Khan, seeking approval of your plan to strike against Kedraal. While we wait for a reply, we set our trap, exactly as we will in Kedraalian space. We practice fleet operations and analyze past engagements with the enemy. And once we have approval, we will pack everything up and head at full speed for Kedraalian space."

The younger officers once again turned away from their cameras, no doubt to communicate with each other again.

Zohar's face was inscrutable, but Satrap had no doubt he would be chatting with the captain soon enough. It would be hard to see the plan as anything but a concession to the impetuous duo, but with a little effort, the captain could be shown the wisdom of the plan.

If Satrap was right, within the two-month round trip of the message, the combined enemy fleet would almost certainly have discovered the Khanate fleet, and the real plan would be put into play.

The young captains turned back to their main cameras, each of them beaming. It was Sudin who spoke. "This plan is acceptable."

Satrap sagged in relief. "Very well. My captains, thank you for your time. Zohar, thank you for inviting me. Now, gentlemen, we begin our preparations."

With a bow, Satrap disconnected.

Ikhama rose with some effort. "*The tongue as sweet as honey brings more fruit from conversation than that befouled with hate.*"

Her damned parables. "The wisdom of our Khan knows no bounds."

The old woman lifted the hem of her robe with a harrumph, shook her head, and shuffled to the hatch. "You are the one who could find value in wisdom."

When the hatch shut, and he was alone, Satrap nodded. "How very true."

He squeezed his eyes shut and connected to his life support device, activating biological purification protocols that had powered down for some reason. His body was failing him, and it had been doing so with alarming speed. With the automated systems failing, he would be fortunate to live long enough to see his own plan through.

The hatch to his cabin opened, and the Jakkara captain poked his head in. "Your life support system has sounded alarms, Satrap."

"Yes. I'm sorry for the bother. I found some parts had shut themselves off."

"You are well?"

"As well as I can be. Thank you for asking."

After a moment, the captain bowed. "Zohar is here."

Exactly as expected. "Please send him in."

At that, the leader of the Jakkara bodyguards disappeared back into the outer cabin. A moment later, Zohar stepped in.

The captain was agitated, brushing down his jacket sleeves. "You made concessions to the most junior commanders."

"Ikhama warned against annoying them."

"You are Satrap. They are merely captains."

Satrap shivered as the life support system injected drugs into his veins. "They are captains commanding ships our Khan had chosen to hold in reserve until now. They're well aware of the status that sort of distinction carries."

Zohar stopped fidgeting with his uniform. "These ships were obviously meant as reinforcements all along."

"I'm not so sure. In my interactions with our Khan, he made it clear that our fleet was expected to succeed as it was configured."

"Bluster and nonsense."

"I thought so at the time."

"Something has changed your thinking?"

"Yes. The tone of the recriminations and chastisements. You receive communiques from our Khan when the Fold Space transmissions come through. You haven't sensed the change?"

The captain squared his shoulders. "In the last one, yes."

"It was there in the previous ones, too. I'd missed it until it became so obvious. When I went back and reviewed the others, it was there, too. In repeated viewings, you can hear a growing sense of desperation."

"A coup attempt?"

"I've thought of that. Who could challenge him? His most aggressive leaders are here or were, before their ships were destroyed."

Zohar stroked his chin. "His health, then."

"Does he look any less satiated and swollen from the lusts of the flesh?"

"Careful."

"It is only you and I, Zohar. Even if she were here, Ikhama knows that the fleet relies on my abilities. She has turned a deaf ear to my blasphemies."

"And has powered off her recording devices?"

Satrap rubbed his aching belly. "I wouldn't be alive otherwise."

"You should still be careful. There are too many enemies around us."

"And if they have their predecessors' skills of command, they won't be around us for long." A message flashed inside Satrap's eyes: The system purification process was done. There was less pain and fatigue in his system, and he could actually focus better. "Have you had a chance to visit your son?"

The captain's shoulders sagged. "No. Sudin has refused the request."

"Did he say why?"

"It's his prerogative as the commander of the *Stroke of Vengeance*."

"If you would like me to intervene—"

Zohar waved the idea away. "I said my goodbyes to my son when our fleet departed. He chose not to listen to my advice. Nothing I could say now would change anything. Sometimes, a father can do nothing but mourn the lack of wisdom of his children."

Satrap wondered if his own father had thought that when his son had fallen too deeply in love with forbidden technology and been drawn into the web that would eventually entangle him and turn him into the sad ruin he was now.

Another message flashed in Satrap's eyes. "We approach our exit from Fold Space."

"And how long will we hold our fleet together once we find ourselves in normal space?"

"You fear Portis and Sudin might try something?"

"They have a full complement of security forces. Their ships have suffered no damage in battle."

"But—"

The *Might of the Khan* shuddered, and Satrap felt the tug and twist that came with passing out of Fold Space and back into the universe where time and distance were normal. Outside the ship, the stars would be as expected once again, and things would be as predictable as he could ever hope.

Except for this idea of another mutiny…

Yet another message flashed in Satrap's eyes, but this one sent cold through his body. "Now, *that* is interesting."

Zohar's neck craned his head forward. "What?"

"A Fold Space message from our Khan—waiting here for us for a few days now." Satrap processed the connection request, then sent the message to the large display.

When it lit, the captain turned around. "Should I leave?"

"I would imagine this will involve more painful accusations of incompetence and threats to replace me. You'll hear of it on your own."

The message began, and Khan's bloated, wild-eyed face stared out from the screen. "Satrap! Listen!"

The old man's head jerked upward, and his eyes danced across whatever ceiling was above him—probably his private quarters.

Satrap couldn't hear anything as the old man's head jerked one way and another.

Then Khan's eyes were back on the camera. "The spirits of the desert!"

Zohar took a step, as if he'd lost his balance. "What?"

"One second." Satrap rewound the recording.

Again, Khan's eyes were back on the camera. "The spirits of the desert!"

Satrap froze the image. "He's gone mad."

"He's been mad for years."

"But he's worse now. He's frothing at the mouth."

"What spirits of the desert? What's that mean?"

"I don't know." Satrap resumed the playback.

Now Khan's eyes bulged. "Our time is short. We must marshal our forces. Bring back my fleet. Return to Azh Shivan." The old man groaned softly. "Someone approaches the Place of the Fallen. Maybe they are within. Hurry! Return home now, or you will be decreed a traitor and your family butchered. You will be boiled alive and your flesh eaten before your living eyes. All of your captains will be recalled. Do not resist me!"

The old man whined and looked around again, wild and on the verge of terror.

And the recording ended.

Zohar turned, his attention now on the data pad he'd pulled from a pocket. "I have a personal call awaiting me."

Which meant the other captains would as well. Satrap rubbed the hard surface beneath the sagging flesh of his gut. Whatever technology Khan's people had installed in his chosen Satrap after breaking him felt inadequate—failing. "Portis and Sudin will convince the others that we must return."

"We have no choice."

"This is the old man's chance to remove me from power."

"You think he would go to such lengths for that? Why not simply tell the Jakkara you are no longer Satrap? Hurl you out an airlock and put someone else in charge. It would be easy."

Maybe not so easy as the captain imagined, but it *would* be easy. Satrap had taken precautions against brute force mutiny. An order from their Khan? It would be a problem for the Jakkara. At the least, it would break their morale.

Satrap brought his legs up and curled his arms around them despite the pain of needles and savaged joints. "It could be worse."

"Worse than you being executed?"

"When you view it objectively, yes."

"And what could be worse than your own death?"

"Everyone's death." Satrap waved at the blank display. "What if these spirits are some other enemy—worse than the Azoren and Kedraalians?"

Zohar shoved his data pad back into its pocket. "Such seems unlikely."

Satrap nodded. "True enough. Have you heard of the Place of the Fallen?"

"No."

"Neither have I." Satrap watched the other man for a reaction. Zohar was distracted by something—the recording on his device. "We'll be facing another of those dreadful conference calls soon. The children will have sharpened their teeth and will need some flesh to sink them into."

The captain grunted, but his eyes were narrowed, and his attention was far away. "I'll advise the crew of our need to prepare for another jump into Fold Space."

"Thank you."

Satrap waited until the captain was out of the cabin, then brought up the records stored in secret places long ago, before blows had stolen his health and freedom.

The Place of the Fallen was trouble, a ruin in the desert far from the Khan's palace. It was a place of darkness and death, a place where the last of the Khanate's best minds—scientists and engineers—had gone to die.

Not as execution. No.

They'd gone there in search of ancient knowledge that might give the Khanate an advantage. This ruin had been explored many times before by the Kedraalians, and when the first Khan had taken the last of those explorers prisoner, he had drawn from them what little they knew of the place.

Were the spirits of the desert the murderous machines that had disappeared in the ruins decades ago? Were they now a threat to the Khanate's existence?

It seemed preposterous, but it also seemed quite possible.

They might be returning to Azh Shivan to face something that couldn't be destroyed, something ancient and terrible.

For some reason, the idea didn't frighten Satrap like it should have.

## 17

———

"You are the favored child."

The message was as old as Faulk could remember, as ancient as the null space he was now in. It was probably the first complete thought he'd ever had. Maybe the voice had changed ever so slightly, but it was still the same simulated, feminine warmth in his head. Each word was like the beat of a mother's heart, giving over emotional nourishment for the soul.

"You are the favored child."

As far back as floating in synthesized amniotic fluids, compressed by an artificial womb wrapped in the pressure of a tank, the message had been there.

He had a destiny as surely as the liquids of the womb were salty.

"You are the favored child."

How could he make a mistake? How could any choice be challenged? If thousands died under his command in an attempt to slay a few hundred, wasn't that the work of the chosen one? If the war effort stalled because he eliminated doddering old fools to enable his ascendance, who could look at it as anything other than another form of victory?

The favored child had all the intellect the Supreme Leader could want.

It stood to reason that the decisions that child made would please his father.

And yet, that intellect had troubled Faulk. He questioned his own decisions.

What had he done with the Kedraalian ship? What had happened with the remote-controlled *Derfflinger*?

Something had gone wrong.

It had been his order to take control.

It had been his order to put his ships in the path of the Kedraalian ships.

Why?

Because he was the favored child, and this Kedraalian captain would not do as told.

Could it be that simple? Could her stubborn independence be such an irritant?

Yes.

He was, after all, the chosen one among all chosen. Born to greatness among those also born to greatness.

He was the final solution.

The reassuring voice and the heartbeat carrier wave faded.

That alone told him what he needed to know: He was receiving treatment. Something had happened, and the maddening headaches that plagued him had pushed him too far. Even after eliminating Colonel Amanda Karlson—his damned doctrine officer—someone had risen up to manage him, to act as his minder.

Ah! Yes! Hart's android—Commander Aidt. Famke.

Dull pain replaced uncertain awareness. Grays took on paler tones, and those quickly gained color and depth, until he recognized the crisp corners and tidy surfaces of his cabin aboard the *Warsaw*.

A light flashed, and now he caught the painful rise and fall of the general quarters alarms. In the chair attached to his desk, Commander Aidt slumped. Dark fluid leaked from the ruin of her face. The valise she packed her treatment gear into rested on the floor beside her, the fall apparently sufficient to pull the gas mask from his face just enough to allow fresh air in instead of the gas.

Karlson had preferred to make her sessions…intimate. Perhaps Aidt was too damaged to have forced herself onto him.

Faulk tugged the mask the rest of the way off. He was woozy, his head full of the remnants of the sharp tang of the gas. His mouth was as dry as any desert, his tongue thick and sticky.

With some effort, he sat up and closed his eyes. He croaked, although he wasn't sure what he was trying to say. It was a terrible sound, regardless.

The hatch to his room opened, and two of his bodyguards entered. "Field Marshal!" The one on the right seemed relieved but frightened, face stiff but eyes wide. "There's been an explosion—a terrible explosion!"

There was every reason in the world to shoot the two men. They had left their commander to the machinations of a doctrine officer other than his own.

Yet what else could they have done? Even with him awake, she could have ordered him into her custody for as long as she saw fit to condition him and correct him. She was there to ensure functionality.

So Faulk pointed to the small sink built into the bulkhead opposite his bed. "Water."

The bodyguard who'd spoken gaped at the destroyed android as he made his way to the sink. He fumbled around for a cup, spotted the tumbler knocked onto its side on the desktop, and grabbed that. Water hissed from the spigot, and the young commando noisily rinsed the glass before filling it and handing it cautiously to Faulk.

He wrapped shaky fingers around the slick glass, nodded that he had a grip, then emptied the contents into his mouth.

Things were coming back to him now.

He'd sent Hart off to his cabin, but the doctrine officer had charged the bridge. She had knocked aside Faulk's bodyguards, then she'd knocked him out. He could vaguely recall her carrying him down the passageway, synthetic flesh and blood dropping from her tattered face onto his.

She'd had a reason, an agenda. Hart. It had to be the captain.

Faulk handed the glass to the bodyguard, glaring. "What has happened?"

"The commander ordered us—"

"Yes, yes. What has *happened?*"

"Captain Hart resumed command. We have rendered ships to the rescue efforts. And just now, the explosion and fire."

An explosion. That would require attention. "This rescue—for the *Derfflinger?*"

"There was nothing left of the *Derfflinger*, Field Marshal."

Nothing left. It had accelerated and maneuvered dangerously and had impacted a larger ship. Could that be enough to completely destroy it? The idea had merit, but Faulk liked to think the Kedraalians must have done something. Maybe they'd fired on his task force after all.

He waved the young men in. "Help me up."

The bodyguards helped Faulk to his feet, then to the sink, where he washed the disgusting bits of android from his face. Next, they helped him into his jacket. He felt wobbly and weak, but his cabin—meant originally for the captain—wasn't so far from the bridge.

After assuring himself that his balance was sufficient to get him around without aid, he waved the two men to the android. "Dispose of it, then join me on the bridge."

"Yes, Field Marshal!"

Faulk had to keep one hand on the bulkhead the entire way. When he reached the bridge, he was met with stunned looks from the crew. Shift turnover was underway, and they seemed agitated.

The explosion. Yes, the explosion.

Shift change meant he'd been out for ten hours or more. A check of the data pad in his pocket confirmed nearly eleven hours had passed.

Hart stepped away from his counterpart—a young commander who wasn't templated at all from his captain—and made his way over stiffly. "Field Marshal—"

"What is this explosion about? Why are we on general quarters?"

The captain bowed his head. "The terrorists. My men stumbled upon another one. He nearly detonated one of the missiles. It would have killed us all."

*Incompetent!* Faulk nearly lost his balance. "How is this possible?"

"Field Marshal, you refused to allow me to do further investigation—"

"You should have had security watching the missiles!"

"We did. Your men nearly stopped the terrorist. We have video of what happened. They shot him, but he still managed to detonate his bomb, which blew up the missile's maneuvering fuel and—"

Faulk wavered again. *His* men. Of course it would have been his commandos. Who else could be trusted? "This fire is under control?"

"Nearly. We're short of people trained in fighting this sort of fire, but we have experienced people leading the teams now. It won't be long."

"Good."

"Unfortunately, the explosion—"

"Yes?"

Hart took a step back. "Ou-our missile launch systems were damaged."

"*All* of them?" A weight as terrible as a neutron star settled on Faulk's chest. He needed the missiles if he were to get this Benson under control.

"The primary control systems. We could launch a few with a more cumbersome process."

"And how long before the repairs are completed?"

"Once the fire is under control...maybe three days."

*Days?* Faulk needed the missiles *now*! He held his breath. His plan would have to be changed. "What else has happened?"

"Things are generally under control." Hart smiled. "You look rested."

"Your android is being disposed of at this moment."

What might have been a look of disappointment settled on the captain's face, then was gone. "She served our leaders well."

"Perhaps you still needed her guidance. I did not."

"Of course, Field Marshal." Hart glanced around at the officers muttering softly. "If you would like an update on the rest in private—"

"We can speak openly here, Captain."

The smaller man bowed slightly. "Rescue operations are complete—"

"Aboard our ship?"

"In space."

"I was under the impression that the *Derfflinger* was completely destroyed."

"It was. All hands were tragically lost."

"Then what rescue?"

Hart's lips pressed into a thin line. "We were assisting the Kedraalians."

"I have no concern about Captain Benson and her people."

"Obviously."

Faulk puffed his chest out. "Then why were our resources wasted on efforts to assist them?"

"I—" Hart looked his superior over, sucked in a breath, and smiled. "I had hoped we might repair relations after the accident."

"I'm not so sure it was an accident."

"My officers wouldn't fly a ship into—"

"Your officers are not my concern any more than the Kedraalians are." Faulk shoved past Hart and his younger second shift officer. At the command station, the field marshal hauled himself up and accessed the control panel. He needed a symbol, something to hold up for Benson to see. "What matters is a proper restoration of order. I will see to that now."

Hart stopped short of the raised platform. "I met with Captain Benson—"

"Although ill-advised, I am somehow not surprised." Faulk glared down at the captain, then scowled at the main control station, where youthful officers quivered. "I will have a connection with Captain Benson. Now!"

An almost boyish ensign—the second shift communications officer, no doubt—slipped his headset on and bowed.

Sneering, Faulk turned back to Hart. After so many hours under the android's care, the field marshal realized that he had a clarity of thought that usually eluded him. The ever-present stinging headache was a distant discomfort for now. With that clarity came a plan for dealing with Benson.

What Faulk needed—this *symbol*—would be in the tactical records. It took a bit of work to find the exact moment of the *Derfflinger*'s destruction as captured by cameras throughout his task force, but when he found it, he enhanced the image with sensor data and projected that onto the large display at the front of the bridge.

Everyone turned to consider the image: the *Derfflinger* slamming into the Kedraalian ship.

"Do you see?" Faulk jabbed a finger at the frozen image. "Do you see what we did?"

Furrows creased Hart's brow. "We…destroyed a Kedraalian ship?"

"Look closely, Captain. What of this ship's size? What of its capabilities?"

Hart stepped closer to the giant display. "The *Seattle* was a cruiser—a newer one."

The man knew the Kedraalian ship by name. "Look at the *fire*." Faulk loomed over the others. "Does no one understand?"

The captain squinted, then his eyes flew wider. "Yes." His voice trembled.

"We have struck them a mighty blow. We have shown that even a destroyer such as the *Derfflinger* could eliminate one of their cruisers. And this one was full of traitors, those planning to flee my command!"

"But Supreme Commander Graf—"

"I am the only member of the High Command here. Or is someone else among us without me realizing it?" Faulk looked around. "Hm?"

"The High Command would want to honor the agreement with the Kedraalians and Gulmar, don't you think, Field Marshal?" Hart swallowed. He didn't want to challenge his superior, not at this point.

"Sabotage." Faulk clenched his jaw tight. Supreme Leader Graf had undermined his own favored child. Why? "Agreements such as this are more like guidelines."

Except…

The *Warsaw* had been damaged by another Khanate spy. It wouldn't take much to dig through the record, to interrogate a few officers, and Faulk would be made to look bad. Despite warnings and evidence, he had refused to consider the possibility of more Khanate spies being mixed in among the Azoren crews. It seemed impossible there had been a handful before. But the fire, the timing of it—

He stepped down from the command station. "My task force has been badly damaged already. Now this Kedraalian captain undermines cohesiveness."

"But Field Marshal, she has offered sound tactics and advice."

"You allow her to poison your mind, Captain. You are to no longer deal with her. Do you understand?"

Hart chuckled—a confused sound. "She commands the combined fleet—"

Faulk grabbed the captain by his jacket and slammed him against the command station rails. Breath wheezed from the field marshal. He blinked away spots. "There will be no more challenges of my authority, Captain Hart! This fleet is under *my* command! I have done everything possible to find a course to victory! This is *my* legacy, *my* right to rule that is being imperiled. You and your feigned disinterest in climbing the ranks—"

"It is authentic, Field Marshal. My views are on the long goal, not killing every imagined competitor."

"You are weak!"

"I'm loyal. My intent is to hold our task force together and to execute Supreme Commander Graf's will." The captain had his hands on Faulk's wrists, and it looked like there might be enough anger in the smaller man's eyes to threaten a fight.

"Captain! Field Marshal!" The youthful communications officer whipped around. "The Kedraalian captain is hailing us!"

Ah! Finally! Faulk pushed Hart away and climbed back up on the raised platform, doing everything possible to hide the shivering that had settled in. "Put Captain Benson on the display, please."

Rather than immediately follow the order, the young man glanced at Hart, who nodded.

Insolence. It was time to make an example—a reminder—for people.

When the call was done.

The field marshal leaned his butt against the support rail behind him and hoped that it wasn't obvious just how weak he was.

Benson's face filled the large display, then the image split, and the Gulmar captain appeared beside her. They were like old lovers, inseparable and operating with the comfort and certainty of decades.

Faulk blinked. *Were* they lovers? Maybe that was why Benson held a superior specimen—a *field marshal*—in such low regard. "Captain Benson." There was just the right amount of condescension in Faulk's voice to annoy the captain. Good.

The Kedraalian captain leaned back from her camera. "You requested to speak to me, Field Marshal?"

"It would appear communications between our ships has been garbled. I made no request."

Benson and the Gulmar captain glanced at each other.

Yes. They had an almost smarmy familiarity about them. Lovers.

Now the Kedraalian shrugged. "Then if you'll excuse me…"

Faulk sucked in a breath, held it, leaned forward. "I *ordered* you to call me, Captain."

That seemed to get the captain's attention, freezing her where she'd been ready to close the connection. She lowered her gaze. "Field Marshal, I think I need to be clear here, because you're showing a limited capacity for understanding."

It was Faulk's turn to blink at the sting of words. "Your impertinence is—"

"After what you did to the *Seattle*, I was ready to destroy your ship."

"Are you threatening—?"

"I'm not done talking. You've endangered a mission that your Supreme Leader deemed critical—*existential*. You've tried numerous times to complicate what doesn't need complicating. And your efforts have unnecessarily endangered not just Azoren lives but the lives of my people and Captain Thiessen's people."

All around the bridge, the young officers turned to stare down at their console stations. Hart looked away.

Heat built in Faulk's jaws and rose up into his cheeks. "I am your superior—"

Benson wagged a finger at him. "Stop! *You* contacted *me*, so now I'm setting things straight."

"Captain Benson—"

"That's enough out of you, Field Marshal. From here on out, I'll work with Captain Hart, and *only* Captain Hart. If you want to imagine you hold some relevance in our war against the Khanate, then you can convey your thoughts through Captain Hart."

Faulk was sure he must be red-faced and shaking. He felt like he was on fire. If he'd had missiles available, he would've launched them against the *Valor* and destroyed this woman!

She lifted her chin. It was an imperious attitude. "That's all, Field Marshal."

Their connection closed.

The bridge hatch opened, and Faulk twisted around, panicked for an instant. Was this Hart seeing his conspiracy through? Were these some of the captain's officers coming with knives to finish what the assassins had failed to complete in the stairwell?

But it was only Faulk's bodyguards, standing in the entry, slack-jawed.

Because their commander looked like a mess, obviously.

Faulk stepped down, adjusted the hem of his jacket, ran a finger around the inside of his collar, and took a step toward the hatch. When he was directly in front of his men, he cleared his throat. "Bring the captain along."

The words were only for his men, and they jumped to action, rushing forward and grabbing Hart by the shoulders and wrists.

They fell in behind Faulk as he stalked to the lift.

Hart's breathing was loud. "Field Marshal? What are you doing?"

"What needs to be done, Captain. You've become the plaything of Captain Benson. She has you wrapped around her finger."

"My loyalty is to Supreme Commander Graf and to our Azoren Federation."

"But Captain Benson will only speak to you."

When the lift arrived, Faulk waved for his men to bring Hart into the car, then punched the bottom deck button. Hart's normally pale face was almost white. His breathing was labored. "We all have the same objective."

"Not true, Captain. In fact, our objectives are quite different, yours and mine."

The lift descended, and Hart relaxed. "I can talk to Captain Benson—"

"Yes. That is exactly what you will do. You will talk to her and explain that your role is no longer as the captain of the *Warsaw*. Instead, you will provide her what she wants: a means to not have to interface with me anymore."

"She was upset, Field Marshal. She has been troubled by the losses suffered."

"Tragic."

The lift stopped. Its door opened.

Faulk covered the distance to the hangar bay at an aggressive stride. Behind him, Hart gasped. His steps were clumsy and loud.

He made a desperate sound. "Field Marshal, perhaps I could call Captain Benson from my cabin and have her put together an apology?"

"No." Faulk opened the hatch to the hangar bay, then waved his bodyguards through. "You can discuss it with her when you see her."

"Yes, of course. I was simply hoping—" Hart howled when the commandos tossed him to the deck. He scrambled to his feet and came after them, but the hatch closed before he could reach it.

His eyes bulged, and he slammed a fist against the porthole. It looked like he might be begging.

It was unbecoming, so Faulk cycled the airlock with an override, draining atmosphere from the hangar bay quickly and sparing the other man the humiliation he'd been putting himself through.

The tension that had been troubling the field marshal eased, and after a moment, he found himself laughing.

His men stared at the porthole stoically.

Hart slid out of sight, his face already a horrible thing to see.

Faulk spun on his heel, and the commandos fell in behind him. Hart would have his chance to talk to Benson soon. It was only a matter of time.

**18**

---

The bridge of the *Valor* wasn't big enough to hold Benson's anger and heartbreak. She pressed shaking fingers against her damp brow, smoothed the sleeves of her uniform jacket, and closed her eyes against the fading image on the command station display, where she'd just concluded a short discussion with a young Azoren commander —Brummell.

No matter what she did, she couldn't make sense of his words.

*"Captain Hart has been...eliminated."*

The words echoed in her head, louder than the soft murmur of Chopra and his crew. Her XO's gaze shifted from his team to her, but he didn't ask what was wrong.

*Everything* was wrong.

Hart had been an oasis of sanity in a desert of crazed psychopaths. That had apparently been too much for Faulk. The field marshal must have felt threatened. Was that how it was for psychopaths? Did they see regular people who were competent as threats?

Her mouth felt dry. She imagined she could smell death in everything around her. She'd gambled with Hart, hoped to use him to marginalize Faulk and reduce the odds of another Azoren catastrophe.

Instead, she'd gotten the Azoren captain killed.

Benson stepped down from the command station, unsure her knees would hold her weight. "Dinesh."

Chopra hurried over from the helm console. "Are you all right?"

"No."

"Do you want to talk about it?"

She shook her head. How could she burden him with the news? But she had to. "Field Marshal Faulk executed Captain Hart."

The light of the giant display reflected off her XO's bald head when it reared back. "Executed? Was he involved with the terrorists?"

"No. I mean—" She hadn't thought of that. It seemed an absurd idea. Impossible. "—I don't think so."

"Then why?"

"You heard what I told Faulk. I demanded that I only deal with Hart."

"So he...executed him?"

She nodded. What else could she do? "I need to meet with the command staff—you, Alexander, Floyd." Not Karras. She'd gone down with the *Seattle*. "Yuen and Dinh, too."

Chopra nodded. "You need some time? To gather yourself."

"Yes." She'd gotten Hart killed by standing up to Faulk. It was no different than using a human shield. How stupid and selfish of her. "I'll make the appointment."

That was enough for the XO. He took his position at the command station and put on a show of normalcy for the crew.

It was what she needed to be able to slip out without all eyes on her.

There were so many things requiring her attention. Parkinson had pushed himself too hard during the rescue operation and had collapsed at his station. Halliwell had nearly gotten into a fight with Dietrich in front of everyone.

Dietrich.

That was something she couldn't delay any longer. It was a nice distraction, in a way. What better thing to pull your mind from the guilt of getting someone killed than to ruin someone's career?

Except Dietrich had done that himself.

She pulled her data device out and connected to him. His face was puffy, with a day of growth hiding the wrinkles and pockmarks on his cheeks. "Ernie?"

He grunted and looked away. Maybe he said something, but it came out wordless.

"We need to talk." She thought she'd gotten the tone of authority she'd tried for, but she couldn't be sure. Dealing with someone older, someone with more experience—how could she pull off authentic authority?

"I'm in my quarters." His voice quavered.

"I'm on my way."

His cabin was close to hers. He rated a small, individual berth, like an economy apartment. When she pressed the button beside his cabin hatch, she imagined him staggering around and struggling to remember how to let her in, but the door slid aside with an efficient, quiet hiss.

He slumped at his desk, which was covered with trinkets and physical images. Benson already knew what would be on those prints.

She settled on the corner of his bunk. "I've seen the video."

The doctor let out a soft snort. "The performance of a career. The final curtain call."

"Why?"

His head came around, but his watery eyes didn't seem focused. "Why go through with career suicide?"

She crossed her arms.

"It was inevitable, don't you think?" He turned back to the desk and plucked one of the images up, holding it so that she could make out a younger version of him and his wife Melissa. "It's been a long, slow burn. She was what held me together."

"You've had access to online counseling. We have clinical treatment."

"And you think that's all it takes? An AI simulating concerns about my feelings? Some pills to close off nerve receptors? I'm a physician. I know better. I'm quite capable of healing myself, if that were all there was to it."

"Then—?"

He dragged a fingertip across the photo. "I'm too far broken. When she left me, she took everything with her."

"Isn't that making excuses?"

Dietrich's eyes lit up. "Excuses? A doctor can't believe in something beyond the body?"

"You think she…damaged your soul?"

"That's as good a description as any. We were connected, and I allowed the military and my own fears to tear us apart. Further, that ultimately led to her decisions and…" He set the photo back on the desktop.

"Have you sought counseling?"

"You mean seeing a *human* analyst?" Dietrich snorted. "Centuries after misguided men set down the basic tenets of a more human treatment of the mind, it's all still witchcraft—no better than my belief in my damaged soul."

"It can be effective."

"Too late. The damage is done. As you said, you've seen the video. And dozens of people lived the experience. The drunk and irresponsible surgeon. Usually, it's something more complicated than…" He ran a hand over the images.

Benson sighed. "If you could give me something to work with—"

"Something to work with?" Dietrich's face contorted into a bitter smile. His face quivered, and tears trickled down his cheek to disappear in his stubble. "I need closure."

"Closure? Melissa's dead."

"I *know* that. But it's the way she died. It's the improbability of it all."

"Ships experience failures all the time. Space travel is still one of the most dangerous things we can do, even with all the advances we've made since humans launched themselves from Earth centuries ago."

"Lecturing me is inappropriate, Faith. Scientist, remember?"

She glanced around the cabin, taking in the starkness of his footprint. There were no digital frames running through an array of images to connect him with loved ones and precious memories. Plaques, diplomas, certificates—for someone with an outsized ego, there were no signs of his accomplishments. His personality only showed in the moderately tidy way he kept the place.

It was hard making a connection with someone like the doctor, but she had to try. "If you don't believe the report that her ship suffered a catastrophic failure—"

"Absurd! It was a newer ship. The company had spent a good deal of money not just on upgrades but on the people to maintain it."

"Then hire someone to investigate it. There are experts who could tell you—"

"I *did*. I paid someone to research the whole thing. They took a ship out to where the accident happened. They reviewed all the evidence." Dietrich pressed his back against the seat. "I talked to Will about it. Do you think there's a more expert opinion?"

"Chief Parkinson?"

The doctor nodded. "I asked him if it was feasible for the reactor to have a cascading failure, like the evaluation team posited."

Benson hadn't known about Parkinson's involvement. "And?"

"He looked the report over. And he said the same thing my investigator said: No. Whatever it was that destroyed her ship had to have been violence."

"Why would pirates attack a research vessel?"

"Pirates?" Dietrich shook his head. "It was military. A warship. It had to be. They were close to Azoren space. Her ship must have had something they wanted."

With all Benson now knew about the war in shadow—the intelligence efforts and counter-efforts—the idea didn't seem so preposterous.

But Dietrich's behavior couldn't go on.

She pushed up from the bunk. "I'm sorry about your loss. I am. But you've been given numerous opportunities."

"I know."

"And this happened in front of so many people."

Dietrich's chin rested against his chest. "I'm all too aware."

"If you can't handle the military—and this is what I'm hearing you say, Ernie—then you need to move on."

He rubbed his eyes with the heel of his hands. "I think we've both seen enough. It's time."

That stubborn resolve of his, the determination to crater his own career—she could punch him right then. Instead, she squeezed his shoulder. "I'm going to put together a reprimand. You don't have to accept it."

"No. I understand."

"When we return to Kedraal, I'm going to recommend you either seek counseling or tender your resignation."

Dietrich chuckled. "We'll all be doing that, won't we? That or a firing squad?"

His words seemed painfully true.

She let herself out. The talk had taken her mind off what she'd done to Hart, but it wouldn't last. And even if it could, she had too much work to do.

So she swung by Parkinson's cabin. He was napping, but his roommate let her in.

She and his roommate talked in whispers, him sharing that Ensign Kohn had come by to check on the frail-looking engineer and had administered an injection. That had seemed to help.

Benson asked the roommate to pass along her best wishes, then she left. She would draft a reminder to Parkinson later that he needed to take care of himself.

Something had changed about the little man. It seemed tied to Chief Taylor's death. Or maybe it was more accurate to say it was tied to Taylor's interaction with him before her death. Parkinson held those interactions almost like a spiritual awakening.

Did *he* understand Dietrich's self-destructive need for closure?

Benson stopped and leaned against a wall. The way death left such a terrible mark on people—

"Captain?" It was Grier's voice. The sergeant's booted steps were clear now, and when Benson looked up, she saw the young woman coming closer, her own shoulder hugging the bulkhead. "Is everything okay?"

"Yes." Benson sucked in a breath and squared her shoulders. "Thanks."

"I was coming down to check on the chief."

"He's sleeping. He's been pushing himself too hard."

"Oh." Muscles worked along the sergeant's jaw. "I guess I can check on him later."

"That would be good."

"Y'know, what he did…on that gunship? That was really brave of him."

"It was."

"He was really sweet on that Chief Taylor, I guess."

"I'd gotten that sense of it."

"Emotions can be crazy like that—meeting the right person and suddenly realizing what you've sort of wanted all along and never knew."

Heat shot through Benson. Was Grier trying to apologize or antagonize? "It...can."

"Um. About Clive—"

Benson shook her head. "No."

"I'm really sorry—"

"Sergeant—" Benson's voice sounded wrong to her own ears. She couldn't dress Grier down. "Toni. I want..." Was it possible to know what anyone wanted right then? Benson doubted it. More importantly, Grier probably didn't know herself what she wanted. Giving her any hint of a fight would likely lead to exactly that. Benson knew better than to let expectations determine the outcome in a social interaction. She had to be bigger than her base emotions. "You two should be happy. That's what's important. But you also have to be safe."

"We're being careful."

"People can be nosy and petty. They can whisper things."

"I—I know."

"The rules on fraternization keep changing, but what you're doing—direct supervisor and subordinate: That's the one that can cause the most trouble."

Grier's head drooped. "I—we know. Are you...?"

"I'm not going to do anything. I know Clive. He's a professional. He wouldn't let anything get in the way of the mission. If he had to send you into a situation that was certain death to see the mission through, he would."

"I wouldn't let him stop me, ma'am."

The sergeant's thrust-out jaw brought a smile to Benson, even though she felt terrible. "That's because you're a professional, too."

Grier straightened. "Thanks. Captain."

Benson waited until the younger woman was out of sight before finding the strength to push off from the bulkhead.

There were too many threats facing them all and too much pain to sink into the guilt and bitterness that teased at Benson's thoughts right then. Sure, it hurt to lose Halliwell to another woman, but the rational part of Benson's mind knew the relationship had been on life support since she'd taken command of the *Valor*.

And now she had a more likely future with Thiessen, although exactly what that future looked like was murky with both of them probably facing charges upon their return to their home worlds.

And all of that assumed they even had futures with a murderous monster like the Khanate captain on one side and a madman like Faulk at their back.

Faulk was the immediate threat, the one that made basic survival seem doubtful, even before engaging the Khanate forces again. But the first hint of a plan to deal with the field marshal was starting to take form. It would be tricky—risky—and involve too many people, but it was the only route she could see to success.

There were calls to make, and so much to explain, and she would need to get Halliwell's buy-in if they were to be successful.

She had to hurry, before things spiraled out of control.

---

For the first time since Stiles had been revived, the skies over Dramora were clear. Moonbeams painted the back of the Patel building in silvery shades. Her stealth suit felt snug and warm against the chill. After three checks, she finally accepted that the systems were truly operating without any problems. The evidence was right in front of her when she sent the suit's data to her mirrored sunglasses: data on the building security; multiple sensor feeds; a measure of her own vital signs.

She was ready.

McLeod wore a simple black bodysuit with light armor woven into the material. It made him look bulky, and not in a good way. Then again, at his age, it was a small miracle he could fit into such a suit.

He adjusted the fit of the outfit for the thousandth time. "Ready."

"Ready?" She raised her voice over the wind, which apparently picked up enough intensity at night to take on a high-pitched whistle. That wind brought a foul, chemical stench in with it, something she assumed was related to the mining operations. "You're not going in, Colonel."

"Of course I am." He patted the big pistol holster nestled just below his left shoulder.

"I can get in and out on my own without detection."

"You're forgetting that I've seen your workouts for the last week, Lieutenant. You'll be a while before you recover your speed and balance. That means you'll need backup."

"No offense, sir, but you'd be more of a hindrance."

"I've probably gone on more operations than you have." He didn't sound confident.

"When was the last one?"

"Some things you never forget."

He wasn't going to budge, so Stiles sucked in a deep breath and let the point go. She pointed to the rooftop. "They've got pressure and motion sensors all over the rooftop. Normally, I could get past them, but these are really good."

"And you're not at your best."

"I'm not, sir. That means we go in through one of two places."

"The front or back entries."

"The ground floor entries or the maintenance tunnel."

McLeod squinted. "Maintenance tunnel? I didn't see anything about a maintenance tunnel on the blueprints."

"An anti-government world like Dramora, I wouldn't trust blueprints."

"But they would show—"

Stiles pivoted to where a squat building rested against a retaining wall at the west end of the rear parking lot. An outer wall surrounded the building, rising a little higher than the roof. "That generator room."

"What about it?"

"It's three times as big as their registered generator requires, even with extra batteries."

"All right. I don't see how that matters."

"In the past week, I've seen five people go into that building and not come back out. I've seen three people come out without going in. They've all been building engineers."

"You didn't mention that."

"With all your years of experience, I assumed you saw it, Colonel."

He winced. "So we go in through the generator building?"

"It's our best chance of getting in undetected. Everything on the exterior is crude physical security. Getting into the maintenance tunnel will be the hard part."

McLeod grunted. "Lead the way."

She hugged the retaining wall and moved in a low crouch, keeping her pace moderate. The colonel kept up well enough, although he stumbled over a brick that had come free from the wall.

At the edge of the building, she climbed the outer wall and jumped to the roof. There was a camera over the door and another at the rear of the building. She disabled both, then dropped to the front door, which was padlocked and had a sturdy door handle with a lock of its own. They were the sort of things that a typical thief would resort to a crowbar to get past. Except a thief wouldn't have any reason to break into a generator room. It didn't hold anything particularly valuable unless generators were suddenly worth a lot.

Stiles had spent months training on physical locks. She wasn't quite the expert Caville had become, but she was good.

The colonel poked his head around the opening in the outer wall. "All clear out here."

"Thank you, sir."

His breathing was fast. "I probably need to do more squats."

"You did fine, Colonel."

"How about you?"

She popped the padlock and dropped the heavy lock to the ground with a metallic *thunk*. "My heart rate could be lower."

"Okay." There was a hint of annoyance in his voice.

"Colonel?"

"Yes?"

"Where do you go when you think I'm asleep at night?"

"What?"

"Around two in the morning, most nights. You go out. You're gone about two hours."

"I..." He swallowed.

"The way you smell, and the way you limp—if I had to guess, you've been—"

"You followed me."

"After the first two nights. Hiring a prostitute isn't going to get you in trouble, but a prostitute shouldn't make you limp." She pulled the door open, releasing a strong, gasoline smell, and returned her tool set to the sheath on her boot. "That place *is* a prostitution business, isn't it?"

McLeod's cheeks puffed out. "Could we talk about this some other time?"

"You were forced to risk your life to rescue us. You nearly lost your job a few times. Was all that because of this? You're need for...whatever?"

He looked away. "That's very personal."

"If you're going to be protecting my back—"

"I've gone through multiple background investigations. I've submitted to more tests than you'll ever know. My loyalty can't be questioned."

"I understand, sir. I think the concern with this sort of thing is blackmail."

"I'm not compromised. My...*needs* are documented within appropriate groups."

*Needs.* There was shame in the way he said it. He might not be compromised, but it wasn't the sort of thing that built confidence. "I've already been shot once by someone on my team."

"Caville was doing his job. My job is to *protect* you. I would never shoot you."

The conviction in his voice—she could trust him. If anything, the way he bowed his head and looked away, she might have more influence over him than she had before.

But that wasn't what she wanted.

There was a light switch just to the right. When she closed the door, she flipped the switch, lighting the room. The generator dominated the center, the exhaust assembly climbing to a hole in the ceiling and rising up to the roof. Racks of batteries lined the walls. They were big, powerful— what she would need soon.

She had to go to the opposite side of the generator to find the trap door. As she'd expected, it had more sophisticated security mechanisms.

McLeod whistled. "Okay, I was actually skeptical until now."

Stiles held up her data pad. "This won't take long. The tunnel itself might be a problem."

There would be cameras beyond the trap door. And there would probably be a device configured to track off-hours use of the door—something magnetically triggered by the latch. Maybe there would be a pressure plate at the bottom of the rungs leading down.

Those were all things she could mitigate with the software on her device. And if someone had made the mistake of leaving them accessible via a wireless connection...

Her device pinged. It had detected the security network below, and now it was probing the devices riding on that network.

The colonel cleared his throat. "I—um—I grew up in a home...in an environment where I was exposed to power from a very young age. The McLeod family is influential and wealthy."

Stiles craned her neck to look him in the eye. "You don't have to, sir."

"No. I do. For trust." He still couldn't meet her gaze. "You could say I was born into a life of ease. Nothing like the Patels, but we never went without...anything. My schooling was the best, and if I wanted onto the student council or wanted to run for president, that's what happened. It was all easy. Everything."

A beep brought Stiles back to the data pad. There were cameras, as she'd expected, and they were now overcome. The pressure plate would be taken offline soon.

McLeod's head was bowed, and his eyes were squeezed. "It was the same up through university. If I wanted to date a young woman, all I had to do was ask. I saw the way other people lived—being given orders, being told no, having to *work* for things. I—I wanted that. So I went into the military. And I did that on my own. I didn't tell anyone where I was for a year."

The pressure plate was offline, as was the system that would track the trapdoor opening.

Stiles didn't budge.

After a soft exhale, McLeod continued. "But that wasn't enough. Not to satisfy me fully. Women still knew who I was. They still were easy to pick up. I had to turn to something else."

His hesitation…

He was done. The rest was there for her to infer, unless she pressed him.

She pulled the door up. "We're clear."

The tunnel had a dank smell about it, almost like a poorly maintained locker room. It was well-lit and big enough for the two of them to walk abreast, but the colonel hung back. His steps were loud, which was fine. They weren't going to be heard by anyone.

McLeod was apparently unable to face her after the revelation. It was an odd behavior considering part of her training was not to judge anything sexual. If there was a vulnerability to be exploited with one of her targets, she would exploit it. Judging it was a waste of time. He had to know that.

Humans and sex—it was always awkward and messy. That was the easy explanation.

Exiting the tunnel was straightforward, since it opened into the basement, not far from the main elevator equipment. The door wasn't even secured.

Stiles held up a hand at the bottom of the stairs that would take them up into the main building. "You could stay here—make sure that our exit's covered."

"I'm not leaving you, Lieutenant."

"You'll need to be more cautious. Security guards are going to be on patrol."

"I realize that." He was gritting his teeth, but at least he was looking at her now.

She exited the basement and slipped into the elevator that would take them to the top floor. McLeod's description of how he'd gotten to the top made the security mechanisms pretty obvious, and it was something Stiles had planned for. She had a card she'd stolen from a building that used the same security systems. Programming in the appropriate security spoofing had taken a bit. Now it was just a swipe of the card to test her work…

The elevator door slid closed with a whisper, and the car began its ascent.

And with that, they were committed.

## 19

One thing Faulk had never been good at was reading the subtle signs of those around him. It was especially problematic with simple humans. The Children were much more clear and assertive about their feelings. And why wouldn't they be? Shielding your perceptions of others was the first step toward treachery. Every one of the Children knew from the moment they managed awareness that there was simultaneously an unbreakable bond with their brothers and a need to subdue, break, and often kill those brothers to rise through the ranks.

After disposing of Hart, though, even the Children were becoming hard to read.

Faulk could feel it when walking the passageway: catching the gaze of one of the dead captain's officers when it lingered a little too long; hearing the whispers when those officers thought their true leader was out of earshot; noticing the distancing that happened—a barely perceptible lateral step—as they passed.

It was like an intentional creation of a bubble to give their field marshal a sense of rejection and isolation.

Well, he didn't need to smell their fear to know it was there, sometimes hidden by soaps and colognes. Of course he made these weak-willed functionaries tremble. He was a constant reminder of the exceptionalism that was expected of them from birth.

When all was said and done, Hart's entire group of officers and maybe even his sniveling enlisted men would be eliminated. They were a pathetic disgrace.

But they were needed for now. Faulk could see as much.

He abandoned the *Warsaw*'s corridors and spent his time in his cabin. His bodyguards—now never fewer than four—were just outside the hatch. He had access to the bridge systems and cameras. Anything that happened, he would be able to see. Amphetamine-laced coffee helped him extend his work day to twenty hours. The heartburn and constant taste of bile on his tongue was a price that had to be paid.

When he wasn't watching the new bumbling captain or the young, rudderless officers manning the main control panel console, Faulk threw himself into analyzing the repair data from the Kedraalian and Gulmar reports. Their ships were hours—maybe a day—away from full operational capabilities.

His task force?

Faulk sneered.

Calling Hart inept wasn't enough. The man barely managed to rise to the level of a simple human. His officers were constantly complaining about people being overworked, parts failing while being installed to replace destroyed components, and completely incompatible parts being discovered in the spares compartments.

That was an obvious attempt to smear Faulk.

The captains might not say it, but it was implied: He was the one who'd approved all the last-minute systems upgrades.

They were ignoring the obvious truth that without those upgrades, their task force would be so much debris, like the paltry Moskav defense force.

The Khanate fleet must have been surprised at the primitive ships the Moskav had protecting their home world.

And there would be a more unpleasant surprise if the Khanate ships came for Faulk and his task force! His ships were the best the Azoren had ever launched! The weapons were dangerous, the armor thick. Even if he had to operate every ship remotely, he would stop this Khanate threat!

He closed the latest damage report and rubbed his eyes.

When he stood, spots danced in his vision, and he caught a whiff of his own foul stench.

How long had he gone without cleaning himself? A few days. Since Hart's death…

Faulk grabbed his data pad and checked the date, then he realized he couldn't recall when he'd killed the captain and searched the records for that.

Five days.

Yes. That wasn't good.

The field marshal's teeth were filmy. His tongue was worse. And when he ran a hand over his face, there were whiskers.

That was odd. He could almost go a day without shaving, and no one would notice. He kept himself scraped clean out of discipline and control. A uniform was only as sharp as the man…as the man…

How had he come to find himself pacing in his cabin?

He braced himself against the sink, and the light overhead winked on. Bleary, bloodshot eyes looked back from the mirror.

A change. He needed a change of uniform. Maybe a nap.

But when he lay down, all that came was the roar of thoughts and voices and data.

Hart's people were out to kill their rightful commander.

Benson and her Gulmar toady were conspiring.

Supreme Commander Graf was behind all of it, architecting the demise of the one man—the Chosen One—who could strike down his father and take the throne.

Hadn't that been a myth, a tale, that Karlson had spoken of back when she'd still had influence over him? How had she described the story?

A father fearful thanks to prophecy that he would one day be slain by his son. The only option was to kill the son, setting into motion a series of events that instead protected the boy and saw him return and take the crown the king had hoped to keep from its rightful heir.

And what had Karlson's sick little twist been? That the boy had been driven to lay with his mother without even knowing that was who she was.

As if Faulk hadn't realized that Karlson had seen her and her sisters' role as that of mother to Graf's Children.

Faulk chuckled. He scratched at his beard and leaned closer to the mirror.

Of course he wanted his father's throne, but Faulk's mother had been a synthetic womb inside a fluid-filled cylinder. Maybe Karlson's voice had been the one in his head going all the way back to the days before cognition. Maybe she had even raised him, if indoctrination counted as parenthood.

That didn't make him part of this myth cycle that she fancied.

Ascending to the throne and ruling over the Azoren Federation was a matter of fate and hard work. Faulk had hit the genetic jackpot. Almost as important, he'd managed to develop a work ethic greater than that of his peers.

Intellect, guile, and hard work: He had everything necessary to win out.

What would Karlson say to that?

He hurried back to his desk and searched through the data pad. Yes, he still had the copy of Karlson. Her body was gone, but her personality and knowledge still existed in the device.

His finger hovered over the button that would summon her.

The tablet beeped, and he dropped it in surprise. He was still fumbling for it when the second beep came.

Finally, he had it in his shaking hands. "Yes?"

Nothing.

He'd forgotten something. A button…

Faulk fumbled through the interface that seemed so alien and inefficient to him.

Ah!

He tapped the button to accept the call as the third beep came. It was one of the ensigns from the bridge—a comms officer.

Now Faulk stared at the young man, wondering why he just stared back.

*I didn't say anything.*

The field marshal cleared his throat. "Yes?"

"A call from Captain Benson, Field Marshal."

Was there a sneer on the young man's bland, pudgy face? Maybe a visit to an airlock would address that. "From...Captain Benson?" So she'd gotten past the idea that she didn't need to talk to her superior, had she?

"She requested an update. On the repairs?"

"Oh. Yes. Yes, yes, yes." Faulk thought he might have tittered. "Please connect—" He straightened. "Wait. Have her hold for five minutes, then connect her."

"Y-yes, Field Marshal."

"And don't tell her. Simply let her wait."

Faulk disconnected and set the data device down. Should he hastily shave? Did the beard make him look wiser and more capable? The face staring back from the mirror didn't look wise but...tired.

He turned the hot water on and splashed his face, then he took the razor from its brace above the sink and...

How did he shave? There was a blade. And he was holding the handle.

Water dripped from his cheeks onto his soiled and wrinkled shirt. The fluid gurgled as it swirled and disappeared down the drain.

It came to him—the angle to hold the handle, the pressure to apply to the blade, the speed to move at.

A stroke that drew blood and felt like tugging each follicle from his face.

He gasped, then rinsed his face. It was a shallow but bloody cut. There was medicine for that. Something in the medicine cabinet that stung and pinched off the blood vessel...

The data device chimed even louder than his wild, frantic search through the cabinet. He couldn't even remember what he was searching for, but he could remember who was calling him: Benson.

High and mighty Benson. Tall and graceful and pretty Benson.

Faulk slammed the cabinet door and strutted to the desk. He dropped into his chair, inhaled loudly through his nose, then leaned back before tapping the button to accept the call.

She wore her white dress jacket, which added even more color to her cheeks and drew out the jade of her eyes. Those eyes went wide.

Was she surprised he'd accepted her call? "Captain Benson. Good—" Was it morning? Evening? He'd just looked up the time, but how long ago had that been? Time seemed to be creating its own circuitous path.

"Field Marshal Faulk?"

"Good to hear from you again." He smiled, then remembered the way his teeth had appeared yellow in the mirror. Had she reared back in revulsion? "To what pleasure do I owe this call? Hm?"

"It's nothing to do with pleasure, Field Marshal. My ships will be ready to depart in twelve hours. Captain Thiessen's ships will be ready before that. I'll be conducting a final inspection tomorrow. Assuming everything passes, we'll be ready to launch."

"Excellent!"

"Thank you. I was hoping you would have an update on your own task force."

"An update? On the most dangerous component in our combined fleet?" It sounded like a trap to him. "Of course I do."

He shrank the window with the Kedraalian officer's face into the upper corner of his device, then dug around for the report. He thought he must have been looking at it. Something about that sounded right. Hadn't he…?

There! Opening the report felt like a repeated motion, something he'd done a thousand times before. He'd never cared for reports, of course. Some of his peers spent their entire day doing nothing *but* that—read, create, summarize, discuss.

There were wars to be fought. People to be led. Schemes to be hatched—

"Field Marshal?"

The pretty captain stared at him. Did she look confused? Maybe. He'd never been particularly good at reading human emotions. Why would someone concern themselves with something—

Her eyes narrowed. "Are you all right?"

Faulk's lips curled up at the corner, despite his concern about his teeth. "Of course I'm all right, Captain. I have—" He realized he was shaking the data pad by the corner. Benson wouldn't be able to see him or to understand that he was trying to make a point.

He set the device on the desktop and cleared his throat. "I have the damage reports."

"Good."

How was he supposed to parse that? It came across cold and uncaring. He was getting the report for *her*. She had to care! Now, if only he could make sense of it. Maybe with more coffee and amphetamines…

"Field Marshal Faulk, are you well?"

Without meaning to, he half bolted out of the chair. "I am perfectly fine."

"You're behaving erratically."

Ha! He'd drawn it out of her!

This is what she'd been wanting to say all along. She had to challenge him. She had to *frame* him and undermine him. They always did—peers, subordinates, those who imagined they were superiors.

But he was the superior now!

"Captain Benson, I can assure you that I am quite fine." He stomped a foot for emphasis.

She scowled. "And you have your report?"

Was that what she was going on about? All he needed to do was rattle off the executive summary. "We should have all of our ships operational within a week."

That seemed like a long time, didn't it? Was Hart playing games to seek out sympathy again?

No. Wait. Hart had been hurled into space after the depressurization killed him. There was nothing better than to toss a body into hard vacuum to make a point to the crew.

Benson leaned closer to her camera. "A *week*? Your ships weren't even that badly damaged."

"We're short of qualified personnel. We've also run into problems with spares." Faulk realized he was just repeating the embarrassing excuses Hart and his officers had been lobbing around. That wasn't how one ran a professional organization. "At least, those are the excuses being offered up by my captains."

"We need to be ready to launch the second we have a destination."

She was challenging him! The problem was his incompetent captains, and—

That didn't matter. What mattered was she was Kedraalian. She was female. "Captain Benson, your tone of voice is ill-advised."

"My tone of voice? I can't believe we're going through this again."

Her tone!

His fingernails rasped across his beard and came away with blood. Had he dug so deep…?

The cut. The razor. Something had happened to his blades.

Faulk paced. This captain was forgetting her place and so soon after he'd used Hart as a lesson. "Captain Benson, you will show the respect appropriate to my rank and accomplishments—"

The woman shook her head. "You've already showed what sort of accomplishments I can expect from you."

"What does that mean?"

"It means that you've put the combined fleet—*my* combined fleet—at risk. You're out of your league."

"Out of my—"

She held a hand up to cut him off. "Consult with your captains. See if there's a way to speed up the timetable. I expect us to be able to launch within three days."

"Three—!"

He was staring at a blank screen. She'd disconnected. She'd cut *him* off.

This was Hart's fault. It was…

Faulk squeezed his eyes shut. Amphetamines and coffee…he needed more of them. That was something his loyal bodyguards could take care of for him.

He gave the order and paced until the hot drink and pills were delivered. The bitter drink burned his tongue, but he swallowed it down and blinked away tears while the pills made their way down his tortured throat.

While he waited for the buzz, he washed the blood from his face.

Finally, his head cleared. He needed to talk to Hart. No. To Hart's replacement. Some commander. The name was in Faulk's data device. He'd recognize it…

He called the unimpressive young man, who snapped to attention. "Field Marshal!"

"We need to get our repair work done quicker, Commander."

"We…" The imbecile obviously couldn't comprehend even the simplest of concepts.

"The executive summary. From the damage report? You have seen the damage report, haven't you, Commander?" Faulk's fingers felt like they were vibrating.

"Yes, sir. The other captains and I consulted—"

"Perhaps if you did less consulting and more actual work, these projects would move along more quickly, hm? What's holding up the repair work?"

"A lack of qualified—"

Faulk waved the other man's words away. "When there aren't enough people, you reallocate from other areas. These are basic concepts."

"But we lack trained—"

"Captain Hart liked to make excuses, Commander."

The young man sank in on himself a little. He was such a forgettable and sad shape to begin with. "Commander Pelham suggested pooling everyone."

"Pooling?"

"Take every able-bodied and experienced hand from each ship and send them to one damaged ship. Focus all resources on one ship at a time. It has the chance of speeding the process, but it also—"

"That's exactly the idea I was looking for. Let's do that. See to it immediately. Also, see to it that Commander Pelham oversees this himself."

"Yes, Field Marshal. We can start with the troop transports."

"What? No. Have them start with the *Warsaw*."

"But the ships we can fix the quickest—"

"The *Warsaw*, Commander. If it sounded as if I was seeking your input, there must be a malfunction in your headset."

"Of course, Field Marshal." The commander bowed and disconnected.

Faulk leaned back in his seat. It was tiresome dealing with people like…whatever the ensign's name was. The Azoren ranks were full to overflowing with even suboptimal Children. When he complained to leadership, the argument was always that everyone couldn't be the best, that the rank and file had to include the mediocre, and that these people only appeared inferior because Faulk failed to acknowledge their strengths.

Even those excuses were weak.

Karlson had accepted his view while consoling him that the arguments were anchored in truth. She had…

He picked up the data pad and poked around until he was at the interface that would allow him to access his former doctrine officer's mind. It was so strange that he suddenly missed her.

Or maybe it wasn't. Maybe it was programming that was creeping to the front.

His fingertips dragged across the image of her face. There had been something with her, some strange connection. Once. Encoded.

Faulk opened the connection to Karlson's mind. "Amanda? Can you hear me?"

"Dietmar?" There was a stutter and jag to her voice. "Why can't I see you?"

He activated the device's camera and smiled. "How is that?"

"Yes, I—" Static—a hiss—dripped from the device. "I no longer have a body."

"You met with an unfortunate end."

"We were driving back from Supreme Commander Graf's countryside manor."

"And an ambush led to your destruction. Tragic, but here we are."

"Why haven't I been put into a new body?"

"Time. The world moves far too quickly. War takes me from home."

Now the static was a whisper. "War against the Khanate?"

"You remember. Yes. War against the Khanate."

He closed his eyes and tried to remember a time where he'd been content with her affections. When you rose through the ranks and proved yourself special, you were given a more deluxe model like Karlson. The bond extended beyond instructor. Having such a woman—even if an android—carried prestige. It generated jealousy. Children didn't have women to choose from. They were all male, and human women would never be good enough, not even one such as Benson.

Karlson's voice turned into a choppy stutter, then went silent. "I'm sorry. I have a hard time being disembodied."

"I can imagine. If it helps, I remember you exactly as you were."

"Good. You look tired. Are you unwell?"

"I am perfect." He grinned. "You remember how you challenged me when I said that?"

"There is a fundamental flaw with a belief in perfection. When the belief is that the self is perfect, the flaw has arrived at its peak."

Faulk chuckled, but only after a moment of annoyance passed. "Of course you would say that. It is a flaw in your own design."

"Might I share something with you?"

"Please do." He almost slipped and said he missed her.

A video played on the device. It was one of Faulk's first commanders, a Child who had been one of the first created. The man was a freshly made general in the video, maybe six months away from death while leading a failed Moskav assault. His pale hair was going silver, his eyes as gray as fog. There were wrinkles on his pink face.

Mannheim. Viktor Mannheim.

The view pulled back. He sat in a chair opposite King—the Minister of Purity. King looked much younger, his back straighter, the light in his jade eyes more energetic. How could a human give off the appearance of such intellect?

King crossed one leg over the other and rested clasped hands on the raised knee. "You prepare for the assault on Moskav."

Mannheim nodded. He appeared tired. "We will succeed."

"Good. Confidence is a promising sign."

"Unless it is misguided, yes."

"Misguided?" King tilted his head. "Can you explain this to me?"

"I can try. The easiest thing I can think of is to point to the Children."

"The children? There are so few of them now."

The general shook his head. "Not the offspring of the dying humans. Your species holds no concern for me."

"Good. That is the belief you should hold. What is it that concerns you about your brothers?"

"I hesitate to call them that."

"But it is what they are. You all are derived from the same DNA design. It is a design specified by our Supreme Leader. In many ways, you are closer than brothers."

"Yes. The purity ideal. I understand. I have studied this theory."

"Your doctrine officer can help you to understand."

"I have no need of someone to tell me what to think, Father."

King bowed his head, but there was obvious pride in the smile he tried to hide from the other man. "Your concern, then?"

"My concern is that I have lived long enough to see three generations born since mine. With each, the product grows more pure."

"Refinement is the means to greatness."

"If you say so. What I see is a trending toward fragility, not greatness."

The purity minister's shoulders stiffened. "Fragility?"

"Less capability. Rigidity. Self-infatuation. Entitlement. A lack of critical thinking. I see it in all of my subordinates. Take this Lieutenant Faulk."

"What about him?"

"You said he is to be considered the future."

"He is."

Mannheim snorted. "He's a self-obsessed buffoon who never questions anything that aligns with his own views."

"Adherence to our belief systems runs counter to that, don't you think?"

"But where is the healthy skepticism? Where is the curiosity?"

King frowned. "Those are more human values."

"Then we are being engineered toward doom rather than supplanting our creators."

"You are being engineered toward what Supreme Commander Graf desires."

General Mannheim leaned closer. "Then Supreme Commander Graf is wrong."

The video ended, and Karlson's face appeared on the screen again.

Faulk heard his own breathing: loud and agitated. "Mannheim was a fool."

Hissing static leaked from the device again. "His successes were unrivaled prior to his death on Moskav."

"But he was a fool. Our design isn't flawed. Minister King is the pre-eminent genetic engineer in all human space. His understanding of the human genome is unparalleled."

"The minister based his design of the Children on his understanding of the specifications provided by Supreme Commander Graf."

"Understanding or interpretation?"

"That question makes no sense. Interpretation is based upon understanding."

Karlson's words were irritating. They reminded Faulk of why he'd grown tired of her. He powered the interface off and pushed up from his chair, seething. How *dare* Mannheim speak in that way.

*Self-obsessed buffoon? Did he ever make field marshal?*

Faulk laughed.

He crossed back to the sink. There was still blood in his stubble. His eyes were wild and bloodshot. How could someone call him anything but brilliant? He had outlived—*eliminated*—so many of his rivals.

And yet...

What was the plan he'd approved—the plan to repair the *Warsaw*? Was that brilliant? Was it consistent with his own doctrine of keeping the number of potential threats in any one area low? How had he come about approving the idea?

There had been a suggestion. It had been set up in a way that he obviously would counter it: fix other ships first.

Manipulation. That's what he'd fallen for.

He reconnected to the ensign he'd talked to earlier.

The young man blinked anxiously. "Yes, Field Marshal?"

"The combined work crews from the other ships. How long before they arrive on the *Warsaw*?"

"Forty…forty-two minutes, sir."

"Good." Faulk smiled as reassuringly as he could.

Forty-two minutes. Long enough to clean up and put on a fresh uniform. Long enough to gather his commandos and assemble outside the hangar bay. If there was a conspiracy at work, he would show his enemies just how dangerous such an idea was.

**20**

Time had become impossible to track for Benson. Night, day—it didn't matter what the clocks and lighting of the *Valor* told her. Everything was stretching out, running together.

Her mouth was dry, her breath foul. She got up from the conference room table and poured herself a drink of water, the sloshing splash thunderous in the silence.

At least the water was sweet and cool.

In an instant, the wall display flipped from black to a static gray, which was quickly replaced by Thiessen's drawn face. He was apparently as anxious as she was about her plan. Once he spotted her, a slight smile crept across his face. Like her, he was in uniform, but his was the typical deep blue coat, while she wore her dress white uniform.

He couldn't possibly feel as stifled and awkward in his suit as she did in her uniform.

For once, it wasn't the outfit that was making her feel so bad but what it represented. Officially, what she was doing now was independent of the Kedraalian Navy.

She'd gone rogue. The uniform wasn't who she was, not anymore.

"Hard to believe we're doing this." He chuckled, but the tension was audible.

"We don't have a choice."

"I know. This lunatic…"

There was no sugarcoating it: Faulk was insane. As bad as he'd been back on Himmel, he was going over the edge now—gone over the edge. Destroying the *Seattle*, whether by intent or not…

It was too much. And after murdering Hart, Faulk's own people were terrified of him.

That was her and Thiessen's deliverance, their opportunity.

The window framing the Gulmar captain shrank to fill the left half of the screen, and another opened to fill the right. Halliwell stared out from it. He had his combat gear on, the visor pulled down. His breathing sounded hollow and loud, and there was the slightest hum on the line.

His eyes darted around, then he scowled. Apparently, he'd spotted Thiessen. Halliwell squinted. "You reading me?"

Benson relaxed as well as she could. "Clear enough. How're you doing?"

"Hanging on to the hull. This better work."

Thiessen nodded. "I think we all feel that way."

"Yeah, well, your asses aren't drifting out here, exposed. And you won't be in the line of fire."

"Actually, Lieutenant, if things go wrong, we'll all be in the line of fire."

Benson caught the invocation of rank and the subtle shift of Thiessen's posture—the squaring of his shoulders and raising of his chin. Halliwell had thrown out the challenge, provoking her counterpart unnecessarily.

She set the glass down on the conference room table. "If Commander Pelham doesn't connect soon, this will all be—"

Halliwell's frame shrank to fill the top right quarter of the display, and a new window opened in the bottom right quarter. In that window, Pelham's narrow face appeared. There weren't many similarities in his appearance and that of Hart, but there hadn't been much to connect Hart to Faulk. Apparently, the Azoren ideal still had some range to it.

Pelham dabbed a handkerchief against his brow. "I hope I am not too late, Captain Benson."

"No. You're good. We just started."

"The encryption shows clean, and I have personally confirmed we are connecting using a point-to-point system. This is as secure as any communication can be."

"Excellent." Benson pulled a chair out and sat down. Her knees felt unsteady. "I think it's best we get straight to it."

"Yes."

Halliwell's head bobbed up and down in his helmet; Thiessen smiled. They were all committed.

A tingling sensation ran down Benson's back. "You've all had a chance to review the plan and make comments. Any last updates?"

The Azoren commander winced, as if he expected to be backhanded. "It is bold. Some might call it audacious."

"Are you changing your mind?

"No." Pelham's head sank. "Our best hope relies upon exactly this."

"Lieutenant Halliwell's Marines are in position. Are your shuttles launching?"

"Even as we speak. The pilots and technicians are our most capable and trustworthy. If they betray us, we never had a chance anyway."

Sweat dampened Benson's palms. The statement was true, but she would've preferred not to be reminded how precarious things were.

She swallowed. "What about your hangar bay situation? Your sensors?"

The Azoren commander dabbed his brow again. "Yes, yes. Your idea was clever. We have a maintenance problem being looked into at this moment. No need to concern ourselves with the possibility one of Faulk's commandos sees something."

"And the hangar bay?"

"There are no commandos stationed in that area. We have people waiting in compartments nearby on the off chance something should draw the commandos there."

Benson turned from the Azoren officer to Thiessen. "Captain Thiessen, your people are in place?"

"Six shuttles. They're not Marines, but they've all been trained in corridor-to-corridor combat. With the help of our Azoren naval allies, we should be prepared."

Pelham leaned forward. "We will need weapons. Our armories have been sealed off by Faulk's commandos."

Thiessen didn't flinch. "We'll have some sidearms."

"But the armories—"

"The armories will be our first objective. And if everything goes right, we'll have weapons to claim from your fallen commandos."

That seemed to calm Pelham. "Yes. Of course."

Halliwell's head shifted. "I've got shuttles incoming."

Pelham looked off to his side, then the glow of a display lit his face in blue. "They approach. They are on time."

"Great. Look, one thing I want to be sure of: Those troop transports aren't a threat, right? No chance we head in and then find a bunch of extra commandos on our ass?"

"Oh. No, no." The Azoren commander seemed on the verge of chuckling. "There are two things working to our advantage here, you see. One is that the troop transports have very limited capabilities. The attached shuttles are crude. They are rockets with compartments to stuff soldiers into—built for rapid surface deployment. They would do very poorly attempting what you are doing, even if they could fit in the already full hangar bays."

"Okay."

"And the other thing—" Pelham's face lit up even more. "—is that most of the remaining soldiers are not Faulk's commandos at all but regular Azoren. They are veterans of wars against the Moskav, and they have no love of Faulk and his Silver Wolf butchers."

"We're fine facing Faulk's people straight up, but no one wins in a crossfire."

"Yes. This is a good question to raise."

Halliwell's camera switched from the one facing inward to an external one showing an Azoren shuttle coming to a stop maybe a hundred meters away. When he looked left, there were five more of the shuttles in a line. Another twist of his head revealed forms launching from the port-side hull of the *Valor*.

Marines. His entire available contingent. This was risky, and Benson couldn't in good conscience order the Marines to take this job on. Instead, she'd pitched the idea to Halliwell and let him present it to his troops.

And they had all volunteered. Readily.

This was—exactly as he'd said—what the Marines trained for.

On top of the job being what they were paid to do, there was a sense of readiness to go up against Faulk's feared commandos. Halliwell wasn't so sure they had a reputation that had been fairly gained. Fighting against poorly trained and worse-equipped Moskav soldiers wasn't a fair gauge of a unit's effectiveness.

Benson could only hope he was right. The Marines would be outnumbered after the losses they'd suffered attacking the Caliphate ship. She had no doubt of what the Marines could do. They were deadly and fearless. But the numbers had her worried.

Halliwell's camera shifted again as he pushed off from the hull and followed the dark forms of his troops to the waiting shuttles.

The jump ended with a series of deft maneuvers to the aft airlock, which cycled open to let his people in three at a time. In that airlock light, the black liner covering the Marine armor was more apparent. It was something they would peel off once inside the shuttles, to be replaced by a liner provided by the Azoren crew.

There was nothing to do but wait as the seconds turned into minutes, and the process of boarding, stripping off one liner and tugging on another, dragged on. Weapons were passed from the Marines to the waiting Azoren, and Halliwell's camera caught the quick training session that was hopefully taking place on the other shuttles.

As the process took place, the shuttles headed for the *Warsaw*.

Benson wiped her palms against her pants legs. "Captain Thiessen, any updates?"

The Gulmar captain glanced to his side. "Shuttles away. We're minutes out."

Pelham pressed a knuckle against his thin lips. "This is the only opportunity we will have to change our minds, Captains."

Thiessen's eyebrows rose. "Are you in, Commander?"

"Yes." The Azoren officer gulped. "We are committed. It is either face death now or face death later."

Benson's stomach flipped. It wasn't the sort of optimistic view she preferred, but it was true.

Of course, it ignored the implications of killing off their commanding officer. Would there be a way around staging a mutiny? She would do what she could to take the heat, but an officer removing a senior officer?

It was the end of a career, at best. And the way the Azoren favored firing squads…?

She would never again complain about her own situation.

As if needing something to distract from that gloomy eventual outcome, Pelham held a finger up. "Captain Benson?"

"Yes?"

"Your plan mentioned our next step, once this is completed?"

"It did." If he needed something to distract him, was there really any reason to delay the discussion? After all, if all went well, they would have to move quickly to hold everyone together.

Benson found her attention drifting back to the interior of Halliwell's shuttle, where everyone was now strapped in and waiting, as if they really were just Azoren technicians come to help with repairs and not Marines come to assassinate a field marshal who put the mission at risk. She wished Halliwell would turn the inward-facing camera back on, but she understood his intent: He was letting them see what was happening as it happened.

She took another sip of water. "The Khanate fleet is no different than any other. We've looked over the debris of their wrecked ships. They have the same sort of reactors we do for power. They have the same sort of propulsion and maneuvering systems that we do. The only unknown is whether or not they cart around enough reactor fuel and other expendable resources to be fully self-sufficient for a lengthy period of operation or if they have to seek out resupply."

Pelham blinked. "You have determined this information just from wreckage?"

"And from the destruction of one of their carriers."

"The bombers?"

"Yes. They're more like remote-controlled missiles, but as far as we can tell, they have a human aboard, too. We've had a few cameras capture close-up images, and they have someone strapped inside the cockpit."

"It is not unheard of. The Moskav have used such tactics. On the ground."

At least they shared desperation, the Moskav and Khanate. "Well, when that carrier went up after the ambush coming out of Fold Space, it went up with the sort of explosions that point to reactor fuel being near the explosions or maybe even near munitions."

"The carriers have the fuel reserves, then?"

"They had *some* fuel reserves, yes. Were they exclusively for the carrier? That's what we don't know. That fleet has tenders. They could be carrying fuel or shuttling fuel from Khanate space. We don't have the ability to determine that."

The Azoren officer's brow creased. "Then your plan would be to track them?"

"It's not as crazy as it sounds. We have some theories about where they might go. Their targets have been poorly defended—Moskav and Radetta." She glanced at Thiessen to be sure she hadn't offended him; he nodded in agreement. "If they're looking for another easy target, we have some ideas. If they're looking for a refueling target, we have some ideas. But there's also a target that meets both criteria."

"An easy target that has fuel?"

"In Gulmar space."

Thiessen tugged on his jacket sleeves. "Petrovan."

Pelham made a little sound of acknowledgment. "Yes! I had heard such an assessment before. A very small defensive force."

"My leadership didn't believe it was prudent to actually put in the effort to project force."

"Our leadership has done nothing but project force." The Azoren pursed his lips. "For us, it has meant only a constant state of violence."

Thiessen shrugged. "That's the peril of life with advanced technology."

Benson didn't believe that. Humans had faced warfare when there was nothing but sticks and stones available to bludgeon each other to death, and the arc of human advancement largely involved the advancement and refinement of those weapons. Whether a matter of survival—a hunting ground, a fertile valley, oil, minerals—or ideology like the Azoren, Khanate, and Moskav embraced, there had always been war. The only alternative was allowing the enemy to end a way of life or to commit genocide to survive.

Still, Thiessen's point was valid enough. Just as ships and then aircraft had shrunk the importance of distance on Earth, starships shrank the importance of distance in space. If Fold Space engines continued to advance, it was feasible that going from one star system to another might one day be days instead of weeks. What would the implications of that be?

But for now, she was faced with weeks to get to her next destination. If she could figure out how to trace movement through the Azoren detection network, maybe she could find where the Khanate fleet had gone.

Or she could find where it was going. She had the codes now.

But none of that mattered until Faulk was removed from the picture, a task that rested on Halliwell's shoulders.

She hoped he was up to the task.

<hr>

The Azoren shuttle executed a sharp maneuver, and Grier found herself instinctively wrapping an arm around the old, scarred harness she'd taken. Everything about the spacecraft felt ancient and tired. She could hear—feel—the air recycler through her armor and the seat she was braced against. And that air? Stale. It left a nasty layer of dust in her throat that caught in her saliva. The recycler needed work, and the interior of the shuttle needed a good scrub. Paint peeled in spots, and there were stains that might be lubricant or might not.

Maybe that was just one of the many differences between the Kedraalian and the Azoren Navies. The shuttle should have been retired or refit years ago.

To her right, a corporal she'd taken onto her team nodded enthusiastically at nothing.

He was a young man who said he was ready to chew nails and glass. He was short and burly, with the sort of mahogany skin that almost glistened in the light.

Maybe he was someone she could enjoy working out with under different conditions, but Grier told the kid to stow that shit. They were here to close down a real problem, put an end to someone who'd killed comrades.

To her left was an Azoren technician who told her to call him Ralf. His environment suit's name tag—scraped and ragged—showed that his last name was Hütter, and she thought maybe he was a petty officer of some sort.

He was definitely old, though. Like, old enough to be her father. She half expected the guy to pull a walker of some sort out from under his seat. Graying hair, wrinkles on soft cheeks, yellow teeth that were pressed together and over each other like happened with old people…

*Old.*

Ralf tapped her shoulder. "You know, we don't have many women in our military."

She smiled. "That's too bad."

"Especially not pretty ones." He chuckled.

Yeah. Okay. She'd never been called pretty in her life. The old geezer was either trying to hit on her or be sociable.

It better be sociable.

He held the pistol she'd given him up. "This is a nice gun, yes?"

"We normally use our carbines." She tapped the butt of hers. "You can cave a skull in with this. See?" She rubbed a worn spot. "It can be tough digging the bits of bone out."

The old guy's eyes widened. "You've killed before?"

"Maybe a hundred guys."

It looked like the old geezer lost some color. A nervous chuckle drifted out of the corner of his mouth. "Most of my time, I am tearing apart communications gear and repairing antennae."

She took the pistol from him. "This is really easy. Flip off the safety, point this end at your target, brace, hold your breath, and slowly pull the trigger. Not fast. Nice and slow. Okay?"

"They wear armor sometimes, these commandos."

"If they're wearing armor, aim for here." She tapped the spot above his collarbone. "The neck is usually exposed or the armor is lighter."

"Ah!" He took the weapon back and turned it in his hand. "This field marshal, he is mad."

"Yeah."

"Many of the Children…" The old man gulped. "They killed so many of my comrades."

"I'm sorry." But she wasn't sure that she was, even if Ralf was human. From what the captain had said, there were people in the Azoren military who'd been forced in, and there were people who actually believed the junk about racial purity. How could someone tell where this old geezer stood?

"My father was a boy when they came. He thought of fighting them."

"He didn't believe in what they taught?"

"No. Not many do. Not from our people. I don't. When I was young, they gave me a choice: Army, Navy, or I could never have a wife." Hütter grunted. "I had my eyes on Zara since I was a young man." He dug something out of a pocket: an old, scuffed data pad. "Here."

An image filled the screen: A woman who must have worked the fields for most of her life smiled over the heads of three children. The woman had dark hair, full cheeks, and a thick nose, but the children looked more like their father.

He beamed. "There were happy times."

Grier handed the device back. "What do they do now?"

"Do? My boys were killed fighting the Moskav. Zara died not long ago. My daughter?" The old man wiped a tear from his cheek.

It wasn't what Grier had expected. Maybe the guy wasn't so bad.

The shuttle shifted and groaned, and for a moment, she thought they'd been detected and the *Warsaw* had opened fire. But it was just maneuvering.

That maneuvering was apparently in preparation for landing inside the *Warsaw*. It felt like the shuttle's ass swung around, then it seemed like the nose came up, then the ass again. Maybe the shuttle was in worse condition than she'd realized.

To her left, the corporal drew an imaginary pistol and fired at imaginary targets. Grier wondered if he'd ever seen action at all. His rank might just indicate years of good service rather than actual experience. After all, training was all most people in the military ever had to worry about. Many people hoped that was the extent of things. Train hard, keep your weapons systems as lethal as possible, and no one would be stupid enough to attack you.

Except the universe was full of psychos like Faulk and the Azoren and the Khanate.

If the corporal had never seen combat, that was about to change.

The shuttle settled to the deck with a shudder, and Grier held up a hand to get everyone's attention. "Visors down enough to hide your faces. If someone tries to get a look at you, put your head down. Do your best to blend in with our Azoren sailors. Keep your weapons out of sight as long as possible."

Her team nodded. They'd run through a simulation of Halliwell's plan. Mixed in with the technicians, they should be able to make it out of the hangar bay and to secure several targets before their first engagement. This Commander Pelham had provided detailed deck plans for the *Warsaw*, and Captain Benson had confirmed what she could from her trips aboard the ship.

But Grier didn't trust the Azoren, and neither did Halliwell.

Still, they had enough information to make a basic plan. Move forward with as much speed as they could, keep the Azoren techs in front and let them do the talking, kill quickly and silently—using knives—if possible, hook up with more sailors and arm them, and sweep the commandos clear of the ship.

Easy.

Except that a best case scenario had Grier and her Marines outnumbered almost two to one. Surprise and planning could only do so much.

She checked her leg pouches for spare magazines and the flash-bang grenades that might come in handy. There were even a couple real grenades, just in case things turned ugly.

Things always turned ugly.

The green light came on, went off, then came on again. They were clear to disembark.

Grier pushed out of her seat, then edged to the airlock. Everyone had their environment suits on and helmets sealed. She waved the technicians forward, allowing them to grab their toolkits and other gear, some of which they handed to the Marines. Carbines were wrapped with tarps. Or the weapons were set in empty trays in the rolling toolkits.

She followed the Azoren technicians down the ramp, head down, thankful for the bulk of her armor. Anything form fitting would've been a problem. She was never going to be mistaken for a man, but the armor helped.

At the base of the ramp, she huddled beside the corporal as the rest of her squad came down. A couple of them were carrying a case marked with some sort of panel—a display or something. But the case held their assault weapons and a couple shotguns. Closer to the hatch that would let them out into the passageway, Halliwell's towering form stood out over everyone else.

He nodded toward her, and she nodded back. Things were going okay.

The Gulmar shuttles weren't far out. That was the second wave—reinforcements.

Then the amber warning lights cycled on, and the groan of the external hangar bay hatch opening rumbled through the bay.

And the atmosphere rushed out of the huge compartment.

## 21

The halls of the ancient underground facility were quiet and dark, just like they were every time Caville scouted the Place of the Fallen. Everywhere his lamp turned, the walls reflected back black and dull. Gallo limped along behind him, now able to move with a shushing hop and slide. It wasn't as much noise as she'd made the first few forays. Her ankle was healing, the swelling diminishing, but it would be another week or so before the last of the tenderness was gone.

She'd demanded the chance to accompany him, hating their safe room for the lingering stench of the long dead and his and her own smells. There wasn't enough water to bathe, after all. In fact, there was barely any water at all, and every drop of the sweet stuff was as precious as air.

That was a real problem. He was already cramping from rationing so much, and his gut rumbled with hunger. The alien sentinel had done nothing worse than scrape outside their room on occasion. Now the greater threat was dehydration.

His light caught a sign he'd cut into the wall at eye level in one of his earlier searches: shallow and silvery.

He waved her closer. The old map had indicated this was an opening into a chamber filled with scientific gear, but he'd tried twice and couldn't get the door to open. That was assuming the door was still there. He'd already confirmed his suspicions that the alien place had changed over the years. Maybe it was still changing.

But this place? This room? He needed access to it. Their lives depended on it.

Gallo ran fingers over the shallow cuts in the wall. "You're sure this is it?"

"Positive."

She took his flashlight from him and shone it along the wall. "I'm not seeing any creases."

"The doors don't always have creases. The best ones—"

"Yeah, well, no crease, no door." She bit her bottom lip and banged her head against the wall. "Shit. I'm sorry. I think I'm going stir crazy." Her voice cracked, and she swallowed. "No. I'm definitely going stir crazy. It's just a matter of time now."

"Don't give up yet."

This was why he'd intended all along to come alone. His mind was meant for something hopeless like this. Just finding the ancient facility had been deemed a likely suicidal mission. Getting into it? Finding the ultimate objectives? Those were given almost no chance of success at all— less than one percent.

He accepted those odds without complaint. It was what he'd been designed for.

Someone like Gallo, though…

All she saw was the long odds growing longer each day. She complained about the cold metal of the floor they slept on. The challenges brought on by their change in diet and slow slide into dehydration were an ever-present misery that extended beyond the hunger, cramping, and fatigue he was mentally prepared for. After getting used to sneaking out to the hatch he'd come in through to relieve herself, constipation had brought her to tears more than once.

And then there was the threat of the sentinel. Every time they left the safety of their room, they ran the risk of encountering the thing. It was supposedly immune to small arms fire, but Caville always had his weapons nearby.

That immunity was something he was ready to test.

Gallo turned the light off, and her fingers hissed softly over the wall. "You know, we could always try to climb out. I mean, before the cramps get so bad that we can't. It won't come outside, right?"

"According to the reports I've read, it stalked for kilometers in all directions when this place was aboveground."

She made a sound that might have been a sigh. "You said we'd die here."

"Odds were, yes."

"I actually kind of thought we'd have this romantic adventure out in the desert. There might be an abandoned base or something where we could just bask in the late afternoon sun until it heated us up, then make love as the moon rose."

"Are there bases out here?"

"I don't know. I only knew about this place because it's talked about in legend."

"It's an important—"

"Sh!"

Caville tensed. He craned his neck and strained his ears, but he couldn't hear the telltale metallic scraping of the thing that had killed so many before.

He leaned close to where Gallo had been. "I don't hear it."

"Listen closer."

He heard it then: a whispery scratch, like fingernails on metal.

She'd found something!

The light flashed—weaker than it'd been a few days ago. She was farther back in the passageway, beyond the sign he'd cut into the wall, up on her tiptoes, and her index finger's nail was partly sunk into the wall up high.

A worried smile played over her features. "Is this it? It's really high."

It was, but maybe that was part of the place changing. Caville pressed his hand over hers, then he traced the faint impression of what might be a big door. He'd been off by a meter, and he'd been looking too low.

He manipulated the wall the way he'd been trained to, feeling for the almost imperceptible controls.

The door slid aside with a grumbling hiss, and the light reflected off a familiar, black crate: a Kedraalian research team's cargo container.

Caville waved the young woman in and followed after, then closed the door behind them. He choked back the urge to laugh triumphantly at their discovery. Exactly as described, the chamber was huge and filled with gear. Everything was sealed. Nothing had molested the crates—opened or closed. Equipment that had been taken out was still wrapped in plastic.

He'd finally managed a success!

Gallo limped to one of the larger cargo containers. "What *is* all of this?"

"Research gear. Test equipment, mostly." That was a lie, but she wouldn't know.

"There's so much." She slid onto one of the crates and lay back. "If I didn't feel like such an animal, I'd say we should just celebrate right here."

It was a tempting thought, stench and all. He set his weapons down. "If everything's still intact, you just might get what you want."

"What's that mean?"

He took the flashlight from her and prowled among the crates, stopping to brush dust off a few labels. Finally, he found what he was looking for and undid the butterfly latches.

Gallo sat up. "Should I even ask?"

"What this is?"

He pulled a green pressurized tank out of padding, then another. Another container held yellow tanks. From a third crate, he pulled out a heavy, boxy metallic device that had a panel of dials, gauges, and knobs. One of the crates that had held the tanks had flexible metallic hoses that he fit first to the tanks, then to the metallic device. A fourth crate held batteries that still showed a reasonable charge. Those he hooked to the device.

All along the panel, the gauges lit up. He flipped a couple switches, and the gauges spun around, then centered.

While the device finished coming to life, he dug through the crates until he found what he was looking for: a clear, heavyweight plastic drum. That he secured to a spout at the top of the metallic device.

Then he stepped back and folded his arms.

Gallo leaned forward from her place on the crate top. "What—?"

Hissing escaped from the plastic drum, then droplets of water sprayed across the inside. More droplets formed. Then the fluid trickled down the side to collect at the bottom. The process was remarkably fast.

The former Khanate spy got to her feet. "Is that water?"

"About as pure as you can ask for. In fact, we'll need to add some minerals to it before we drink. You don't want to drink a lot of pure water. It strips minerals from your body."

"I think I'd be okay with that right about now."

"Sure. We can all spare a few minerals."

"H-how much will that make?"

"If I can find all the tanks, and if there's not too much lost to leaks—fifty liters. And there's a device to recycle wastewater. It's hooked in directly to a shower." He ran the light across deeper sections. "They may have already built—"

A soft thud echoed through the ceiling overhead.

Gallo staggered back, eyes locked on the shadows above. "Is it in here?"

As Caville backed toward his assault weapon, he trained the light on the general direction of the noise and swung the beam in a broad arc to increase the odds he might catch any hint of movement.

Nothing seemed out of place on the black metal surface.

Another soft thud shuddered through the metal.

He slung the weapon over his shoulder. "That's not inside the room."

"You can't know that."

"Think about it. The sentinel always has a metallic scraping sound when it moved on the surface. Its claws are harder than this material. It wouldn't make that noise. And if it had gotten in here, the door would've been open, and all this gear would've been stripped."

"What?"

"I'll explain later. The point is, that's not the sentinel."

A third muffled thud vibrated through the metallic surface.

Gallo's eyes drifted to the water, then back up to the ceiling. "What is it, then?"

"I think your Khan sent people for us."

Something louder rang through the surface, which vibrated noticeably.

The young woman's eyes scanned the ceiling. "What was that?"

"A demolitions charge. A powerful one." Caville hurried to the hatch, which opened at his command.

He stepped into the hallway, flashlight beam tracking back toward the room they'd been using for safety. Something glinted oddly in the glow.

He froze.

The strange glint shifted, moving along the wall with the softest sound of a metallic scrape. Caville caught the slightest movement along the ceiling, a faint reflection of a reflection.

Gallo came toward him. "What is it?"

"Don't move." He barely managed a hiss, maybe thinking that would be enough to keep the thing from coming toward them.

But it slithered along the ceiling with movements that were part feline, part serpentine, and fully alien.

He stepped back toward the room, and he sensed that Gallo backed up as well.

Then another deep thud ran through the walls, and every surface vibrated.

The thing creeping along the ceiling dropped to the floor with far too little noise for its size. It rolled or tumbled or writhed, and the flashlight beam caught more angles and surfaces—one second clear as glass, the next chrome-like, and then blacker than night. A sense of its size became easier to estimate: twice as big as a large human.

Now it was up on its legs—

Except…its appendages had shifted from its top, pointed up, to its bottom, pressed against the floor. Or maybe they'd been regrown. Caville couldn't be sure. But it looked like its head was now turning away from him, looking back toward the hallway fork that could take it toward his shelter or up higher into the ancient structure.

That head slowly craned back toward Caville, and he felt an inexplicable coldness, like an alien intelligence reaching out to him.

Then the thing sprinted away, taking the fork that would carry it up.

Caville ducked back into the equipment room and grabbed his assault rifle.

Gallo stood in the doorway. "Was that the sentinel?"

"Yes. And I think it's pissed." He pressed a hand against the small of her back. "Stay here."

"What?"

"I'm going back to our little hideout."

"Then I'm coming with you."

"I'm not staying there. We can make this room our new home. It has everything we need."

She looked back inside. "I could drink all that water right now."

"We'll have the chance to drink all we want. But that thing was waiting to ambush us. I don't want to move around any more than we have to."

"But where'd it go? It could be hiding, waiting to ambush you."

"I think it's more interested in Khan's men. If they keep at it, they might be able to blast a hole in the roof."

"Why not just come down to one of the openings?"

He shrugged. "They might not even know there are any. If all the old teams that came out here were killed, their orders might be just to destroy the place. I need to go."

She nodded and hopped back inside.

Caville closed the door behind him and at the fork ran the flashlight up the way the sentinel had gone. Maybe it wasn't immune to gunfire, but he could now appreciate how it would seem to be. It had been pure luck that he'd spotted it, and it could apparently be more quiet than he'd expected when it wanted to be. That spoke of adaptability and intellect that was greater than he'd been led to believe.

At the door to the old sanctuary, he paused to listen, then let himself inside. It didn't take long to gather up their belongings, although he paused when another deep ringing ran through the structure.

More explosives.

The Khanate forces might be brutish and simple, but they had the resources to eventually get what they wanted. How long before they simply brought out a nuclear weapon?

His window of opportunity was closing.

On the way back to the huge equipment room, Caville stopped at the fork and listened intently. His imagination had been playing with him the whole way down the hallway, each shadow taking on a serpentine, then feline aspect. Scrapes, scratches, and squeals emanated from each open door or hall. Now, he had to be sure the path was clear.

He pressed his head against the wall and held his breath.

Human screams echoed down from the upward-leading fork. They were distant and distorted, but there was no mistaking them.

Gunfire drowned out the screams. Then there were more explosions.

And more gunfire.

Then there was only the screaming.

Until even that stopped.

The sentinels wouldn't go through doors. That's what the records said. It was meant to patrol corridors and open spaces. So the Khanate forces had managed to blast or cut or otherwise create a hole.

If it killed them all—and it would—then another group would come: larger and more ready.

Caville sprinted to his marking on the wall, then backpedaled to the hidden door and searched for the seam. It was an eternity before he found it—long enough for the ancient guardian to return to the depths and finish off the annoying intruders that had eluded it so far.

But it didn't come.

Finally, the door slid open, and he jumped inside. He didn't relax until he was safely sealed back inside with Gallo.

***

Normally, hauling batteries from the basement of a building to a lift wouldn't have done more than leave Stiles winded. These batteries were large and heavy, and there was the complication of being shot in the head and left for dead for weeks. She was wheezing by the time she had the two boxy power units in the lift car, and spots were dancing in front of her eyes.

McLeod looked worse, his face a splotchy red and his hair dampened by sweat. He set his one battery down with a groan that boomed in the silent building. "Why didn't you...make the security guards...do this... before killing them?"

He glanced at the two corpses with blood slowly pooling around their heads.

"The risk of them activating an alarm was too high."

"You said the computer security…was already triggered."

"It will be. The next step I take, there's no way around it. When I log in, the computer's going to prompt for a password or code phrase that only Patel knows. When I fail to respond, that security software I told you about is going to try to zero out all the storage devices."

"And we lose everything. I understand."

"So we take the computers off that network with the storage wipe software and run them off a network we power with these batteries." She stretched her back out and studied the dead guards stretched out on the marble floor.

With anyone other than the Patels, she would have relied on nonlethal force to dispatch the guards. Innocent people often took jobs to keep their families alive. These guards worked for one of the most corrupt and terrible organizations in all known space.

There was no way they were ignorant of the illegal acts of their employers.

She brushed grime off her palms. The batteries had come from the generator room and were coated with a slick, brown tacky substance that smelled like some sort of primordial grease. Maybe the batteries had been installed shortly after the planet had been discovered a century ago.

The colonel wiped sweat from his brow. "How many more?"

"This is it."

"Enough to keep her computers online?"

"Enough to last us until more of her people arrive."

McLeod braced himself in the corner of the lift car. "Oh. Right."

Stiles took one of the guards' cards and the card she'd previously prepared for the break-in, swiped the two in the card reader, then tapped the button for the top floor.

The doors slid shut, and the car climbed, but it seemed to be on a time-line of its own.

Sweat dragged grimy slicks down the colonel's face where he'd wiped himself. "How long?"

"Before the main force arrives? Fifteen minutes at most."

McLeod looked older now, and there was a weariness in his face that hinted he might be reconsidering the operation. "She'll come with them."

"She has to. We're penetrating her systems."

The lift car stopped, and the door opened. They'd propped Devanshi's door open on the first trip up. Now they only had to haul the batteries in and hook them up to the converter Stiles had rigged after spotting the security system.

It was an uncommon thing, finding a security system that couldn't be defeated. In the case of Devanshi's private computer system, even the design was anachronistic, with the storage maintained on a local network in her office. That sort of paranoia was expensive, but it was also the most effective means of securing her criminal activity.

Stiles plugged the batteries in, then settled into the chair that held Devanshi's perfumed scent. Once the password prompt came up, Stiles flipped the computer over to the batteries and the hardwired network she'd put together.

She waved McLeod over. "You need to take over in a minute."

"Take over? I don't have anywhere near the training—"

"Colonel, this is going to take longer than fifteen minutes. I can leave the rapid reaction team to you and sit here while this process cracks the last of her security, or I can deal with the Patel security team."

He nodded. "Show me."

"This is the decryption and capture step. All the prompts are clear. Mostly, you respond with whether or not to proceed."

"Why bother with that?"

"Because it's designed to let you know when it has a batch of data. If we have to leave with incomplete data, it won't be corrupted."

He rubbed his chin, smearing it with grime. "Okay."

"Last thing to worry about: battery power."

"You said those three—"

"Those three will be enough to get what we need. Yes. But I have everything set to run at top speed right now. I want as much data as we can get as fast as we can get it. If we stay at this speed, we'll burn through the batteries before they finish. This indicator—" She tapped the display where three simple battery icons flashed a bright green. "—tracks how hard the computer processors are hammering the batteries. When these dip into yellow, take the processor speed down." She pointed to a set of three drag bars that were all pushed up to the top, then dragged one down by putting a fingertip over the icon and swiping down.

"I can do that."

She pushed out of the seat and did her best to hide the wooziness that washed over her. "I'm counting on you, sir."

At the office door, she paused to glance down onto the parking lot. Fifteen minutes was a conservative estimate. The alarms would've already gone up at the nearest security facility. A crack team would have piled into vehicles minutes ago.

Bright lights flashed on the road leading toward the building complex.

That would be the teams. They wouldn't wait for Devanshi, who was probably already rushing to her air car.

The second wave would come with her.

Stiles took the lift car down, checking her weapon. On the ground floor, she took the pistols off the guards and stuffed the guns into her belt.

These weren't keyed to biometrics, which was surprising.

There had been two vehicles. Vans. Four people each.

She paced the interior of the lobby. The approaching team would already be aware that building security was out. They would assume the guards were dead or disabled.

One team would probe through the front. The other would take the rear.

They would enter at the same time. No stealth.

This attempt would be brute force. It would rely on speed.

Her best option was the security desk itself. It provided cover and she would be able to turn her attention from the front entry to the rear quickly, but it risked a crossfire.

Everything would come down to taking the front entry team down fast.

Did she still have the accuracy to do that?

Stiles crouched beneath the desk and closed her eyes. This was the sort of thing she'd spent years training for.

She could do it.

Cool, even breathing…focus and calm…letting the body do what it knew to do.

She had to put aside the fear of death. That was history. This was now.

Tires screeched on the pavement outside. The outer door dully opened, then the inner door followed.

A radio squawked; a deep voice growled.

These weren't innocent people. They were part of the Patel private army.

Boots stomped alongside the desk. An armored helmet poked over the top as the others hurried past.

"I've got two men down!" That was from the entry to the lift hallway.

The person above the desk sucked in a gasp.

When Stiles looked up, she saw a thick, female face, eyes wide in surprise.

That was the signal.

Stiles fired, sending a round through the woman's chin and rocking her head back.

The boom of gunfire would bring the others around. They were meters away and would have weapons out and ready.

So Stiles tucked and rolled, moving away from where she'd been and coming up on the opposite side of the desk, beside the body slumping to the ground.

Exactly as expected, there were three others. They had their weapons up.

But they were focused on the other side of the security desk.

She fired three times, dropping two of the security team immediately.

The third staggered but whipped his gun around.

Stiles was already rolling away when the burst shattered the interior breezeway window. She stopped rolling long enough to put a round into the man's crotch.

He fell with a deep moan.

Now gunfire came from the other end of the hallway. The security team had submachine guns, and they were firing them on automatic, counting on a hail of lead rather than accuracy and discipline.

Wood cracked, and glass shattered.

Stiles dropped her pistol and sprinted for the wall that provided cover from the gunfire. Her heart pounded, and the strength went out of her legs.

There were too many. She'd been too slow eliminating the first team.

*Rely on the training. Remember who you are.*

A pause in the gunfire betrayed the lack of discipline: The security team was going to have to reload all at once.

She pulled the two security guards' guns and popped around the corner.

For an instant, terror registered on the private soldiers' faces.

One woman was what they saw. Just one woman.

Then her training kicked in, and she squeezed off shots with the same accuracy as before her death.

And the Patel security detail dropped to the floor with a clatter.

**22**

———————

Benson leaned against the rail of the raised command station. A second ago, she'd felt alert and refreshed. Her skin had tingled with the clean and sweet touch of soap. She'd been ready for this horrible thing with Faulk to come to an end. Her world had been constrained to the small screen on the top support rail ringing the raised platform, where the aggregated video feed of the Marines Halliwell had led onto the *Warsaw* had played out.

In that panoramic view of the Azoren hangar bay, she'd almost felt present, as if standing beside one of her people, maybe with an assault weapon of her own hidden in a toolbox.

Then the image had broken into a million pieces chewed at the edges by static before fading out completely.

She looked up from the display, rubbing her eyes to make the abrupt change stop.

But the screen stayed the same gray-black.

Silence fell over the bridge crew, then Ensign Grehan hunched over her communications console and began tapping and swiping through the interface furiously. She turned her pudgy, panicked face to Benson. "It's something on the *Warsaw*, Captain. They're blocking the communications channel."

Nuñez wouldn't have been so shaken by the problem, but she had been a dancer—fit and disciplined. Grehan was pampered and soft.

"Get me reconnected, Ensign." Benson was pleased at the calm in her own voice.

Of course, she didn't *feel* calm. All the panic Grehan wore on her sleeve pulsed through Benson. All of it and more.

Those were her Marines on the *Warsaw*.

They'd gone across at her command, been left exposed and vulnerable. They'd agreed to do something unthinkable...unconscionable. Assassinating the commanding officer of an allied force was as mad as refusing to follow the order of a commanding officer speaking for the prime minister.

And here Benson had chosen both things out of a need for expedience.

Chopra drifted to the command station on quiet soles, eyes jumping from the darkened giant display to the young communications officer. "He must have known."

Benson tensed. "How? Pelham wouldn't betray us."

"Perhaps not. There were many other Azoren involved."

"They were all hand selected. They loathe Faulk and his commandos."

"Do they feel so different about us?"

"It has to be something else. I mean, yes, you're right—they might still consider us inferior, but hatred can be held in isolation and people can have priorities to how that hate drives them."

"The enemy of my enemy...?" Chopra's eyes drifted to the red-haired ensign.

"Exactly. Faulk terrifies them. He keeps provoking us, looking for a fight. They're not stupid. They know we would wipe their task force out."

"Meaning they will be our friends at least until the field marshal is dead."

"That's the gamble." Had she made the wrong call? It seemed so certain.

"Then maybe Faulk is somehow prescient."

"Paranoid, more like."

The field marshal could certainly have seen through the plot. It was simple and intended to exploit his ego, which seemed ideal.

But he wasn't *stupid*.

His intellect could have overcome his ego.

It was just as possible bad luck had worked against them.

Grehan held a hand to her ear. "Captain—"

Mahama spun on his heel, eyes bright against his dark skin. "Captain! There's been an explosion aboard one of the Azoren ships!"

The communications officer nodded vigorously. "Yes, ma'am. That's what's coming from the Gulmar ships—an explosion aboard an Azoren ship. One of the troop transports!"

Another act of Khanate saboteurs?

Benson stepped down from the command station and pressed herself between Grehan and Konrath, who was craning his neck over Maham's weapons station. "Ensign, I need a connection to our forces aboard the *Warsaw*. That's your number one priority."

"Yes, ma'am."

Now Benson placed a hand on Konrath's shoulder. "Find me Chief Parkinson."

The helm officer nodded and stepped back from his station, head bowed as he tried to contact the engineer.

Benson shifted over to Mahama's side. "I need to know what's going on aboard that troop transport. Sabotage? An attack we missed? Is it full of human soldiers or these Children?"

"Ma'am?"

"Ensign Mahama, this is simple. We're in the middle of attempting to assassinate Field Marshal Faulk. Some of those troop transports have his commandos aboard. I need to know what we're dealing with."

"Yes, ma'am." The way his cheeks shook said he wasn't so sure, though.

Was she being a savage, like Faulk? Her priority as the head of the combined fleet was to keep it at peak effectiveness. A troop transport ship full of human Azoren soldiers wasn't so different as one full of Azoren commandos.

Except that the commandos were loyal to the man she was trying to kill.

A glance at Chopra showed he might have the same doubt she did. He sucked on his bottom lip and fidgeted.

She stepped back and tugged his arm so that he would accompany her to the command station where she turned her back on the big bridge console. Her heart was out of control—hammering far too fast. "Honest opinion, Dinesh."

Chopra hunched. "About this explosion?"

"All of it. Do you think Faulk figured it out? Is this part of his plan?"

"We have so little data—"

"Opinion. Analysis can come later."

"Opinion? This field marshal is wily by all accounts, but he's not a genius. He's shown irrational behavior more than tactical and strategic competence."

That was a relief.

"Captain?" It was Mahama. He'd twisted around at his station, searching for her.

Benson stepped around the command station. "What do you have?"

"The Azoren transport? Those are…humans inside."

"Thank you." Benson noticed Grehan's pinched face, as if she had something to say, too. "Go ahead, Ensign."

"The *Warsaw*? There's no transmission of any sort coming out of it."

There were too many redundancies in system design for that to be possible outside of taking damage in battle. And that meant whatever had happened was definitely planned.

But if her Marines were still transmitting from their suits, they didn't have to ride on the *Warsaw* communications systems. The signals would still be coming out of the Azoren shuttles. Sealed up inside the hangar bay, those signals would be attenuated, but they would be there.

That meant getting one of their ships closer to the *Warsaw*. Benson pointed to Grehan. "Good job, Ensign. Have the *Sinclair* move closer to the *Warsaw*. Exercise caution—don't provoke. But get there as soon as they can."

"Yes, ma'am. What about the Gulmar shuttles?"

"They won't have the gear, but the *Sinclair* can work with them." Benson squeezed Chopra's wrist. "Faulk had to be behind this. Cutting off all the comms? It was his doing. That and the explosion, they have to be connected, don't they?"

"They could be. There could be saboteurs aboard this troop transport."

"I was thinking about that myself. But why act now?"

"I don't know."

"But what about what we're doing—killing Faulk?"

Chopra bowed his head. "Are we? We try right now, yes, but are we actually killing him? I think we might be better served asking a different question."

She suspected she knew the answer, but… "What question?"

"How far are we willing to go if the assassination attempt fails?"

<hr>

Parkinson sat up in his bunk in the dark. Somewhere far away, he'd heard a buzzing sound. It had been soft and almost teasing, but it had been tenacious, drawing him out of his time with Chief Taylor. That had been the worst of it, having to excuse himself from another intriguing round of simulations and post-simulation dissection. The way she smirked or sometimes laughed when he made more outrageous guesses about the data from those results had a ticklish playfulness about it. That was a feeling he could grow to love so intensely.

Except…the buzzing was his computing pad. And he was in his cabin. Alone.

There was no cherry syrup soap smell mingling with Taylor's warm scent. Instead of the bitter film of coffee on his tongue, there was the sour hint of vomit he never seemed to shake.

Nausea doubled him over. He'd slept through the alarm to take his medication.

His pad buzzed again—insistent, impatient.

He threw off the covers, stumbled to the foldout desk, and plucked the device from the corner, shivering. His vision was blurry. Who was calling?

Ensign Konrath? That was one of the navigation officers.

Parkinson backpedaled to his bed and settled on it. "Hello?"

Konrath breathed softly. "Chief Parkinson?"

"Yes."

"Sorry to bother you, but we've got a problem."

That was the last thing Parkinson needed to hear. He shouldn't have agreed to take time off. "Did something go wrong? Is my team okay?"

"Not on the *Valor*, Chief. Sorry. Um, Captain Benson asked me to call you. She's probably best to explain this. Can I transfer you?"

"Sure."

Parkinson padded to the little sink he shared with his roommate, who must have been on duty. Yes, the time showing on the device's display was about right for that.

The chief engineer splashed cold water onto his eyes and cheeks helped with the nausea and helped more with the remaining fog of sleep.

He stank, and his T-shirt was damp with sweat. That would never have done—

Benson's voice came out of the computing device speaker. "Chief?"

"What's wrong?" He toweled his face off.

"Everything. We've got a puzzle. It's the kind you're good at."

The words weren't meant to stroke his ego. Benson seemed to be past manipulating him to behave. More importantly, he was past the need to hear how necessary he was.

Dying sort of corrected a lot of problems.

He returned to his bed. "Should I come to you?"

"Are you up to it?"

"I need to clean up. After that, I should be okay."

"I'm on the bridge. Hurry, please."

She disconnected. Not that long ago, he would've griped and moaned about how she was demanding too much of him, pushing him until he couldn't take it anymore.

He'd been petty and whiny.

Taylor had seen right through that and had called bullshit on him. Now he felt embarrassed to remember that version of himself. The old Will Parkinson was still there—a constant troglodyte in his memory, a pleading and groaning little jerk who insisted that his expertise and intellect made him more important than anyone else.

How had he made it so long like that?

He showered, dressed, and made his way to the bridge as quickly as his shaky legs could manage. In the lift, he realized he'd forgotten his medication.

Again.

The captain had sounded too stressed to worry about something like treating a symptom. This was a problem. She'd said everything had gone wrong but the *Valor* was fine. That meant one of the other ships was having a problem.

What did they call it when you trained up your team? Deepening the bench?

That's what he needed to do. If he still had a career. If he lived. No more expecting everyone to work to acquire the knowledge he'd gained the hard way. That was selfish and petty, and he was past that.

Benson was circling the command station when he stepped onto the bridge, too caught up in what was going on to even notice his arrival.

And he could see why. On the giant display everyone used for a shared reference, the image was split into two windows. On the left half was one of the blocky, weathered Azoren troop transports. On the right was what looked like the *Warsaw*—the Azoren flagship.

Something was odd, and he felt stupid for not being able to see what it was.

Why were they looking at Azoren ships? Those had to be the problem.

The captain turned, straightened, then hurried to his side. "Chief. Thank you."

"How can I help?" The words felt so good.

"I made a call. You might say it was a risky decision."

"That sounds like your job description."

She smiled. "We were trying to eliminate Field Marshal Faulk."

Parkinson realized his jaw had dropped. "Wow."

"The Azoren captains were terrified for their lives, and we couldn't afford another incident like what he did to the *Seattle*."

"I understand." But assassination? That's what she was describing.

She exhaled. "Unfortunately, our Marines went into an ambush, and we lost contact with them."

"I could send Telly over."

"Telly?"

"My drone. Telly's decked out with advanced comms gear."

"I've already sent the *Sinclair*." She pointed to the right side of the big display. "They've had to slow their approach. The *Warsaw*'s sensors are active and they've got lock-on."

"Our shadow tech should be better than theirs."

"The *Warsaw* isn't the only problem." Benson pointed to the other half of the screen. "We think a bomb might have gone off inside that troop transport at the same time Faulk shut off comms coming from the *Warsaw*."

"Exact same time?"

"It seems like. As far as we can tell, there's a big fire raging in there. People could be dying. I've scrambled all of our shuttles for rescue operations, but I'm not sending anyone inside without knowing there's someone to save."

Parkinson tugged at his soul patch. "Because it could all be part of a trap?"

"Yes."

He tugged harder at the little beard. Benson looked like she was coming apart. She was radiating a fever heat, like she'd just finished a workout. But it was all stress.

Anyone would have freaked out. The Azoren were psychotic. "Did you have someone confirm the exact timing of the cutoff and explosion?"

"No." Her eyes narrowed. "Why?"

"Because if there were terrorists working in coordination, they might have set up a bomb to go off when comms signals dropped. Use the persisted comms signals as your dead-man switch. The signals stop, the explosives go off."

"Okay." She bit her lip. "Then this is the worst of it."

"You mean no other ships blew up?"

"Only this one."

"That's not all that bad—losing a troop transport. They could've lost everything. You said he refused to do the sweeps you suggested, right?"

She nodded. "Can you hack into their internal systems and get a look inside?"

"Inside the troop transport?"

"Yes. Those are humans inside there, or at least we think they are."

"I'll send Telly over. It won't take long."

Benson touched his hand. "You could be saving lives."

Unless they were the freakish Children.

He did his best shuffling run to the lift, taking it down to his office in Engineering. The excitement and activity actually pushed his awareness of the nausea into the background, until it was bearable.

Hu looked up from her workstation but didn't scold or challenge him.

By the time he was seated and sliding on his VR helmet, he sensed her hovering outside his door. "Just doing a little work for the captain."

"Okay." Hu's soft voice sounded reassured.

Telly sped toward the transport, passing close by the *Warsaw* and *Sinclair*, burning through the drone's small fuel supply at a terrific rate. Acceleration mattered, not endurance.

As the transport grew closer, Parkinson noted the shuttles hanging back, waiting for the signal to go.

Benson hadn't mentioned putting Marines in the shuttles.

Wait. She'd said the Marines were inside the *Warsaw*. All of them?

If so, her anxiety made even more sense.

He brought up the hacking tools he had loaded in his computing device. This was the suite of software programs and utilities he'd acquired throughout his lifetime. Some were illegal, but they could be explained away as part of his job.

Maybe one of those tools would be what he needed to crack the Azoren security.

If it worked, what would that mean? Like she said, saving lives.

But those were *Azoren* lives. Even if they really were human, *were* they? Hadn't they held her captive? That wasn't what civilized people did to diplomats and dignitaries who'd come in good faith.

He decelerated Telly, bringing it alongside the troop transport.

Pockets of heat glowed on the drone's infrared sensor. Without a doubt, fires were burning inside. Maybe it was too late to pull off a rescue.

That wasn't his call to make.

Parkinson went for some of the more basic utilities to start with. If the Azoren security software was too powerful, he didn't want to waste his best tools right off. A low-percentage approach seemed the best first swing. Hit the most hardened systems, then work down the list.

He sent a simple ping utility, attaching an unsophisticated viral package with it. There was no way something so crude could work, but—

The Azoren transport's comms system accepted the ping, and the virus slipped into its systems.

Impossible. It was rudimentary, brute force, clumsy—

His computing pad vibrated, and a dump of the Azoren ship's systems data came across. Every functional system…

He was in!

A strange thrill settled in his gut, almost crushing the nausea: The Azoren ships—the transports at least—were running ancient software. They were vulnerable. He'd never even thought to try to hit the ships with such an approach! Comms systems usually shut down what amounted to stupid, brute-force attacks long before they had a chance to actually get into the network.

But he was in.

And the security systems? Cameras?

He poked around, finding ancient and unprotected systems everywhere he looked. It was worse than when he'd gone through his first week of technical training and found the school's systems running software he'd hacked as a pre-teen.

Benson would need to know about this. Maybe it could help with the *Warsaw*. Maybe it could help with the Khanate.

For now, though, he needed to see what was going on inside and who these people were.

He brought up a passageway camera on the top deck.

And gasped.

Flames spat from a partially open hatch. Men in silvery, flame-retardant suits sprayed foam at the fire. The metal around them seemed to buckle from the heat, and the camera blacked out.

He switched to a camera on the deck below. The same scene was playing out, but a couple of blackened hatches showed where there had been some success.

But there were bodies on the deck. Some wore the firefighting suits and had collapsed, maybe simply unconscious. Others were charred black.

This wasn't a ruse. It was sabotage.

And everywhere he looked, the people were human—like him—rather than Children.

He closed down the hacking suite and connected to Benson.

She was right. There were lives to save.

---

Grier had created a mental list of all the things that could go wrong with the plan to assassinate Faulk. Him being ready to kill his own people when they arrived hadn't been in the top five.

It hadn't been in the top ten. And she'd only come up with ten.

Now her Marines were pinned down, slowly burning through their environment suit oxygen. She was sitting at two hours remaining, but it seemed to her like the air was going stale. That was her head playing with her.

Her helmet radio squawked, then Halliwell was in her ear. "You hear me okay?"

He was at the other end of the hangar bay, near the hatch that would open at any minute and let in the Azoren commandos. She was huddled among her own squad and the Azoren techs who had been with them, closer to the bay door that opened into space.

Ralf squeezed the pistol in his hand, unmoving.

She wanted to turn her head around, to see where Halliwell was, but the only way their desperate plan would work was for everyone to stay on the deck, still. "If I'm playing dead, can I hear you?"

"Must be. Look, it's been five minutes since the last of the atmosphere went out. Either they fell for it or they're trying to figure out how to blow this place."

"If they fell for it?"

"Then that door by you is going to close, and they're going to re-pressurize this—"

Something rumbled through the deck: The hangar bay door was closing!

Grier snorted. "They fell for it!"

"The door's closing?"

"Can't you feel it?"

"Maybe. I kind of fell on top of one of the techs. He panicked and needed some help looking like he was suffocating."

"Nice. Anyway, it's closing. That means they fell for it, right?"

"I think so. And that means they're going to come in here and check the bodies."

"We have to hit them the second that outer hatch opens."

"Yeah. I've got some flash-bangs. It's a tough throw from here."

Grier swallowed. "I've got a clean shot—almost a straight line."

"That means they've got a straight shot on you."

"I'll be fine."

Halliwell sighed. "I think I should make the throw."

"Nope. One, I've got the best line of sight. Two, I've got some real grenades."

"What?"

"I know, I know—no explosives. They were only for emergency. Let's not fight about it right now. The door's closed. Another five minutes for them to re-pressurize, right?"

"Yeah."

"That's all the time we've got to plan. This almost works out better for us, right? A bunch of his commandos are going to be squeezed into a tight space."

"And we're out in the open, unless you count these toolboxes."

Grier had been in a firefight training scenario once where a platoon was caught in the open when ambushed by a squad with cover. The entire platoon had been killed in the simulator. "Any luck reaching the *Valor?*"

"No signals going out. Maybe we could use one of the shuttle radios if we could get inside. Those systems aren't line-of-sight like our suits' short-range radios."

Those short-range radios were the only thing they could use to avoid the people on the other side of the hatch picking up radio traffic. It had been the short-range radios that had kept everything from falling apart. The second Grier had realized what was going on, she'd broadcast to everyone to look away from the outer hatch, go to the ground, and pretend like they were suffocating. In their bulky suits, with only the small porthole to see in through, it must have been somewhat convincing. Whatever cameras were in the hangar bay were positioned along the ceiling, so they didn't provide a more detailed view.

But they had to know the shuttles had closed their inner airlock doors, so some of their targets would be alive.

Would the commandos make a run for the shuttles? Did they have breaching charges?

Whatever the commandos did, Grier couldn't see them staying clumped together for long. "I'm thinking they're going to come in fast and disperse. Staying out in the passageway… I don't see it."

"I know."

"So let me make the throw. During the confusion, we get everyone to cover."

"Let me think about it, okay?"

He was being ridiculous, but she couldn't just shout him down. She had to approach it the way Benson would. "Clive, we don't have a lot of choices, and time's running out."

"I told you not to do that."

Grier wanted to punch him right then. "And I told you not to tell me not to argue like the captain. She's right when she does it, and I'm right."

She squeezed her eyes shut. His stubbornness was wasting time.

Finally, he sighed. "You're right. I'm sorry."

"We need to get the word out, squad by squad. What's the signal?"

"Your grenade detonating."

That made sense. She would look like the lone survivor. When the grenade was out, panic would make everything else irrelevant.

Halliwell made a low, frustrated growl. "If we get out of this, we're having a talk."

"We are. A talk and listen."

"Tell your squad."

His disconnect was a deafening pop, an authoritative declaration that they were down to business.

He could've said he loved her, but maybe that was too much so soon.

Or she could've said she loved him.

That was her incentive to stay alive, then.

Now all she needed to do was brief her squad and pull a grenade out without giving anything away.

She sent a text message to keep things easier: *When my grenade goes off, grab your guns, drag the sailors to cover, then kill the commandos.*

The affirmative texts came in one at a time, and all the while she slowly edged her right hand closer to the thigh pouch where she'd put her fragmentation grenades.

Her fingertips were on the flap to the pouch, slowly tugging.

Then she slid her forefinger and middle finger inside the pouch. She probed around, slowly bringing her thigh closer to make the search easier.

There. The grenade was in one of the smaller interior compartments.

She pulled the weapon out, then the other.

The spinning amber warning lights powered off.

Five minutes. There was atmosphere. She had to hurry.

Her helmet picked up noise now: the outer hatch unlocking, activating.

It was too late for anyone to notice her. She hefted the grenade, shifted it around in her hand until she was ready to activate it.

The second one was ready, too.

A metallic grinding noise boomed in her ears: the outer hatch opening.

She activated the first grenade, imagined the huge bay as she'd seen it before the Azoren field marshal depressurized everything. She'd have to get to her feet to throw over the toolbox less than a meter away from her. And she'd have to throw...

Now!

Grier hopped up, drew her arm back, spotted the clump of commandos charging through the door, saw the spot just beyond them where the grenade had to go, and threw.

Then she activated the second grenade and threw that...

Just as a burst of gunfire caught her in the chest and knocked her to the deck.

## 23

Waves of pressure washed over Satrap—the signal of the *Might of the Khan* transitioning from Fold Space to regular space. The machinery under his flesh registered the change more quickly and more fully, so that it actually came in two waves: an excitement of miniature computer systems and a disruption of organic matter. That feeling radiated out from his chest to his eyes, leaving behind a sickly, burning smell that spoke of fresh and dangerous energy.

They were close to the home world of Azh Shivan and to the Khan.

Satrap's eyes fluttered open as he swallowed back the bitter taste that came with the transition to normal space.

His awakening was just in time for the bright, sharp chime from the bridge and the subsequent connection from Zohar.

Satrap pinched the bridge of his nose. "We have arrived, Zohar?"

"We have. Surely you must feel the light of the Khan even this far out."

The captain was being surprisingly ironic and biting. At least he seemed to be focusing his hostility on Khan.

"Actually, this close in, my systems are vulnerable." Satrap clenched his teeth. "And Ikhama's systems can no longer be hidden from our guiding light and sword of justice."

After a pause in which Zohar must have digested the meaning, the captain cleared his throat. "Of course. We do have problems, though."

"So soon?"

"My fellow captains voice concern for our Khan's health and safety."

"The last transmission *was* disturbing."

"I did not mean to imply their concerns are unwarranted. They are, however, *your* captains."

"Until the Khan says otherwise." Satrap massaged his legs.

His position came with great power, but that power was hollow without the constant assurances of support from their source of light and wisdom. What happened more often than not was that the power became a fragile shell that was ready to collapse at even a hint of a whisper of disapproval from the glorious leader.

But the expectations never diminished.

Infinite responsibility, uncertain authority. That was the way of the Khanate, the burden and terror of being in power at any level other than that of the Khan himself.

Pain from Satrap's joints became a growing fire that sapped his focus when he most needed it. There had been something he'd intended to do—

The systems! There were so many little failures piling up in his systems!

"A moment, Zohar."

Satrap paused the connection. The pain was so intense now that tears trickled down his cheeks in a steady stream. What had been an instant of burning in his sinuses was now a continuing stream of char and ash, of computers cooking themselves to blackened powder.

With so much pain, concentration was almost impossible. He stretched out on his pillows and breathed deep, trying to control the oncoming panic.

Something inside was roasting him alive, boiling away his blood and baking his brain.

Data was his salvation. Escaping the rigors of the flesh.

His world went black, sliced abruptly by bright colors: cyan, magenta, yellow.

Numbers and letters flowed past: not the ridiculous alphabet created by the first Khan, but straight conversions of binary spat out by processors and converted back into microcode and data blocks.

This was Satrap's world—his language.

Swimming through that, he picked out the relevant modules and flows. What mattered to him at that moment was survival, and that required a correction somewhere in the life support systems.

Things were bad, and they'd continued to worsen since the fleet first launched.

He'd found the systems before, so it was easy to find them again. However, their information flow was chaotic and puzzling.

Where were the changes he'd made? They had been temporary, yes, but they had been simple and good enough to keep the systems running…

Except they were gone now. Someone—some*thing*—had undone his work.

A sensation pricked at his awareness, drawing him almost out of the data stream. He stopped near the surface that would take him back to his failing body and studied the input.

Zohar was worried about the other captains causing an insurrection. Support was building for a demand that the fleet return to Azh Shivan.

Now!

Even before the captain's fingers had retreated from his input device, Sultan replied from within the machine: *Just a moment more.*

That moment in Zohar's perception was a small eternity inside the machine.

Satrap drew the systems data together and filtered through the contorted and winding information.

Something was telling the regulation systems to reduce dosages.

Something else was telling the monitoring systems to ignore the alarms and alerts and to accept older readings as valid results.

Another something was shutting off stimulation mechanisms that kept flesh from complete failure.

Software. Firmware. Hardware.

When the Khan had broken Satrap and remade him in a desirable image, the ruined organs and failed systems had been replaced with machinery. Now the inbuilt obsolescence of those systems was shutting down the host.

Had there been a consideration at the start that Satrap represented a risk after a short while, or was this something external and virulent striking him?

His electronic avatar laughed at the idea.

This was Khan and his servants creating an assurance of temporary power, nothing more. There could be no permanent military leader to threaten the mighty Khan!

It was something Satrap would have to permanently reverse at a later date.

Maybe it was something he would have to seek vengeance for.

For now, though, he had greater and greater crises building all around him.

Once again he programmed the systems to return to baseline processing. Once again, or was that a failing brain's imagination going wild?

Medicines and nutrients flowed through lines, and the pain and poisons faded, leaving him shaking.

His eyes fluttered, and he pushed up from the pillows.

Tingling spread from his chest to his fingertips and toes. Breathing became possible without straining. The black that had encroached on his vision from the edges pushed back out.

Khan had many assassins, and not all of them were flesh and blood.

*Remember that. Remember that!*

Satrap pushed himself upright again and resumed the connection. Zohar was on the screen now, squinting in concern.

Or maybe it was a measuring look, testing the viability of eliminating an opponent.

Something more for Satrap to remember.

He waved the captain's concern away. "These troublesome captains, is this part of a coup?"

"Do you ask whether they intend to eliminate you?"

"That much is assumed. What is unknown is whether their plan is to return to Azh Shivan with their ships flexed as a threat to our dear Khan or perhaps to simply use their power outright."

Zohar stroked his chin. "This was always a concern for the Khan."

"You do not build a fleet with too great a commander, unless that fleet is deployed against the enemy immediately." *And that commander is slowly poisoned.*

Satrap jumped when his hatch opened.

It was the Jakkara captain. The man bowed. "The Ikhama."

When the bodyguard stepped aside, Ikhama entered, her robes whispering across the deck. Head bowed, she took a seat on the pillows across from Satrap and beneath the giant display. *"The lion rests easy atop the escarpment, contemplating the hyenas scurrying beneath. No fear seizes the majestic heart. No villain threatens the power of heaven."*

Another of her ridiculous allegories, but the intent was clear: She had heard the conversation.

And so had their Khan.

That was something Satrap could use. "Ikhama. You are well?"

"My bones are frail, and my heart is weak. Only the light of our Khan may preserve me."

"And I will do what I can in that regard. Zohar and I worry that our fellow captains might have forgotten their primary duty and which master they must serve until their Khan says otherwise."

*"Knives out, the assassin stalks his prey in darkness. Beware the encroachment of light, dog! In the fullness and purity, the traitor will taste his own blade."*

"Yes." Satrap glanced at Zohar's face on the display.

The captain was unreadable other than looking down ever so slightly toward Ikhama.

Had he caught the undertone Satrap had? Was Khan already signaling his intent to break any conspiracy before it had the chance of taking root?

Satrap had never had a chance to dig deep into the newer ships' systems. Could software poisons reside within their systems as they did within his life support and basic cybernetic hardware?

Or was he reading everything wrong, and he was the hyena and assassin?

With a paranoid and delusional leader, that seemed just as likely an interpretation.

What mechanism remained in the arsenal to prevent bloodshed?

Satrap could only think of one: preemption. "Zohar?"

The captain bowed. "Yes?"

"We will be within range soon of a lag-free connection to our Khan."

"In less than an hour."

"Perhaps we should inform our fleet that you and I will soon engage our glorious Khan for guidance."

Zohar arched an eyebrow. "No update awaited us upon exit."

"For fear of interception or corruption of the recording. So it is best to let our Khan know we have returned for his words of wisdom."

Now the captain's chin and other eyebrow came up: he understood. "I will direct the fleet to full acceleration to hear our Khan's wisdom."

Satrap bowed. "Thank you."

Once the captain disconnected, Ikhama clasped her hands in her lap. "You hold concerns in your heart."

"Out of respect for my captains. To misjudge them based on brash talk—"

"They hold dark thoughts in theirs."

"Possibly. It's one thing to toy with the notion of claiming a throne. Many young men with a hint of aspiration find their minds wandering toward ultimate power. Put those men among others of a similar bent, and the foolishness of blind ambition somehow becomes a romantic notion."

"Or misguided machismo."

"Both are possible. These are young leaders. Obviously, something about them inspired our Khan to give them such power. Now he has recalled them."

The old woman studied her wrinkled hands. "The greater oddity is your concern for them."

"It's more a concern for me—my mission."

"That mission has come to an end."

"Has it? The Khan has spoken to you?"

Ikhama shrugged. "There was an expectation of conquest within a period of time."

"And I've failed."

"Have you? In my eyes, the failure was in those around you."

"So, if the cause for my mission ending is something other than failure—"

"It is." When Ikhama breathed, it was a shuddering sound. "I have shared the Khan's nightmares."

"Nightmares? His claim that the spirits—"

She held up a hand. "No claim, Satrap. *When I wandered the deserts for forty days and nights, the last of my strength was gone. The light descended from the stars and placed a sword within my grip and said to me to stand strong. And in the shadows, the spirits rose and twisted. Only the sword gave me light and hope, shining as bright as the stars. Careful lest you lose that light, for the spirits shall return one day.*"

"I don't recall that one."

"It is in a book that only a few ever see in their lives. The Khan is one."

"A physical book?"

"The writings of our first Khan. It is meant as a guide for those who follow after."

How must that feel? Most who followed after a Khan had his blood on their hands. Were they given time to wash that blood away before the strange threats of the book were made known to them? And the dying Khan: How would he feel knowing that his killer would be the recipient of such an ominous warning?

At least Satrap would never have to concern himself with that. "What are these spirits?"

"*They are shadows in daylight and death in darkness. They are ancient as the stars and born from the abyss.*"

"Riddles." He closed his eyes. "This...struggle has drained me. Would you watch over me while I rest?"

"I will wake you when our Khan speaks."

"Thank you, Ikhama."

It felt hollow and wrong to thank the old woman for the small assistance of watching over him while he tried to fight off the poisons she obviously knew were slowly killing him. That knowledge had been there all along, and she'd never once hinted at the threat.

She had nearly died with him during the first attempt on his life. He'd thought maybe a bond had been created between them.

Apparently, that wasn't so.

Once he closed his eyes, it was easy enough to drift into the data again. The distraction of pain was reduced to inconsequence, and with the proper medications, his mind was sharper.

In his youth, that mind had been something wonderful and miraculous. He had seen things, and understanding had come quickly afterwards. Now that he was broken, and each day accelerated him toward a premature death, his mind was a mere shadow of what it had been.

Yet it was still more than others would ever know.

The question now was whether it would be adequate to the task of saving him from the course the Khan and his people had laid out. Could the solution to reverse the sabotaged machinery achieve a level of permanence?

He had nearly an hour to determine that.

His head touched a pillow, and the press of the moment slipped away. The end was nearing—the end of his command and of his subservience to the man who had broken the body of a child out of psychotic desire.

What could that childhood have otherwise held absent the dark influences of the Khan?

Satrap had once had dreams and desires. He had flesh and health.

Those were times denied him now. To survive, he had to return to the data.

No sooner had he dove into the streams of data—tearing apart origins and destinations, ferreting out designs and modifications, gleaning intent and malevolence from chronologies—than he was shaken physically.

Ikhama's strange eyes stared into his. She seemed curious, maybe even amused. "Our Khan speaks now."

Satrap pushed up from his pillows. "Time passed quickly."

"Your rest was deep. You spoke."

He froze. "I did?"

"Who was Helena?"

The name brought a blush to Satrap's face. "No one."

"You were appointed as a child, like me."

"Yes. Different Khans, but I believe we both knew the same glory, didn't we?"

For once, the old woman didn't look away. She returned to her pillow, an almost wistful smile on her face. "I had a boy I swore that I would marry. Our families were among the early converts, before the worlds were ours."

"When the Khanate was persecuted for the sort of things it did to us?"

She nodded. "How can anyone understand taking a child from her home and killing her dreams? Mutilation in the name of a cause she has yet to embrace…must seem a tragedy."

What she was saying, even couched the way it was—it was sacrilege. Blasphemy.

The wall display flared to life, and Zohar's face filled it. "Satrap, the Khan would speak."

Satrap bowed his head as close to his knees as he could. "I await."

Khan's face filled the screen, and the window with Zohar's face shrank to a corner. The old man who ruled the Khanate with an iron fist looked haggard, confused…terrified. He sat in the dark of what might be a large bedchamber, lit by the wan glow from his display. A high, ornate seat back rose over his head, gold framing some reddish wood.

His eyes searched around. "Ikhama? Where is the woman?"

Ikhama bowed. "Beneath you, Glorious and Mighty Khan."

"Ah!" Khan's fingers wiggled. "I have heard nothing from you these last minutes. I worry when an Ikhama goes silent."

"There were those who tried to kill me in the past, my Khan. Some of my systems were damaged."

"Have them fixed! You are my eyes and ears! The Khan's glory is eternal!"

"Of course, my Khan."

So, she had shut herself off again. Her warning to Zohar might have been a reminder. Or maybe while she watched over Satrap, she felt pity for the indiscretions of sleep.

Khan turned his focus to Satrap. "You! Destroyer and betrayer!"

Satrap bowed even deeper. "Your Satrap, my Khan."

"My glorious fleet! The promise of victory! Honey on your lying tongue has turned to vinegar and nightshade."

"We managed great successes against the Gulmar, my Khan. The

Moskav are a dead people now. That same success was close against the Kedraalians."

"Has close now become another word for achievement?"

"It has not. What was left unspoken was the sad truth: Our failures fall at the feet of those who betrayed their Satrap, the appointed leader named by none other than the Great and Glorious Khan." *The same Khan who would poison me while I serve him.*

"Your lies and guile are only outstripped by your incompetence. With months to refine your apologies and deflections, this is all you can manage—a repeat of your messages?"

"I repeat the truth. The recordings of the battles support my claims."

Khan's chair groaned when he pushed it back. "You were put in power to succeed, not to make excuses."

"I humbly offer my resignation, if that appeases the Khan."

"It does not. I have need of protection. The Khanate faces threats from beyond the stars. Malignant spirits roam the desert. They are enraged. Their sacred graves have been fouled and despoiled. They have slain an entire company of men."

"Command me, Khan. But...I have only a fleet, not an army."

"Protect us from the spirits. That is my command! The spirits will come from space, too. It was in the prophecies, in the dreams!"

Was he referring to the Kedraalians? Were they what plagued the old man's dreams? "Then my fleet will protect Azh Shivan. We have developed strategies to...account for the change in fleet composition."

Khan wiggled his fingers again.

Was it some sort of mystical sign against dark powers?

The old man leaned forward. "Zohar, you listen well."

In his little screen, the captain bowed. "As the Khan speaks, so it will be."

"Good!" Khan's eyes darted around, squinting into the dark. He whimpered, recoiled from something, then muttered under his breath. Once again, his fingers danced around.

It had to be some sort of protective measure—something he believed.

The muttering dropped away to silence, then the old man's eyes came up, wide and darting. "Satrap!"

"Yes, my Khan?"

"Your plan, this scheme to further attribute blame to others—tell me of it."

There was the hint of a trap in the old man's words. "My assumption is that the enemy will be…like the Kedraalians and will share similar tactics and limitations."

Khan waved for his Satrap to hurry. "Go on."

"We found some success using the new missiles you provided us—the anti-radiation missiles that will lock on to their signals vessels."

"Ah! Ah!" The old man nodded enthusiastically. "Even the shadows are not without vulnerabilities!"

The shadows? That made it sound as if the desert spirits were attached to the advanced technology of the fleet and the enemy ships.

Satrap filed that away as another data point to dig into.

*If* he survived. "We seed the likely areas of entry with these missiles and leave them inert, listening only for these stealth signals and counter-measures. When those are detected, the missiles creep forward using microbursts until even that must be detected, then they accelerate."

"That is all?"

"Our engagements with this Kedraalian force have always been different. The last time, they had Azoren and Gulmar ships attached. If not for poor discipline among our captains, we would have dealt a mighty blow to even that force."

Instead of scolding Satrap, the old man hunched forward in his seat and gnawed on his knuckles. When he looked up, blood trickled down his wrinkled hand. "A joined enemy is a dangerous enemy."

"The Azoren seem undisciplined to the point of detriment." Satrap checked himself before pointing out that was what he faced with his own captains.

"Perhaps we should seek a combined force against the shadows. Yes. Strength in numbers. Even great differences can be set aside once the spirits awaken." Khan tittered. "A sword brilliant as the stars to cut through the blackest dark."

Satrap held his breath. Was the old man suggesting an alliance with the same people he'd declared enemies that must be annihilated? "Khan—?"

"No!" The Khan shook his head. "We are the sword. We are the light."

"Then you wish for me to continue with the plan?"

The old man opened his mouth, jerked his head around to stare into the dark, then turned back, breathing rapidly. "What?"

"Should I have my captains set out the traps I described?"

"What of my glorious fighter aircraft and the holy pilots?"

"There is a role for them, my Khan."

"The role was to be foremost in the fleet, striking terror into the hearts of those who have wronged us in the past!"

"We achieve that." Satrap wondered where the notion of terror on the battlefield came from for this Khan. Once weapons capable of vaporizing a hull and killing the entire crew fired, there was nothing but terror among all involved. "The missiles are merely the beginning. Once they've launched, the enemy finds itself quickly overwhelmed."

"Yes. Yes, that is good." The Khan glanced down at the blood dripping down the back of his hand and licked the dark fluid away. "Good."

"If you approve, Khan...?"

"What?" The old man looked up, lips smeared red. "Approve?"

"This strategy—these tactics we discussed. If you approve of them, perhaps a message to my captains to remind them that our goal is the protection of Azh Shivan from this...enemy would be in order?"

"Oh. Yes. To curtail ambition and focus it on the enemy."

"For the glory of our people and our Glorious and Mighty Khan."

A bloody smile spread over the old man's face. "Yes. Such a suggestion is well received. I will record messages for each one now."

"Thank you, my Khan."

The old man blinked. "Perhaps I am now seeing the wisdom in grooming you for this role, Satrap."

Satrap winced, but the old man didn't seem to notice.

The connection ended, and Zohar cleared his throat. "A strategy well designed and implemented, Satrap."

Admiration or at least acknowledgment shone in the captain's eyes.

Then he, too, disconnected.

Ikhama rose with a groan. "Soon, I must have my systems repaired so that I can again be the eyes and ears of our Khan."

"Soon." Satrap couldn't be sure, but the look on her face bordered on conspiratorial.

She paused at the hatch. "Helena is a beautiful name."

When the hatch closed, and Satrap was alone again, he let the weight of those words sink in. Who had ever known about the young girl he had sworn he would one day make his own? With dusky features and sea-green eyes, she had been a beauty in physical and spiritual form.

Why had he dreamed of her now after so many years of pushing her aside?

It was death—the proximity and inevitability of it.

After seeing so clearly the madness in the Khan, leading his war against the Kedraalians felt more wrong than ever. What if everything went as planned? Satrap merely delayed his death.

To what end?

And the life he had? A life where he could only summon up childhood dreams but not remember them? A life where he fought against the dark designs of the man who had snuffed out childhood innocence simply to survive in a different form of pain?

All of it was for the single purpose of spreading the madness and poison of his people.

Did extending life justify such an outcome?

Perhaps not. But Satrap wasn't ready to surrender his life just yet.

He had always relied upon data to guide him. Now there was a new enemy—these desert spirits. Data about the threat must exist in the old computers on the planet he was still speeding towards. That data might unlock greater secrets and possibly the means to his own survival, maybe even freedom.

And Satrap knew of ways to touch those computers.

## 24

From the start, Faulk had known the Kedraalians were outclassed. They might have come to Azoren space acting from a position of strength, but it had all been an illusion. Newer ships loaded with fancy technology couldn't hope to replace superior minds.

And no one had a mind to match the Azoren field marshal!

What more proof did he need than seeing through the Kedraalian attempt to assassinate him? His commandos had the outnumbered enemy pinned down and now it was merely a matter of time. And when the assassins fell, the flagship *Valor* would be next!

Bullets cracked ineffectually against the hatch frame and the bulkhead behind his tight-packed soldiers.

Even accuracy escaped the fools!

He gripped his pistol tighter and looked to his officers. They were as ready as him to end this farce.

Gunpowder stung his nose, and the roar of gunfire filled his ears.

This was war. The belly-crawling enemy in the hangar bay—many of them traitorous Azoren—would all be killed.

Faulk raised his pistol. "Charge!"

It was glorious leading the commandos through the hatchway, like battling the Moskav animals. Only here, there was nowhere to hide, no place for bombs and booby traps.

His superior commandos would win out—!

Something sailed over his head, into the thick of his unit.

Then another.

Grenades!

What fool would use a grenade aboard a starship?

No matter. For the moment, he dropped and skidded across the deck.

But when the explosion came, the impact was worse than he'd expected.

Pain spiked through Faulk's skull, but it was only pain. His body was unharmed by shrapnel.

He got to his feet unsteadily and squeezed his eyelids until something approaching focus resolved from the blur.

The enemy were in pockets, hiding behind rolling toolboxes and shuttles. They were crouched low. Only a few looked wounded.

Why hadn't he thought of something that could hurt them?

Wait. He had. He'd opened the hangar bay to vacuum. This battle was still his to win.

Faulk staggered forward, shouting encouragement no one could hear. His own body only picked up the sensation of noise being generated by his throat.

Here and there, commandos rose. Others who hadn't been affected by the weapons rushed over their dead comrades.

But there was nowhere to rush to, Faulk realized.

It was a slow, stupid thought that took a while to sink in.

The enemy had the cover now, not him. His superior numbers had been counteracted with grenades thrown into the chokepoint. And he didn't need to hear gunfire or see the muzzle flashes to know that the enemy had seized the advantage and turned the tables on his assault.

No sooner did the healthy rise and advance than they were mowed down. When they reached the enemy, it was in ones and twos, and they were readily met with knives or brained with brutal rifle strokes.

Why didn't this enemy fear the commandos? These were the dreaded Silver Wolf elite soldiers!

Faulk advanced, finally able to bring his pistol up.

Three of his commandos rushed past, then fell, twitching.

Two more who had reached a pair of enemy soldiers wrestled them to the ground, their arms a blur of slashes, blocks, and jabs.

Then one of those commandos rolled off of his target, clutching a ruined throat, and his killer finished off the other commando.

Faulk shot the killer. Then he shot again. Then again.

The enemy fell onto her back, bloodied.

There! See? Fear the Azoren! This is the deadliest force in the galaxy!

He twisted around to wave more of his soldiers forward, but none moved. Blood pooled on the deck, and if he concentrated, the reason became clear: bullet holes perforated the fallen.

How many remained?

A desperate search located pockets here and there, many holding positions of cover they'd taken from the assassins, others still involved in close-quarters combat.

Why? Why go to knives and fists?

Again, it took a moment for him to put it together: Many of his soldiers had been drawn past enemy positions. If either side fired, they risked hitting allies.

He shook off the last of the malaise. It was time to call in the rest of his commandos. Leave Hart's people without guards.

In a moment.

For now, his pistol made it easier for him to continue selective attacks, but there simply weren't that many available targets. Bodies were tangled on the deck or in tight melee.

Faulk risked a shot to help one of his officers, but the man shifted at the last moment, and the bullet clipped his shoulder.

In battle, no one cares about the reason for an advantage—it's seized.

And in the next instant, the enemy Faulk had fired at had the wounded officer in an arm lock that drew a high-pitched scream.

Then the officer was on the deck, rolling and moaning, clutching at his ruined arm.

His opponent searched around, then locked onto Faulk.

It was a strange sight: a shorter person with almost feminine hips. But the shoulders, the way it moved—it had to be a man.

Faulk drew a bead on the enemy, which already had a bullet-scarred chest plate, and fired as it advanced.

He missed, then missed again, then finally hit the helmet.

The shorter person fell back.

Once again, proof of the superior—

Instead of twitching and bleeding out, the enemy fighter sat up and wrenched off its helmet, tossing it aside. The visor was splintered and white where the bullet had struck.

But it was the revealed head that grabbed Faulk's attention. The hair was a sweat-matted dark brown—longer and thicker than a man's. And the face was feminine, in some ways attractive.

Then the woman snarled and rolled back onto her feet. "If you're gonna shoot, you'll have to aim better than that."

Faulk snorted. He'd hit the woman in the head!

And he would do so again.

He fired, but the round glanced off her armored chest.

She rushed at him then, darting left and right, left shoulder forward.

There was time for one more shot, again aimed at her head.

He squeezed off a round and—

Impossible! He should have hit her!

But he'd missed, and now she had the pistol by the barrel, twisted away with surprising strength.

Faulk released his grip before she could snap his finger, then kicked at her forward leg.

She bent the leg to the side, losing her balance but sparing her knee.

Too late, he realized she'd intended the move all along, at the same time as grabbing his pistol. Perhaps it was even a trained maneuver, although it seemed inefficient and risky.

Then she rolled up onto the leg he'd kicked with, locked an arm around the calf, and drove her own knee into the side of his knee joint.

His weight was on that knee. His balance was off, because he hadn't expected the maneuver.

Now white-hot pain shot through the muscles and ligaments.

He went to the floor with her.

Even with the pain, it was a stupid move. In fact, attacking him in close combat was stupid. He was bigger, stronger.

He wrapped one hand around her chin and pulled it up, then brought the other down to crush her windpipe.

But she somehow managed to block the blow, grabbing his wrist in the process.

Then she grabbed the thumb of the hand that had her by the chin.

Faulk felt the snap of the thumb coming out of its socket. He clenched his jaw tight to avoid screaming, but snot blew from his flaring nostrils.

This woman—

She was *only* a woman, and a Kedraalian at that—some sort of mongrel by the darker skin tone. How could she do what she'd done?

He twisted his uninjured arm free of her grip when he realized she was going for some sort of arm lock like the one that had crippled his officer.

If she wanted to fight using barbaric means, he would claw her eyes—

The hellion refused to sit still.

She wiggled and twisted and ground herself against his groin. Pain built as she pushed his testicles harder against his body.

And while she did that with her shoulders, then ribs, then hips, she maneuvered around—swatting away his hands when he went for the vulnerable points on her face.

Finally, he got his good thumb just under her eye and started to jab into it.

But she had that wrist again, and this time the grip was unbreakable.

Before he could tear free or claw at her, her hand had moved up to his, and she twisted it with a bestial grunt.

*Twisted* it!

His wrist snapped: dislocated.

Now he couldn't stop the screaming. It came out from deep within, almost a shriek.

How strong was this woman?

She answered that by rising up on her hands so she was looking into his face, then driving a knee repeatedly into his testicles.

There were so many dimensions of pain shooting through him now. It was worse than the assassins attacking in the stairwell. At least then, he'd slipped into shock. Here, the pain stayed just below that threshold, and he wasn't bleeding out.

Faulk shuddered. He could barely breathe.

Where were his men? They would come to his rescue, and this hellion —he wouldn't let death come quickly for her.

Now she straddled his wounded knee and pinned him down with her hips and drove a fist into his face, and all thoughts of vengeance disappeared.

Bone snapped, and he tasted blood.

His nose.

He wasn't allowed to dwell on that, because she struck again, and one of his eyes just…stopped working.

This wasn't possible. It wasn't right. He was the field marshal of the Azoren military! He was the chosen one, the one who would finally kill his human master and rise to the throne!

Surrendering was a humiliation Faulk would simply have to deal with. Survival was necessary for the good of the federation, for his brethren.

Faulk sucked in a breath, nearly gagging on the coppery blood.

Before he could speak, the woman dragged him up by the shoulders, twisted his torso, and wrenched his head around at an excruciating angle.

It took a second for the peril to break through all the pain.

She was breaking his neck!

---

Benson was ready to collapse. Now that the *Sinclair* was close enough to capture transmissions, she'd split the command station display into thirds to keep an eye on the rescue, the assassination, and the field of battle.

Things had spiraled out of control so quickly, and now she was sticky with sweat and feeling foul. When possible, she concentrated on Chopra and his crew to catch snippets of their conversations.

It was all bad news.

The Khanate terrorists couldn't possibly have chosen a worse time to strike the Azoren troop transport. Parkinson's theory made perfect sense: This was a dead-man switch.

On the third of the display tracking the transport, the heat was rising.

Those soldiers were being cooked alive.

Inside the *Warsaw*, the battle between Halliwell's Marines and Faulk's Silver Wolf commandos was down to close combat.

That probably favored the Marines, but they were still outnumbered.

And in space, the combined fleet seemed on the edge of disaster as a line of shuttles headed toward the damaged Azoren troop transport.

At least no ships were firing…yet.

She jumped from screen to screen, magnifying to fill the entire display with each press against the playing video.

Trying to keep track of everything at once was more than a human could hope for. If Chopra weren't already overwhelmed, she would delegate to him.

Parkinson requested a connection. It was his drone that was making the rescue operation possible, so she had to accept the request.

"What's up, Will?"

The chief swallowed—a wet sound that told Benson just how bad the nausea was. "I've got Telly in place."

"That's excellent. Captain Thiessen's rerouting his shuttles."

"I don't know how many we can save. They're fighting the fires, but…"

"I know." This was all Faulk's doing. His arrogance, his stubbornness—

"I was scanning their systems—the Azoren. You know, just trying to see what we could learn about how they operate."

"The rescue is our first priority."

"I know; I know." His breathing was ragged. "The thing is, they're vulnerable. I mean *really* vulnerable."

She jumped back to the video of the *Warsaw* hangar bay. "Can you give me an idea what that means?"

"It means I could shut down their weapons systems remotely. Maybe I could do more if I wasn't feeling so crappy."

Benson pushed everything else aside for a moment.

What would it mean to have the *Warsaw*'s weapons shut down? She didn't have the resources to send more people across to help the Marines. The destruction of the *Seattle* had left her shorthanded.

And it had been a gut punch for the Kedraalian task force.

Faulk had to be eliminated. If he survived Halliwell's assault.

But, still…

Benson lowered her voice. "Will, could you get life support to shut off in the *Warsaw?*"

"The entire ship? That'd be easy."

"Could you evacuate the atmosphere in the hangar bays?"

"I think so."

"Work on that. Keep it in your back pocket, okay?"

"Is it looking bad for our people?"

That was the first time Benson could recall hearing the engineer so clearly embrace the idea that they were all one team. It was a huge step forward, but she hated that it had taken something so terrible for it to happen.

She sighed. "It's a close fight."

"I'll work on it. How long before those shuttles arrive?"

"A few minutes."

She hated saying that, when seconds counted saving lives. Her time on the *Pandora* had taught her to value time.

Parkinson mumbled something, then disconnected.

*Work on your little miracles, Chief.*

Benson connected to Thiessen. "Any chance those shuttles could speed up?"

An anxious smile flashed across the Gulmar captain's face. "They're already pushing the limit."

"I know. The temperature keeps going up, and Will says they're fighting the fire."

"Which means the bomb was very targeted. I understand." Thiessen chewed on a knuckle. "I'll tell the pilots to ignore safety precautions."

"Not if it puts them at risk."

"This whole rescue operation puts everyone at risk."

It did. "We can't just let them die."

"I know. But we're stretched as far as we can go, and the best-case scenario is that we're bringing Azoren soldiers aboard my ships. I don't have the crew to handle them if they turn out to be trouble."

"I'll…" *What? What can I do?* "I'll send people over to supplement your security."

Thiessen relaxed a little. "I'd appreciate it."

Benson mouthed a thank you, then disconnected.

The fire was the problem. Whoever had set the bomb had found the perfect place to maximize damage. Maybe it'd been another engineer, like on the *Lyon*. There just wasn't much that could be done when a fire—

Life support. Fire needed oxygen.

She connected back to Parkinson. "Will?"

His face seemed sunken and pale. "I haven't had a chance to figure the *Warsaw*—"

"Could you evacuate the atmosphere on that troop transport?"

"What?"

"We need to kill that fire. It's no good getting the shuttles there if they can't get to the survivors without fire killing them. So, we evacuate the atmosphere just before our rescue teams go in."

"People will suffocate."

"Not as many as would burn to death."

The engineer winced. "I can do that. I can't work on both, though."

"The *Warsaw* can wait." An ache settled into Benson's heart.

She was condemning her Marines to death if she didn't send reinforcements.

No. Halliwell could still succeed. And this was a risk he'd accepted.

And with what Parkinson had discovered, as painful as losing her Marines was, she could still cripple the *Warsaw* and destroy the ship, if necessary. After everything Faulk had done to his own people, it didn't even seem likely there would be pushback from his fellow Children.

The stress of the mission had clearly destroyed whatever last shred of sanity he'd had.

On the split screen showing the dying transport, the first of the shuttles arrived. Rescue teams would be crawling onto the hull to create emergency entry points. If Parkinson couldn't come up with a way to evacuate the atmosphere, those shaped charges were going to do the job, but it would be riskier to the rescuers.

Thiessen connected to her. "We've got teams on the hull."

"I saw that."

"They're in position to set off the first charges. They can't use the portable airlocks if there's a big fire."

"I know. Blow the outer hull." She put him on hold and connected to Parkinson. "Will?"

The engineer's hair was a mess, and his eyes were bleary. "Almost done."

"The rescue teams are making entries at the points you identified."

"Another—" He sagged in his chair. On the command station screen, fire vented from the transport's belly. "Done."

"You're saving lives."

"I get that. It's just…sloppy. I wanted a more refined solution."

"This entire mission has been sloppy."

"Killing always is, isn't it?" His eyes locked with hers; he looked as drained as she felt. "I'm sorry. I don't feel well."

"Get some rest."

Once Parkinson disconnected, she reconnected with Thiessen. "Your teams are a go with the portable airlock. People are going to need oxygen."

Tension eased from the Gulmar captain's posture. "We'll rescue as many as we can."

"And I'll get security to you."

He nodded, then the connection winked out.

Like her, he had too much to manage and too little time to do it properly.

Now came the part that would anger her officers: assigning critical staff to security aboard the Gulmar ships. And it wasn't just the staff. Only gunships were available to transport them. That was only going to add to the confusion in the combined fleet.

She waved Chopra over to her station—his station, really. He straightened his back, whispered to the communications officer, then stiffly approached.

Even her most loyal officer was being stressed.

If something didn't break in their favor soon, the fleet would come apart, and all the lost lives and ruined careers would have been for nothing.

———

Grier had recognized the lunatic Azoren field marshal the second she'd torn her helmet off. She'd hoped for the chance to at least take a shot at the asshole in combat. Getting to mix it up physically?

Hell, yeah!

With the man she'd injured screaming behind her, she advanced on the field marshal.

His pistol roar was almost lost in the jolt of energy that rocked her head back and took her legs out from under her. She hit the deck with the back of her head, which stung despite the helmet.

He'd shot her in the face!

It took a second for that to sink in, probably because she'd banged her head.

The bullet had shattered the visor without puncturing it—not a straight-on hit, then.

But she didn't need the helmet now.

She sat up and tore it off, then tossed it aside and sucked in the hangar bay air—thick with gunpowder and death. "If you're gonna shoot, you'll have to aim better than that."

Faulk's eyes widened. His lip curled in a snarl.

He took more shots. They came close—real close.

Okay, so the guy was a good shot, but he was worrying too much about shooting her in the face.

And when she got in tight with him, he was easy to disarm.

In fact, his entire approach to hand-to-hand seemed clumsy, almost backwards, as if he'd never undergone intensive training.

She took his knee out easily, then countered his attacks.

He was a tall man and quick, and he was fairly strong, but she'd trained with Halliwell. This Faulk guy didn't compare.

In seconds, she had dislocated one of his thumbs.

Give the guy credit, he kept fighting. Some people lost it the second they suffered an injury like that. Kneeing him in the nuts didn't stop him, either.

But when she finally snapped his wrist, it was over.

No matter how much he wanted to fight her off, he was too broken.

She pressed herself against his bad leg, then pummeled his face, stunning him. This was always the last of the struggle, the part where some part of the opponent's brain signaled it was time to give up. How many guys had she forced to tap out in sparring sessions?

Except this wasn't sparring.

They'd come here with a simple mission: Kill this Faulk bastard.

So when he blubbered and made a sound that might have been the start of begging for mercy, she dragged him up by the shoulders and maneuvered to get him into a neck lock.

The guy had to be close to shock with all his injuries, but he tensed.

It was easier to snap someone's neck if they weren't resisting. Even with leverage and with all her training and conditioning, the spine and neck muscles could be sturdy.

Grier looked past Faulk, for the first time seeing the entire battlefield.

Across the deck, her comrades were hanging tough. They were still outnumbered, but they obviously had better training. Little pockets of Faulk's men were moving like packs, overwhelming individuals.

She needed to fix that. "Get into groups!"

No one was going to hear her, though. Every battle was small and desperate now.

One of the small packs—two men—turned toward her.

Recognition settled on their faces.

She smiled. "That's right. I've got your boss."

Faulk gasped and flailed weakly, but she was choking him out now. It was only going to be another second or two…

His arms sank limply.

The two commandos sprinted toward her.

With Faulk unconscious, she could drop him and deal with the approaching attackers.

Except the mission was right there: Kill the field marshal.

Snap his neck, and the mission was complete.

She shifted her grip. "You can't take back a completed objective, assholes."

Then she twisted Faulk's head around until she felt the snap of bones.

His commandos slowed for just a second.

That was enough time.

Grier released Faulk's corpse and dove for his pistol.

The commandos came at her again, holding up bloody knives, eyes wide in fury.

She dropped the closest one with two quick shots.

Howling, the final one leapt at her, knife aimed at her face.

With a twist of the torso, she took the point on her armored shoulder. The blade scraped across the rigid surface and gashed her cheek. Salty blood flecked her lip.

But she had her forearm inside his knife arm...there were so many options.

Grier smashed the flat of her palm into the crook where the throat went into the jaw.

The Azoren commando rocked back, face contorted as he tried to gasp and couldn't. He dropped his knife.

She plucked it from the deck and drove it halfway up to the hilt through his eye.

Before he hit the deck, she had the field marshal's pistol raised and was charging another of the small clumps of Azoren commandos—this time a trio who had backed a Marine and an Azoren technician into a corner.

Grier shot one of the commandos in the leg, then shot another in the face before her Marine jumped on the third and turned the Azoren's knife on him.

She stomped on the wounded Azoren's arm, snapping it, then took his knife.

There were other pockets of fighting around them.

When she handed Faulk's pistol to the Azoren technician, he took it.

"You are quite the killer!" It was Ralf!

She pointed to the closest struggle and waved for the other two to follow. "If you get a clear shot, take it."

Once again, the battle was over in seconds, and she had another Marine—a young, pale woman with spiky hair and a broken nose. She had a nasty cut in the gap between armor plates covering ribs and hips.

Spiky Hair smeared blood from her lip with a gory glove. "Where to, Sergeant?"

There were fewer groups now, and the tide had turned.

Grier pointed to where Halliwell and a small group of Marines were holding a section of wall against a larger group of commandos. "I guess it's time we save our commander."

With a howl, she charged toward Halliwell's position.

**25**

---

S ealed off from the outside world, it was easy to lose track of time. Caville had been trained against anything like that happening.

It started with a strict schedule that he adhered to, no matter what. He woke before what would be dawn at this time of year, cleaned before eating some bland rations, then went to work assembling gear. Every hour on the hour, he stretched, then at noon he went out on a recon.

His movements were cautious, his attention focused on the sounds.

In a place as big as the ancient underground facility, there were always sounds—creaks and pings of the structure settling or adjusting to the world above.

But what he was listening for was the telltale metallic scrape of the sentinel.

*That* was the danger that would get him killed in this cool, subterranean tomb.

Falling for the misleading comfort was how you became one of the dead. Always watching for a glint of metal that was out of place in his lamplight when he played the beam across the ceiling and walls was his only protection.

A few days after the Khan's soldiers died breaking in somewhere overhead, winds sometimes blew the stench of their bodies into the deep hallways.

Caville used that as another reminder of the danger and of the press of time.

When he scouted the place, he kept his data pad in his left hand, checking it every few meters to be sure he knew where the nearest doors were. He could get into any room and seal the door before the sentinel reached him…

…if he was fast enough.

And so, he established a routine.

Eighteen days after the Khan's people died breaking in, a distant, deep thump woke Caville.

He checked his data pad: twenty minutes before dawn.

Gallo stirred beside him, pulling her robes on as she rolled off the mat they'd been sharing. "What was that?"

"They're back."

He strode to the shower, which had become their favorite luxury from the crates of loot and rinsed off while his partner paced, lamp pointing to the ceiling, as if she might see through the thick metal floor.

She sighed. "Why? Why come back? If the first team failed, what makes them think this will end any differently?"

"They'll have heavier weapons. There will be more of them."

"But you said this thing is an advanced robot."

"It's more than that." He toweled off. "Even the most advanced weapon system can be defeated. You just have to be willing to throw enough resources at it."

Another distant thump reverberated through the metal skin—louder.

When her light beam dimmed, she squatted next to the mini-reactor that had become their second-favorite piece of loot and pulled another battery from the charging station, then swapped it into a spare lamp device. Once that was on, she put the fading battery into the recharger.

Caville checked his clothes to be sure they'd dried after washing them the night before. The underwear was growing stiff and rough, but the outer clothes were holding up.

He took a battery from the charging station and tested another lamp, then grabbed his assault rifle. "I need to head up."

"What? That thing's going to be on patrol."

"It's going to be prowling the upper area."

"It could be hiding in one of the passageways. If it gets behind you, you won't have a chance."

He held up his data pad. "Look at this." He powered it on and showed her the updates he'd made.

She squinted at the display. "Is this accurate?"

"As accurate as I can make it. Blue lines for hallways; red squares for doors."

"Is this a ramp up?"

"Three." He took the device from her and shifted the view. "And three more on the floor above."

"You've gone up a level?"

"I went all the way to the top to get you, but I didn't map that out. We have to know the layout of this place. There are rooms on the level above with their doors open. I have to figure out why."

Gallo laughed. "Are you crazy?"

"This is what I came here for." It was close enough to the truth.

She waved at the pile of gear he'd been assembling for the last few weeks. "I thought you came here for…whatever that is."

"That's the primary reason, yes. I need to know this place, though. I need to understand what really happened."

"What happ—?" She groaned. "You said everyone who came here died."

"They did."

"What more do you need to know? Dead is pretty final."

He checked the assault weapon. It was intact, the magazine loaded.

That would've been an inefficient but simple way for her to betray him. It would've been easier to club him to death after he slipped off to sleep.

Paranoid thinking was creeping in. She'd proven her loyalty.

He set the weapon down and crossed to the device he'd spent so much time assembling. "You want to know what this is?"

She hugged herself. "Only if it's okay."

"I trust you."

"But do you care about me? If you keep running around out there with that robot stalking you, you'll get killed, then I'll be alone down here."

"I care about you. And I'm only doing what I have to do."

Gallo came closer. "Why can't we just sneak out instead of mapping this place? Those soldiers in the first group had to have come here in vehicles. We could've taken one."

"We will when the time comes."

She scowled, which somehow made her more attractive. "Those guys are going to be inside soon, and that thing's going to kill them. That's the perfect time."

Caville knelt before the big device. "I can't go until this is ready."

Lights came on along the front of it, revealing a small display and several panels with buttons and switches.

The former Khanate spy leaned close enough that he could smell her breath. "Are those physical buttons?"

"They have to be."

"I didn't even know devices still had knobs and buttons."

"This isn't a computer or simple entertainment gadget. Those physical components are safeguards."

"Safeguards? For—?"

A series of quick, barely detectable rumbles ran through the floor.

He craned his neck and listened, imagining he heard gunfire.

The first team from the new force had been sent down to probe the structure the Khan's people called the Place of the Fallen, and they had apparently been introduced to its guardian.

How long before the commander aboveground sent another team in to check on the first?

What would they find?

Not much, according to everything Caville had read about the sentinels. They were expert hunters, and whatever technology survived on the dead would be...

That part was hazy.

As far as researchers had been able to tell, technology was repurposed in one way or another. Sometimes damaged parts were replaced. At least one theory promoted the idea that new capabilities were added.

If there were a limit or a specific direction, not enough observational data existed for conjecture.

He pushed a panel, and a physical keypad slid out. That keypad was the only way to enter the commands necessary to finish his mission.

For now, he typed in a code.

A new image filled the display.

Gallo pressed against him. "What's this?"

"A bomb." He traced his fingertip along the lines that connected the different components, then pointed to each physical component he'd assembled. After a second, he pointed to an empty chamber at the bottom of the device. "Or at least it will be, once I find what goes there."

"That hole? It looks like a cabinet."

"That *cabinet* has some pretty critical components connected to it. But it's what goes in there that makes all of this into a bomb."

"What—uranium?"

"Antimatter. Several grams."

Gallo's head rocked back. "Antimatter?"

"The research teams that came here long ago figured enough of this place out before they died to know what it isn't. This isn't some temple from an ancient species or whatever it is your Khan—"

"I keep telling you, he's not my Khan. These aren't my people." She was emphatic about that.

"That doesn't change anything. This is an alien outpost. We harvested technology from it, but that technology's dangerous."

"And now you don't want anyone else to have it. You told me."

"It's too late for that. Strategically, we've been sharing bits of it."

"You gave up a competitive advantage. Now you want to blow it up?"

"To stop our enemies from poking around on their own. Every time someone comes into contact with what these aliens left behind, we run the risk of something going very wrong."

"But...antimatter? That's a bit much."

"It's just to fuel a nuclear bomb."

"Oh, that's so much better."

"It won't destroy the whole planet. People will be able to come back here once things settle back down. But I need the antimatter first."

"And you don't know where this antimatter is?"

"The team that got all this gear into here went off the grid before confirming they had everything in place."

"That thing could've gotten to it."

"I wouldn't be here if it had. Neither would your Khan."

Gallo brushed the front of her robes. "My ankle's almost healed. It barely hurts when I walk."

"You're not going with me. I can't risk you."

"But you can risk yourself?"

He powered the bomb back off, taking his time with each step. "I never expected to leave here. Now I'm planning on it."

Her eyes widened when she realized what he meant. "You'll take me back?"

"You can't stay here."

"I wouldn't want to."

Caville took his lamp back to where his assault rifle leaned against the wall. "Then let your ankle heal. When the time comes, I'm going to need you at your best."

He let himself into the hallway, listened, then quietly headed for the nearest ramp.

The sentinel was above him somewhere, hopefully focused on their common enemy.

Otherwise, this excursion might be the last.

---

In the quiet of Devanshi Patel's executive suite, Stiles checked her weapon. She had two more magazines, then she would have to switch to the weapons taken off the security guards or rely exclusively on getting in close. At that moment, she didn't like her odds in a drawn-out melee.

McLeod hunched over the desktop terminal, apparently ignoring the old woman's perfume, which was bonded to the seat. Sweat beaded on his forehead despite the almost frigid air conditioning, the one thing Stiles hadn't turned off. "Not much longer."

She paced the spacious office as she pulled her data device out and activated the security camera feeds.

Lights flickered in the distant sky—this time not lightning.

She counted: four distinct sets of lights, so four cars.

Upwards of twenty-five people, rounded up to thirty, if she wanted to be pessimistic.

This was one of the most powerful and dirty business executives alive. Stiles *had* to be pessimistic.

The numbers were too big.

She put the device away. "I need to head to the roof."

"The roof? What about—?"

"Everyone other than us is dead, Colonel. You're safe. Keep the data extract going."

He nodded, but he didn't seem to relax.

She rolled her shoulders. "I shouldn't be long."

Realistically, she couldn't be. Devanshi and her killers would be on-site in minutes.

After a quick stop on the bottom floor to visit the building maintenance office, Stiles headed for the rooftop.

In her hands were bundled a cable cutter, drill and bits, a squeeze tube of adhesive, and another of silicone lubricant and application cloth, a tarp, and some heavy cable.

Everything else that she needed was already on the roof.

The rooftop could handle two air cars easily. At least one would set down up there, probably two. The others would come in the way the alerted security teams had: one group through each bottom floor entry.

She hurried over to the air conditioning unit. It was a big beast, designed to handle the load of a huge building that turned into an oven each day in the planet's brutal heat.

What she needed first was the metal paneling covering one side of the main unit. She had a drill and bits for that, removing the screws as quickly as she could.

Those panels were laid out in front of the door to the stairs, then covered with a light tarp, which she glued down.

The distant lights were closer now.

Stiles lifted the tarp corner and twisted the leads of a cable through one of the panel screw holes, then covered it back up.

She played out the cabling, running it around loosely rather than straight to the air conditioner.

McLeod wasn't going to like what she did next.

Stiles pulled out her data pad and powered the air conditioner off, then shot the rugged pipe where the power line ran into the air conditioning unit.

She kicked until the cable housing cracked, then snipped the cables. After that, she hooked the exposed cover wire of the heavy cable and lowered it toward the exposed power line, promising herself that she was just imagining the sound of humming and the threat of electricity in the air.

A couple centimeters up from the power line, she dropped the hooked lead and backed up.

Then she powered the air conditioner back on.

For a second, the smell of heated insulation was thick and sharp, then the wind carried it away.

It wasn't ideal, but it was something.

Stiles powered the unit back off and jogged around the opening to the stairs, where she hopped onto the steps partway down. She crept a few steps shy of the entry and applied the silicone liberally.

Outside, the approaching air cars gave off a high-pitched shriek.

She had to leave the door open. Anyway, it would look like she'd come in that way.

With the air conditioner offline, the hot night air filled the stairwell.

Equilibrium. Everything would tend toward balancing when it could.

Before heading back down, she powered the air conditioner circuit back on.

One benefit of Devanshi's office being so large and prominent was that the hallway outside had a clear view of the elevator and the stairwell. Those were the only entry points.

The downside was obvious: the potential for concentrated fire from both areas.

Stiles ran back to Devanshi's office door.

McLeod's head came up, and he pointed a pistol at her before lowering it. "The air conditioner's out."

"I know. Sorry."

He licked his lips. "I don't really need to watch over this."

"And I don't need you out here, sir."

"If they get through you, I'm dead anyway."

"If they get through me, I won't be worrying about you, unlike what would happen if you were out there with me."

The colonel winced, then pointed at the terminal. "I'll stay on it."

Stiles dragged furniture out to where she had a clear line of sight. There were dirt-filled planters with real plants in the hallway. She pushed those in front of the furniture.

Then she waited, pistol in hand.

It didn't take long. The fans of the landing air cars sent hot air swirling into the stairwell, rattling the door in its frame.

The rooftop team would be first. Their objective would be to secure the office.

But the other teams wouldn't be far behind.

She focused on the stairwell door.

Seconds dragged on.

They turned into a minute.

Would they wait and coordinate? That seemed—

A loud thump came from the stairwell, then another.

Softer impacts followed.

She smiled: The heavy noises were people slipping on the silicone; the softer noises were teammates jumping past the threat.

At least two were down.

The door burst open, and two forms flashed out of the opening, weapons raised.

Stiles fired immediately, dropping both.

More forms rushed out, these firing in her general direction.

She dropped to the carpeted floor and settled for low shots: shins, thighs, the crease between groin and leg.

Five were down now.

There was a pause as the wounded writhed.

Stile swapped in a fresh magazine and turned toward the elevator door. It had opened silently, without a flash of light.

She'd expected that.

Three people rushed out, heads turning rapidly.

Instead of actively searching for a target, you let your eyes pick out anything odd: movement, shapes that were out of place.

Her little fortress caught their attention, and the three of them opened fire.

Automatic weapons chewed through the plants and the piled furniture.

Stiles rolled away, taking cover against the far wall for a second. One of the team would rush wide to get a look—and draw her attention— while the others more cautiously came to the corner.

When the obvious target bolted out wide, she held fire, waiting until the head and shoulders of one of the other two poked around the corner.

She put a bullet in between that person's eyes, then scrambled back and around the next corner.

Only two remained in the first wave.

An experienced coordinator would call them back, but this team was desperate. The person who paid their bills was probably calling all the shots.

They would keep coming. In fact, the second team was probably already incoming.

Something rustled: one of the plant leaves.

Stiles glanced over her shoulder: The two would be coming from opposite sides.

She put her gun away and strained to listen, catching the whisper of booted feet on carpet.

Close.

Now!

Aching muscles launched her into a tight tuck as she flipped over the gunman just as he swung around the corner.

Stiles kicked out, knocking the man against the wall and sending herself against the opposite wall.

The difference was that she was ready for the impact.

While she slid down, her opponent bounced off with a grunt.

She got to her feet and lunged at him as he brought his gun up.

He made the mistake of trying to fight for control of the weapon, allowing her to wrap her legs around his hips and twist him to the ground.

Once again, he made a mistake—this time trying to control his fall.

Stiles let go of his gun and punched him in the face, then punched again, and again.

He went limp just as his partner came around the corner.

The instant of delay caused by seeing a partner battered by someone who had already killed several comrades was just enough for Stiles to draw her pistol and shoot.

But the gunman fired a burst as he fell.

A bullet grazed her thigh, and another punched through the flesh above her hip.

Pain jolted her.

That was good. Pain meant she was alive and awake.

The last gunman fell.

She took a knife from the man she'd beaten unconscious and cut cloth from his outfit: black latex that did a pretty good job resisting the blade.

Armor. Not bulletproof, but it was still armor.

After wrapping her wounds, she kicked the unconscious man in the face and took his weapon.

It was biometric-keyed: useless to her without time to hack the system.

But she had his knife.

She pulled out her data pad, activated the security cameras, and staggered back into the office, where McLeod had his pistol raised.

He swallowed at the sight of her and lowered the weapon. "The download's complete. I've already started the transfer back to Kedraal."

"We need to find a better position—" She froze.

On the security cameras, the roof was clear other than three still forms near the door. In the parking lot, one of the air cars was lifting off.

The colonel stepped closer. "What is it?"

She showed him. "They're giving up."

He laughed. "She knows I've got the data. It's over."

Stiles hobbled for the door. "I need to finish this."

McLeod grabbed her arm. "Whoa! Wait! Devanshi's right. It *is* over."

"But she'll just start—"

"Let her go. She's finished. With this data available to the Kedraalian government, she's as good as dead."

"Only real death can stop her, Colonel." Stiles swayed but caught herself.

He wrapped an arm around her. "Settle down, Lieutenant. Her business is ruined."

"But she has money."

"Some, certainly. It won't save her. All the influence and power she's used to? That's gone, and she'll never get it back."

"Then where—?"

"That's a good question." He hooked Stiles's arm around his neck. "The places she can still find safety and possibly exert influence—there aren't really any to speak of. Safety…I guess she could call in some favors."

Stiles wanted to argue the point, to challenge the idea that anything short of killing the matriarch of the Patel family was surrender.

But Stiles herself had just recently been close to death, and now the blood loss had left her feeling as weak as a newborn.

McLeod picked her up. "After all you've been through, I'm not letting anything more happen to you."

She nodded. "I appreciate that, Colonel."

"I think it's time we hide for a bit, while I call in some reinforcements. When I'm sure we're safe, we've got a nice, long trip back to Kedraal."

"I'll be on my feet in no time."

"I don't think so. You've earned a rest."

**26**

———

Benson couldn't remember a time where flying in a shuttle felt so vulnerable and ripe with danger. After reaching agreement for negotiations with the senior Azoren staff, she'd accepted a single volunteer pilot—the Marine Captain Patanga—to carry her and Thiessen to the *Warsaw*.

Now the three of them were hurtling through space, a lone, little craft moving among giants capable of blasting them to pieces.

Even with the display turned off, she couldn't forget that she was protected from hard vacuum by a relatively thin hull.

Of course, there was more than that: diplomacy and decency were at play.

That almost made her snort, but she sucked in the cold recycled air and squeezed the padded armrest until her fingers ached.

One small spacecraft, the lights low, her, a pilot known for his fearlessness, and the Gulmar captain she had fallen for, all wrapped in anticipation-laden silence.

Thiessen patted her hand. He smelled clean and bright. "It'll be fine."

She pressed her back against the seat and told herself to relax. The freshly printed uniform scraped against her flesh. "Rationally, that makes sense."

"But you can't convince yourself to let it go."

"Not even a little."

"We've got nearly two hundred of their soldiers under our medical care."

"And we killed their field marshal and who knows how many of their commandos."

Thiessen balled his hand into a fist to lean his chin against. "I think it's fair to say those were the big problem, weren't they?"

"They're still Azoren. He was their commander."

"I think Hart was their commander."

She powered the display on again and squinted at the nearing *Warsaw*. "Do you think I was wrong to have our ships keep sensors offline?"

"It shows confidence. And I'm sure these commanders know it would only take a few seconds to have those sensors back on and to turn their ships into slag."

"You took sensor reads before everything shut down?"

"All in the cache. Really, it's a matter of seconds."

"Alexander demanded the same. Dinesh backed him."

"They're just as vulnerable as we are—even worse. They've sent their most senior officers to the *Warsaw* for the meeting. You have three people on your staff who could step into your shoes."

She glared at him, then frowned.

It was true. From years in space alone, she was junior to half her captains.

The shuttle dipped below the Azoren flagship, which had opened its hangar bay.

A minute later, they were on the deck, waiting for the atmosphere to cycle back in.

Their escort consisted of a sharp-looking young lieutenant and a handful of navy crewmen, all in the Azoren Navy blue. They looked uncomfortable with the weapons on their hips.

It was hard for Benson to get used to seeing nothing but men in uniform.

The architect behind the Children wasn't just a racial purity lunatic but someone who couldn't appreciate how meaningless it was to see differences when looking at the sexes. Women might on average be smaller and weaker than men, but aboard a ship? A button activated weapons systems exactly the same, whether it was a male or female finger pushing.

Not understanding that basic concept went back to the part where Supreme Leader Graf was a lunatic, she supposed.

Four commanders rose when she and Thiessen entered the small conference room. The Azoren officers didn't look quite as sharp as Hart had. They had the same sort of pushed-to-the-limit haggardness about them, though—something that extended to the musty odor of uniforms gone too long without cleaning.

Still, they looked better than Faulk had: shaven, pressed uniforms.

Some people held to the belief that those were what won wars, after all.

She tugged on the hem of her jacket and took the seat offered to her— the head of the table.

That was a good sign.

So was them putting Thiessen to her right.

It really was looking like they weren't going to murder the people who'd killed their field marshal.

Benson glanced around the room: small, with scuffed paint, hot and stuffy.

This was the pride of their fleet, and it had the same worn and tired aspect as the officers.

Where the Kedraalian military was on constant alert and readying to defend itself, the Azoren had been at war nonstop. Fatigue was in their eyes, their clothes, and their gear.

These people looked ready for something different, maybe nothing more than a respite.

She clasped her hands in front of her. "Thank you so much for making the time for this meeting so soon after our situation was resolved."

Nods; a quick smile come and gone; a look of relief…

But there were no winces or angry tightening of the face muscles. In fact, they leaned in a bit, as if encouraged.

Faulk had truly been seen as the root of all their troubles—an unhinged despot more concerned with advancing his career than helping the Azoren toward their twisted goals.

Maybe in net, that was a good thing. It certainly was at the moment.

One of the commanders—an older man with thinning dark blond hair and a cleft chin—leaned forward. "Captain Benson, we hoped you might have an update about our next move."

It was a strange thing to ask of another nation's officer after what had just happened, but it was also a good indicator that they weren't conspiring.

She smiled at the man. "Commander Terboven—is that right?"

The man had smiled earlier and did so again, this time revealing a gap between his top incisors. "Yes, thank you, Captain."

"I think our priority is conducting the search for Khanate terrorists that was refused previously."

"This has begun, Captain." Terboven straightened his back.

"Excellent. When that's done, we need to coordinate with you to effect repairs on your ships. My engineers are stretched thin at the moment, but I know some of your vessels are still behind on addressing maintenance."

The four Azoren officers muttered agreement, but they looked away when doing so.

It must have been a blow to their pride having their effectiveness brought up.

She needed to give them something, to do repairs of her own. "Once you're where you feel you're space-worthy again, the next step is figuring out your destination."

Another of the officers raised his thick eyebrows. He had thin lips and a nose that could kindly be described as "strong."

This was Brummel—Hart's most senior commander. The man would now be captaining the *Warsaw*.

His eyelids narrowed over dull blue eyes. "Our...destination?"

"Well, we'd like you to accompany us on our attack against the Khanate fleet, but..." She glanced at Thiessen.

The Gulmar captain nodded. "You *have* just lost your operational commander."

Brummel's brows raised again. "Ah."

The four Azoren officers exchanged looks for a moment, then Brummel squared his shoulders. "Field Marshal Faulk's death provides a complication for us."

"We thought it might."

"If we return to Himmel following his...death, then we signal that we have surrendered. It is the Azoren way to continue the fight and to rise to the challenge. Surrender is...suicide."

"I understand. So, our next step is to locate the Khanate fleet."

That seemed to assuage the Azoren officers' fears, because they once again leaned in enthusiastically.

Benson's gut said they were operating out of self-preservation as much as a hatred for or fear of the Khanate. At this point in the war, she was willing to use any motivation.

She ran a finger along the inside of her coat cuffs. "I'm not sure how many of you were aware that Captain Hart gave me access to your Fold Space Detection Network?"

A couple of them nodded.

"Yes, well, our people have used that to test out the theory that we could track large fleet movement through Fold Space, even beyond the assumed limit of the sensors. We think we've found proof that this works."

The Azoren officers seemed genuinely surprised.

Brummel raised a hand. "You are saying that you have located the Khanate fleet?"

"Well, no. There's no way for us to *know* that. What we did find was five different indications in the records of large fleet movements in the network. Two of those were ours. One was the Khanate fleet just before we engaged it. I'm assuming the other two were Khanate movements after that."

"I see. And where would this put them?"

When Benson glanced at Thiessen, he gave a slight nod: She had their attention. More importantly, she had their buy-in.

"We believe they're on their way back to Khanate space."

Brummel and his fellow officers leaned in to whisper to each other.

This was the tricky part. Pursuing the Khanate ships closer to Azoren space—maybe into Gulmar space, as she'd expected—would have been more palatable. Instead, she was asking the battered Azoren task force to follow her out to Khanate space.

And it wasn't just the distance. There was always a chance this was an ambush. If the Khanate military had more ships that they didn't feel safe allocating to the fleet when it left their space, those ships could still be deployed defensively.

When Brummel turned back to her, she went to the one piece of information she felt she could disclose. "There is one other thing."

The Azoren commander's mouth hung open for a second, then he closed it and nodded at her.

She had to get this right. "We believe we have a way to cripple the Khanate fighter threat."

A smile crept across Brummel's face. "Then we should depart as quickly as we can, Captain."

---

It took a minute and a glare from Halliwell for Grier to realize that she was mimicking Benson.

Not in voice—Grier was listening intently, which meant no talking. But she had adapted the captain's posture. Grier now sat stiffly, erectly, with her legs closed rather than spread wide. She kept her eyes locked on one thing—the presenter—and blocked out the comfort of the conference room.

There were no dead bodies here, spilling out blood or emptying their bladders on the white surfaces. And there were no screams of the wounded and dying, either.

It was just three people, with Benson's steady voice guiding them.

Grier took a sip of water. Maybe her subconscious felt that sweet, cold refreshment would wash away the memories of the hangar bay fight.

Or maybe she needed distraction from Halliwell's gaze.

A part of her resented the unspoken scolding. Benson looked professional, didn't she? Crisp white uniform instead of their battle dress, bright face framed by shiny hair, darting eyes that connected when she looked at you.

But Grier remembered how Halliwell felt.

If she wanted to avoid fights with him, she needed to respect the pain that remained over his breakup with the captain. That was like a live wire, and brushing against it was unpleasant as hell.

Grier relaxed, slumping just a little, and letting her knees drift apart.

Somehow, that made the listening—the actual hearing part—a little easier.

Benson was still talking about the big problem: what to do with the Azoren. The combined fleet was about to come out of Fold Space, right into the Khanate system. They would be hours out from the capital world of Azh Shivan.

This would be the battle to end the Khanate threat.

And the captain was right: The Azoren were a huge unknown once that battle was over.

They'd fought alongside the Marines, but that was really just self-preservation, wasn't it? Would they flip back to being murderous racists when that was over?

Halliwell pressed a palm against the conference room tabletop. It wasn't a slap or a hammered fist but a soft press.

Good. He had his temper under control. Sort of.

He shook his head. "If you really think they're a threat, we should've blown them apart when we had the chance."

The captain pulled her cup of water closer. "We still have the chance."

"You mean hit them when we jump out of Fold Space?"

"That's an option, too."

"But it's not what you want to do."

Benson clasped her hands. "They're a resource at this point. I don't think it's a good idea to waste resources, especially when we don't really know the enemy fleet composition right now."

"You're going to know in a few minutes. You might want to come up with some contingencies."

"I have. And I think our best approach is to use the Azoren in a way that serves everyone's needs."

Halliwell's hand drifted to his chest, where the piece of shrapnel that had nearly killed him dangled. He always massaged that when he became stressed, like it was a good luck charm.

There wasn't much luck there, as far as Grier was concerned. He carried that survivor's guilt like a two-ton boulder.

He settled for pinching his bottom lip. "You want them to take the capital."

"It gets them out of our hair, and it draws part of the fleet's attention."

"Meaning they take the brunt of the attack."

"Maybe. After talking with Chief Parkinson, that might not be true."

Grier realized too late that her jaw had dropped.

The captain arched an eyebrow. "You have something, Sergeant?"

"Oh. Well. Um. Nothing, I guess. It's the way he looks. I think that radiation sickness's tearing him up pretty bad."

Benson's eyes dropped to her water cup. "We're doing everything we can."

"Maybe he could go into cold sleep?"

"He refused that. And we're out of berths at the moment."

Rather than respond, Halliwell looked away. More than half of their Marine comrades were waiting for a shot at revivification. The rest were walking wounded like her or still fighting for their lives in infirmaries. Maybe Dietrich's people could do some revivifications themselves, but it wouldn't be today.

That dry, hungry urge to settle down with a bottle of booze hit Grier again. In the past, that was how she'd handled so many losses.

Mourn the dead; celebrate the living—that had been the Marine way.

But she was off the booze and free from the partying now. Instead, she carried that pain with her.

It was her own two-ton boulder.

She swallowed. "If this is something the chief's cooking up, are you sure you can count on it? When I'm sick like he is, I don't think so straight."

Benson curled her long fingers around the water cup, cradling it. "We don't have a choice. We'll need him to pull this off."

But the wrinkles on her brow, and the way her eyes looked watery…

This wasn't her choice. She was just as desperate as anyone else, Grier realized.

That familiar sense of distortion—like time got all dilated and you weren't you but a string of you from across a bunch of seconds, looking at the same frozen point in time—punched Grier in the gut.

"We just exited Fold Space." She couldn't help stating the obvious.

Benson clenched her jaw, then looked at Halliwell. "I know you're down to almost nothing, but I need you involved to make this work."

He pushed his shoulders back. "You want me to lead a team down."

"The Azoren have to see that we're invested in this."

"I can get twenty-one Marines in combat gear, but it means stripping every ship bare."

The captain shook her head. "That's too many. It's just a show of support. You won't even touch down on the surface."

"We're just waving guns around and giving rah-rah speeches?"

"This is diplomacy."

"It's misdirection."

"They're the same thing. I want to hold Sergeant Grier and the others in reserve."

Grier took another drink. This was pushing Halliwell. It was pushing him *hard*.

Before he could respond, Benson's data pad chimed.

She tapped the screen, revealing the face of her XO, Commander Chopra. "What is it, Dinesh?"

"Not good, Captain. The Fold Space exit went well—no losses. But the enemy has once again done their mining. We have detected twenty or more objects where the odds are unlikely naturally occurring objects would be."

"Did you try Chief Parkinson's attacks to shut down missiles?"

"We have."

"Self-destruct?"

"Unfortunately, none of these attacks seem to work."

Grier had to fight back the urge to point out she'd been right. Parkinson was a brilliant guy, and before falling for Chief Taylor, he'd been just as much of a jerk. That had been proof right there that he was human. This failure was further proof.

You can't outsmart a failing body.

Benson massaged her temple. "How long before those missiles detect us?"

Chopra cleared his throat. "It would appear one already has. We've detected movement."

"So, they all have."

"Soon, yes. It hasn't radioed or otherwise signaled yet."

"They're probably designed to detect the movement of other missiles." Benson frowned. "Thank you, Dinesh. We'll need to be ready to go to battle stations."

"I was awaiting your confirmation."

An amber light flashed in the conference room.

The captain smiled weakly. "Keep me informed."

She disconnected, then tapped the display a couple times.

A moment later, Parkinson's pale, gaunt face appeared. He'd shaved the ridiculous little soul patch beneath his cracked lips. His breathing was deep, and his skin was damp, as if he'd just washed his face. "I saw the lights go on after the Fold Space exit."

Color drained from Benson's face. Maybe she hadn't expected him to look so bad, or maybe the reminder of his condition hit hard. "Something's gone wrong, Will."

"It always does." The engineer sighed. "They detected us?"

"One of the missiles is moving toward us. It's not responding to shutdown or self-destruct signals."

Parkinson toweled his face off. "So they've patched up their systems, or they did an upgrade. We can still take out their antenna arrays. That's the blunt-weapon method."

"On their control ship?"

"Yeah. That's going to flood their network with failure messages. I can attack their systems during the confusion."

"Are you sure?"

That old spark of resentment at being challenged flashed in his eyes, then was gone. "They couldn't have changed their entire network infrastructure—not this fast. It took me weeks to upgrade the Gulmar systems."

"You're sure of this?"

"Positive."

"Thank you, Will."

"I'll suit up."

Benson bit her bottom lip. "All right." She disconnected, then focused on Halliwell. "I'm going to need two teams."

"Of my Marines?"

"Yes."

"On top of the force going down to the planet?"

"You heard the chief. They've modified their systems. We'll need to take out the antenna arrays on the control ship if we hope to cripple their fighters."

Grier almost dropped her water cup while raising her hand. "I'll lead them."

Halliwell twisted around, glaring at her with more heat than before. "With me out, you need to—"

Benson bowed her head. "No. She's the best choice."

"I thought you said we had their systems figured out." Halliwell sounded like a petulant little boy arguing after getting caught breaking curfew. All that was missing was his bottom lip jutting out.

"If we can't disable or destroy those missiles, then they've changed something. All of our planning and strategizing was built around crippling the enemy shadow technology."

"Change your strategy. Come up with new tactics."

"It's too late. Will said that we have to flood their systems with errors to get in. Knocking out the fighter control ship will do that. He's been running simulations nonstop."

A lump of fear caught in Grier's throat. She was tired of all this fighting, but she was just as tired of Halliwell's behavior.

She pushed back from the table. "I'll get my people ready, Captain."

Benson sank in on herself a little, as if fighting Halliwell had taken something out of her. "Thank you, Sergeant. If you could help the chief—"

"We'll take him to the hangar."

"Use the stealth shuttles."

"Roger that, ma'am."

Grier spun on her heel sharply and exited the conference room without meeting Halliwell's gaze. There would be a big blowup about her circumventing his authority.

It was a fight for later.

At least she hoped there would be a later.

---

If Parkinson had a regret, it was that he'd never really thought about what it would be like to be old and infirm. As far back as he could remember, he'd always seen a clear path through life where he was eternally healthy, and his mind was as fast and sharp as when he was a teen.

Now, here he was, strapped into a chair aboard a racing stealth shuttle, eyes squeezed shut against the awareness he couldn't manage, trying not to spray bitter, acidic vomit against his visor.

And he hadn't been able to suit up all on his own. He hadn't even been the one to strap the harness into place.

Nausea was a constant twist in the gut that was beating the snot out of him. The only nutrients he could rely on were injected, maybe from sugary drinks, or sometimes from fast-dissolving pills. Shaking made programming a challenge, so he now mostly relied on clumsy dictation.

He cranked up the heat in his environment suit and tried some deep breathing exercises, hoping the anti-nausea meds he'd taken would kick in soon.

That breathing became his focus: ragged, hollow, desperate.

Trapped inside the helmet as he was, his rancid breath became his world.

If he had a good vein to poke, he could've gotten some fluids before they launched, but the nurse couldn't find one fast enough.

It was almost funny for someone who hated needles to actually look forward to having one stuck into him, but the relief that came with a bag of saline and sugar administered was almost orgasmic.

He opened his eyes, despite knowing that the shuttle's interior lights would feel like the midday sun on Kedraal.

Grier was across the aisle, staring right at him through his face plate.

The purpling around her eye and slight scabbing on her cheek simultaneously infuriated him and made him feel like an ass.

Parkinson wasn't a violent man, but if he had a gun and a clean line of sight on the guy who'd injured Grier like that, he wouldn't have hesitated to pull the trigger.

Part of what made him feel that way was the gnawing sense that it wasn't just physical marks left on people that mattered.

Looking at it that way, Parkinson had left plenty of marks of his own.

Psychological wounds was the proper term, he guessed.

His heart ached remembering Greta—Chief Taylor.

He wasn't sure he really knew her well enough to be allowed to remember her as Greta.

He hoped so. The woman had known exactly what it took to put him in his place, and the lesson left him hurting for her. She was as close a kindred spirit and peer as he'd ever known.

A few of the Marines strained against their harnesses to talk to each other privately. It wasn't really loud inside the shuttle if Parkinson opened his visor. There was the soft roar of the engines that he could feel vibrating through the deck and seat and the whisper of the small air recycler.

That was still too much noise for him right then.

So instead of listening in, he watched the big, dangerous people he'd once called brutes as they joked and checked their weapons.

He needed these warriors now, because he'd missed something somewhere in his research.

Or maybe it was because the Khanate forces had incidentally fixed a vulnerability with an upgrade. That kind of thing happened—bad luck for him.

The point was that his pride had taken another hit after failing the captain.

Grier tapped the section of helmet that covered her jaw: She wanted to chat.

He nodded and accepted her connection but couldn't manage a word. She did fine on her own. "You okay?"

"I should be. Soon." Did she see the sweat on his face? How feeble that had to look to her. She'd slaughtered a legion of commandos with her bare hands, and he had to take medicine to keep fluids from leaking out.

"We're coming up on the big cruisers. Just so you know, they've launched fighters after the Azoren ships."

"The ones escorting the troop transports?"

"Yeah. Clive's got a couple gunships carrying his team down to be with those soldiers when they drop. I mean, to fly over."

It sounded like a suicide mission, but Parkinson wasn't about to say that to Grier. He'd never seen anyone as loyal to someone else as she was to the towering Marine commander.

Parkinson waved weakly at the shuttle ceiling. "We've been maneuvering."

"Random fire from the Khanate ships. They know the fleet's out there, but they're not doing a very good job of putting an organized defense up."

"Their captain must be an idiot."

"Either that or they're crazy. Captain Benson says she thinks it's the crazy option. Sometimes, they make some smart maneuvers. Like, really smart. She said."

If Benson said it, he believed it. After working around her for years, he was finally coming to terms with the idea that she wasn't someone who relied on a pretty face to open doors. The woman was smart in her own way—emotional intelligence, organization, strategy.

She saw the big picture quickly, and she adapted to it. There was a lot to respect about that, especially once he realized just how poorly he'd adapted to things throughout his life and the damage that had done.

Grier pointed to the computing pad strapped to his hip. "Is that the secret weapon?"

"Unless I screwed up again." He patted the pale blue brick.

"You're our miracle worker." Her smile could melt a glacier.

That was funny. He'd never really seen her as anything but a muscle-bound jock with a nice rack. Now, done up in stealth skin covering bulky armor and an environment suit, she was positively glowing.

It shouldn't take sliding toward death to bring on those sorts of lessons.

He squeezed his eyes shut. "Your team doesn't have to take out the whole array. Just a couple will do."

"We've got enough explosives to tear out fifty square meters of hull."

"They'll have defensive weapons. That stealth gear can only do so much."

"We got this, Chief."

Her confidence was misguided. Maybe she knew that, and it was a show for him.

The shuttle lurched to the side and then decelerated hard, and his stomach nearly shot its contents up.

He swallowed and opened his eyes just as they came to rest.

That sort of piloting…even computers couldn't match it.

Captain Patanga. Parkinson remembered the guy by reputation now.

Grier popped her harness and slammed down her visor. She added Parkinson to the general channel. "Let's go, Marines!"

It was easier to focus on her and her team than to focus on his own misery. They took bricks of explosives from the cases secured next to the airlock hatch, then headed inside.

She waved before the hatch closed.

Parkinson frantically switched to the external cameras and to Grier's feed.

In the consolidated view, it was easy to watch the Marines sneak across the ship's skin and hook up with the second team.

The hull between the shuttles and the antennae looked new, untouched by battle or years in space. Even those antennae had the appearance of something freshly installed.

It had to be a new ship, which meant the Khanate could pump out capital ships as fast as the Kedraalian Navy. That took the advanced robots, technicians, and engineers Parkinson had considered unique to the Republic.

Or it meant that someone had sold a lot of technology to the enemy.

A *lot*.

Grier's team split off from the second team and spread out toward the antennae cluster on the right…if they were looking aft—which he thought they were—then it was the port side. The second team headed to the starboard cluster.

*Just two antennae, Grier. That's all I need.*

Her team broke into pairs.

Okay. Sure. Three teams, three antennae. That increased the odds of success. Parkinson got that. But it increased the odds of detection. They were walking on the hull of a ship. They'd *landed* on the hull of a ship.

It was only a matter of time for someone or a system to notice the artifacts created by stealth technology: blurs, gaps, the odd duplication.

And then there was the timing. Each antenna targeted needed to be blown at the exact—

Something flashed in the shuttle's forward camera: a gun emplacement.

That hadn't been there before! It was partway between the shuttles and the antennae arrays…a rail gun nearly the size of a shuttle.

The gun spun around, pointed at the other shuttle, and—

Before Parkinson could shout a warning, the other shuttle was shredded, atmosphere and clumps of debris rising in a silvery cloud.

"Rail gun!" He leaned against his harness.

Patanga hissed. "Can't fire. It's between us and our teams."

Even as he spoke, the gun spun around and tracked uncertainly: Sensors were picking up the Marines.

Parkinson punched against his harness. His thumb was rubbery, flimsy. Finally, he activated the release.

He staggered back to the explosives case. "That's going to tear them apart. Grier! You see what happened?"

Her camera perspective shifted. "Shit. We've almost—"

The rail gun opened fire, tearing apart the second team of Marines without damaging the antennae.

It had a clean, precise lock, a computerized lock.

Parkinson fast-cycled through the airlock. His lungs burned. His knees shook. When he ran across the hull, he had to hang low to avoid spinning debris.

One of Grier's Marines opened fire on the gun and was quickly turned into…nothing. Just chunks of flesh and armor floating away.

The gun returned to scanning, trying to pick the other Marines out from the antenna mounts and cables. Even a computer had its limitations.

Fatigue hammered Parkinson. His legs gave out.

He fell, and the explosives brick bounced off the hull.

As clumsy as a newborn, he stretched and caught the brick by the corner.

It tumbled back toward the hull.

Parkinson covered the brick and pressed it against his chest with shaking hands.

The rail gun found another target and fired, splitting the Marine in half.

After a deep breath, Parkinson got back up. He staggered forward.

Only a few more meters—

But the rail gun stopped tracking the Marines.

It spun around, targeting him.

Then it shifted left. Then right.

Something had the targeting computer confused.

Prioritization. Threat analysis. It couldn't see him clearly, and he wasn't around critical gear.

Muzzle flash from the antenna array preceded sparking along the gun's armored shell.

It spun around and fired again.

Parkinson barely had time to hear Grier's agonized scream, then he was on top of the weapon, slapping the brick against the unprotected joint between the mount and the gun proper.

But the Marines were down; only a couple even had life signals.

He ran past the gun, felt it tracking him as he fought off nausea.

At five meters, he detonated the brick.

In the part of the video coming from the shuttle, the top of the gun tore free of its emplacement housing.

There was still a chance.

He stumbled and slumped until he reached the first Marine—a big guy with a hole in his gut. Blood covered half of the visor and most of the man's brown skin. His eyes were unfocused, and his life signs were dropping fast.

Resuscitation wasn't really an option. The guy was dead but his body was fighting.

Tears floated from Parkinson's eyes as he ran to Grier's side.

She was on the deck, pressing a quick-seal patch against the side of her arm where a shell had grazed her. That had been enough to melt the armor and dislocate the shoulder. He imagined the bones were shattered, too.

He pulled her other arm over his neck and hauled her up.

This time, he couldn't hold back the vomit, which sprayed everywhere. *Clean it later.*

Grier howled as he dragged her along. She shook her head. "Leave me!"

"No!"

He'd lost Taylor. That hurt enough for a lifetime.

Five meters out from the antenna, he squeezed her hip. "Blow it!"

On the shuttle camera, sections of several antennae launched away from the hull, and the assemblies came apart.

Debris spiraled through the void, and something nicked his environment suit.

His suit flashed a warning: He was losing air.

Parkinson laughed. The universe was going to have to try harder if it wanted to kill him.

**27**

———

"F" ailures come in threes."

Satrap muttered that to himself as the fleet data washed over him in streams of green, yellow, and red.

Mostly, the data was red at that moment.

Of course, that was nonsensical old wives' tales perpetuated because it was convenient.

People think in threes. Good luck comes in threes. Ill fortune comes in threes.

How comforting, and also how ridiculous a notion.

And yet, here he was, deep into the data flow coming in from the fleet, staring straight at three consecutive failures.

First, the enemy fleet had come in exactly as expected, but they'd detected the anti-radiation missiles, despite the upgrades he'd ordered put into place to increase the odds of success. Now those missiles were clutters of debris, hardly any threat at all for ships with deflection fields.

Second, the *Purity of Fire*'s communications systems were completely crippled, which meant the fighters they'd controlled from launch were now speeding toward nothing. With all the resulting network traffic flooding communications, it would be minutes before Zohar could seize control of those fighters. By then, the enemy would have started its ground assault.

The third failure was more personal, a cluster of red that spoke to his stuttering heart and the fever cooking his body. It flashed with each burst of shivering brought on by his twisting innards.

Once again, his life support systems were failing.

An irritation dug at him—a summons from the world of dying flesh.

He exited the comforting digital world, wrinkled his nose at his own thick musk, and gritted his teeth against the pain. This wasn't an abstract digital representation of suffering but real pain.

His vision cleared enough to realize he had two messages waiting: one from Zohar, the other from Ikhama.

The captain wanted an update now that their tactics were foiled.

Ikhama wanted to sit with her satrap during this crucial battle.

Of course she did. The Khan must have his eyes and ears.

Satrap approved her request and unlocked the hatch to his room.

Zohar…that was going to be more work.

Satrap connected to his senior captain.

The man's jaw was set and his chin raised. "Satrap has found the time to speak to his senior captain."

"I've been studying the data."

"And what has the data told you?"

"Nothing good, I fear. Our missile trap failed. Either the upgrades weren't all that I'd hoped for, or they've made advances to counter the technology we were told would win us the war."

"They have several ships dropping shuttles planet-side."

"Unless they plan for a lengthy fight, they can't get the numbers on the ground to make a difference. Once you have the fighters under your control, sweep the troop transports from the sky."

"We have yet to silence the *Purity of Fire*'s systems." The captain looked agitated—less in the way of a captain grappling with problems than—

*Of course!*

Satrap had forgotten that Zohar's son had been selected to fly in the fighter group launched against the targeted Azoren ships.

It was terrible enough for a father to watch his son die in war. How devastating it must be to control the craft that launched the child at the enemy.

But this was something Zohar had been expecting.

Still…

Satrap sent an encrypted text to his senior captain, offering sincere condolences for the loss. That would fire off whenever it was the boy's fighter detonated.

Even in death, there would still be an honest extension—a connection—between the two men.

Zohar glanced away. "We still have the main body of their fleet coming toward us. If we focus on the ground assault—"

"Leave them. The Khan has a loyal army to defend against such a threat."

"His loyal army is not so large as you think."

"They must hold their own. Our focus is protecting the fleet. Without us, that planetary assault force will have time to grow into a threat."

The captain seemed ready to argue further—mouth opened, brow knitted. Then he shrugged. "It is the other captains who protest, not I."

There was no surprise in that at all. "What do they suggest? Would they fly their ships down to the planet and have their crews hop out to fight on the Khan's palace walls?"

"One has suggested exactly that."

"The Khan has damned us with fools."

Zohar's eyebrow climbed in warning.

The hatch to Satrap's quarters opened, and Ikhama floated through, her white robes whispering behind her.

She bowed, then took her customary seat beneath the large display. "Satrap. Zohar."

The clap of the captain's heels coming together matched his bow. "Ikhama."

Satrap leaned back against the wall. "Your presence brings comfort at a time of pain, Ikhama."

"You are unwell?"

"My systems fail me again. Poisons course through my blood."

"This must be addressed."

"When I have a moment." Satrap wondered just how sincere her words were. "The system is a gift of the Khan, as is the body I live in now."

Her face remained flat and emotionless, but she stiffened.

*She is recording, as the Khan commanded.*

Zohar cleared his throat. "Your guidance, Satrap?"

He, too, realized everything was being seen or listened to, assuming the old Khan actually had the faculties to watch over his spy network at that moment.

Satrap massaged his legs, which burned with the toxins leaking from his failing life support systems. "Protect the fleet. Once we have control of the fighters, those ships will come for us. Have our captains coordinate—"

Zohar's connection froze.

It wasn't a communications failure but an intentional pause. Something was going on.

Ikhama's eyes drifted up to the display. *"A master tactician is like a painter, each feint a stroke necessary to complete the portrait."*

This didn't seem to Satrap to be a tactical play.

Pain lanced through his gut again. He could wait for Zohar to return, but the pain was making concentration impossible.

Satrap closed his eyes and dove into the data once more.

It was comforting there, free of a body that only knew collapse. Here, in seconds, he could do the work of hours.

This time, instead of expending himself on the fleet, he focused on his vital signs.

Every indicator was dropping: endocrine operation, blood pressure, kidney filtration...

He pulled up the system operations panel, the one he'd adjusted before.

How could everything be failing at once? He'd corrected things the last time he'd checked...

Yet there they were: All the settings he'd modified were back to where they'd been.

Dangerous settings. Lethal settings.

This wasn't an accident or sloppy coding; it was malicious.

He opened the different modules—code, configuration, security.

Everything had been changed since his last system scan, undoing all he'd done. That pointed to either an external agent attacking him or something inbuilt, some sort of self-destruct that would ensure his slow, agonizing death.

Why would someone create such a system? The Khan had spent substantial sums introducing cybernetic replacements for everything he'd destroyed.

Could it be the work of a rival?

Satrap almost laughed at that.

His rivals were simpletons who feared technology unless they could use it as a weapon.

So this had to be a remote attack from the Khan's people.

Or it was the design from the start, something Satrap had tried hard to convince himself wasn't possible.

What sort of twisted lies and deception led to that sort of thinking? Assault a young man—a boy—and destroy everything he was or could be, then promise him a better life for his loyalty and service. *Then* install a system that would fail once that service was near its end.

It was incomprehensible.

Yet it also made perfect sense with this sick tyrant.

But there was one thing the Khan had never done: destroy his victim's mind.

Satrap knew data. He knew systems. The hardware was functioning just fine. As promised, it could outlast a human body. And if the hardware had been installed with defective software, that could be rectified.

There were files that tracked operations. He dug through those, tracing back anything that might have come awake around the time of the file changes.

He traced those processes back to anything that could have spawned them.

Then he traced those spawning processes back to see what triggered them.

It was an interesting web, a series of connections that looped back on itself for redundancy: check if running; if not running, then spawn; shut down; launch erase.

Why hadn't he ever dug into this?

Because he'd been struggling for his life, trying to keep the lunatics and zealots from getting everyone else killed with their irrational behavior.

And because Satrap had never thought for a second anyone—not even the Khan—could be the sort of monster who manipulated and lied and deceived even the ones he'd broken.

That was dangerous naiveté.

A distant buzz ran through Satrap: He was being called back to the real world.

That could wait. This was his *life*. This was him striking back against the monster who had taken everything.

Satrap slowly pulled the web apart, replacing each strand with a strand of his own. He corrected the modules with optimal settings and code. He created backups of those optimized modules, then backups of backups, then he overwrote the poisoned modules with the optimized ones. Finally, he added a new layer to check the modules against clean values and to alert him if anything changed.

Only once all of that was done and confirmed did he return to the real world.

Zohar's face shook with rage. "Did you not receive my connection request?"

"I did. The data looked troublesome."

"The data!" The captain sighed. "Here is the data you should consider: Your captains have once again refused your commands. Even now, they speed for Azh Shivan, each proclaiming louder than the other that their act is for the glory of the holy of holies."

Satrap wasn't surprised by the words, but the fury he should have shared with Zohar couldn't come to the surface. Instead, it boiled somewhere far, far below.

The betrayal would undo the fleet, but there was an almost symmetric beauty to it.

Khan's insistence upon keeping his subjects weak and being caught up in schemes to advance their careers had created a situation where his own safety would be undone, where the great sword he had crafted with the help of his enemies would now be shattered before that enemy closed for its own death stroke.

"Symmetry." Satrap laughed, but it was a sputtering sound.

Why had he said that?

He sucked in a deep breath, burning his lungs. "I was never going to be given a chance to escape my fate, Zohar."

"What?"

"Toxins. Systems within systems, failing, robbing me of a life promised in return for service. Let the body kill itself." Satrap whipped his head around, searching for the cause of his outburst.

Sweat dripped down his face.

"Too late." He whispered that, but it felt like a roar in his head.

Something had collapsed before he'd corrected the settings. Or he'd missed a key component. Perhaps the architect had been smarter than given credit for. A real poison could have been left for the eventuality of the Khan's betrayal being discovered.

Zohar leaned closer to his camera. "Satrap?"

"I've done all I could do. Where there is no honor, serving a monster gains me nothing." The pounding was in Satrap's chest and in his head.

Then it slowed, and the burning became a cooling.

He'd done all he could to keep his fleet alive. He'd done all he could to survive the Khan's machinations.

Now came the end.

The last strength of Satrap's body faded, and he slid to the pillows that had been his only comfort.

His breathing was a soft wheeze. The light became a pinprick in the abyss.

Ikhama was beside him, hands on his chest. "His heart fades!"

Zohar released a sound close to a tortured howl. All things considered, the man had been decent and honorable. "We cannot stand alone against this fleet."

Ikhama's hands lifted away. "This is the war that was desired. Seize your opportunity to show the Khan your loyalty. Slay the infidel. Stand your ground and fight to the end."

Her voice grew stronger as she spoke, even as she drifted away from the nonsensical parables.

Satrap wished he had the strength to tease her about that.

Far away, Zohar started to speak, then his voice caught. He coughed. "Without the satrap, we are undone."

"Our Khan has said forever, through each incarnation, that he fought others alone."

"Parables, old woman. These enemies are real. They fire upon us even now. Missiles race toward us as our allies flee. Do you understand?"

"I hear abandonment of faith and weakness."

"There is no weakness, Ikhama! My own son lies strapped into a missile, enveloped in explosives. What more can a father give than his own child?"

It sounded as if the old woman cried. "What more can be given? Satrap once asked if I had been touched by this Khan. I said I had not. This is truth within a lie. He may not have abused me as a child, but his predecessor did."

Zohar gasped. It was the crash of thunder to Satrap, stronger even than Ikhama's confession. The captain was resolute, yet here it sounded as if he had been confronted with too much to deny anymore.

"I do apologize for such behavior." The captain's voice shook. "Even the Khan is only human."

Ikhama's breath caught. "No one should hold such power."

"No."

Even in death, Satrap caught the pain in the other man's voice. That was his love for his children, the acceptance that everything he'd stood for was a lie.

Satrap wished he could reach out to the others before total darkness fell.

Ikhama's tears were a soft patter of rain on Satrap's face. "Will you fight, Zohar?"

"The odds have always been against us. Only Satrap's strategies have kept us alive."

"Will you fight?"

"Not for this Khan, no. But I will fight for the survival of my family. And if I live, Khan will die."

As the last sensation fled from Satrap's body, he thought he might have smiled.

**28**

---

On Benson's command station display, the impossible played out in real time. Khanate ships retreated toward the Azoren task force. Khanate fighters had launched the moment Brummel had taken his destroyers and transports out of the combined fleet to make a run for the planet. Now those fighters sped off toward nothing, while Brummel's transports had already dropped nearly three hundred soldiers to the surface of Azh Shivan.

The only explanation for the Khanate captain's behavior was madness.

Why expend the fighters if they were only a ruse? If there was a malfunction, and they could be brought back around, then why throw the entire fleet at the Azoren instead of engaging the much larger fleet still coming head on?

She took a sip of her stimulant drink, the cold, bittersweet, citrusy tang that normally made her think of lemon blossoms barely caught her attention.

This was *her* drink, a thing she'd used for years to keep her edge. Now it felt like someone else's memory, same as the comfortable jumpsuit she'd traded out for her dress whites.

Was that because Thiessen had complimented how she looked in the whites?

Maybe.

A part of the crew's chatter—just one component of background noise against the humming air recycler and other ship sounds—brought her head up.

Chopra was hunched over the shoulder of Ensign Grehan, the round-faced communications officer whose anxiousness manifested as a perpetual patch of red on her soft cheeks.

The XO murmured something to the young ensign, then edged along the wide console station, talking to the helm and weapons officers before drifting back to the command station.

Benson stepped down from the raised platform and turned away from the console. "What is it?"

Chopra was a ball of agitation, wiping sweat from his brow. "The Azoren."

"Are they calling for help?"

"Not yet, but Chief Parkinson's hacking has given us access to their chatter."

"And?"

"It would appear that they're panicking."

"Wouldn't you? They can't stand up to that Khanate force."

The XO clasped his hands together. "They will call for assistance, though. Soon."

She turned back to squint at the main display. "They left a capital ship behind. That's a cruiser."

"It seems an odd tactical decision."

"Or a trap. Do we have lock-on?"

"Not at this range."

"But how does it look? Did Parkinson's ploy work?"

Chopra nodded at the weapons station. "Lock-on looks likely."

She tugged on her the front of her outfit. This Khanate captain was completely unpredictable. Splitting his forces… "Talk to Alexander and—"

Benson had almost said Karras, but the commander of the *Seattle* was dead.

Chopra caught what had happened and nodded his head. "I'll pass along to the captains to continue on course for this cruiser."

"Thank you."

Benson climbed back up to the command station. She didn't trouble Grehan with a request for a connection to Thiessen. He'd established a connection early, and Benson had kept it active but muted.

She put her headset on and unmuted. "Floyd?"

He didn't answer immediately.

When she pushed the video to the command station display, he was talking to someone outside of camera range.

Then he noticed the line was active and put his own headset on. "Faith?"

"I assume you saw the ships head for the Azoren task force."

"We can't react. Not yet."

"That task force isn't going to last long against the Khanate fleet."

Thiessen's eyes darted around, then he turned slightly and dipped his head lower. "Every Azoren ship that comes out of this battle undamaged increases the odds of future trouble." His voice was soft but firm.

"We need them to drop that landing force."

"Need?" He shook his head. "Look what the Khanate did on Radetta. Not a foot soldier put at risk."

"You're saying we should let the Azoren take the brunt of this attack, and when this is all over use missiles on the city?"

"I can't say that without someone calling me a savage."

"I see. But it's the ideal outcome. Is that right?"

"What these people did to my people…" Thiessen leaned closer to the camera. "How would you have reacted to that happening to your capital?"

Benson brought the battle display back up. The Khanate ships would be within range in minutes to begin harassing the Azoren task force. She'd been ready to work with the Gulmar to destroy the Azoren after what they'd nearly accomplished with their stealth fleet.

She bit her lip. "We can stay focused on the cruiser."

"And when it's done, we can support our Azoren allies."

"I'll pass that along."

Her palms were damp. What Thiessen was saying was absolutely valid, but it was also the exact sort of thing that couldn't be said in civilized company. Killing an enemy actively attacking you was fine. But the second they surrendered, even if they had done terrible things and been the aggressor—

Politicians didn't understand what Thiessen—what she—was feeling. They saw war as a loathsome thing, a last resort.

But for the last resort to truly have value, it needed to be brutal, total.

She waved Chopra over and leaned down. "Begin evasive maneuvers."

He glanced at the big display. "Yes. Of course."

"Have Ensign Grehan connect me with our captains. Also, have Lieutenant Halliwell return to the *Valor*."

The XO's eyes widened. "You've reached a decision?"

"We'll discuss it."

Chopra returned to the communications officer's post, then edged over to the helm station.

A warning went out about the imminent evasive maneuvers.

Then Chopra pointed to the headset he wore: They had their call.

Benson joined and brought Thiessen into the call, too. "As you might have noticed, we're beginning evasive maneuvers."

Tuleyev harrumphed. "They flee toward the planet."

"They left a cruiser behind."

"It will break soon."

"It hasn't yet, so let's not make that assumption. We're going to focus everything we have on it and take it out of this fight."

"But the bulk—"

"I understand, Alexander. I intend to warn our Azoren allies of the need to hold their position until we arrive."

Chopra blinked rapidly as realization settled in.

Then the soft catch in Tuleyev's voice indicated that he, too, understood. "Yes, Captain. We must not leave the cruiser to strike at our rear."

"Thank you, Alexander."

No one was going to voice the obvious.

Good. She had their support in this, if only implicitly.

Benson disconnected and sucked in a breath. They were committed.

Chopra pulled his headset off. "Evasive maneuvers have begun for the combined fleet."

"Let's box that cruiser in, please."

The XO slid up next to the weapons station. "Open fire at maximum optimal sensor range."

With the entire Kedraalian and Gulmar fleet sharing lock-on and firing on the ship, even a cruiser wouldn't last long.

She stepped down from the command station and stood just behind Grehan. "Ensign, please open a connection to the *Warsaw*."

The red splotch on the ensign's cheeks darkened. "Yes, ma'am."

Benson fiddled with her headset until Brummel's face appeared in the corner of the large display.

His nose was red, as if he'd been rubbing it, and his eyes looked watery. "Captain Benson. The Khanate fleet has abandoned its defense."

"They've left their biggest ship behind."

"One ship would be easy to maneuver around, Captain."

"We can't risk it fleeing or flanking."

"But—" The Azoren commander licked his lips. His eyes narrowed, his shoulders slipped back, and he swayed for a second as he took in the meaning of her unspoken message: He was on his own. "I...understand. The Azoren fleet will protect the assault force and will send as many soldiers to the surface as possible."

"Thank you, Captain Brummel."

The Azoren officer bowed, then the connection ended.

Chopra followed her back to the command station. "It seems they are used to such treatment."

A cold dread settled in Benson's gut. "And now I'm like them."

"Not at all. Not even close."

She couldn't manage even a quick smile as she mounted the steps. Her XO wasn't going to say it, but she was doing exactly what the Azoren would do in the same situation—

—because she had to.

On the large screen, the computer system was lighting space up with flashes of light to reflect weapons fire the human eye couldn't perceive. The enemy ship had begun its own evasive maneuvers, and its weapons systems were similarly lighting up the display.

Damage reports for each ship popped up on the screen.

The *Mississippi* took a hit that dropped its forward shields.

The *Nairobi* lost a forward rail gun when a shield failed.

Despite the improbable hits, there were no major injuries.

Those hits were the result of a big ship bristling with weapons landing a few lucky shots. Missiles sped across the battle display as the cruiser put everything it had into play as quickly as it could, but nothing else touched a Kedraalian or Gulmar ship.

That was because the Khanate ship couldn't get lock-on.

For her group, that wasn't the case.

On the giant display, her ships laid down what amounted to a lattice of withering fire that boxed the cruiser in and rapidly shrank once it adjusted maneuvers to avoid the constraining fire.

It was the death spiral of space combat, where lucky hits didn't destroy you but reduced maneuvering capabilities did.

Within minutes, her fleet's coordinated firing solutions had the cruiser operating within a rough cube of space where computers could start to calculate likely movement and fire with reasonable accuracy.

A few of the bright lines representing weapons fire traced through the enemy cruiser.

Lieutenant Mahama turned to Chopra. "Direct hits." The young officer's dark skin glistened with sweat when he beamed at Benson. "Damage to the enemy cruiser, Captain."

"Launch missiles. Let's wrap this up before we take any more damage."

Mahama bent over his station and spoke into his headset.

Chopra slipped back to the command station, eyes locked on the giant display. "Do we take prisoners, Captain?"

She scraped a thumbnail over what might have been a stain on her jacket sleeve. "We're in the middle of a battle."

"I meant it more as a question of how much firepower—"

"We need to ensure it's not a threat and can't escape." Her stomach knotted when she looked her XO in the eyes. *Don't make me say it explicitly.*

He stared for a moment, then returned to the console.

War should have an element of honor to it, or so the academy taught. Never kill when crippling would do. Use only so much force as is necessary to secure victory. Remember the value of diplomacy and the ultimate objective of peace.

Those tenets were the influence of politicians, though, the lingering poison of a culture that had formed after fleeing barbarism and destruction on Earth.

It wasn't that she disagreed with the concepts. Killing was revolting, dehumanizing.

But fleeing Earth hadn't allowed the Kedraalian people to flee *humanity*.

With humanity came inhumanity—like the Azoren and Khanate.

So she clenched her jaw tight and stared at the missiles tracking through space. And when those missiles slid through the crippled defensive short-range weapons arrays to blossom against the cruiser's unprotected hull, she fought back the images that threatened to come forward—images of her own ships being blasted apart.

Only when the last missile struck did she look away from the fires and floating debris coming out of the mighty enemy vessel.

She cleared her throat. "Threat assessment, Lieutenant Mahama."

"Significant damage to the hull. They've lost engines. No weapons fire. If it has any sort of explosives stored aboard it, that ship's going to come apart at some point, Captain."

"Thank you."

A quick glance at the Azoren task force showed a near complete reversal. Three of the destroyers were out of action, and a fourth was taking fire. Only the *Warsaw* seemed relatively unscathed.

But the second wave of soldiers was away, headed for the capital below.

She tapped a finger on the command station console. "Commander Chopra, let's do a complete damage report assessment before we proceed, please."

The XO went rigid, then nodded. "And after that?"

"After that, I believe we have a mission to eliminate all threats to Kedraalian peace."

She shuddered at the coldness of her own words.

If her career hadn't already been cut short by politics, she would have ended it herself upon her return home.

War necessarily created monsters, and she had reached her limit.

The rumble and shake woke Caville before his alarm again. It wasn't the intensity of an earthquake, but he was well aware of what the soft pinging and groaning meant.

He ran a hand over Gallo's shoulder, letting his fingertips linger featherlight on her throat, taking solace from the pulse there.

They shared each other's musk now, something he would miss. But their intimacy was gone; the time for action was upon them.

She stirred, and he kissed her cheek, shushing her. "They're here again."

Tension tightened the muscles of her neck. "You're sure?"

Once again, the deep rumble ran through the walls and floor.

Caville chuckled. "I'm sure."

He hopped from their bed and cleaned up, already running through the plan. Today was the day: Find the antimatter or die trying. During the fighting, they'd ventured as far as two floors above their safe area. The combat was deeper inside the structure now.

Three rooms remained unexplored, but they were near ramps. That made them risky. Khanate soldiers or the sentinel—either would kill them if they were spotted.

As Gallo cleaned up, he dressed, then set out food and drink.

All they had was water and the simple sustenance the research teams had left behind, but the bland paste and sweet water were to him like living in a palace.

Having Gallo around influenced that notion.

While she ate, he packed his bag: one bottle of water for the two of them, and the last of their energy bars.

He stuffed the bag just inside the door to the passageway, then returned to the device he'd spent so long configuring. When Gallo wasn't looking, he checked the logs to be sure she hadn't accessed the system.

It was clean.

The odds that she was a true Khanate spy were so close to zero that he put aside the last of his reservations.

She was just a dumb kid, someone raised on a hateful ideology and twisted into a traitor by a bad parent.

*Traitor* was a tough word.

Everyone made bad decisions. He'd had the luxury of being insulated from choice and opportunities to fail.

Caville smiled.

When puberty had come, he'd developed a troublesome rebellious streak. He'd started challenging his trainers and asking questions that annoyed them. Stiles had warned him to be careful, even though she had the same questions.

Their accelerated aging helped them through that period quickly, but if he'd been outside the rigid control of his trainers, would he have been so different?

Gallo looked around their little paradise. "What if we don't find it?"

"It has to be in one of those three rooms. If it were somewhere above, those Khanate soldiers would've found it by now."

"You don't know that. Not every door was left open."

"If it's not in one of the rooms, then I go up and check the next floor."

Her eyes narrowed. "That robot's going to be up there."

"Killing soldiers."

"You can't—"

"Denise, we're running out of opportunities. If it's not down here, it's up there."

"Then let's wait until the soldiers retreat and sneak out the way we came in. We can find the hole they've made at the top and search from there."

"The sentinel's a threat either way."

"I—"

Caville pointed at the ceiling. "That battle's only going to last for so long."

She followed him out the door, lamp in hand. He held the assault rifle at low ready. Gunfire was more clearly audible this time, but there were still the occasional screams of wounded men.

Those screams didn't last long.

At the ramp to the level above, Caville hunched low and listened, then he hurried up to the floor above. He did the same a little later, when he was sure the weapons fire was still ongoing but farther away.

To their credit, the soldiers hadn't simply abandoned their objective. They'd adapted, and they'd brought in reinforcements.

Battles ran for minutes, sometimes an hour.

And they'd reached the ramps down. They hadn't taken them all the way down yet, but they'd reached them.

That meant the sentinel was being cautious, hunting them rather than charging them. It also meant that the sentinel had to be moving up and down the levels to keep the invaders off guard.

But so far, he and Gallo had avoided the robotic creature.

Caville stopped at the crossway just before the final three rooms he'd spotted. It was a fifteen-meter sprint past the intersecting passageway, then they'd be at the first door. The next two were at the end of the hall.

The one problem was where the intersection ran to the left, ending at a ramp that led up to the level above.

When he poked his head around the corner, there was movement near the top of the ramp.

*Not the sentinel.*

He dimmed his lamp and pulled Gallo after him, darting down the hall until they reached the door. It opened without trouble, and he rushed her inside. Even before he brought the lamp light up to full, he knew the room wasn't what they were looking for. The faint remnant of rotting bodies hung in the air.

It was a small group—two or three Khanate soldiers. They'd been wounded and retreated into the room decades ago. Now they were mummified skeletons and ruined clothes.

Caville signaled for her to stay put, then opened the door.

Voices echoed down the passageway, and a bright light reflected off the walls of the intersection.

A Khanate team had reached this level.

He hurried down the hallway and tried the door at the end.

When he was inside and brought the lamp light back up, he froze.

Sitting on the floor was a shiny, metallic pot with a black handle. The whole thing was more than a meter in diameter and a meter high. A small indicator slowly flashed a sickly green-amber.

Even the best batteries would run out eventually.

It only took a moment to confirm this was the storage container he was looking for.

He dimmed the lamp again, clipped it to his outfit, rolled his shoulders, then braced his legs. There might only be a small amount of antimatter inside the device, but the batteries and the system maintaining the containment fields bumped the weight well past thirty kilos.

Because of the size of the thing, the best he could manage was a waddle. His assault rifle threatened to slide off his shoulder with each step.

The doors were thick, but he pressed an ear against the cool metal anyway.

No one was banging on the door, at least.

It opened with a whisper, and he shuffled out.

Just as he reached the door where he'd left Gallo, he stopped.

Voices grew loud enough that he could make out words. Then he heard boots clomping.

The Khanate soldiers were near the intersection.

Caville could abandon Gallo and risk a clumsy run down to the bomb apparatus, set it up to detonate in an hour, and make his getaway.

Or he could risk trusting her and pull her out of the room now.

He popped the door and jerked his head for her to follow.

At the intersection, he paused, peering down the hall to the intersection long enough to see the room the Khanate soldiers were huddled in. There were at least three, one of them wounded. That one was on the floor, and it looked like the other two were trying to patch him up.

Caville took a step to the other side of the intersection, then stopped.

Deeper down the intersecting hallway, beyond the room with the Khanate soldiers in it, something moved along the floor. It was barely visible, a strange glimmer from the Khanate soldiers' flashlights.

The sentinel.

It seemed to stare at him.

He glanced back at Gallo. Would she give them away? Would she shout a warning?

She squeezed his arm.

The sentinel crept closer to the room with the Khanate soldiers.

Caville hurried down the hall, away from the imminent slaughter; Gallo followed.

They weren't even down the ramp when the screams came.

He moved as fast as he could, coming dangerously close to stumbling twice.

Gallo was crying by the time they knelt in front of the instrument console. "It could've killed us."

"We're not the current threat." He slid the container into the device.

"But it saw us!"

"And it's going to come for us when it's done with them."

He programmed the device to detonate in two hours. That was cutting it close, but everything they did from this point forward was going to be risky.

Caville got to his feet and activated the timer. "Two hours. We have to go *now*."

She knuckled tears away and nodded. "Is that enough time?"

"It'll have to be."

At the door, he grabbed the bag and listened again.

Scraping. A rasp against the door.

The sentinel was outside, waiting. It knew somehow.

Caville checked the assault rifle. It wouldn't be enough. An explosive might work, but the Khanate weapons hadn't stopped it.

Gallo pressed against him. "It's going to keep us in here."

"Maybe." He kissed her, pressing the taste of her into his memory, as if that might be something that carried on after he was dead. "I might be able to distract it, and you could make a run—"

She scowled and swatted his arm. "We go together."

Then they would wait until the bomb detonated.

Except...

Except that the scraping against the door stopped...and it sounded like the metallic noise of the thing's movement was farther away.

He pointed for her to open the door. "Better to die making a run for it, right?"

She smiled, then activated the door.

The passageway was clear in the lamplight.

He put her hand against his back and led her out, padding down the hall until they reached the room where they'd taken cover that first night.

It was deadly quiet.

They headed for the door to the outside shell of the structure. He expected the sentinel to jump out of the dark at any moment, until the sound of gunfire and explosions came from above.

It was fighting the invaders again.

Caville helped Gallo out, then up the ladder, stopping when they reached the edge of the sand-covered top they'd fallen onto so long ago.

The fighting was more intense now—a constant thunderous chatter of small arms fire and what might be heavy-caliber weapons coming from below. The roof was unoccupied but littered with gear. There were two wide holes in the roof, where sand had been cleared away. Metal ladders ran up and out of sight.

He pointed up. "We've got a way out."

With the fighting intensifying, it didn't matter if they made noise getting to the surface.

Gray moonlight illuminated the desert. Wind tossed sand at Caville's head when he poked it out of the hole.

Two things jumped out immediately.

Maybe fifty meters to the right were the lights of an encampment—a *big* encampment. The Khan was serious about taking this place.

About twice as far to the left was a less brightly lit airstrip.

*That* was their destination.

A scream echoed below, then went silent. There was no more gunfire, either.

Gallo paused before climbing out. She looked down, then scampered up. "I think it's coming."

Caville hadn't planned on that. "It'll go for the camp."

He wasn't going to gamble on that assertion, though.

Eschewing stealth, he sprinted for the airstrip, pulling Gallo behind him.

It was the first full-on, long-distance sprint in a while, and it left his damaged toe aching.

As they approached the airstrip, things resolved in the moonlight: two aircraft and a small shack.

Someone leaned against the shack, staring toward the camp.

There were screams coming from there now…and gunfire.

The man leaning against the shack turned. He had a weapon, but it wasn't raised.

Caville fired a burst, and the man slumped against the wall without a sound.

The two vehicles were the same: low-profile, short-range, high-speed aircraft meant for rapid deployment.

He popped the door on the first and looked inside.

It was meant to pile twenty soldiers into and smelled like it. Crude, frayed seats lined the scuffed walls.

A quick peek inside the other revealed a dignitary's aircraft, probably a very senior officer. There were only ten seats—cushy and clean. In fact, the whole interior gave off a pleasant aroma that indicated frequent cleaning.

He dragged Gallo inside that and rushed to the cockpit.

Lights winked out at the encampment.

Caville brought systems online and overrode the recommended prelaunch checklists. The whine of engines spinning up was deafening after so long underground.

The light coming from the aircraft belly caught something shiny, almost transparent, sprinting toward the airstrip at inhuman speed.

He punched the launch button, and the aircraft lurched up and forward.

The thing that approached sparkled one second and shimmered like water the next. It was larger than when he'd first seen it.

*Repurposing technology.*

Caville gained altitude but never took his eye off the thing until it disappeared completely.

Gallo shook in the co-pilot's seat. "It's coming after us."

"It's not fast enough. Just hang on."

The thrust of the engines pushed them back against their seats. As they sped across the desert, it seemed as if new stars lit up the sky.

Whatever was causing that, he knew it couldn't be good.

**29**

Tremors woke Satrap. His eyes opened to white-hot fire curling up and around him. Hunched, shadowy forms rushed beneath a golden, flaming arch that stretched on forever. Agonized screams warred with the roaring inferno, only to be swallowed and suffocated. Stinging acid burned the back of his throat.

There were stories in the Khanate's scriptures—parables about the punishment for betrayal and the unbelievers. Pits of fire and agony awaited the condemned, where all they knew was pain and the stench of flesh burned away.

Satrap sucked in a hot, dry breath.

Had he somehow been wrong all these years? Was the Khan's teaching true?

A section of burning wall fell away, revealing a sealed-off compartment aboard the *Might of the Khan*. Men in environment suits were spraying a freshly patched bulkhead with sealant, while other men covered ruined corpses with blankets.

This was no hell but the ship that had once commanded his fleet.

The heat, the stink of cooked flesh, the brilliant fires...

He was alive!

Satrap squinted against the blinding light and realized that he wasn't being transported by demons to his eternal torture but by his Jakkara. Their sealed armor protected them from the inferno, no doubt.

Something must be protecting him, too. Otherwise, he would be dying.

With a straining effort, he raised his head enough to see the silver foil blanket covering his chest, arms, and legs.

Then he was protected as well.

Except for his face, which felt sunburned, as if he'd spent a day in the desert.

So, he had survived. The toxins Khan's machines had built up hadn't been the end.

And the *Might of the Khan*? Fallen or falling. He couldn't be sure which.

The Jakkara at Satrap's right shoulder gently pushed his head back down.

His captain, or so it seemed in the intense light and stark shadows.

A metallic groan preceded clanking and squealing, then the flames overhead shifted, flowing in the direction they were running. A moment later, they sped through a wide hatch that shivered and grated shut again.

Immediately, the air took on a familiar coolness and the dull, chemical quality of a hangar bay.

For a moment, Satrap thought the Jakkara might simply run to the giant hangar bay deck door and leap out into space. It would make a strange sort of sense, as their vows of protection and still-incomplete conditioning left them with no concern for their own lives, so long as they kept him alive.

But they came to a stop rather than killing themselves along with him.

A motor lowered a ramp, and Satrap turned.

Ikhama stood between him and his corvette, replaced now after his previous one had been destroyed during the failed mutiny.

She bowed. *"Only through death is there release. Only through release is there life."*

He breathed in the comforting cool air as the Jakkara set him down and pulled off the protective blanket to reveal the portable system that regulated his body functions.

That simple act of taking in air was easier than he could recall in some time.

The old woman smiled. "The end has come for some of us."

"You knew." The realization was painful coming so late. "I was right: You knew I was being poisoned."

"To tell you would have meant my own death."

"And what happened to me? Was that planned?"

"It was convenient. Your body went into shock, yet your systems were already fighting to counter it. The same cannot be said for the fleet."

With the help of the Jakkara captain, Satrap sat up. "What happened?"

Tears welled in Ikhama's eyes. "*The coward flees. The lion holds. The spears strike down the noble. Life may belong to the weak, but sleep eludes them forever.*"

"The other ships fled. Zohar held his position."

"So it is."

"And now? The *Might of the Khan* dies?"

"*Our enemy has pulled its spear out of our heart, and our blood spills onto the sands.*"

He looked to his captain. "Where will we go? Return to Azh Shivan, and I will be executed for my fleet's failure."

The captain stood erect but didn't respond.

What it must be, this total lack of fear. Satrap wondered if there was resentment at some level for what amounted to the removal of agency. Perhaps warriors preferred that freedom from base emotions that would otherwise quickly leave them vulnerable and ineffective.

Not Satrap. The way fear dug its claws into his heart—that had kept him alive.

Ikhama waved toward the ramp. "Your ship might take you anywhere."

"But would you be willing to go anywhere? I can't offer you protection. I have no influence outside of this fleet." Satrap winced at the irony in that statement.

His influence within the fleet had been tenuous from the start.

The old woman shuffled closer. "Satrap, where you go, you must travel alone."

"Alone?" His heart raced.

"We are dead already—your Jakkara and me. Even you are dead. So far as the Khan knows, we died with the strikes that crippled this ship."

Satrap held a hand out for her. "Then come with me. We can find a new home."

"I am too old and too near the end. Your Jakkara have already chosen their path."

The corvette seemed so small, so frail. How could one person hope to survive in such a thing? He'd nearly died in one already.

Of course, he could do that without effort. Once connected into the ship computer, piloting was native. His systems could keep him alive for weeks with connections to the galley's water and integrated nutrient packs.

But his mind…?

Ikhama squeezed his hand. "You hesitate. You convince yourself that this cannot be done. It is only fear of a new life. Look at me. Free of the Khan's ever-watching eye, my life is now and forever mine. I can speak without concern of his presence evaluating all that I say. What glorious freedom to be authentic and unregulated. My fellow Ikhama would be jealous."

"So come with me. Taste wine and experience blasphemy."

She chuckled. "The Khan's death would not undo the poison that courses through the veins of our people."

"Our people? If that fleet kills the Khan, the religion will wither away."

"One day. When I speak of our people, I mean humanity."

"This religion exists apart from the human species. It only lives because the believers have a desperate need to feel relevant. The might of the military—"

"The might of the military has been an illusion for years. Even this fleet has been…" She shook her head. "He went mad with his hatred. The first Khan and all the rest who followed. It has been interwoven into what should have been an uplifting belief system."

"You've known? You've known and served?"

"All the Ikhama have known from the moment we become eyes and ears, Satrap. We have no freedom. Knowing a collar encircles your neck does not shatter it."

"But that chain is broken now. They're going to destroy this tyrant."

She waved for the Jakkara to come forward.

Two of them lifted Satrap between them, gently wrapping his arms around their shoulders.

It was always awkward going up the ramp, but normally they used a wheeled device. That was probably lost in the damage, or maybe there had been too much debris to use it.

Satrap let them strap him into his seat and connect his system to the ship. Cool fluids dripped into his veins.

That was a relative coolness, of course. His body was tender and hot.

One of the Jakkara brought a wheelchair up from Satrap's private cabin and secured that to the nearby bulkhead.

The bodyguards saluted with arms crossed over their chests, bowed as one, then left.

Ikhama stayed behind, looking around as the ship's lights grew brighter.

Without the oppressive mass of the Khan's dogma crushing her and driving every aspect of her life, her back seemed straighter, and the wrinkles of her face were, if not diminished, then less defined.

He tested the padded harness that would hold him through the launch and maybe more. "Don't you want to know a life—a real life?"

"As I told you, the Khan's poison will remain for a time. Unlike you, the devices within me cannot be undone. I would be tracked down by the last of his loyal assassins, assuming I even survived that long. This short taste of freedom was sweet enough, and it was made sweeter by outliving him."

"He's dead?"

"Something…terrible has happened on Azh Shivan. I felt it. I heard radio traffic before our systems failed here."

Satrap tried to feel shame for his failure. He tried to feel pain at the loss of his family.

Except the failure hadn't been his. The Khan had architected that.

And Satrap's family had abandoned him long ago. They had chosen this twisted religion over their own child simply by remaining when there had been opportunities to flee to someplace sane.

Ikhama knelt beside Satrap. "His machinations, the damage done—it will all heal one day. See to it you outlast them."

She bowed, then rose and exited the ship.

As the airlock hissed shut, the ship shook in the giant cruiser's death throes.

He connected to the corvette's systems, bringing up the Fold Space drive and star maps, checking the reactor and environmental indicators, ensuring the communications and navigation systems were fully operational.

Everything flashed green.

Another shudder ran through the small ship as Satrap triggered the hangar bay deck hatch.

Seconds were an eternity when you were surrounded by imminent death.

He checked the helmet attached to his seat, ensuring the swivel worked easily. In emergencies, he could swing it down, and it would deploy a blanket of material that would seal around him. That wouldn't keep him alive long, and even an advanced ship like the little corvette didn't have the capability for self-repair.

That was the fear talking again, the self-preservation instinct.

Those fifteen minutes or maybe even a few hours sealed with the helmet—maybe it was enough for another ship to rescue him.

*Good enough.*

Finally, the deck hatch opened.

Through the corvette's cameras, he had a sense of the space outside. That sense took on detail as the ship slipped from the *Might of the Khan*'s battered belly. Sensors translated the barrages of weapons fire into visible beams. A few ships registered as Khanate remnants, but fire bloomed along their hulls, bright in the void.

Other ships suffered as well. Enemy ships. Smaller ones.

He should have taken solace in that, but the war was lost.

More importantly, it wasn't his war. It never had been. The implicit bargain with the Khan had been a false construct from the start. Satrap had never been willing to come to terms with the obviousness of this lie.

*Where could I go to escape the Khan once I delivered all those systems, wiped clean of his enemies?*

At the very edge of perception, Satrap thought he might have spotted huge dust clouds over the planet surface.

Then a giant hand shook the ship and tossed it around.

Systems died, and klaxons rang before dying, too.

*The Might of the Khan.* It had to be. Something had finally given out, and the corvette had still been close enough for the explosion to have taken its systems out.

But he could breathe the recirculated air. He could hear things.

He was spinning in the dark, out of control, but things hadn't completely failed, and the ship hadn't lost its atmosphere or artificial gravity.

Yet he was still doomed.

How was he supposed to undo whatever damage had been done?

Satrap pressed the tender flesh of his face against the harness padding.

There was always the option of filling his bloodstream with painkillers. He would slip away fairly quickly and with no suffering.

Except…

Except that was letting Khan win.

The wicked man had taken away Satrap's identity and his body, but he still had his mind.

He pulled the wheelchair free of its brace and rolled it around until it was in front of him, then locked the wheels. His breath raced from the exertion, and the inner crease of his elbows stung from the needles secured there.

Satrap powered his life support system down, then pulled the lines from the needles and detached the cables from their plugs.

That took a couple unpleasant minutes that left him damp with sweat.

Getting into the wheelchair…

Long ago, he'd learned how to do this. It had been part of the training he'd undergone for self-sufficiency after the Khan had finished his brutal work and left the favored young boy a broken rag doll.

Ever since, though, Satrap had fallen into the trap of relying on others.

That was going to be rectified, starting immediately.

He wrestled free of the seat, then slid across the arm of the wheelchair and lowered himself down.

The wheelchair was sturdy and balanced, and he weighed so little without his life support system, that it never seemed much of a threat to tip over.

Once in the wheelchair, he guided it to the bridge.

The corvette was built for a small crew to manage easy maintenance. He found an emergency battery switch under the console and powered critical systems on just long enough to troubleshoot the problem. That necessitated interfacing through buttons, consoles, and other crude interfaces, which slowed everything down.

Fortunately, the problem proved easy enough: a reactor failure, no doubt caused by an EMP burst from the *Might of the Khan*. His own systems had better shielding, apparently.

However, the solution wasn't so easy.

He opened the hatch to the reactor area, then powered the batteries off to preserve them.

When he reached the reactor room, he was shaking from the exertion.

The worst of it remained.

To restart the reactor, he had to operate a manual pump to re-seal the coolant system, then use mechanical claws to reconnect the elements that had been decoupled as part of the rapid shutdown.

Both pump and claws were designed for an average person to be able to operate them without too much effort. Satrap had suffered years of atrophy.

He fought the pump lever like a madman, grunting and growling as he pulled it down, then pushed it up. Blood stained the sleeves of his robes where the needles had torn his skin.

Ikhama would have given up; he refused to.

And, finally, the reactor was reconnected.

Satrap wheeled himself back to the bridge, brought the batteries back online, and fired up the reactor. When it was online, he brought everything else up, one system at a time.

The corvette once again showed green.

Ha! He'd done it!

He pushed the wheelchair back to his seat, laughing even when reconnecting the tubes and cables of his life support system.

*This* was freedom! The bleeding, the pain, and the sweat.

The ship presented the Fold Space interface and the star map to him.

Anywhere he wanted, he could go. He was a no one, erased by the Khan.

Satrap thought back to the destruction he'd brought to Radetta and almost brought to the refueling planet Petrovan.

Could he go there? Could he face the result of his work in service to the Khan?

It could at least be a starting point to rehabilitation.

He programmed in the course to Petrovan and sent the ship away from Azh Shivan at full acceleration.

There was a great deal to pay penance for and no reason to delay.

One of the Khan's parables came to mind: *As the wind is cultivated, so shall the whirlwind be harvested.*

Finally, there had been truth in all the nonsense.

## 30

The Himmel sky was a bruised, steel gray, dashed by freezing rain. As Benson's escort vehicle sped through the streets, she had the sense that the city might not have known sunlight since she'd left. The way Thiessen scowled, she thought maybe he was thinking the same thing.

When their vehicle stopped, it was a few blocks past the building where they'd met the Azoren High Command. That brutish structure and those around it were sunken ruins.

Howling wind carried the smell of ash into the vehicle rear.

Her escort climbed out of the Night Leopard—slow and awkward. Like the vehicle, these soldiers were worn and drained. Their youthful faces were sunken, their pink cheeks scruffy with days of growth. Dark bags made their pale eyes stand out even more.

She waited when signaled by a sergeant, whose foul breath could only come from diseased gums and rotting teeth.

Fortunately, he hobbled away, dull boots scraping the chipped sidewalk.

Steam rose when Thiessen blew into his hands. "Things change quickly."

Benson nodded toward the dark pools collecting in the chewed-up street. "It feels like years since we were here."

"It felt like years when we came out of Fold Space."

"Azh Shivan wasn't even two months ago."

That's all they referred to their dark work as: the dead planet's name.

But it had been more than that. It had been…genocide.

According to the GSA agent they were transporting back to Kedraal, the cause was an anti-matter device. She was still trying to make sense of the rationale behind it.

In the end, did it matter?

The Khanate was gone, or it would be soon enough. She was hauling the nation's robotic shipyards behind the *Valor*, and the *Lyon* and three Gulmar destroyers were conducting mop-up operations against the other planets.

That sounded so much more palatable than "purifying."

A harsh bark broke through her contemplation and put an end to her shivering.

She turned in time to see a stooped young man in black trench coat stomping past the sergeant toward them.

Close up, the young man was barely her age—probably younger. He smelled like he might have showered in the last week, and his cheeks weren't quite so hollow as the others'.

*A general. Rank has its privileges.*

Benson extended a hand. "General."

He sneered at the offering, then blinked slowly. "You return from the hunt of the Khanate fleet, yet you come alone. Not even one Azoren ship survived?"

She nodded toward Thiessen. "Captain Thiessen and I felt it would be inappropriate to simply radio the outcome of the war. We all suffered losses."

Thiessen put on a solemn frown. "We have a good deal of data for your leadership, if they're interested."

Rain collected on the Azoren general's cheeks.

Finally, he barked at the sergeant again.

It was a name, but with the clipped Azoren speech pattern, Benson couldn't make it out.

The sergeant understood. He jogged away, but with the effort of someone sprinting.

Thiessen pointed in the general direction of the fortified starport. "Hey, General—looks like you guys launched some pretty intense artillery into the woods out by the starport."

"Does it?" The Azoren turned away.

Benson stepped back to find a little cover next to the Night Leopard. The stench of the interior was better than the miserable cold.

Thiessen huddled beside her. "This one went to charm school."

"Don't they all?"

"I guess the closer they drift toward psychosis, the more training they get."

Before she could comment on that, she caught the deep gurgle of a combustion engine. A long, blockish black car shot past the Night Leopard, kicked up a spray of water braking, then swung back around.

She craned her neck. "Isn't that one of the Supreme Leader's cars?"

Thiessen squinted. "Looks like."

But instead of the old man stepping out, the general strolled past them, waving for them to follow. He pointed them into the back, then settled on the wide bench seat facing theirs.

The vehicle engine roared, and they launched forward.

With the vehicle moving, the Azoren general relaxed. "You did not come with conditions and threats, then?"

Pieces clicked into place for Benson. "You're worried about our ships having lock-on against your defensive task force."

"It seems unprovoked, Captain."

"The last time we visited, we weren't necessarily treated as guests."

"Field Marshal Faulk voiced concerns about your intent. It would seem his concerns were warranted."

"If we meant your task force harm, General, it would be fiery chunks raining down on Himmel."

Muscles bunched along the Azoren officer's jaw. "You mentioned data?"

Thiessen reached inside the blue slicker covering his uniform and pulled out a storage device. "Mostly, it's video and sensor readings from the major engagements. We're well aware that you wouldn't trust our analyses. Unfortunately, we weren't able to retrieve data from your ships."

The general took the device and studied it. Barely the size of his palm, but it held petabytes of information. He sniffled, then pocketed it. "I shall review it tonight."

"Supreme Commander Graf and Minister King might—"

"You'll have your chance to meet with them." The general turned his attention to the dreary haze outside the window to his right.

Benson took the signal and looked out the window to her right.

Other than stopping to pass through a security checkpoint anchored by a heavy tank with fire-blackened and dented armor, they moved through the city at a frightening clip.

An hour after arriving on the planet, they were sloshing down a rutted dirt road. Muddy water splashed against the undercarriage.

Several minutes after turning, they came to a stop again.

The rhythm of the windshield wipers thumped through the car.

A soldier in gray uniform glanced through the windows, saluted the general, then waved the car forward.

Once they passed through the gate, Benson sat up.

This wasn't some old countryside manor with rustic stone walls. The fence and gate were wood and heavy-gauge wire. Machine-gun towers pointed inward, not out. Simple wooden structures sank into the muddy ground.

They stopped outside one of those buildings, and the general nodded toward it. "You have half an hour. Spend it as you will."

Benson's muscles froze.

Sensing her unease, Thiessen pulled her out with him.

What had been a vague scent of smoke became a choking, clinging reek, as if they were downwind of a foundry.

He pulled her up to the wooden slats rising above the mud and knocked on the crude door.

A voice boomed from within. "Come."

Thiessen squeezed her hand and pushed the door inward.

King sat at a rickety wooden table, the glow of a display making his face ghostly. His stylish outfit hung loosely off of him, now threadbare and dirty.

He stood. "The conquerors return!"

Benson staggered forward. "What's going on?"

"Come now. You're a bright woman. It's obvious enough."

"Why? What did you do?"

"What did I do?" The old man chuckled. "Child, this is architectural realization."

Thiessen turned back to the door. "They're killing you after you created them?"

"They're killing me because I'm an embarrassing reminder of their origin."

Benson swallowed. "And Graf?"

"He and I have our appointment this afternoon. Perhaps we shall hold hands. The last, if there's honor with that."

"The last?"

"Humans. Enablers. Naive fools who imagined themselves gods. I think it's safe to say that Graf might be conflicted about this outcome. He never did see the end game, I'm afraid."

"But you…knew?"

"Death is inevitable, my child. When you work so closely with toxic materials, the odds of them killing you are quite high."

Thiessen shook his head. "What happened? The High Command building was collapsed. The woods out by the starport were just craters."

"It would seem that General Weber's association with the locals was much stronger than previously suspected. Once the fleet—do allow me the vanity to call it that—left, a more organized assault than anyone had anticipated was even possible pushed deep into the city. It's only a matter of time now."

"And these Children have been exterminating any humans they could get their hands on?"

"Fellow soldiers, research scientists, laborers—all obsolete now."

Pain was like a spike pounding into Benson's skull. She rubbed her temple. "We can get you out. We can declare you a diplomatic asset."

King made a ticking sound. "That is both impractical and unnecessary."

"We already have the defense task force targeted. The *Valor* alone could destroy that force, and a few missiles would turn the capital to rubble."

The old man clapped and laughed. "You do a father proud."

Thiessen's eyes flew wide. "What?"

Benson bowed her head. She hadn't been ready for this, but there it was. "He's my father."

"The second most powerful man in the Azoren government is your father? How did you...?"

King held up a hand. "This is something that predates her, Captain. It's something I've spent decades bringing to fruition—something my cause has spent generations bringing about."

The old man reached inside his shirt and pulled out a gold necklace, which he unclipped from his neck and handed to Benson. "These animals would only loot that. Thank goodness gold and silver are no longer used for dental work."

She held the chain up and turned the thing dangling from the end of it around in the glow of the display. "What—" She could barely breathe. "What's this symbol on the ring?"

"An old Earth bird. An owl."

Thiessen's arm was around her shoulder. "You said you architected this?"

"Going back decades, yes. The Azoren have had a poisonous infatuation with racial purity and idealized versions of the perfect human. For someone with a track record creating exactly that, I became the perfect recruit."

"You...what?"

"I'm a geneticist, Captain. More, really, but that became my focus. My career was modeled upon the idea of crafting perfect humans—perfect servants. Androids, originally. As Faith can tell you, the Kedraalians have their own Children."

Benson cringed. "Stiles."

"Then you've worked with one of my Generation 3 creations."

"Genesis 3."

"Ah! Rebranding. Good. They're a worthwhile variation from my previous work. The difference between them and the Children wasn't just in the toxic insistence of an incestuous, closed genetic sourcing but in the way they were raised. The Generation 3s weren't given families as I had proven wise, unfortunately, but they were shown something close to it. The Children were only shown the value of hatred."

Thiessen paced. "But you gave them the technology to create these monsters?"

"I accelerated and refined work they were already doing. At some point, they would have arrived at the solution."

"You created this situation!"

"Not at all. What I did was help them to end it. Feed the fire until the fuel is gone, then it can do nothing but expire."

The Gulmar captain turned away. "That's inexcusable. This army of…things—"

"Ah, ah, Captain! Careful with your judgments. I've seen the look in your eyes when you get close to my daughter."

"What—?"

King tilted his head. "Didn't you hear what I said earlier? Genesis 3? There must be a predecessor, mustn't there?"

Thiessen's jaw dropped. "Faith?"

King's brow wrinkled and his lips turned down in a frown as he turned to Benson. "My Genesis 2 child. The only way we could have successfully had a child, Sargota and I. Do tell your mother that I've missed the thrill of her intellect."

Benson's headache flared even more dangerously. "I—"

Her father hugged her awkwardly. "The headaches still trouble you all these years on? Talk to Old Man McLeod. Damon McLeod."

"Damon McLeod? Is he related to Avis McLeod?"

"That boy must be a man of some years now. His grandfather, yes. He has my notes, or he can put you in contact with one of my colleagues from MartGun. It's a minor chemical imbalance. You should've outgrown it. It's easy enough to treat. Cinnamon can help."

*Cinnamon!*

She could have stayed in that awkward hug forever, but there was a knock on the door.

Benson pushed away, gasping, trying not to cry. "We have to go."

"Surprisingly, I will as well." There was no fear in her father's eyes. "I was never going to be the sort of father who could watch you grow tall or wipe away all your tears. My ambitions—my obligations, I suppose—from the start took me away from your side. Yet that never diminished my pride in what I created."

The door opened, and the sergeant who had driven Benson and Thiessen waved them out. "We must go."

She stuffed the necklace inside her jacket and headed out into the rain.

Another car like the one they'd come in was parked behind theirs. A woman climbed out with help from a poshly dressed, beefy young man who had the look of a bodyguard.

Benson recognized the woman. "Devanshi Patel?"

The older woman turned, smiled smugly, and drew in a deep breath. "Captain Faith Benson. How surprising to see a senior Kedraalian officer in the headquarters of the Azoren High Command."

Thiessen pressed a hand against Benson's back. "Headquarters? Does she—?"

Benson gave a quick shake of her head. "Did you have business with… the High Command, ma'am?"

Patel's smile turned cold. "We have a long, hard-earned history."

One of the camp guards jogged over and waved for the Patel matron to follow. "We are ready for you."

She waved over her shoulder at Benson. "If you'll excuse me, Captain."

As Benson lowered herself into the vehicle, a squad of soldiers with rifles ran toward the area where Patel was being escorted.

Benson closed her eyes. "General, if you could get us to the starport, I believe our business here has concluded."

"Of course, Captain."

They sped out of the camp, but they couldn't outrun the sound of rifle fire.

It was the sound of a snake eating its tail.

Grier tried to focus on the conference room's large screen, but for the life of her, she couldn't be drawn to the signals. She knew the symbols and the colors and all of that, although with some of it she had to think back to training.

Halliwell, though? He was absolutely absorbed in it. He was hunched forward, one finger crawling over a control surface to drill down on the image of Himmel's capital city, where a red triangle sped along a long brown line.

He ran fingers across his furrowed brow. "What the hell is she doing?"

Grier leaned in close, as much to breathe in his cologne as to study what he was looking at. She enjoyed the heat coming off of him and imagined she could hear his heart beating just below the soft hum of the air recycling system. "Looks like they're headed back to the starport, right?"

The Marine lieutenant tapped the control surface twice, flipping back to imagery from the *Sinclair* signals ship, which was now in a low orbit. From its high-powered camera feeds, a long, black, blocky car moved down cratered and cracked streets.

He leaned back with a frustrated sigh, nearly brushing against her. "But why'd she go to that camp outside the city?"

Scowling, he flipped back through cached imagery, stopping when he found a high-resolution blowup of Benson headed into a wooden shack.

She looked regal in her whites, her long hair let down.

Was that why he'd focused on that image?

Grier's injured arm itched.

Despite Commander Dietrich's reassurances that everything would be fine if she were patient, she scratched at the flesh around the top of the cast. Bone could regrow stronger than before, and atrophied muscle could be rebuilt with time and effort. But every time she removed the cast to clean the grody skin it covered, her heart plummeted.

Those muscles were a part of her identity. They were something she'd worked so hard to craft, and they were shrinking so quickly.

Maybe that diminished her in Halliwell's eyes. It felt that way.

She set her good hand on his. "You don't have to get all worked up about this. She's fine."

He yanked his hand away. "I told her exactly what I could support."

"I think she's the captain, Clive." Grier pulled her hand back and tried to hide her pain. "Maybe that allows her to, y'know, make her own calls?"

"I can get ten able-bodied Marines in gunships. That's it. If she doesn't follow my plan, I have no idea what to expect."

"All that battle damage we're seeing—do you really have valid plans?"

His scowl deepened, then he turned back to the live data feed. "You see these signals?" He indicated a wide circle of gold squares around the heart of the city. There were a lot more of them than the red triangles representing Azoren positions.

"Unknown forces, right?"

"In this case, they might as well be listed as hostile. That circle's been closing in since she landed. It's closing faster now." He flipped back to the *Sinclair*'s live camera feed. "There. See?"

At the extreme edge of the camera's field of vision, clumps of people in uniform and civilian clothes moved between buildings. They were armed with a mixture of assault rifles and hunting weapons. Some had bows or axes.

Grier flexed her good hand. "Rebels or something."

"Yeah, well, rebels don't care if you're a visiting dignitary or the king. They're out to kill anyone they see as a threat."

"I get it, okay? You don't have to snap at me."

"Toni, my point is I've got ten people on standby, sitting in gunships. They might have to head down there and pull off a rescue—"

"I said I get it."

He glared. "Fine."

She thrust herself back in her chair. "Actually, no it's not."

Halliwell groaned. "This isn't the time for one of your fits."

"One of my..." She snorted. "Did you just say that?"

"Not now."

The edge in his voice said he was ready to escalate to calling her out by rank.

Fine. She could let it go until the captain was in the air, but it was long past time someone talked frankly with him about his temper.

*One of my fits.*

If her arm wasn't such a wreck, she would've punched him in the shoulder.

She propped her good arm on the table and leaned her chin against the fist. "They're past that circle now, headed for the starport."

He grunted, flipping from imagery to symbols. "That city's going to fall."

"Good. They're assholes."

"How do we know these other people are any better?"

"At least they won't be the threat the Azoren were."

Halliwell tapped on his data pad, and the chime of an accepted connection came through.

"Lieutenant Halliwell?" It was Chopra, Benson's XO.

"Hey, Commander. Are we seeing any activity with the Azoren ships?"

"None whatsoever."

"Are those human crew or Children?"

"It is my understanding they are humans. When I've talked to the task force captain, he looked nothing like the Children. Is something going on?"

"We're monitoring the situation on the ground, and it's turning ugly."

"Ah. Then the Home Defense ships not intervening is curious."

Halliwell rubbed his chin. "Captain Benson's almost to the starport. What would you think of our gunships acting as escort?"

"A sound idea, if there's trouble. I'll see to it."

"Thanks, Commander."

Halliwell disconnected and drummed his fingers on the tabletop while Benson's signal moved inside the fortified compound.

Green circles sped down toward the area: the gunships.

He bowed his head. "I know you think I've got a temper problem."

"Think?" Grier took a long breath. "Clive, everybody *knows*. It's the only thing holding you back."

"I don't have—" His voice was rising, and he apparently realized it.

"Stress is a bitch. I get that."

"It's not stress. It's…" He massaged his forehead. "Nothing."

She straightened her back and sat like Benson. "You can talk to me."

"Don't do that."

"C'mon. I'm trying to get you to open up. I know you resent how your family was punished and how you didn't have fair and equal access—"

He waved her away. "That's not it."

"You said—"

"That was just…an excuse, I guess."

"But it makes you mad, right?"

"It did. Does. It's not the *real* problem."

She let him stare at the display until Benson's shuttle was off the ground. "Then you know what the problem is?"

He shrugged his thick shoulders. "I think so.

"I'm listening. I'm always listening."

"I know. I don't say it, Toni, but I appreciate everything you do."

She offered her good hand again.

He took it, engulfing it in his powerful grip. "It's Dramora."

"Oh. Yeah. I get nightmares, too."

"It's more than that. The way they tried to sweep the whole thing under the rug so they didn't upset all those important people, like our battalion didn't matter." He squeezed his eyes shut.

"It's politics, right?"

"It's betrayal. My whole career, I've been asked to be honorable and to take orders without giving lip. Now I'm asked to lead, to send my Marines into deadly situations."

"That's our job."

"It is, but look what we're doing. I mean, look what we had to do. Everything we've learned. This spy blows up a planet because there's alien technology on it? And we gave that technology away, we gave away weapons systems responsible for killing all those people on Radetta? They don't just want us to shut up and follow orders. They want us to live without a voice."

"It's screwed up. I get it."

"It's eating me up inside, every time I find out more. We've got a prime minister who's rotten. He's talking about not giving up his power."

"Make me a promise, okay? When the captain gets back, and we're out of here, talk to her."

"She can't change this."

"I think she can. She's going to have a lot of power and influence when this is all over, even if her military career is over."

He turned from the screen. "You think?"

"What she did had to be done. They were hanging her out to dry, setting her up to take the fall. But she pulled it off."

"It's still going to end her career."

"I don't know. But she'll be able to do whatever she wants. And if she gets into power, she's going to be the one who can fix these problems."

Halliwell relaxed a little. "I'll talk to her."

"Good. And when we get back to Kedraal, you can start therapy. Okay?"

A weak smile tugged the corners of his mouth up. "If you say so."

She squeezed his hand. "I do."

<hr>

Nausea was a block of ice in Parkinson's gut. He folded his coveralls into a neat square and set them on the examination table. The medical center was always cool, but now it felt like he was slipping into a cold sleep container.

Beyond the privacy curtain, the hiss of respirators and the soft moans of the other patients undergoing intensive care acted as a background noise generator.

Nothing could protect him from the smells of mangled bodies, though —alcohol, unguents, and dry blood.

Ensign Kohn gently probed a discolored patch of skin that was flaking. "You've been taking your medication?"

"It doesn't always stay down."

"We could administer it intravenously."

"Does it matter now?"

The intern pointed to his patient's prominent ribcage. "You've lost significant mass. The bruising, the nausea—it's best if we put you in sleep immediately or administer more aggressive treatment."

Parkinson tugged a patch of hair from his scalp. "It's a little late. I mean, my gums are bleeding."

"Then we should definitely go with cold sleep. We get you back home, the treatment regimen is going to take care of all these problems."

"All of them?"

"It won't be pleasant, but your odds of survival go up significantly."

A part of Parkinson wanted to rebel against that diagnosis, to challenge this young man who'd been a quietly suffering subordinate for years. Fortunately, there was a rational part of the brain putting out an unmistakeable warning.

That warning was a frank "no," an acknowledgment of damage done and a level of behavior that could already justify a small, lethal mistake during treatment.

Parkinson chuckled at that without meaning to. "Sorry."

Kohn's thick eyebrows arched. "Is everything okay?"

"I was just thinking how things have changed for us—me dying and you starting on a career path that...you deserve."

For just a moment, there was a tension on the young man's face, then it was gone. "You'll be fine."

"That doesn't mean I don't owe you an apology."

The intern smiled. "I'm past that."

"I appreciate that. I didn't realize it at the time, but you're sort of intimidating."

"Me?"

"Don't act surprised. You made me come to terms with being a big fish in a small pond. That's tough on an ego."

The intern shrugged. "I understand. I always felt growing up that I was less than everyone else. I wasn't sure who I was supposed to be."

"Looks like you got that sorted."

"I hope so. We'll see how my parents feel. It was always tough just..." His jaw clenched. "They never cared what anyone else thought of me."

Parkinson's gut twisted. "My problems were the other way around: I never deserved love. In my head, I mean. I had to constantly work to earn even a little. It's screwed up how parents can be so unreliable."

"At least you had them. Those Children the Azoren created never had parents at all. Neither did Stiles, apparently."

"She told you that?"

"Sort of. Indirectly."

"I need to make amends with her, I guess."

"She might not care?" Kohn shrugged. "She was sort of using both of us."

"Not as badly as I did her. That sick need to feel superior, having a pretty woman as a conquest? I see it now."

"At some point, everyone does terrible things—intentional or not. Accepting responsibility for what you did is what matters."

"Fair enough." Wisdom from someone so much younger…

It would've been painful for Parkinson before. Not now.

Plastic rings scraped along the shoehorn railing surrounding the examination area, then Dietrich stepped through the small gap, data pad in one hand. He closed the curtain back.

He'd lost a little weight in the trip back from Azh Shivan. Rumor was, he hadn't handled the destruction of the Azoren and Khanate ships well, and that all of the deaths caused by some secret weapon detonating on the planet had sent him back to the bottle.

Now, though, he seemed fine: bright-eyed and almost pleasant as he studied the data pad. "Chief."

Parkinson tried to match the doctor's positive vibe, then gave up. "Ensign Kohn here was giving me the cold sleep sales pitch again. I think he's just tired of my visits."

"Ensign Kohn knows what he's talking about. Your numbers look horrible."

"Thanks, Doc. So, if I go under, do I wake up in a military hospital with the two of you as my caretakers?"

Dietrich's eyes darted over to Kohn, then back to the data pad. "I think Chuck's going to be able to choose whatever path he wants. I've already submitted my retirement paperwork."

Kohn looked down. He obviously wasn't surprised, not like Parkinson.

The engineer tried to figure that out. "Retirement sounds like a pretty big change for you."

"I'll get used to it. I need to dedicate myself to something bigger."

"You opening up a research clinic?"

"I've never been good at research, I'm afraid. No, my focus will be on finding out what really happened to my wife."

Before, Parkinson had never connected with Dietrich over that tragedy. It was just a thing people talked about. Yeah, the report about the ship's reactor blowing up was nonsense, but now, after feeling the pain of Chief Taylor's death...

It was like a shared scar.

Except Dietrich had been in a long-lasting relationship, and Parkinson's had been...what?

Potential? Imagined?

It had to have been potential. Taylor had sent signals. She'd warmed to him.

And that had really hurt. That hurt kept piling up.

A part of Parkinson realized that death would just be the end of all that pain accumulating, but it was shouted down by the part that enjoyed life.

*More scars. Toughen up. Get over it.*

Dietrich powered off the data pad. "Well? What's the verdict, Chief?"

The chief shivered. He'd done his part for the war, paid the price for his cowardice, hadn't he? "You think I deserve one of those cold sleep spots?"

"Of course you do. We've got a few now that we've gone a while without a constant onslaught of dying. We'll be able to pull some more people out and work miracles before we get back to Kedraal."

Parkinson licked his cracked lips. "Then I guess it's time to sleep."

**31**

---

Citizens packed the Avenue of the Founders, a sight Benson couldn't recall seeing outside of videos of the armistice celebration after the War of Separation. For all she knew, those videos were doctored.

What she saw now? The deafening shouts, the aroma of funnel cakes and grilled protein sausages? The throngs of whooping and hollering people waving flags?

It was real, brilliant in the intense, broiling sunlight.

"Quite the sight, wouldn't you say?"

Benson twisted her head around in the crowded back seat of the open limousine to get a clear look at the man who'd spoken: Prime Minister Zenawi.

Sweat trickled from the giant, barrel-chested man's wiry gray hair to glisten against his copper-brown skin. He never stopped waving enthusiastically or flashing his polished white teeth, and the look of jubilation in his pale brown eyes was as reptilian and calculated as ever.

She followed his lead, ignoring the damp of sweat beneath her white jacket and smiling a little less resentfully while waving at people on the other side of the car. "They're the first people in generations to know peace."

"And they have the great and wise Captain Benson to thank for it."

Zenawi's smile was like a permanent fixture, only disappearing in the instants where his lips moved.

"You resent me circumventing your office."

"Not at all. A brilliant tactical maneuver. You have a bright future."

"She should be in prison." Admiral Ames's voice was recognizable without having to look at him.

She did anyway, smiling brightly at the Chief of Naval Operations. "Who should be in prison is an interesting discussion point, isn't it, Admiral?"

The old man twisted away, his heavy jowls shaking before he threw a perfunctory wave at the assembled Kedraalians.

But there was no hiding how he'd aged since issuing his orders to her to abandon her attack against the Republic's enemies and return. His gambit had puffed out the bags under his dark eyes and dug deeper the wrinkles crisscrossing his chestnut skin.

If he'd dreamed of ending her career with that order, he would die unsatisfied.

The car continued down the avenue, then along for another three kilometers, before coming to a stop in the parking lot of Heroes Green. Security officers rushed over and opened the car doors, helping the two older men out. A few of the officers—young, sturdily built women—smiled at Benson.

Were they signaling approval or gratitude? Did they see themselves in her?

She hoped that might be it, that she might have done something that one day could be seen as aspirational and noble.

In her heart, though, there would always be the nightmares of killing.

When she climbed the stairs to the stage, Sargota was there, quick to move in for a hug. Benson felt a flash of cynical resentment, questioning the old woman's sudden need to show affection after a lifetime of cool disconnect.

Even if it was all orchestrated, it could be forgiven. Until Sargota finally had her little scepter of power, she would never be satisfied, and it was so close now.

They took seats behind and to the right of the podium as Zenawi rushed to the front of the stage to work the crowd. He glad-handed and pumped his fist like the showman he was, soaking in the adulation that apparently acted like a mythical elixir, rolling back the years.

Finally, he settled behind the podium.

This was going to be the excruciating part.

Benson pretended to listen, nodding and even clapping when it seemed appropriate.

Sargota leaned in. "Give him his due, I suppose."

"That he knows how to manipulate people already susceptible to manipulation?" Benson clapped as the crowd roared.

"He rose from humble enough beginnings."

"Ambition can overcome any barrier."

The old woman cocked her head. "I sense you had more than one target with that comment, my dear."

"Think of it as a cluster bomb. It's a target-rich environment."

"You should exhibit more discernment with your attacks."

"The attack goes no further than a commentary about blind ambition."

Her mother adjusted her blue coat. It was the same deep color as the prime minister's jacket, varying only in the marginally feminine cut. "Would it be fair for me to make an observation about the competitive nature of a child who finds it necessary to upstage her mother?"

"Upstage? That's how you'd describe someone going off to war to end decades of instability with crazed enemies? That seems a bit much, even for you."

"I have my coalition. Any minute now, that blowhard's going to wrap his speech with the somber announcement of his necessary retirement so that he might spend more time with his family. I think I've earned my moment."

Benson thought back to the Azoren death camp. "I almost forgot: My father wanted me to convey how much he missed your intellect."

The old woman stiffened, and the color drained from her cheeks. "You talked to him?"

"Twice. He's dead now."

"The galaxy's a better place, then."

"Your empathy overwhelms."

"All you have are the memories of a spoiled child. How could you possibly appreciate the sort of monster he was?"

"I didn't get the impression he believed the Azoren ideology."

"Of course he didn't." The old woman shook her head, as if offended. "But he cared more about his career than mine, and he only ever saw you as a science project."

Benson almost laughed at the old woman's lack of self-awareness. "He definitely missed out on all the years of warmth we shared."

"Don't be an ungrateful boor, Faith."

"I don't know what I was thinking."

A sad moan went through those assembled, and Benson realized Zenawi must have announced his retirement.

He waved the boos down. "Now, now. While your response is certainly appreciated, I think it's important to remember that I've dedicated forty-two years to public service, and in that time…well, I have six grandchildren in need of spoiling."

The old politician let out a heartwarming chuckle that brought a long round of applause and screams of thanks.

Sargota sniffled. "I should have forced him to resign publicly and ridden in the limo with you. I earned that much."

Benson concentrated on the prime minister as he launched into his buildup.

"And after all—" He turned, that same fake smile plastered on his face, and waved toward Sargota. "—we have more than capable hands waiting to take the reins and drive our great Kedraalian Republic to new heights. Sargota, come on up here."

As if she'd been bursting with joy all along, Benson's mother hopped out of her seat and hurried to the podium. She squeezed Zenawi in a bear hug that signaled warmth and compassion—let bygones be bygones.

The old couple held each other's hands aloft in victory, beaming as if this was a spontaneous love fest rather than the outcome of brass knuckles negotiations.

Zenawi settled in the seat Sargota had abandoned while the old woman launched into an awkward but impassioned speech.

He clapped when the first cue came for it, but most of the crowd seemed to be parsing her words.

She didn't notice, instead plowing on with her focus on minutia and esoterica.

The old man leaned forward and without letting his ecstatic facade slip glanced at Benson. "You know what's worse than being undone by you, Captain?"

"Losing to my mother?"

"By many, many kilometers. Would you be offended if I called her a ball-breaking bitch?"

"I think it's a fair assessment. I'm not brittle."

"A lot of people take offense."

"You know what I call a man who uses her tactics?"

"An ass?"

"A ball-breaking son-of-a-bitch." Benson clapped when the crowd finally signaled they'd grown warm to Sargota. "Or an ass. Sex doesn't protect you from condemnation. She has unnecessarily sharp elbows. So do a lot of men."

Zenawi looked at Benson through slitted lids. "You really are something."

"It's taken me a few years to see it, but I agree with you."

"Well—" He nodded toward the podium. "—I'll concede the point that she can be convincing. I was ready to contest this coalition to the bloody end."

"Until you saw the GSA's case against you?"

"I prefer to present it as accepting the value of embracing solidarity, forgiveness, and seeing the way ahead for our great nation."

"So she did offer you a full pardon?"

He chuckled. "After some concessions. Admiral Zane might not say that he's stepping away to spend time with a bunch of snot-nosed brats, but he's going to enjoy his new opportunity to enjoy his yacht and all the deckhands he can afford."

Benson glanced over at the seething admiral, who was staring daggers at her mother's back. "I guess her promise of transparency will have its limits."

"One would hope. Dismantling the spy agencies..." The prime minister tut-tutted. "You might want to speak to her about that."

"I already have."

Zenawi bowed his head. "I'd hoped you might be more rational."

"That's not what I meant. I warned her that maybe it's not a good idea shining a light into all the dark corners. Sometimes, the light reveals things too terrible for people to know."

His head came up. "You told her that?"

"Almost in those exact words. I've had the chance to work with some very insightful individuals, Mr. Prime Minister."

"The Genesis 3 agents?"

"Including them." She pulled her father's Owl ring out for the prime minister to see.

He nodded. "Some legacies are better left buried."

"It was a different time, and we were struggling to survive. I understand."

"Do you? You weren't even born when the greatest mistakes were made, when we failed to stop the worst of humanity from escaping Earth with us."

"I've seen those people firsthand now."

"You have, I suppose." Zenawi thumbed sweat from his upper lip. "In many ways, your father was a patriot."

"I don't think I like that term. I prefer to see him as a flawed human, same as the rest of us. His flaws just enabled him to do things I wouldn't have, and those things led to the survival of our people."

"That's an almost emotionless analysis."

"Arrived at only after days of crying and wrestling with who and what I am."

Zenawi clapped and whistled as the crowd roared, then he patted Benson's knee. "Can I tell you something, Captain?"

She flinched. "I guess so."

"What you did? I know it's eating at you. I know you're taking meds to deal with the trauma of betrayal. No one can fairly call all of that heroic. I wouldn't pretend to. But the bravery behind seeing your mission through? There isn't a word powerful enough to capture that."

"Thank you. Now let me ask you something."

"It's only fair."

"If I hadn't used my connections to get the word out through the Parliament that my task force had returned victorious, what would you have done?"

A dark grin split his face. "I wouldn't be the one stepping down, obviously."

"Your office had a public relations project built out already, I assume."

"A noble officer gone off the rails because of stress. A terrible choice made when faced with nothing but terrible choices. We had many possible scenarios to play with. If you accepted a quiet retirement, that would've been the end of it."

She nodded. "I don't think I'm quite ready for retirement, Mr. Prime Minister."

The people on the stage rose and applauded; Benson did the same, as did Zenawi.

When Sargota waved Benson forward to the podium, she accepted, putting on the same false smile Zenawi had managed. All the cheering, the waving, the chanting—it had an intoxicating element to it.

Benson soaked it in.

She wasn't ready for retirement. Not yet.

But there would come a time where new leadership was called for, and she would be ready.

**32**

———

Robotic construction vehicles beeped shrilly as they crunched over debris, grinding it beneath heavy treads before scooping it up and piling it into the back of trucks that lumbered away, laden with the remnants of the once great city of Radetta. The operation tossed dust and ash into the air, and even with her mask on, Benson coughed.

Thiessen pulled her along, his fingers clasping her hand tightly. "We'll have to scrub this off when we get back. That's the remains of hundreds of thousands of people."

She pressed his hand against her hip, enjoying the strength and warmth of it in the cool morning air. "We can't let something like this happen again."

"We won't. The Khanate's gone."

"It wasn't just them. The Azoren, probably even the Moskav—they would've been fine turning any opposition into radioactive waste."

"They're gone, too."

They passed through a cloud of the choking dust, which settled in their hair. She shook it out and brushed fine flakes from her coveralls. She would've preferred wearing her whites, especially on what amounted to a critical diplomatic mission, but no one was watching them, and she preferred throwing out a work uniform to something Thiessen admired.

She could always dress up for him later.

He came to a stop beside their vehicle—a bright red corporate shuttle that was gray from the ash. "Have you put together the first set of announcements?"

"Maybe we could work through them tonight."

"Over dinner, I suppose? I know someone who could get us some really good linguini and a bottle of wine."

"I don't have any plans. When I took on this envoy position, I guess I threw open my schedule."

"Then we could hash things out. You up for an all-nighter, Admiral?" His wink was almost lost behind the powder covering his mask.

The shuttle ramp dropped, and they climbed up, peeling off their masks, then brushing the dust from each other's outfits. Rather than a pilot awaiting them, a computer chimed when they stepped into the passenger seating area.

Thiessen pulled his data pad out and tapped the display, then the shuttle engines came to life.

He strapped in beside her, throwing an arm over the top of her chair. "Mind giving me a preview?"

She kissed him, tasting the rubbery remnant of the oxygen mask assembly on his lips. "Or were you talking about policy?"

Thiessen rested his chin on an open palm and studied the ceiling. "I had been thinking policy, but..."

That made her laugh. "All right, *Mr.* Thiessen."

"Appropriate."

"The highest priority is going to be bringing the corporations to heel."

"Highest and toughest. I know that's obvious, but it has to be stated."

"Noted. Hand in hand with that is dismantling the lack of access for the poor. People are going to have access to training and cultural rehabilitation—"

"That's a tricky phrase."

"Isn't that what it is? You've had generations who went without fair access and opportunity. Some of them have given up. It's going to be a significant effort to change their mindset, but it's been done before."

"What was the example you cited?"

"Absorbing the former East Germany back into Germany after the fall of the Soviet Union. That was centuries ago. If they were able to do it, we can do it."

The shuttle engines whined as it lifted off the ground.

"It's going to be an ugly fight. The elite aren't going to just give everything up."

"They don't have a choice. Without the old Gulmar leadership, your nation is on the verge of economic ruin. They can't recover, and every one of your executive leadership members acknowledges this. We can't give you big enough loans to keep you afloat. You'll need to rejoin the republic."

"And you know the argument: Why can't we just do that now? You have an answer?"

"Well, I have Sargota's answer, and I have my answer. Which do you—?"

"Yours, thanks. Your mother's too much for me right now."

"That's odd. She said the same thing about you."

His eyes twinkled. "Thank you."

"So, my answer is simple: If we bring you in without these changes, your elite just replace the Patels and their comrades. We don't have enough prison space for another group of corporate criminals. That means we fix the problem first."

"And the impoverished? You want them to suffer?"

She kissed him again. "I know those are your people. The problem is, even if everyone means well, if we dump millions of low-wage workers into the economy, it's going to be too disruptive."

"It's okay for my people to suffer so that yours don't?"

"Try not to put it that way. We're talking about opening schools and universities to everyone who qualifies and shows an interest."

"A small percentage."

"We can build out educational opportunities here in parallel. That short-term demand for instructors will generate hundreds of jobs."

"For *your* people."

"Eventually we're all one people, Floyd."

He crossed his arms over his chest. "Only after my people go through years of starvation and suffering. It's not a fair exchange."

"I'm not through yet." She pulled on his elbow. "Stop closing me out. Please?"

He sighed, then relaxed. "Go on."

"It's not just a concern about people in our economy being displaced by low-wage labor. There's also seeing that labor pool exploited. We can't regulate out greed. Well, we can, but this is the best approach. Greed is still a part of human nature, no matter how hard we try to kid ourselves we're enlightened."

"Speaking as a former low-wage laborer, I think we're fine being exploited. A roof over your head, clean clothes—it beats the alternative."

"We're going to get there. Your people just need a chance to catch up."

He tensed. "And your mother has agreed with this?"

"All of it. Not without fighting, but I have it in writing. She'll make a provisional decree next year about the Gulmar Union returning. The loans, the educational programs, the relief programs—it's all budgeted."

"And her support?"

"She has a big enough group in the coalition to back it all. Going against all the provisions would mean the representatives would have to vote against their own best interests."

Thiessen snorted. "Like that would ever happen."

Benson leaned against him. "I don't think I like this cynicism cropping up in you."

He looked away. "I think I caught it while we were firing on defenseless ships."

"Do you mean that?"

"I don't know. I'm still trying to come to terms with it. I hadn't had a good night's sleep until you came back, and now I'm not even sure I'll sleep well tonight."

"We can try for physical exhaustion again."

"Ha." He pinched the bridge of his nose. "Seriously, it hasn't haunted you?"

"Of course it has. But I'm dealing with it. We could have left those Azoren and Khanate ships to fall into the atmosphere. The crews would've died before that happened, though. The EMP from that anti-matter weapon was what killed those people. We just ended their suffering."

"Ouch. That's a nice way to rewrite history. I don't think I'm up for that."

"It's not really a rewrite. What would you have had us do? Did you really want a bunch of Azoren Children mixed in with your wounded Azoren soldiers? Neither of us had the personnel to keep them all under control."

"Their ships could've been repaired."

"Maybe. Same problem, though. If we sent teams over to help with repairs, they would've needed Marines and security officers for protection."

The shuttle banked, pushing Thiessen against her. His frown didn't fade. "It was a terrible mission, regardless."

"That's the main thing we have to accept. Those people forced this onto us."

Thiessen sighed. "It's hard to condemn an entire planet for the acts of what might not even be the majority."

"Actually, I didn't even get a chance to tell you about that."

"About what?"

"Your old friend Ambassador Manshaus—"

"Anders? What about him?"

"He contacted Sargota. Apparently, the old regime's collapse has brought about a significant shift in ideology. They're proposing a normalizing of relations."

Thiessen shook his head. "I never thought I'd see the day."

She brushed her fingers through his hair. "Did you ever expect to be the de facto leader of your people?"

"You mean benevolent dictator?"

"Is that your plan?"

"No. I agreed to oversee this return to the Republic. After that, I'm done. I know enough history to see how power holds onto you if you don't push it away. There's always the next crisis to justify extending the length of your rule. Not me."

"But when it's all over, will you come to Kedraal? You could be the first representative of your people."

"It sounds like prison."

"It's not that bad. I'm thinking of giving it a try myself when I finish up."

"Hanging up the admiral stars? I thought you dreamed about being in command of a fleet."

"I had a lot of dreams. They're not always what you expect."

Thiessen bit his lip. "I guess there are worse things than having to negotiate with someone like you."

She smiled. "Let's see how you do tonight."

---

Stiles rested her elbow on the deck rail and took in the brilliant Kedraal sunset as the waves lapped against the yacht's side. It was different seeing the colors stretched across the horizon when she wasn't on duty—when she didn't have a duty anymore.

She took a sip from her glass, then rolled the fruity alcoholic drink over her tongue. It was hot going down, and it made her legs tremble. She breathed in the salty sea air and closed her eyes as a warm wind hugged her skin. Rehab was over, as was her career.

What was she supposed to do now?

Caville's scent reached her before she heard his steps. He leaned against the rail to her right, skin glistening after a quick swim. "Most of the scars have healed up nicely."

"Your toe, too."

He looked down and wiggled the stump. "I'll have it regrown, I guess."

"Messes with your balance otherwise."

"I've done well enough."

She took another drink. It burned in her stomach, relaxing her. "You figure out what you're going to do?"

"We don't have to *do* anything. The settlement against MartGun and the government hush money should be enough to live comfortably, don't you think?"

"I guess. I'm not sure I can just...*live*, though."

"Give it a try." He nodded back toward Gallo, who was stretched out on a deck recliner. "We're going to."

"I thought you liked your women more athletic."

"How about learning a little forgiveness?"

Stiles squinted at McLeod, who came out of the wheelhouse. He wore a loud shirt covered in jumping fish designs and white cargo shorts. Compared to his three young bathing-suited guests, he was over-dressed.

She imagined that was insecurity. He was old enough to be their father. In fact, he had the easy manner of someone who would have been good at exactly that.

When he knelt beside Gallo to chat, Stiles remembered his admission about his "needs."

Maybe she was being naive about his personality and intent, after all.

She looked down at the whitecaps rushing toward the shore. "You're not worried about her safety?"

"Denise?"

"Her testimony forced Zenawi into retirement."

"So did ours. So did a whole bunch of people's. His history forced him into retirement, not us."

"I'm thinking of taking the prime minister up on her offer."

"Looking for other survivors?"

"We don't know all of our brothers and sisters died. Before McLeod took over, the records were a disaster. All those people deep undercover..."

"Who wants to keep detailed records on their private assassins?"

Stiles set her drink on the rail again and looked at her hands. Muscles moved under her skin when she flexed her arms and legs. Power, agility—it was all coming back.

She ran fingers over her belly, where the alcohol was releasing its chemicals. It was a strange sort of freedom, just enjoying that.

McLeod's sandals flopped against the deck. "Ahoy!"

Caville turned and extended a hand for the older man to shake. "Colonel."

"Mister now." The former head of their group released Caville's hand and raised a glass of clear liquid in toast, then took a drink.

He reached into the pocket of his pants with his other hand and pulled out something that he set beside Stiles's elbow: rings.

She picked one up. "Ravens?"

"And Owls. The last of us."

"Us?"

"I may have told a small fib. It was necessary, though. Until we rooted out everyone else, I had to hang on."

She took an Owl ring from the rail. "It really is over?"

"As much as it ever will be. Under the new transparency policy, if we're going to hunt down conspiracists and the like, it'll have to be done in the open. I'm getting too old for that."

Caville snorted. "You've got years left in you."

"And I'll spend them far out of sight. I have some relationship repair work to do with my family, and it starts with not embarrassing them." He glanced at Stiles, then looked to the horizon.

She blushed, although she wasn't sure why. It had to be the recognition that he was trusting her with his secrets.

After turning the Owl ring around and around, she finished her drink and scraped the metal bands into the cup with a series of sharp tinkling chimes. "I don't have anyplace to put these right now, but I hope you don't mind me keeping them, Colonel?"

He laughed. "Consider them war trophies. Brianna."

Brianna. Not Lieutenant Stiles.

The way that sounded when he said it…was almost intoxicating.

She sauntered off toward her cabin, shaking the rings as she passed Gallo.

They were all former spies, now unemployed, full of secrets and dark knowledge. Maybe that made them dangerous, and maybe it made them embarrassing. That was something they would all have to explore on their own.

But for now, Stiles wasn't ready to leave the shadows.

# EPILOGUE

Viktor Serbsky shuffled down the long, ice-covered hall leading from the garage to the dining facility, his booted steps a soft whisper bouncing off the walls. He kept to the center, avoiding the low light fixtures that threatened to clip his forehead.

Tall, skinny, maybe a little more clumsy than most—this was as good an assignment as he could ever have hoped for.

And yet, he'd hoped for so much more when he'd volunteered to travel to Jotun, possibly to find his brother-in-law still alive here.

Unfortunately, everything pointed to Major Talbot O'Bannon being dead.

In fact, it looked like *everyone* was dead.

No loss if the Children who'd been assigned to the remote planet-sized moon had died here.

Good riddance.

He tugged on the mess hall door, breathing in the warm air that was thick with the smell of cooked sausage and cabbage. His mouth watered at the earthy spices, and a smile broke over his face at the murmur of conversation.

A big, broad-shouldered man turned. "Viktor!"

Viktor waved. "Lunch so soon, Jurgen?"

"I am hungry all the time."

They all laughed, and Viktor took his place on the bench next to the scrawny electronics technician Matilda. She was almost swallowed by her grimy jumpsuit.

When he smiled at her, she brushed a long, curly strand of brown hair over a big ear.

Like him, she wouldn't have been part of the Azoren plan.

But that plan was abandoned now. They'd all heard the radio call: The old government had fallen. The last pockets of Children were being hunted down.

The recovery team was on its own for the moment, the government in full collapse.

He caught Karl Yudin's eye.

The project lead's chubby cheek twitched, and he eyed the radio beside his plate. "I sent the request for extract, Viktor."

"This is good to know."

"There isn't party loyalty here. We're scientists."

"Yes, of course."

Except that Karl had been connected with the Supreme Leader's organization. Blond-haired, blue-eyed—the project leader might be a respectable chemist, but he was still a political officer.

Viktor took a tin plate from the tabletop and scooped sausage and cabbage out, then tucked into the food. In between bites, he jabbed his fork back at the door he'd come through. "The water recycler is operational."

Jurgen clawed at a tooth. "Power is at full now, too."

Karl nodded. "We can live for several months with supplies."

Jurgen grunted. "But we all want to go home."

Matilda took a drink of water, then set her cup down. "This new government. Do you think they might rejoin the Kedraalian Republic?"

Smiling victoriously, Jurgen held up the piece of cabbage that had been stuck between his teeth. "Would they have us, do you think?"

Karl's mouth opened, but the radio squawk silenced him.

"Mr. Yudin?" It was the Army captain, Biedermann.

Everyone set their forks down and stared at the political officer.

Karl activated the microphone. "Yes, Captain?"

"We are at the crater. We are doing preliminary reconnaissance. I have a squad descending now."

"Have you seen anything?"

"Flares are dropping. No corpses so far, but there are definite signs of a conflict."

"Can you send video?" Karl set up an old data pad as a display, propping it against his water cup.

Blue light flared from it, then the image turned red. Shadows flickered along the ice-covered black walls.

Matilda leaned closer to the display. "It is obsidian."

Karl waved for her to be silent. "We're seeing the video."

Now the video showed the descending team, intermittently lit by the flare, then lost to darkness. The signs of conflict became obvious: frozen bits of what could only be blood; cracks in the black stone from small arms fire; the glint of light on shell casings.

Suddenly, the video was washed out by static.

Then it died.

Karl fiddled with the display. "Captain?"

Biedermann's voice was choppy. "I've detected a vehicle at the edge of sensor range. I'm heading over to check on it."

"Your signals are weak."

"—capable vehicle—"

The video moved, now following Beidermann as he stomped across the frozen surface. A second screen opened inside the display, showing the team descending.

Now they had two images that were next to useless, instead of just one. That was progress.

Some of the descending team had reached the crater floor.

One of them waved what looked like a chunk of shrapnel. In between the interference, more images of frozen blood and pieces of cracked composites filled the smaller window.

Jurgen pointed to the display. "Those blackened pieces along the wall —metal, plastic."

Viktor stroked his chin, his appetite gone. "Not just that. Circuit cards."

"You think?"

"There were coppery leads in the light."

The big man shrugged. "Maybe."

Matilda gasped. "Did you see that?"

"See what?"

Viktor leaned over the table. "Movement. Was that it, Matilda?"

"Yes."

"Karl, ask them what that was."

The political officer frowned. "I can't reach them."

"Try."

Karl keyed the mic. "In the crater, can you hear me? This is Karl Yudin."

Static. The image flickered in and out.

"Go ahead." On the display, one of the recon team waved a flashlight.

"Yes. This is Karl Yudin."

"Go ahead, Karl."

"Someone here saw movement." Karl looked at Matilda, then Viktor, eyebrows arched.

Matilda wagged a scrawny finger. "To their left, at the edge of the camera range."

"Did you hear that?" Karl leaned toward the display. "Pan the camera to your left."

The recon soldier panned the camera around. "We didn't see anything. Are you sure?"

Viktor nodded. "Yes, yes."

"Well, there's nothing—"

A scream drowned out the soldier's words. The camera swung around. "Johan? Where did Johan go?"

His camera caught confused stares and a couple concerned looks.

"Everyone, come in. Form a group here. Now."

On the larger window, Biedermann's image became even more staticky. He stood beside the gutted remains of what must have been a large vehicle at some point. Now it was bare metal and tires.

The captain leaned through the dark maw that led into a large compartment. "What's going on here?"

Biedermann stepped into the compartment, blocking out the light from the camera, then screamed.

The noise ended in a wet sound.

Then the video and audio from the reconnaissance team died.

Karl keyed the microphone. "Captain?"

Matilda's jaw quivered. "There was movement."

"Yes, we heard you." Karl keyed the microphone again. "Captain Beidermann. Do you copy?"

Silence.

Karl stood and waved for Viktor to follow. When they were away from the table, the political officer shoved a small radio into Viktor's hand. "The garage doors."

"Yes?"

"Are they secured?"

"Of course."

"Check them again."

Viktor glanced back at the others. They were watching intently. "You're worried something is out there?"

"Secure the doors, Viktor. All of them, please. And hurry."

There was no room for argument. Even if Viktor was sure he'd closed the doors, it was just good security to check.

He hurried back into the concrete hallway with its low light fixtures and jogged back to the garage where Talbot's team would have had its vehicles. The closer Viktor drew, the colder the air became.

That was odd.

Except, of course, he was getting farther and farther away from the warmth of the dining facility, so it wasn't odd.

He took the ramp up to the garage and—

The doors were open.

Now *that* was odd. He had absolutely sealed the doors. There was no question.

He hurried forward, shivering when the cold winds drew tears from his eyes. The metal groaned but finally slammed shut.

That done, he pulled out the radio. Karl didn't need to know the doors had been opened. All he needed to know was that they were secured.

Viktor checked again: closed. He brought the radio up to his lips. "Karl? The garage door is secure."

Static answered.

"Karl?" Viktor breathed on his gloved hands. He keyed the mic again. "Karl?"

Static.

Something scraped from the direction of the ramp.

Viktor hurried back to the top. It had to be Jurgen or—

A metallic dog-like thing looked up the ramp with diamond alien eyes, head tilted curiously. Blood dripped from its mouth.

---

The sentinel sat on the rise, looking down at the base that had been built by inquisitive organisms. The organisms had been dispatched time and again, yet they had returned.

Now the connection to its comrade—a connection going back millennia—had been broken, the chatter of eternities silenced.

It was time.

The sentinel reconfigured itself, unfolding and reassembling, rerouting power and aligning components until it was nothing more than a transmitter and an antenna pointed into the dark depths of space.

It fired off a message on repeat for a while, then it stopped.

The sentinel would wait now.

An answer would come from the darkness.

There would always be shadows.

# ACKNOWLEDGMENTS

*Shadow Fall* is the sixth chapter of **The War in Shadow** saga, which concludes the space opera and military science fiction series.

There are some obvious historical influences from multiple decades on this series and on *Shadow Fall*. These are meant to inform the story and to provoke thought.

If you enjoyed this series, I hope you'll consider posting a review of the books and letting friends know about it. Word of mouth and reviews carry more weight than a neutron star.

For updates on new releases and news on other series, please visit my website and sign up for my mailing list at:

http://www.p-r-adams.com

# ABOUT THE AUTHOR

I was born and raised in Tampa, Florida. I joined the Air Force, and my career took me from coast to coast before depositing me in the St. Louis, Missouri area for several years. After a tour in Korea and a short return to the St. Louis area, I retired and moved to the greater Denver, Colorado metropolitan area.

I write speculative fiction, mostly science fiction and fantasy. My favorite writers over the years have been Robert E. Howard, Philip K. Dick, Roger Zelazny, and Michael Crichton.

*Social Media:*
www.p-r-adams.com
pradams_author@comcast.net